More praise for the work of M.L. Malcolm

"A bold narrative, immensely readable
from first page to last…I was mesmerized."
~ *Jack Valenti, former president of the
Motion Picture Association of America*

"Captivating….One of the 10 best novels of the year."
~ *World Art Celebrities Journal*

"*Silent Lies* stands shoulder to shoulder with the most
gripping and passionate tales of the last several decades."
~ *Curled Up With a Good Book (curledup.com)*

"A romantic rags-to-riches tale and a suspenseful thriller,
full of vivid description and intriguing history…
The writing is smooth and engaging, drawing in
and carrying the reader along effortlessly."
~ *Bookends*

"Malcolm writes with skill and passion, and brings her
characters and settings to life with rich description,
believable dialogue, and expert use of tension."
~ *The Road to Romance*

"Malcolm paints a vivid picture of the time and place,
and gives an excellent characterization of a complicated hero.
This is an excellent first book."
~ *The Historical Fiction Review*

Read more about M.L. Malcolm and her work
at
www.MLMalcolm.com

DECEPTIVE INTENTIONS

Enjoy!
Mary L Malcolm

A NOVEL

M.L. MALCOLM

A Good Read

LOS ANGELES, CALIFORNIA

Published by
A Good Read Publishing
Los Angeles, California

Copyright © 2008 by M. L. Malcolm

1st printing, 2008
ISBN: 978-0-981-5726-0-4

Library of Congress Cataloging in Publication Available by Request.

Printed in the United States of America

Cover and book design by Dotti Albertine
www.albertinebookdesign.com

*For John, Andy and Amanda, who make my life complete,
and in memory of our dear friend Laura. We miss you.*

DECEPTIVE INTENTIONS

CHAPTER 1

THE ASSET

୧ᢇᢁᢇᠪ

TANGIER, MAY 1942

If the city of Tangier had been a woman, she would have been a whore, and a wealthy one. Brazenly straddling the northwest tip of Africa, she brushed one of her sultry thighs up against the undulating waves of the turquoise Mediterranean Sea; the other unfolded west, teasing the unquenchable desire of the gray Atlantic Ocean. Her proud limestone cliffs, created by Hercules himself, granted her patron-of-the-moment a keen view of his seafaring rivals. For centuries men fought to claim this sun-drenched Siren of antiquity: the Phoenicians, the Carthaginians, the Romans, the Berbers, and then, finally, the countries of Europe. For he who possessed Tangier could control the Straits of Gibraltar, the only maritime passage between east and west that did not involve sailing around a continent.

Tangier's charms seduced not only kings, pirates, and warriors, but merchants and artists as well. The merchants came for her magnificent *souks*, grand markets offering spices, silks, exotic fruits, gemstones, livestock, and slaves. The decadent city lured the world's most famous artists with her unique light, a shimmering radiance so bright it could reveal four different shades of green in a single blade of grass, or beguile an unwary soul into a permanent state of lethargy.

But the brightest light casts the deepest shadows, sheltering the creatures who thrive in darkness. Leo Hoffman had lived in sunlight and in shadow for the better part of two years.

He sat at a table in the tiled courtyard of Hotel El Minzah, an unfinished cup of coffee in front of him, watching another customer signal for his check. The man was dressed in a dark wool suit, worn only by those new to the heat and dust of the city. "*L'addition, s'il vous plait!*" Leo overhead heard him ask for the third time, the growing irritation in his voice another sign that he was new to Tangier. One learned patience here. You learned to be patient, or your nerves broke. Then you made mistakes.

Leo was aware of two other men watching the newcomer. The city was an enormous spiderweb of intrigue. One small vibration in one isolated corner, and out scurried the predators with a thousand eyes, ready to feast on the vulnerable.

He glanced at his watch, drained his cup, left enough change on the table to pay for his coffee, and put on his sunglasses. Time to go meet his new boss.

☙

In a dilapidated hut on the outskirts of the city, where orange sand and scrub brush gave way to the desert, Lieutenant Colonel William Eddy stopped reading long enough to enjoy the sunset. This began his favorite time of day: the magical thirty minutes between the moment that the sun dipped below the horizon and the onset of true darkness. He watched as the sky turned a purplish blue, illuminated only by the brightest stars. Lord, how he had missed the enormity of the Arabian sky.

Already his time as president of a small college in upstate New York seemed like part of someone else's life. *If my fate is already written, let the story end here, while I'm doing something more useful than fighting over parking privileges at a faculty meeting.*

Surely there was some guiding hand at work in his life. If he hadn't been at that cocktail party, hadn't offered his services to General Holcomb, he'd still be waiting for the spring snows to melt. But within weeks of that meeting he was back in Marine uniform, as head of the nascent Allied spy network in North Africa.

The first thing he did was move his headquarters from Cairo to Tangier, which in Eddy's view held several advantages. The move got him out from under the British, whom he didn't trust. His operation was now only twenty miles from Spain, which facilitated communication with their contacts on the European continent. The other advantage was Tangier's near-lack of a functioning government. The eight-nation governing council allegedly in charge of the independent city-state had collapsed, and Franco's decision to send in Spanish troops to "protect" the city after the fall of France only added to the chaos. What better place to set up a home base for spies than a city already so overrun with them that no one would notice a few more, or even think to complain about commonplace events like car bombings, kidnappings, and bribery?

One of the young Marines keeping watch for Eddy outside the hut stuck his head in the door. "Someone's coming. On horseback."

"On horseback? Can you get a look at him?"

"Not a good one. Too dark. Looks like an Arab, though."

"That's odd. I'm not expecting any native visitors. If that's not the gentleman I'm expecting, we may have to shoot the poor bastard."

The young officer looked startled. "Sir?"

Eddy shook his head and sighed. "You and Davies come inside. Flank the door, guns drawn. I'll tell him to come in when he knocks. If he shows any signs of aggression, take him down. Don't kill him if you can help it. Just a good knock on the head."

Eddy watched from a crack in the wall as the man dismounted. He stroked the horse's neck and said something into the animal's ear. As he approached the door, he pulled back the hood of his *djellaba*, the long, hooded robe Moroccan men wore over loose trousers.

It was Leo Hoffman, all right. Easy enough to recognize him from his file photograph. About six feet tall, black curly hair, and… those eyes. He looked like the Hollywood version of what a spy should be, or like one of the agency's Ivy League recruits, excited by the possibility of cloak-and-dagger exploits, with no idea what they were doing.

"At ease, boys. It's him."

Leo knocked. "Come in," Eddy answered. One of the yeomen opened the door.

"Good evening, gentlemen. I didn't see anywhere to tie up my horse. Would one of you be kind enough to mind him? He's not likely to wander off, but one never knows."

Eddy smiled. "There's an old Arabic saying, 'Trust in Allah, but tie up your camel.' Men, go see to our visitor's horse." The two departed with a salute.

Eddy and Hoffman shook hands, openly evaluating each other as they did so.

"Have a seat," said Eddy, gesturing to one of the three camp chairs, the only furniture in the tiny hut. Before sitting himself, he picked up a file from a small stack on the floor. As he opened it Leo caught sight of his own picture, taken when he'd first arrived in London in November of 1940, before his fair skin became permanently sunburned.

Why did Eddy have all that information with him? If that stack of files fell into the wrong hands, the whole network could be blown. Not that there was too much secrecy involved at the top levels: there wasn't a single U.S. State Department representative in North Africa who was not a suspected spy. Everyone knew that Eddy, stationed here in the U.S. Embassy as "Naval Attaché," was in Tangier to head up a spy network. Everyone knew that Robert Murphy, the American counsel in Algiers, and the twelve vice-consuls working for him as "inspectors," were all simultaneously gathering intelligence. But the identity of the people from whom Eddy, Murphy, and the "Twelve Apostles" received information, now that was valuable. Leo was one such person.

"Don't worry about the files," said Eddy, as if reading his thoughts. "I'll burn them before I leave here tonight."

"That's comforting."

"And that, Mr. Hoffman, is a perfect example of the type of sarcasm that's noted in your evaluation."

"Is that so?"

Eddy pretended to read the file. He'd already committed the major details to memory. He was not going to interview many of the informants upon whom Murphy and the Twelve Apostles relied. But there were a couple of extraordinary cases, and Hoffman was one of them.

"Born in Hungary, 1900. Spent fifteen years in Shanghai as a businessman and banker. And you speak six languages. That's useful. But tell me, Mr. Hoffman, what are the chances that we were shooting at each other during the previous war?"

"Slim, I'd say, unless you were at the Italian front in 1917."

"Never made it out of France. Went home in 1918."

"With a stack of medals, including two Purple Hearts."

Eddy put down the file. "What else do you know about me?"

"You were born in Syria, to missionary parents, who wanted you completely immersed in the Arabian culture. You prefer to eat Arabian food when you can get it, and you've even been seen riding a camel. Went back to Princeton for your college degree, got out just in time to go to war. Worked in intelligence. Injured hip sent you home, and that's the cause of your limp. Got back to Cairo for a teaching position at American University in the early '20s, and you've been back in academia, in the States, since 1928. And it's said you're the only commissioned American officer who's fluent in Arabic."

Eddy was impressed. "That's pretty thorough, except that it was a bout with pneumonia that sent me home. Hospital infection crippled the hip. So where did you come by all that?"

Leo smiled slightly. "Now sir, isn't it up to you to get independent corroboration?"

The man's sarcasm was beginning to get on Eddy's nerves. "I expect a man working for me to answer any damn question I ask him. Why are you here, Hoffman? What made you volunteer for this duty?"

"It's a means to an end, Colonel. And that's to be able to get back to the States, and live a peaceful life with my daughter."

"And how will being here help you?"

Leo pointed at the file on the floor. "What does it tell you in there? That I was recruited by the U.S. Ambassador out of Shanghai in 1940?"

"And that we obtained a replacement for your passport. A French passport. That seemed a little strange, given that you're a Hungarian national."

"Not strange if it's a passport issued in Shanghai, Colonel. A certain French diplomat there was quite willing to hand out French passports to the right person for the right price."

"Sounds like Tangier."

"The two cities are remarkably similar, in many respects. At any rate, I was recruited by the U.S. Office of Naval Intelligence. But the Americans weren't active in Europe yet, so in light of my language skills I was sent 'on loan' to the Brits, because their Special Operations Executive, the covert angle, was already gearing up. Churchill and company sent me to North Africa as part of the S.O.E. contingent that tagged along with Bob Murphy's little American espionage entourage in early '41. But unlike the Apostles, I was sent in unofficially, so they'd have at least one clandestine set of ears to the ground."

Eddy frowned. "But how does that get you back to your daughter? I'm missing a piece here."

"I agreed to join Naval Intelligence because I was told that if I served for two years, I'd qualify to become an American citizen. Madeleine, my daughter, was already in the States. She went to New York with the woman who was, at that time, her stepmother. An American. I got them out of Shanghai right after the Japanese invasion in '37. But I couldn't leave."

"Why not? If you were married to a U.S. citizen?"

Leo paused. "I had some complicated business arrangements."

"Of what kind?"

"The kind that make me an excellent spy."

"And then there was that little matter of you being wanted for murder."

"Yes," Leo replied, steadily meeting Eddy's gaze. "There was that."

Eddy was about to push for details, then thought better of it. Self-defense, the report said. Hopefully someone at Naval Intelligence had checked out Hoffman's story before sending him to London. If not, well, he wouldn't be the first man with a violent past to work in espionage. Good spies were rarely Boy Scouts.

"So what's keeping you here?"

"At the moment I'm in limbo. When America entered the war, my two-year deal evaporated. The time I needed to serve was suddenly 'unclear.' And I'm technically not even in the Navy anymore. Your Marine uniform and all those sparkling medals provide protective camouflage. If I were registered as U.S. military but turned up in the wrong place at the wrong time wearing civilian clothing, I'd be shot as a spy outright. That's why on paper I'm S.O.E., covert operations, with an 'understanding' that I'll get U.S. naval credit for time served. However long that is. When I'm released, I'll go to New York."

"Somehow that part of the tale wasn't in your file, Hoffman. You're listed as an unaffiliated civilian volunteer. No mention of attachment to O.N.I., or any other military connection. You're not even on the official S.O.E. asset list. My records indicate that you're more of an independent contractor."

Leo's nonchalance evaporated. "That needs to be corrected, sir. The only reason I'm in this game is to earn my citizenship, and get back to my daughter."

"I'll have someone look into it."

"Thank you. I'd appreciate that." Before Eddy could speak again, concern replaced the relief on Leo's face.

"But, sir, then who's writing my letters?"

"Your letters?"

"Letters to my daughter. Once I left London I wasn't supposed to write home myself. My chief at O.N.I. assured me that regular letters would be sent home on my behalf, so my daughter would know that I was all right. If I'm no longer with the U.S. Navy, and not claimed by the Brits, then who's writing my letters? "

Eddy tried to temper his exasperation. "Hoffman, I can't even get a straight answer from the top brass about how we're supposed to prepare for a North Africa invasion that may or may not ever come to pass. And now I'm supposed to check up on your mail?"

Leo stood up, his movements radiating agitation. "Sir, I know you don't want to hear my life story. But I wasn't a decent husband, and I haven't been a good father. I'm not sure I've ever done any-thing decent in my life. For the first time, I'm trying to play by the goddam rules and I'd like some good to come out of it. But it won't mean anything if my daughter thinks I've abandoned her."

"I can appreciate that. So write a letter! We'll throw it in the diplomatic pouch and run it through the censors before it gets to the States. It's no secret to anyone that you're here. Whatever your original agreement was, the only thing that's still a secret is the fact that you're working for us while you twiddle your thumbs in Tangier. But the kind of work we need you to do takes complete commitment. If you can't manage that, if you want out now, you have my permission to leave. What that does *not* give you, unfortunately, is permission to enter the United States."

Leo sat back down heavily. "I'll do whatever it takes to get back to my daughter."

"Then work with us. We'll get you back as soon as we can. As soon as any of us can go back."

"Very well. I will. And, thank you."

To Eddy's surprise Leo was now speaking in Arabic. "How well do you speak?" he asked, also in Arabic.

"Not quite well enough to fool a native. Not yet. But I can eavesdrop pretty efficiently, get through a conversation, and negotiate a deal when I need to."

Eddy slapped his good leg. "That explains how you were able to get the information on those fortifications at the border. You used a native, didn't you?"

For the first time during their meeting, Leo gave Eddy a genuine smile. "For the right price, he proved very helpful. I also persuaded him to loan me that beautiful horse."

"That disguise almost got you shot."

"It also got me here unnoticed."

Eddy switched back to English. "Fair enough, Hoffman. That should do for now. Thank you for coming tonight. You'll be hearing from me."

"A pleasure, sir." Leo took his leave.

Eddy took the time to look over Leo's file once more, making sure he'd missed nothing. "We'll have to watch that one," he said, mostly to himself, but Davies, coming back into the hut, overheard him.

"How's that sir?"

"I'm not sure we can keep him, Davies. His heart's not in it. And that's dangerous."

"Dangerous?"

Eddy picked up the next file. "Because if his heart isn't in it, he could be turned. Become a double agent."

CHAPTER 2

THE NEMESIS

᠑᠊ᢙᢦᢙ᠊᠑

NEW YORK, MAY 1942

Who the *hell could that be?* Amelia lifted her head off the pillow just high enough to check the time on the small Cartier clock decorating her nightstand. *Christ almighty!* It wasn't even nine o'clock. Who'd have the energy to be out and about at such an indecent hour of the morning? And why wasn't that stupid maid answering the buzzer? Oh, that's right. She'd fired her yesterday. *Damn, damn, damn.*

The buzzer sounded again. Amelia knew there wasn't a doorman in the building who would dare summon her before noon—not for anything less than a five-dollar tip. That meant the visitor was not only unexpected, he was also the owner of a fat wallet.

She threw back the silk comforter, grabbed her dressing gown, and headed toward the buzzer, jamming her thumb down on the response button while working her way into her satin robe.

"What is it?"

"A visitor, Mrs. Hoffman. A Mrs. Bernice Mason is here to see you."

A woman? Bernice Mason? The name was not the least bit familiar. Wait, had one of the guys from last night been named Mason? Could the woman in the lobby be an angry wife? No. Not one of the handsome threesome with whom she'd wined, dined, and danced the night away knew her address or her real last name. And by now they'd be headed to San Francisco, and then across the Pacific, to fight the Japs.

"I'm not expecting anyone. Ask her what she wants."

"She says she'd like to talk to you about her niece. Should I send her up?"

Her niece? "I'm sorry, I don't know this woman or her niece. She's made a mistake. And I'm not dressed. Tell her I can't see her."

Amelia barely had time to light a cigarette before the buzzer sounded again. Now the doorman sounded anxious.

"I'm sorry to bother you again, Mrs. Hoffman, but she says that her niece is Madeleine Hoffman, and that the girl is your step-daughter. I'm not sure that Mrs. Mason is going to leave until you see her, Mrs. Hoffman. And she doesn't seem like the type what gets tossed out, if you get my meaning."

Amelia stared at the innocuous electronic box as if it has just sprung to life.

"Mrs. Hoffman? Are you still there? Should I send her up?"

"Give me... give me ten minutes." Madeleine Hoffman. She hadn't heard that name for nearly two years. Little Maddy. How old would she be now? Twelve? Thirteen?

And who was Bernice Mason? As Amelia headed back to her bedroom to change, she caught sight of herself in the huge, art-deco mirror hanging on the wall behind her sofa: tousled blond curls, prominent cheekbones, cigarette dangling out of a sensuous mouth. Amelia moved closer to her reflection. She was still slim, and her years as a dancer had helped keep everything up where it was supposed to be. But those small lines around her lips... hadn't she just heard that smoking causes wrinkles? She grabbed a crystal ashtray off the coffee table and stubbed out her nearly untouched cigarette. Soldier-boy playmates were delightful, but she needed to find another husband. Soon. A rich one. Preferably a rich one headed off to war, so that Amelia could mind his fortune until he returned. Or better yet, until she became a widow again.

To improve those odds, I really ought to go back to San Francisco. The government was positively herding eligible men out to the west coast, like cattle lumbering off to the Chicago stockyards. And Amelia could make a man's last days ashore very, very pleasurable.

Once widowed, and once divorced. Well, as good as divorced. She'd kept Leo Hoffman's name, although legally she probably shouldn't have. Bastard. He'd had their marriage *annulled.* It hadn't been much of a marriage, but she'd counted on having a chance to make it real. She'd taken his little brat with her to New York, and kept her out of harm's way for three years, while he dallied in Shanghai, all because... *not now.* She had to throw on some make-up, find something relatively demure in her closet, and slip on a pair of low heels.

Bernice Mason. Madeleine's aunt. Was she Leo's sister? Or Martha's?

Precisely ten minutes later Amelia opened her door to see a woman who looked nothing like either of the people to whom she was allegedly related. Martha, Maddy's mother, had been a petite, auburn-haired beauty. This woman's face was almost masculine: short brown hair, thick, unshaped brows, dark brown eyes hovering over a long nose. And her conservative gray suit did nothing to show off a trim figure. She was, in a word, plain.

Yet there was nothing ordinary about the way she handled herself. Bernice Mason looked at Amelia, then behind her. She seemed to be evaluating everything she saw with scientific precision: the mohair furniture, the satin drapes, the lighting, Amelia's clothes, her shoes, maybe even the temperature and barometric pressure, before she looked again into Amelia's face. The level of scrutiny was unnerving, so much so that Amelia neglected to say hello.

"Mrs. Hoffman, I'm Bernice Mason. May I come in?"

She spoke with a distinctly German accent. Amelia recovered her composure and opened the door wide enough for her visitor to enter. "Yes, of course."

Bernice Mason did not offer Amelia her hand before walking into the foyer. "What a lovely apartment," she remarked, making the compliment seem irrelevant. "May I sit down?" Without waiting for an answer she stepped into the sunken living room and took a seat on the sofa.

Amelia followed her into the room, but remained standing. She'd lost the first round, somehow, and wanted to regain the upper hand. All Amelia knew was that she must have some information that this woman wanted. How could she use that fact to her advantage? She leaned one hip against a credenza on the opposite side of the room, and crossed her graceful arms in front of her chest.

"This is quite a surprise, Mrs. Mason. I wasn't even aware that Madeleine had any surviving relatives, other than her father." *And he might be dead, too, for all I know. May he burn in hell.*

"Where is Madeleine? Is she at school?"

Hmmm. If you thought you'd find her anywhere around here, there's a whole lot to this story that you don't know. The question is, if I fill you in, what's in it for me?

Amelia cocked her head. "Well, who are you, exactly? And why are you here? You're presuming quite a bit, Mrs. Mason."

"Forgive me," she replied, in a tone empty of contrition. "My sister, Martha, is—was—Madeleine's mother. After considerable effort, my husband and I learned that Martha was killed in Shanghai during the bombings in 1937, at the time of the Japanese invasion. We also discovered that you and Madeleine's father, Leopold Hoffman, were married just a few days after Martha's death. It took some time to learn that you and Madeleine sailed from Shanghai that same day, and even more time to locate you, here in New York. But now that we have found you, we are hoping we have found Madeleine as well."

"Let me get this straight. You've been trying to find your niece for five years?"

"That is correct. Is she here?"

"Where have you been all this time?"

"Mrs. Hoffman, I appreciate the fact that this is a very unusual set of circumstances, but before I elaborate any further, would you please tell me if Madeleine is living here with you?"

Amelia knew the value of a dramatic pause. *Screw the wrinkles. Time for a cig.* She picked up her enameled cigarette case, selected a cigarette, lit it, and blew out a lungful of smoke before turning to look Bernice directly in the eyes.

"No. She isn't living with me."

"Oh." Disappointment barely registered in the woman's voice. "Then, can you give me any information that might help me find her? Is she with her father?"

Amelia made her way over to a chair facing the sofa. "I'm not sure what I should do. This is really quite a shock, having you appear out of nowhere, demanding information. It's a bit melodramatic, wouldn't you say?"

For some reason the older woman seemed to find this comment amusing. "My life has been nothing if not melodramatic for the past several years, Mrs. Hoffman." Then her humor vanished. "What information do you need from me in order to secure your cooperation? Or, may I reward you for what you have to tell me with a check?"

Amelia paused, torn. She could use a windfall, especially now that she planned to begin husband-hunting in earnest. On the other hand… she stayed silent for some time, struggling to resolve her competing desires. Then, decision made, she leapt up.

"How dare you imply that I can be bought? I took care of Madeleine for three years because I loved her and I loved her father. I don't know even where you come from, or what your intentions are. Good Lord—you've got a German accent! We're at war with Germany! For all I know, I could be putting Madeleine in jeopardy by letting you know where to find her." She gestured towards the door. "You may leave now, Mrs. Mason. Keep your money to pay your private detectives, or whoever it is that's gotten you this far."

Bernice rose, showing no signs of distress. She removed a calling card from her jacket pocket. "I am sorry that I insulted you," she responded, laying the card down on the coffee table. "I assure you that I have Madeleine's best interests at heart. Please, take some time to think things over. I would like to meet with you again in a day or two. I will bring all the documentation necessary for you to feel confident that I am who I say I am. Please call."

Amelia glared at her. "There's the door," she said, pointing.

As Bernice Mason shut the door behind her, Amelia dashed over to the coffee table and picked up her card. Englewood. She was rich, all right. *Well, shove your checkbook up your ass, you ugly Aryan hound. I don't want your money, not this time. I want revenge.*

☙❧

Margaret O'Connor kept her rosary in her apron pocket. Or hanging over her bedpost, or in the bathroom, in a little glass bowl placed on a shelf she'd put up just for that purpose, for those moments when there were no pockets available.

In the four months that her youngest son had been gone, she'd completed the rosary thousands of times, her plump calloused fingers touching each bead as if she were stroking the fuzzy patch of auburn hair crowning his head on the day he was born. She even found herself reaching for a cooking spoon or a feather duster with her left hand, in order to keep the other quiet in her pocket, moving bead by bead, prayer by prayer, along the sacred circle. She never lost her place. And every time she completed it, she added a prayer of her own. *Holy Mother, I've got no right to ask ya this, for you gave up your own Son to pay for the sins of all mankind. But I'm askin' ya just the same, dear Mary. Protect my boy. Please protect my boy.*

She'd not had a letter for six weeks—not that the scribbled notes her Jamie sent were proper letters. He had none of the poet in him, that one. But even a few lines about the bad food, or his bragging about winning a handsome pot in a poker game, was proof enough that he was alive.

Her husband had died so suddenly, there'd been no time to torture herself with terrible pictures of how he might go. He was there one day and then he wasn't, leaving her with seven children in a home on the upper west side, nearly paid for by the life insurance policy she'd called him an idiot for buying. Margaret piled her family into two rooms and took in boarders. There was no time to mourn. She kept her tears for the pillow, and on many nights was too tired to stay awake long enough to cry. If idle hands were the devil's workshop, Satan would find himself permanently unemployed in Margaret O'Connor's home.

But Jamie! He was her Patrick all over again, with that crooked smile and his deep-throated laugh, ready to throw a punch when necessary, soft-hearted when it came to helping anyone who needed it. For three years she'd suffered through Jamie being on the police force, fearing he'd come home with a bullet in his back or his skull cracked open, comforted only by the fact that he was close to home.

And then he'd *volunteered.* That was the rub. After they'd all seen the newsreels about Pearl Harbor, Jamie had signed up without so much as a by-your-leave. A grown man, all set to fight for his country.

It was her punishment, she knew, for having a favorite. But surely the constant worry was punishment enough. Asleep and awake they came to her: the visions of him floating, terrified and helpless in the cold, dark ocean, surrounded by the screams of his shipmates as the sharks moved in, praying that he'd freeze to death before the beasts got to him. Or she'd see him looking across a ditch at a leg that used to be his, knowing it was the last thing he'd ever see as his blood poured out of him like water. *Hail Mary, full of Grace, the Lord is with thee. Blessed art thou among women…*

"Ma! We're home!"

Margaret slipped the rosary back into her apron pocket as the two girls popped into the parlor. "As if I couldn't tell from all the gigglin' and stompin.' About time, too. Or do you think I can make dinner for eight people in less than an hour with just two hands?"

"Ma, I told you. We had to put the baby to bed."

"The baby! Merciful heavens. That's what yer callin' it now?"

Mary Katherine Anne O'Connor shot a sidewise glance at her best friend, Maddy Hoffman, who stood silent during this mother-daughter exchange. But Katherine saw one of Maddy's shoulders lift slightly. She was on Katherine's side.

"Ma, you know what an honor it was for me, a rising freshmen, to be chosen as an assistant editor. I can't just let all the seniors do the work on the days the paper goes to press." She looked down at her ink-stained hands. "Journalism sure is a dirty business."

"Oh, off with ya both. Get cleaned up and meet me in the kitchen. Potatoes don't peel themselves. At least not in this house."

Margaret stood in the doorway, watching as the girls scampered down the narrow hall. How much they'd grown this year! They were closer than sisters, though no one would ever mistake them for blood kin. Katherine, tall and lanky at thirteen, with red hair and an Irish temper to match, would charge hell to put out the fires with nothing but a glass of water. Half a head shorter and a year younger, Maddy had her father's black curls, but there her resemblance to Leo Hoffman ended. She gazed at the world with her mother's green eyes and, Margaret suspected, for she'd never met Martha Hoffman, moved with her mother's grace.

Margaret's right hand found her rosary. At least those two were still here, where she could keep an eye on them. Not like Jamie. Not like Timothy or Mark, in the merchant marine, liable to get blown up by a submarine at any moment, but not, thank God, slap in the thick of the fighting. *Hail Mary, full of Grace...*

Maddy and Katherine burst into the bedroom that they shared with one of Katherine's sisters. Katherine immediately flung herself to the floor, pulled a newspaper out of her book bag, and disappeared under one of beds.

"You know, I think you could go to jail for keeping that stack of newspapers under there. It's not only hoarding, it's a fire hazard," said Maddy, tossing her books onto the same bed and plopping down on the second one, barely two feet away.

"Maddy, I keep telling you. These are for research."

"Researching what? You're not exactly working for the *New York Times*. How much research do you need to do to write about the school field trip to an art museum?"

Katherine's muffled voice responded. "But someday I will work for the *Times*. I'll be a famous foreign correspondent, and these files could come in handy."

"If your Mum doesn't find them first."

"Why would she look under here?"

"Oh, you know. She has some kind of radar."

"Yeah, she knows everything, all right. Ma Maggie and her Magnificent Irish Boarding House. There's days I'd rather take on the Nazis than live here another minute."

"Everyone fights with their mother, Katherine. Just be glad you've got one to fight with."

Katherine's head shot out from under the bed. "I'm sorry, Maddy. I didn't mean—"

"It's okay. But you know—"

"She loves you as much as she loves any of us."

"It's okay, Katherine. Really. I'm just glad to be here."

"I'd go crazy without you around."

"I'm not going anywhere." *Where would I go? There's no one else who wants me.* "Let's get to the kitchen, Miss Pulitzer. Your mum sounded like she meant business."

CHAPTER 3

THE STRANGER

❧⌒⌒❧

NEW YORK, MAY 1942

Eight-year-old Casey O'Leary saw the man first, just as he rounded the corner. He tapped his friend Kevin Riley on the back. Riley looked up from the bag of marbles he was inspecting, the spoils of a victorious afternoon. "Oh," he said, and shoved the coveted marbles into his pocket. They watched as the man stopped, looked down at a clipboard, looked up at a house number, and continued down the sidewalk.

The boys were up off their front stoop and following along a split second after he'd passed by. Two more boys stopped roughhousing and stared from across the street. O'Leary jerked his head, inviting them to join the surveillance team. They dashed over and fell in alongside. Half-jogging to keep pace with the man in front of them, the four of them traded curious looks. Where was he going?

Oblivious to the small posse forming behind him, the messenger stopped in front of a brick two-story house. It looked squat and stubborn in its shabbiness, out of place on a city street now full of four-and-five-story apartment buildings.

"Good law, no. Not *here*," muttered Finn. As if on cue, the boys backed away a few feet, their eyes reflecting anticipation and dread.

Margaret O'Connor opened the door. The color drained out of her face, until her skin very nearly matched her gray hair. The boys backed up even more.

"Don't you be comin' to see me," she said to the young man on the doorstep, in an icy voice the boys knew all too well. No one could deliver a scolding better than Ma Maggie.

"I'm sorry ma'am." He held out an envelope.

Margaret looked at it as if the devil had just tried to hand her his tail. She didn't move.

He jiggled the envelope. "Ma'am," he said again, pleading. "I've got a lot of people to get to today. I'm sorry."

"Ma? Who is it?" Katherine peered out from behind her mother's stout shoulder. Her eyes locked onto the telegram. "Oh, no."

"It's no one. It's no one fer us," replied Margaret, still motionless.

Eyes wide, Katherine edged out the door and reached for the envelope. The Western Union employee handed it to her and bolted, scattering the boys behind him like frightened mice.

Katherine took a deep breath and ripped the telegram open. Margaret winced. Katherine read the short sentences written there, and shook her head.

"Which one is it, Mary Kate? Which one?" Margaret demanded, looking ready to collapse despite the strength of her voice.

"It's not, Ma. It's not about any of them. It's about Maddy."

"Me?" Maddy squeaked from behind them.

Margaret snatched the paper from Katherine's hand to read it herself. Katherine looked at her friend, her features etched with confusion.

"It's from Amelia. She says... she says your mother's sister is here, in New York. She's here in New York and she wants to see you."

৩৽৩

Amelia loved traveling by train. What was the point of flying? Why get to where you were going so quickly? Train travel offered so many… possibilities.

She took another sip of champagne, savoring the effervescence on her tongue. With the war on, it would soon be damn near impossible to enjoy a glass of bubbly. How very nice to have some right now. Champagne was a perfect accompaniment for gloating; and Amelia had a lot to gloat about.

Three years she'd waited, and when Leo finally showed up, they'd spent less than a day together before Madeleine screwed everything up. The stupid girl hadn't listened when Amelia warned her to keep her mouth shut. Leo had believed everything that whining, lying brat told him about how Amelia had *supposedly* mistreated her during the three years he'd kept them both dangling on a string. The brat's outburst ruined the one chance Amelia had to get Leo back.

Now Amelia had made sure he'd never have the one thing that he seemed to love most: his precious little Maddy.

Once that Mason woman made it clear that she wanted to protect Madeleine *from* her renegade father, Amelia had added another layer of untruthful, unflattering information to Leo's dossier, such as the fact that he and Amelia had been lovers for years while Leo was still married to Martha. How would Bernice Mason find out otherwise? Leo was the only person who could contradict her, and she doubted that Martha's sister would believe the man who had abandoned her niece. When Leo came back, *if* he came back, he'd soon discover that his domestic situation had changed quite dramatically.

Best of all, Bernice Mason knew how to express her gratitude. Amelia got everything she wanted: revenge, a check, and a start on a new life in San Francisco, where the men going to war made brides and widows out of beautiful women every day.

Amelia closed her eyes and smiled. Trains, champagne, and a city full of desperate men.

So many interesting possibilities.

⟨✦⟩

Mrs. O'Connor called Bernice Mason that evening. She wasn't about to let Maddy meet any woman sent their way by Amelia Hoffman without investigating the whole matter. Who knew what that wretched tart was up to?

Waiting for the hotel operator to connect her with Bernice Mason's room, Margaret thought about the first day Maddy had come to live with them. She and Katherine had been friends for nearly a year before Margaret discovered that Maddy had only come 'round on Thursdays because she'd been sneaking out of the convent school where that awful woman had stashed her, like an unwanted piece of furniture. If the Sisters hadn't locked the alleyway entrance that day, Maddy might've never come to live with the O'Connor clan. But when Margaret took Maddy back to the iceberg Amelia called an apartment, and felt the sadness in the child as she walked through the door, she knew she couldn't leave the poor broken-hearted lass in the clutches of that she-devil. Margaret had taken Maddy in, and never regretted it, not for a single minute of the nearly two years the child had lived with them.

"Hello?"

Margaret was startled by the woman's heavy German accent. Of course she knew that Maddy's family had come from Austria, but Leo Hoffman, well, the man's accent had been so completely British, why, the German aspect of things sort of slipped out of the back of her mind. Maddy always insisted she couldn't speak German at all. Said they'd spoken only English and French when she was growing up in Shanghai.

But this woman spoke with the voice of the people determined to see all the O'Connor boys dead.

"Hello?" she said again.

"Yes, good day. This is Margaret O'Connor. Amelia Hoffman sent me a telegram sayin' that you were Maddy's aunt."

"That is correct. May I speak to her?"

"Well now, just hold yer horses. We've no idea who ya really are, do we? Maddy's never laid eyes on ya, and, to be frank, we've had enough dealings with that Amelia woman to know she's not the kind that any decent person would want as a reference."

"That, I can understand."

Margaret thought she detected a note of amusement, but she wasn't sure what it meant. Just who was this Mrs. Mason laughing at?

"So," she said, clearing her throat, "It seems to me the two of us ought to meet."

"Yes, of course. Are you free tomorrow?"

"No, no. It'll have to be on Sunday. Sunday afternoon."

"I don't mean to be overly insistent, Mrs. O'Connor. But I've waited twelve years to meet my niece. May I at least talk to her?"

The woman's accent set Margaret's teeth on edge. "No. She'll not be havin' anythin' to do with ya until I'm sure… until I'm comfortable with the whole situation."

"I understand."

"Yes, well. Where should we be meetin,' then?"

"You're more than welcome to come to my suite at the Regent."

Come into my parlor, said the spider to the fly. "No, I don't think so. There's a coffee shop just down the street from ya. The Brew Stop, it's called. Look for me there at three o'clock."

"And how will I know you?"

Margaret paused. "Oh, I'm just sort of normal. It's a small place, and it shouldn't be very crowded that time o' day on a Sunday. I imagine we'll find each other easy enough."

"Very good then. Until Sunday. And… thank you, Mrs. O'Connor. Thank you for taking care of Madeleine, and for agreeing to meet with me."

Don't be thanking me just yet. "Maddy's never been any trouble to us, Mrs. Mason. Her father left plenty of money for her keep, and she helps out besides. She's like one of me own."

"I cannot tell you how good it is to know that. I look forward to seeing you on Sunday."

"Until Sunday, then."

Margaret didn't say anything to the girls until after breakfast the next morning, and they knew better than to ask. Margaret O'Connor would talk about a subject when she was ready to talk about it, and not a moment before.

She brought in the last pile of dirty dishes and stacked them next to the sink, where Katherine washed as Maddy dried. "I don't know how you could possibly in a million years think Cary Grant is better looking than Humphrey Bogart," Katherine was saying, elbow-deep in gray dish water.

"Shake them off a bit more, will you please Katherine? I think it because it's true. Bogart isn't even *handsome.*"

"It's not all about pretty-boy looks. It's about *impact.* It's about a man who can look at you a certain way and—"

Margaret took a seat at the heavy oak table that served as work counter, desk and table for the family, and bore the scars to prove it. "About that telegram."

The chatter stopped. Katherine pulled her hands out of the dishwater and grabbed Maddy's towel to dry them as she spit out questions. "Is Maddy going to meet her? Where's she from? How did she find Maddy? Does she know anything about Maddy's father?"

Margaret held up her hands. "Mary Katherine Anne O'Connor! Calm yerself. This isn't some news interview. Now, the two o' ya sit down a moment."

Katherine leapt to a chair. Maddy stood still for an instant, like a gazelle on alert for a predator, before cautiously taking a seat.

"I don't know anythin' yet," Margaret began, "I just want to let the two o' ya know that I'll be meeting with this woman tomorrow.

This Mrs. Mason. And to ask, Maddy, well, you were so very young when ya lost yer mum, but if there was anythin' ya can remember that might be helpful, ya know, in figurin' out what's what…"

Maddy shook her head. "Nothing I haven't told you before. I remember my mother did sometimes talk about her sister, Bernice. I know that their mother died when my mother was, well, my age. And they grew up in Munich, where my grandfather was a professor. *Wait until we get to Germany, Maddy. There's so much I want to show you. Like the wildflowers in the spring, cherié! And the streams that run so clean and clear through the mountains. Not like the river here, Maddy, all yellow and slow and stinky. She held her nose and Maddy laughed. The Whangpoo did smell bad.*

Her mother's voice retreated. "I never went to Austria or Germany. I never met anyone in my mother's family. Or my father's. It was just… us."

Margaret nodded. "Okay, then. Well, we'll see who this lady is, and what she's up to." She reached across the table for Maddy's hand. "I'll not be lettin' anyone take ya away, Maddy, unless and until it's yer own heart and yer own two feet showin' me it's what ya want, and me own good sense tellin' me it's the best thing for ya."

Maddy gave her hand a squeeze. Katherine started to say something, and then, quite uncharacteristically, seemed to think better of it, and remained silent.

"Good. Now, it seems to me there's still a load of dishes to be done. So the two o' ya get back to it."

෴

There were only three customers in the Brew Stop when Margaret entered, and only one was a woman. She sat in a booth in the far corner, facing the door. Margaret took a deep breath, and unconsciously patted the tight bun into which she'd pulled her once-red hair. Time to find out what was going on here. She prided herself on being able to spot deceit in a person. In the many years she'd run her boarding house, she'd not once been cheated. If she didn't like the looks of you, why, you were quickly shown the door. And, more often than not, she caught on when one of her brood tried to pull any sort of trick. She had a sense for these things, she did. And she intended to use it now.

The woman was standing now, headed toward her, hand outstretched. "You must be Margaret O'Connor," she said.

Margaret was not used to this new business of women shaking hands. She grasped Bernice Mason's for an instant and let it go.

"Yes. And you're Bernice Mason, then."

"Yes. Please, sit down. Shall I order some coffee?"

"I'd have a cup of tea, if you don't mind."

Bernice signaled to the waitress behind the counter. "Miss? We will take one coffee, black, and one tea, please." Except the "will" came out as "vill," making Margaret wince. Bernice did not seem to notice.

"So," said Margaret stiffly, once the two were seated. "Who are you, and what is all this about?"

"I'm Madeleine's mother's sister."

Margaret's raised eyebrows communicated her skepticism. "Is that right? Well, you'll pardon me for sayin' so, but ya don't look a bit like Maddy's mum. I know. The child has a picture. Her parents' wedding picture."

"I should like to see that." The waitress brought their drinks. Margaret tended to her tea. Bernice pulled a small leather satchel up from the bench and put it flat on the table. As she talked she pulled out two official-looking documents and several photographs.

"I understand your concern. Martha inherited our mother's beauty, and her… what shall I say? Her restless nature. Here. You see? There's Martha, and me, with our father. You can see who I resemble."

Margaret took the photograph. A young lady with a heart-shaped face, large almond-shaped eyes, and a petite build stood between a younger version of Bernice Mason and a stern-looking gentleman. "Merciful heavens! Maddy is the spittin' image of her mum."

"Is she really? Does she look like Martha?"

"Like a twin, but with darker hair. How old was she in this picture?"

"Fourteen. I was seventeen."

"Well, you look like yer Da, that's for certain."

Bernice smiled. It was a fact she'd long ceased to regret. "Yes."

Margaret put down the picture. It was pretty good proof that this woman was who she said she was. But that was just the beginning.

"And where have ya been all this time? Why is it that poor child was left alone for so long?"

"My sister eloped, Mrs. O'Connor. Evidently she met Leo Hoffman while they were both on a holiday in Paris, in 1925. Six months later, Martha just disappeared. It was weeks before we heard from her. She wrote and told us that she'd married Leo Hoffman and was living with him in Shanghai." She handed Margaret one of the documents she'd pulled from the leather case. It was a copy of a wedding certificate. Margaret barely glanced at it.

"And so? If you knew where Maddy was, why didn't ya go and fetch her? Why did ya let her father send her off with that awful woman?"

"My father was ill. I stayed with him until he died. By then it was not easy for Jews to get out of Germany. My husband and I were able to get to France in 1938, but by the time we tried to get in touch—"

"Did you say *Jews?*"

Bernice sat back in her booth. "Does that surprise you? Never mind. I can tell by the look on your face that it does. Yes, our family is Jewish."

Margaret looked down at the marriage certificate she held in her hands. "Leopold Hoffman and Martha Levy," she whispered. *Levy.* She'd never met a person with that name who wasn't Jewish.

That surname was as Jewish as O'Connor was Irish. But Maddy? She studied the document.

"But look, it says right here, 'Religion: Catholic.' And Maddy went to a French Catholic school in Shanghai. She told us all about the French Sisters, how she learned all her prayers in French. Why, she can still say the Lord's Prayer in French, and—"

"I am sure that everything you are saying is true. But none of that changes the fact that Martha came from a Jewish family. Not a religious family, but a Jewish one."

Margaret did not know how to react. Of all things, she had not expected this. Three years of loving the child like one of her own, only to discover that Maddy was, well, she was not an *us*. She was a *them*. How could that be? "But I thought you were German—"

Bernice's voice went cold. "I am German. I also happen to have a Jewish heritage."

Margaret took a deep drink of her tea before she responded. "Mrs. Mason, I didn't mean to offend ya. But you know, we are *at war*..."

"Germany and America are at war. But the Germany that Hitler now controls is not the country in which I grew up." For the first time during their conversation, genuine emotion registered on her face. "You have no idea how intolerable our situation became. My father was no longer allowed to teach. The university was his life. And then there were restrictions on where we could go, on what we could own—"

"Beggin' yer pardon, Mrs. Mason. But I do know. I'm Irish. It wasn't so long ago the newspaper employment pages right here in New York were full of 'no Irish need apply,' and that after we'd come to America, willing to work and work hard, to get away from a place where we were starved and thrown off our own land by the English."

Bernice fell silent. At last, she said, "Yes, perhaps you do know."

For a long moment neither woman spoke. Margaret tried to sort out her thoughts. *Maddy was a Jew.* This woman was her blood relation. What should she do? What was the best thing for Maddy? How much more shock could the child stand?

With sudden shame, Margaret thought about the many times she'd complained about the Jews moving into their neighborhood, with their irritating mannerisms and their mysterious ways. But that wasn't the real problem. For the last ten years, with everyone she knew struggling to make ends meet, Jews were leapfrogging right over the Irish, taking away the very jobs that Margaret's people had fought for three generations to win and hold.

Most of the Irish blamed the new mayor. *We ran the city, and ran it well, until the Little Mongrel was elected, courting the Jews and Italians like a shameless rooster tempting chickens out of the hen house.* Margaret shared many Irish New Yorkers' dislike of Mayor La Guardia. He was part Italian, part Jewish, and nothing but trouble for the Irish, whose fifty-year grip on power was slipping rapidly now that he governed the city.

Margaret considered herself a fair-minded woman. She didn't like to see folks at odds with each other, or to judge a person unfairly. It worried her that more and more out-of-work Irish boys joined that so-called "Christian Front," fired up by the garbage that radio priest, Father Coughlin, spouted out, about how all Jews were Communists, plotting to take over the world. They were nothing more than hoodlums, that bunch, going around boycotting Jewish businesses by day and vandalizing them by night. Beating people up who couldn't defend themselves. Awful. The Pope himself had declared that anti-Semitism was wrong. There was no excuse for what they were doing.

But there was always an *us* and a *them* in life, people whose aims and interests competed with your own and the interests of those like you, people from whom you had to protect your family, and the fact of the matter was that the chasm between the Jews and the Irish in New York grew wider every day. She'd never expected to find Maddy on the other side of it. *Would I have taken her in if I'd known? Yes, of course I would've. Maddy is still Maddy, just as lovely as she ever was. Calm yerself, Margaret. It's just the shock of it gettin' to ya, that's all. Go have a talk with Father Cassidy. He'll help you sort it all out.*

"And what about Maddy's father, then?" Margaret finally asked. "What do you know about him?"

Bernice shook her head. "Very little. He is Hungarian, and was in the hotel business in Budapest before moving to Shanghai."

Margaret did not want to seem ignorant, but she had to ask. "Hungarian? And where would that make him from, exactly?"

"He is from the country Hungary. Next to Austria. It was part of the Hapsburg Empire until the last war."

"So, he's not German either, then?"

"Unlike our family, if that is what you mean, he is not German."

"And Jewish? Is he Jewish as well?"

Bernice gave Margaret a look that communicated nothing. "Yes, Martha did tell us that much. Although if they enrolled Madeleine in Catholic school I think it is unlikely that he was very religious. Not a religious Jew, at any rate."

"And you've never met him?"

"No."

"I see. Well, I've met him. Once."

Bernice leaned forward. "When? What was he like? I did not know he was ever here. What is he doing? Why is Madeleine not with him now?"

"Oh, he's a charmer, that one. But I'll tell ya this. He loved yer sister. He loved her so much it almost killed him to lose her."

"I cannot say that I feel much sympathy for him, Mrs. O'Connor. Loving him *did* kill my sister."

CHAPTER 4

THE OPERATIVE

❦

TANGIER, MAY 1942

"It's interesting, isn't it, how quickly the world changes. As of two years ago, only a handful of Europeans had ever sought out my company. Yet here you are, the third such visitor to my home this week."

"And I doubt I will be the last," Leo replied.

They sat in the formal reception room of Hamid Belafej's *riyad*, a traditional Moroccan town house built around a central interior garden. Moroccan tiles created intricate and colorful geometric patterns halfway up the fourteen-foot walls. Soft carpets covered the stone floor. Mahogany shutters filtered out the late afternoon sun, creating a wall of ladder-like shadows across the far side of the room.

Belafej bit into the dark flesh of a fresh fig, and talked while he chewed. "To everyone but the French, Morocco was no more than a flea on a camel's ass before Hitler's invasions. Now, it seems, my beautiful country has become the center of the universe."

Leo, who'd not seen much of Morocco beyond the immediate vicinity of Tangier, did not agree with this description. *This is not a beautiful country. It's nothing but sand and stone.* Aloud he said, "It's common sense. If the British and Americans don't attack Hitler directly through France, then they'll come this way. They'll have to. North Africa will be the footstool they use to reach the rest of Europe. And for men like you and me, that means opportunity."

"Men like you and I? Pray tell, what is it that you think we have in common?" Belafej leaned back against the pile of silk-covered pillows covering the low-slung divan he used as a chair. "I am a Muslim, and you are an infidel. I have pledged my life to winning freedom for my people, who have lived without freedom for over a hundred years, while you—you have no loyalty to your own country, and look for opportunities to capitalize on the weakness of others. The similarities between us escape me, Mr. Hoffman."

Leo took a sip of his honey-sweetened mint tea before answering. "We are both men with goals. Different goals, true. You want the French and Spanish out of Morocco. I want to earn enough money to live securely, no matter who wins this war. What we share is the ability to take advantage of our current situation."

Belafej's wide brown eyes narrowed into slits, and his slight double chin became more pronounced. "Carlton Coon, the American vice-consul, comes here to pay his respects, although I am now the leader of an outlawed political party. He asks if the Americans can rely on me to rally my people against the Germans should they attack through Spain. I ask him if the Americans will, in return for such a promise, ally themselves with us to fight for our freedom from the French. The French! The same people who swore allegiance to their German conquerors, who have vowed to resist any invasion of North Africa by the British or the Americans. And do you know what Carlton Coon says to me?"

"What does he say?"

"He says, in his pretty school-boy Arabic, 'the United States government can make no promises that might destabilize the domestic political situation in North Africa.' We have a saying, Mr. Hoffman. 'The enemy of my enemy is my friend.' The Germans are enemies of the French, and enemies of the Jews. That would make them friends of the Berbers and Arabs in North Africa."

"If you could trust them."

"Just so. And we are better off trusting no one."

"Still, you will fight, when it is advantageous for you to do so. And for that, you will need weapons."

Leo's comment was rewarded by a flicker of interest in the other man's eyes, though his response belied this. "We do not need a war. What we need is the opportunity for education, and to be treated like human beings. And we must have an end to the repressive taxes. The French try to squeeze money from us like milk from a dry goat. Yet, I will ask. What is it you have in mind?"

"Grenades."

"How many?"

"Six crates."

"Where are they? How are they guarded?"

"That is the information that I am willing to sell to you."

"For how much?"

"One thousand dollars, U.S., and some information."

"What information?"

"The name of your undercover German contact in Tangier."

Belafej looked at Leo suspiciously. "And why should I tell you this?"

Leo smiled indulgently. "Because you will need weapons to fight the French, when the opportunity arises. And I can sell that man's identity to the British."

Belafej brushed a few crumbs off the table in front of him. "You will rot in hell, Mr. Hoffman."

"No doubt. And when the time comes, you can send along some Frenchmen to keep me company."

⊛

Leo stood on the balcony of a spacious villa set high up on one of the cliffs overlooking the port of Tangier. The city spread

out beneath him like a Cubist painting, its low-slung buildings reduced to basic shapes and monochromatic tones: squares,
spires, semicircles and rectangles, rendered in white, off-white,
and beige, hugging the flanks of the hills that separated the sea
from the sandy plains to the south. From here one could not
see the city's riotous colors: the fabrics ablaze in red, yellow, and
green; the exotic rugs woven from silk and wool; nor the walls,
floors, and fountains covered with tiles of blue, white, green, and
rose. One could not see the details in the latticework as intricate
as Belgian lace, nor the mother-of-pearl inlay gleaming in deeply
polished wood. Bougainvillea plants added the only splashes of
color, their fragile magenta and orange blossoms hiding the talon-
like thorns that enabled the plants to grip doorways and fences.
From this vantage point Tangier looked deceptively simple and
peaceful.

A man walked toward him carrying two short crystal glasses.
"Single malt," he said, handing one glass to Leo, "with a treat: an
ice cube."

"Thank you." Leo tasted the scotch. "Excellent."

The other man turned to admire the view. The criers of the
Muslim evening call to prayer had just begun their chants. The dis-
embodied voices blended into a complex harmony as they wafted
up the hillside from the city's mosques.

"I was lucky to find this place," he said. "The city filled up like
a barrel after Paris fell. The owner of the villa was able to get out
about six months ago, to Argentina, I believe. Good fortune for
both of us."

"Here's to good fortune," Leo repeated, lifting his glass before
taking another sip.

"To good fortune." They were speaking German, and the
nuances of his accent revealed to those with an ear for such things
that Leo's host was a German Swiss. His name was Rolph Schmidt.
Leo had discovered that the man loved good food and expensive

liquor. He also enjoyed other, less socially acceptable, sensuous pleasures. He was the Swiss representative of the Red Cross in Tangier. He was also an architect, and a German spy.

"So you're from Austria, you say?" Schmidt asked Leo.

"A long time ago."

"And you've been where since then?"

"Shanghai, mostly."

"Were you there during the Japanese invasion? I heard that was an ugly business."

Leo paused. In his mind's eye he watched again as the Wing On department store shattered, then disappeared from view behind a cloud of smoke and dust. Shards of glass, chunks of cement, and bloody bits of human flesh rained down upon and around their car. He heard his daughter's screams, felt his heart and lungs contract in terror. *Martha was in that building.*

He took a long pull on his drink. "Yes. I was there. It was an ugly business."

"So, forgive my curiosity, but why didn't you go back to Austria? Why come to Tangier?"

"Opportunity."

"Opportunity? Of what sort?"

"Desperation and chaos always yield opportunity, Herr Schmidt. I took advantage of this in Shanghai. When the Japanese took over, the opportunities diminished. I left and came here."

"Tangier certainly supplies plenty of both, if chaos and desperation are what you seek. But as an architect, I delight in overcoming chaos. My goal is to impose organization: function, form. What do you have in mind to build?"

"An empire."

"That's ambitious."

"Yes. But as with many things, we start with one small piece. One brick. That's what I do, Herr Schmidt. I take one small piece, one small piece of information, and I use that to connect people who have complementary needs. Weapons with warriors. People with hard currency with those who must travel. People with assets they must sell with people who have money."

Schmidt studied Leo for a moment. "You're not here to give me an architectural commission, are you?"

"I confess I am not. I want to help you."

"Help me? Help me how?"

"I want to help you help the Fuehrer."

Schmidt put his glass down on the top of the balcony rail. "Switzerland is a neutral country, Mr. Hoffman. What makes you think that I have any interest in helping Germany?"

Leo looked him in the eye. "A mutual acquaintance. Someone who is in the position to know."

"This is preposterous. How can you stand there, in my home, and accuse me—"

"I did not make an accusation. I made an observation, and offered to assist you."

"The only assistance you can give me is to leave my house at once."

"No, I don't think that's accurate. I can assist you by telling you some things that the Germans would very much like to know. Like when and where the Allies plan to attack."

Schmidt stopped sputtering. "You're bluffing."

"And that response is an admission of interest."

Schmidt went to pick up his drink, but knocked it over in the process. The two men listened to the muffled sound of breaking glass as it struck the rocks fifty feet below.

"Damn," Schmidt muttered. His face was red, and Leo could see beads of sweat popping up along his brow. *He's close now.*

"I'm sure this must be very disconcerting for you, but I assure you that an alliance will prove advantageous for both of us. And, while I would much prefer to work *with* you, now that I know the true nature of your activities here, that information also has its price, a price others would be very willing to pay."

"And no doubt the services that you are proposing also have a price."

"Yes. But I won't ask to be paid until I've succeeded. And as part of that payment, I expect to receive permission to reside permanently in Switzerland, along with my daughter."

"I can't arrange for that."

"But you know others who can. You're not the only man in Switzerland hoping that the Reich will succeed."

"Very well, Mr. Hoffman. I will... communicate with my associates regarding your... offer. They'll want to know how you're getting your information, of course."

"I'll be happy to let the right people know, when the time comes. Thank you for your cooperation, Herr Schmidt. And for the scotch."

"Forgive me if I don't see you out," Schmidt replied, his voice brittle. "Leave the glass on the table."

Leo turned to leave, then turned back around to face his host. "We all have our weaknesses, Mr. Schmidt. And Tangier has many temptations."

The man's face broke out in a full sweat. "You really are a bastard, aren't you?" he stammered, pulling out his handkerchief.

"I'm sure there are many who think so. But when I get you the information you're seeking, you will find that I am, at least, a very useful bastard. And I believe the German high command will think so as well."

❦

William Eddy sat in the office of Carlton Coon, former professor of anthropology at Harvard University and Arabian specialist, now stationed in Tangier as a vice-consul under J. Rives Childs. He was also a spy.

They'd met only a few weeks earlier, but the two men got along extraordinarily well. Both had spent years living and working in

North Africa; they respected the history and culture of its people. Both came to Tangier from academia, though Coon looked more professorial. Eddy entered a room with the broad-shouldered confidence of a Marine; Coon was denied a naval commission for being overweight, and one of his legs was a full inch longer than the other. Ungainly, with prominent ears and a large nose, Coon's intellect was his salvation, and he knew it.

They got along well for another reason; both men believed that it was necessary, in their current line of work, to bend the rules. Or, if need be, break them.

Eddy was shaking his head. "What is it that Childs said, exactly?"

"That his wife has been complaining about the 'clicking' noises up on the roof of the consulate at night. We'll have to move the transmitter."

"Because the Missus can't sleep? He expects us to give up the most secure transmission site we've got?"

"You know how concerned he is about keeping the Snake Pit out of our 'clandestine' operations. He won't even let me use diplomatic license plates on my car, even though I'm a vice-consul."

Eddy smiled at Coon's use of the derogatory term the espionage team used for the State Department. "Well, he's been pretty good at turning a blind eye. We'll move the set to my place for the time being. Rives should leave us alone for a while. He'll have his hands full with that Hollywood guy in town—what's his name?"

"Zanuck. Darryl Zanuck. Director. Or producer. Or both."

"Right. Zanuck will prove a useful distraction." He skipped on to the next subject. "The weapon transfers are going well?"

"Exceedingly well. I just hope you're right that the tribes will use them against the Germans and French, when the time comes. If the time comes."

"Oh, it's coming, all right. North Africa is the only realistic avenue we have. Roosevelt will come around soon enough."

"And you're convinced the French will resist an invasion?"

Eddy shook his head. "What I think doesn't matter. We have to prepare for a fight. Vichy has eight divisions in North Africa. The leadership vowed to resist an attack, and the Nazis are holding a million French POWs hostage to seal the deal. If the French fight back, we'll need native support."

"And then hope the tribes don't use those same guns against us later, when they don't get the freedom they want."

"One war at a time, Carlton. One war at a time. Now tell me, what do you know about a Leo Hoffman?"

"Hoffman? Hmm... tall? Dark hair? Sharp dresser?"

"That's him. Ever met him?"

"No. I've seen him around. He doesn't exactly melt into a crowd. I hear he's quite the operator. "

"Meaning?"

"You know, always able to put 'interested parties' together. A broker of sorts. Makes money coming and going matching up something someone has with someone else who wants it. Why do you ask?"

"He's one of us."

"What? You're joking."

"It's no joke. I inherited him from the Brits. Now that I think about it, being a wheeler-dealer is a pretty good cover, if everyone assumes he's out for himself."

"He's a Brit? Funny, I thought he was... well, I'm not sure what I thought. French, maybe."

"Hungarian. And he's done some good work. Those grenades we wanted to get to Belafej's group? He arranged for them to be 'kidnapped.' Got half the money from Belafej in advance, then paid off the depot guards."

"That was clever. The French can't be pissed off at us when Arabs succeed in stealing French grenades."

"Exactly. Now it seems he's come up with something that could prove very useful, and we're going to have to be very careful how we work it."

"I'm listening."

"He's uncovered a high-level German undercover operative here, in Tangier. Hoffman has the man thinking he can be a conduit."

"Hoffman can pass on false information? That's great!"

"In theory, yes. But the problem is, we have to make sure that Hoffman won't put his personal interests ahead of ours, given the right set of circumstances. He's a man without a country. No loyalties. Doesn't seem to care much about anything, other than his daughter."

"He has a daughter? Here?"

"No. She's back in the States."

"How did that happen?"

"American wife, or ex-wife. Anyway, to make this work, we'll have to pass along tidbits that are true but not really damaging, and false information that is truly misleading. Hoffman has to believe that most of it's true, and we have to make sure he doesn't find out anything that we don't want him to know. A delicate mix."

"I'd say so."

"I'm counting on you to come up with enough harmless stuff to keep the Germans interested. Travel plans for major diplomats, names of cooperators we've already exposed… that sort of thing."

"I'll get clearance, of course?"

"Of course. We won't communicate anything that hasn't been sanctioned. But I want you to be the point person."

"With pleasure. And do we have an ultimate goal of some kind?"

"Yes. We want to mislead the Germans as to the time and place for the invasion of North Africa, once the date's been set."

"Oh. Is that all?"

Eddy smiled. "Yes, Carlton, that's all."

CHAPTER 5

THE AUNT

NEW YORK, MAY 1942

The three of them had tea in the parlor. Bernice sat in one of two wing chairs near the fireplace. Margaret kept popping up off the sofa, acting like the nervous mother hen she was: straightening a picture, grabbing a runaway napkin, adjusting the curtains so the afternoon sun didn't shine in their eyes. So far they'd spent ten uncomfortable minutes making conversation about Maddy's school and the weather. *Surely the woman would soon turn to the subject at hand.*

To Margaret's considerable surprise, it was Maddy who introduced the topic. It wasn't like the child to charge ahead in a conversation, but then Maddy was always one to surprise you.

Maddy laid her cup and saucer back down onto the small oval table beside her, sat up just a bit straighter, and began speaking with exaggerated formality, in a way she hoped made her sound very sensible and mature. "Mrs. Mason, I've seen the photograph you gave to Mrs. O'Connor. It's very convincing."

"Please, Madeleine, call me Aunt Bernice."

"I… ah… no, no thank you. Not yet,"

"As you wish."

"Well. As I was saying, after examining the birth certificates for you and my mother, and my parents' marriage license, as well as the other family photographs, it does seem that we might be related."

"Indeed. I'm glad that you have come to that conclusion."

"Yes. Of course, I do have some questions."

"I'm sure you must. I have some of my own to ask. But, by all means, you go first."

"Okay." Maddy paused, and when she spoke again, her voice was infused with five years' worth of loneliness and longing. "What was she like? My mother? When she was young?"

"Ah. Well, as you might imagine, she was always beautiful, even as a child. And she was full of energy and enthusiasm. Martha could always see a bright side to things. Very much like our mother."

The two women stayed silent while Maddy took a moment to soak this in. "And do you know why they—my parents—moved away to Shanghai?"

"I know a little. As you might know, we grew up in Munich, your mother and I. After our mother died our father did his best to raise us. I'm afraid it went easier for me than for Martha. My father and I were very much alike. We didn't need… great gulps of life, the way Martha did. Always jumping into situations without thinking about the consequences.

"I was older by three years. I left home in 1925, to study at the university in Graz, in Austria. At the time I thought it a *fait accompli* that your mother would marry a fellow by the name of Harry Jacobson, whom she was seeing at the time. But that didn't happen. Instead, one day, in the summer of 1926, she just disappeared. She left a note for my father, explaining that during a brief trip to Paris, she'd met a man with whom she had fallen in love, and that she was going to Shanghai to marry him."

"My parents *eloped*?"

"Yes, Madeleine. My sister ran away to marry your father. It was several months before we heard from her. From her letters, she seemed happy enough. For reasons that were never really well explained, they told us they could not come to Germany, but invited us to Shanghai. My father hated to travel, and I was busy with my studies, then my work. We never went."

Maddy took a deep breath, clearly summoning her courage. "And then why—why did it take so long for you to find me?"

Bernice looked at Mrs. O'Connor before answering. Mrs. O'Connor looked down and studied her tea. *So she has decided to let me tell the whole story,* thought Bernice. *Very well. At least the child will get only one version.*

"I did not know that anything had happened until months after your mother died, Madeleine. Our lives were very… unstable."

"What do you mean?"

"Well, Madeleine, our family is Jewish, and by 1937, it was becoming more and more difficult for Jews in Germany."

"What do you mean, 'our family is Jewish?'" Maddy interrupted, bewildered. "We're Catholic. We've always been Catholic." She looked to Margaret for support.

"Now, Maddy. You were confirmed with Mary Kate. You're certainly Catholic now. Catholics aren't as—particular as some about what came before. It's yer history she's speakin' of, isn't that right, Mrs. Mason?"

"I suppose." Bernice looked at the child's confused face. "We cannot sort everything out right now, in one conversation. We were Jews according to Hitler, and that meant our lives were becoming very difficult. So we decided to leave. By then I was married myself. You will soon meet my husband, I hope. But my father was ill, too ill to travel. So I stayed in Munich until he died. Archie, my husband, made it to France.

"Around the time we made these decisions, we heard about the war in Shanghai. We tried to get in touch, but with the chaos that war brings, we could not. After almost a year, Archie was able to confirm through the French embassy that Martha Hoffman was among the victims of a bomb blast in Shanghai, in August of '37.

Luckily, my father was spared that news, for he died before we found out. We did not know how to look for you. We did not even know if you were alive.

"By the time the war broke out in Europe, Archie and I were both in the United States. I will not go into the details now, but because of some patents we hold, we were allowed to immigrate. With some money in my pocket, I was able to hire a private detective. I finally found Amelia Hoffman, and then... I found you."

She reached over and touched Maddy on one knee. "You see, I never gave up, Madeleine. I knew that if you were still alive, I would find you. And I did."

Maddy stood up, her eyes fixed on Bernice.

"Madeleine?" Bernice repeated, now hoping for a response.

"I'll be right back," the girl whispered, and raced out of the room.

"Maddy!" Margaret stood up and called after her.

"I'll be right back!" she called from down the hallway. Mrs. O'Connor sat back down on the sofa. "I don't know what to say, Mrs. Mason. It's all so—"

"Melodramatic?"

"Yes, I suppose it is that."

In a moment Maddy returned, carrying a long, gray velvet jewelry box. She reclaimed her seat and opened the box slightly, only to snap it shut again.

"This necklace belonged to my mother," she said in a small but firm voice. "If you can tell me what this is, I will know you are my aunt."

Bernice shook her head. "That is not realistic, Madeleine. The last time I saw your mother, she was just eighteen years old. The only piece of jewelry she owned then was a gold medallion that Harry had given her. There was a bird, I think. It was a sort of nightingale—"

"Mr. Songbird. She would take it out, and let me play with it, and she would sing to me." Maddy opened the box, and taking her mother's golden medallion in her hand, clutched it to her breast. Then came the tears.

ॐ

The Mason's house was immense; bigger, even than the respectably huge Georgian estate Maddy had lived in as a little girl in Shanghai. But this house was unlike anything Maddy had ever seen, or even imagined. She knew nothing of Walter Gropius, or the group of modern architects that had emerged from Germany in the 1920s with the name *Bauhaus*. She did not know that houses could be so completely spare: that windows could line up, side by side, and form a wall; that lights could shine straight down like eyeballs in the ceiling; or that stairs could float, like airy sculptures connecting one floor to the next. She'd become used to crocheted slipcovers covering tattered furniture, to faded curtains hovering protectively over small windows, and overstuffed, squeaky chairs that greeted you upon arrival like an endearingly cranky old relative. But the Mason's home, as unfamiliar as it was, was also intriguing. It was intimidating, but fascinating. Just like her Aunt Bernice.

The Masons lived in Englewood Cliffs, New Jersey, a posh, verdant suburb just thirty minutes from Manhattan. Maddy only had a vague idea of what Mason Industries manufactured. She knew it was a chemical and electrical engineering firm, busily supplying the United States military with some of the staples of modern warfare: smoke screens and components for radar systems, and a special compound that, when added to paint, helped to protect metal from the corrosive effects of salt. She knew her aunt and uncle were doing well. They were rich enough to live in Englewood

Cliffs, they were rich enough to own a brand new Cadillac, and they were rich enough to buy her a whole new wardrobe at Saks Fifth Avenue.

But Maddy soon observed that her aunt and uncle, for the most part, lived very frugally. Bernice did the grocery shopping, had a housekeeper in only once a week, and did the cooking herself unless they had company. She bought her shoes at a discount store, and refused to hire a chauffeur, until she discovered that she needed one to bring Maddy to school and back every day. It was too late in the school year to transfer, but if, by September, Maddy was still comfortable living with her aunt and uncle, she would attend an exclusive girl's high school in New Jersey, with the grandchildren of Vanderbilts and Winstons.

Bernice promised to let Katherine visit often on the weekends. She had already come once and, for the first time in her life, was rendered speechless in the face of such contemporary luxury. At first the two girls talked after school nearly every day, but Katherine was busily involved with the school paper, her studies, and her chores. She lacked the abundance of free time that Maddy now enjoyed.

Bernice was just as involved in Mason Industries as her husband, if not more so; she was a chemical engineer, with a Ph.D., no less, and knew more about the science of what Mason Industries manufactured than anyone else there. Archie met with their clients and handled the contracts. He traveled frequently and worked late. Maddy was usually left to herself from the time school was out until late in the evening.

After a few weeks, a nagging loneliness began to tug at the edges of the joy she'd felt upon being found. She did her school work and then listened to the radio, or prowled around the house, restless and bored, trying to stay away from the one room that drew her like a magnet.

It was a library, but it was obviously designed to be used as a reading room rather than a working office, for it lacked a desk. The room contained two chairs, elongated leather recliners that reminded Maddy of enormous caterpillars. Built-in bookcases lined three of the walls from floor to ceiling. The fourth wall was mostly window, presenting a view to a back lawn that sloped away from the house toward an acre of woods at the rear of the property. A Persian carpet covered the gray slate floor.

And, tucked into the corner, sat a baby grand piano.

The first time that she walked into the room Maddy jumped as if she'd seen a gremlin. Her aunt completely misinterpreted her reaction.

"Oh, do you play?"

"No," was the curt reply.

"Neither do we. We bought the house partially furnished, and the piano stayed. It's handsome, and I thought it would be useful for entertaining. You may take lessons, if you wish."

"No. No, thank you. I can't play."

Bernice gave her an odd look, but said nothing more.

Now, once again alone in the house, Maddy walked to the library and stared at the piano. She could feel her heart pounding. "Stop being a baby," she chided herself aloud. "You'd think there was a ghost in here. Don't be so stupid."

But there was a ghost in there. Her mother's ghost.

Bernice had waited several weeks after Maddy had settled in to her new home before asking about Martha's death. "Madeleine, I know this will be difficult for you, but I would like to know—for you to share with me how your mother died."

"I don't know very much. I wasn't there." *Liar! You were there. And your mother was there, in that store, only because you'd begged her for that doll. Tell her! Tell her how you killed her sister.*

"I see. I realize that you were only seven, and you might not remember much about it, but is there any information that you can give me? We have been in the dark for so long."

The parlor was my favorite room in the house. The walls were made of golden wood, and when the sun shone on it in the after-noon it glowed like Mama's amber necklace. There was a big, comfy couch where Papa liked to take naps, and the chair where Mama and I would sit when she read me stories, when I was still small enough to fit on her lap.

One day Papa opened the parlor door, and there it was. My piano. I knew it was mine right away, before he even told me so. I could already hear the music it was going to make. As far back as I can remember, I could see music in my head. Like fairies dancing. I didn't even need to think about it. The music was just always there.

Then a few days later the first bomb fell, the one that hit the street outside the hotel where Maman and I were having tea. The glass windows burst into millions of sharp raindrops, and for hours afterwards I couldn't hear properly. And people died. All around us. People just... died.

After that Shanghai was horrible. Everyone was so afraid; afraid that another bomb would fall, afraid that the Japanese would come. Mama and Papa tried to pretend that they weren't afraid, but I knew. There were too many whispers. Too many times when Maman and Papa spoke German to each other, because they knew that I couldn't understand.

But I had my piano. So I decided to cheer everyone up. No, I wanted to show off. That was it, really. I wanted to show off. So I made them come in and listen to me play. I knew they'd be surprised. Gaston, who played the piano at the country club, he'd showed me the sound that each key made on his piano, and after that it was so easy! I was a prodigy, Gaston said. I'd never heard that word before. He said it meant that I had a special talent, that I could do something almost no one else could do, not even grown-ups. He wanted to tell my parents, but I made him promise not to tell. I wanted to tell them myself. I wanted to show off.

And they were surprised, and for a few moments it was wonderful, just like it was before. I was so pleased with myself, and Papa was so proud of me. He asked me if there was anything I wanted. A new doll, maybe, he said. And there was a doll… she was a princess, a ballerina, dressed in red velvet and lace. Mama knew just which one I meant. So we went, right away, down to the department store to buy it. But because the street was so crowded the driver couldn't find a place to park the car. Maman jumped out, kissed Papa, and went into the department store to get my doll.

Papa told the chauffeur to circle the block, but we couldn't go in a circle, there were too many people. All the Chinese who'd come into the city to escape the Japanese soldiers. So we had to go down a street that led away from the store. And then there was the noise, that awful thundering noise, and the building disappeared. A hand fell onto the hood of our car. A woman's hand, with pink painted fingernails. I was screaming and screaming. And my father left me there, with the driver. He shouted at the driver to take me home, and he left me there. And then he sent me away. Of course he did. How could he stand to be around me after I'd killed her?

"No, Aunt Bernice. All I know is that a bomb fell on a department store where she was shopping. My mother and a lot of other people were killed."

And she wouldn't have been there if it hadn't been for me.

Maddy walked into the room and sat down on the piano bench. Her fingers laid themselves out in middle C position, as if by instinct. She'd taken lessons during her two years as a boarding student at the convent, coerced by the threat of being locked in a dark closet if she refused. Almost despite herself, she'd learned something about scales, major and minor keys, chords and fingering. But that had been over two years ago. She'd not played since.

Trying to get used to the feel of the keys under her fingers, Maddy practiced a few scales. The piano needed tuning but it wasn't off too badly. Excited and more curious by the second, she stood up and lifted the lid on the bench. Yes, there was some sheet music there. She flipped through a couple of nearly new books, looking for something easy and familiar. Finding a book of Christmas carols, she propped it up on the piano and sat down again.

"Oh Holy Night," she murmured, positioning her fingers. She touched a few notes lightly, then began to play. By the time she reached the second verse she had stopped looking at the music. Some part of her brain, long quiet, stirred. She knew which notes to reach for. Her ears and fingers were connected in some mysterious way. She heard the music in her head, and made her fingers replicate it, until what she heard satisfied her. What she'd told her astounded parents five years ago was still true—*I just play. I know where the music lives.* There was a tuning fork in her head; a string quartet; no, an orchestra. She could reach for the music, and make it hers.

Playing for herself, by herself, she felt a rush of energy like nothing she'd ever felt before. Within an hour she had played every simple Christmas carol in the thin volume.

By the time her aunt came home, Maddy was exhausted but exhilarated. She did not say a word about the piano. Bernice, assuming that her happy mood was the result of a pleasant day at school, asked her niece a few questions about her day, clearly pleased that her choices for Madeleine were working out so well.

That night Maddy lay awake, savoring her accomplishment. But her joy was laced with guilt, as if she had done something delightful yet deplorable.

I won't tell anyone. It will be my secret. My home. My piano. And with a thousand sweet notes playing in her ears, she fell asleep.

CHAPTER 6

THE VISITOR

ᔕᐧᐧᔒ

NEW YORK, MAY 1942

The following Saturday Maddy went downstairs promptly
at eight to breakfast with her aunt. Bernice had already made coffee
and toast, which, along with an occasional piece of fruit, was all she
ever ate for breakfast. It never occurred to her to ask Maddy if she
would like something more for her morning meal.

"Good morning, Madeleine," said Bernice as Maddy took her
place at the table.

"Good morning."

"Did you sleep well?"

"Yes, thank you. And you?"

"As well as I ever do. Were you warm enough? The weather is
changing. I could give you another blanket. I dislike turning up the
heat. It seems a silly waste of money to heat a whole room when a
good blanket is sufficient."

To Maddy, who had not slept in a room by herself since she
was seven years old, the simple act of climbing into her own bed,
under her own blankets, was such a luxury it never occurred to her
that the room itself could be warmer.

"No, thank you. I'm really fine." Five years in America had flattened her English accent, but Maddy noticed it coming back, totally unintentionally, when speaking alone with her aunt. She had no idea why. It just seemed appropriate.

"Very good," responded Bernice. And then, changing the subject in her usual abrupt way, she said, "Madeleine, there is someone I would like for you to meet."

"Oh?"

"An old friend of mine. And an old friend of your mother's. Harry Jacobson. The man who gave your mother that necklace."

"Here?" Maddy looked around, as if she expected him to pop out from behind a door.

"He lives in Chicago, but he is here, in New York, for a few days. He's an architectural engineer and he has a commission here. Because he has achieved some renown in his field, it was not difficult to find him once we arrived in the States. Archie and I visited once when we were in Chicago, and Harry has been here several times." Bernice put down her toast and looked directly at Maddy. "Of course, it was a very long time ago, but he and your mother were once very close. He would love to meet you."

"Of course." Harry Jacobson! The man her mother almost married. The man who'd given her Mr. Songbird. Maddy felt as if a treasure trove had been laid at her feet. After so many years of knowing nothing, she was to be given another piece of the past: someone else to whom she was connected.

"When?"

"Perhaps this evening, if you like."

"Yes, yes. I would like that very much."

"Very good. We will have dinner here. I will make an apple strudel. I seem to remember that Harry loves strudel."

By the time six o'clock rolled around Maddy had tried on every outfit she owned. She finally settled on a plain blue skirt and white blouse. She thought the simple combination made her look older.

Just before leaving the room, she took her mother's necklace and put it around her neck. The chain was too long; the golden nightingale fell well past her budding bosom. Maddy gazed at herself in the full-length mirror mounted on the wall to her very own bathroom. She could almost hear her mother's voice again, as she knocked on the lid of Mr. Songbird's gray velvet home. *Bonjour, Mr. Songbird! Are you there? Would you like to come out and sing for little Maddy?*

Maddy touched the medallion and closed her eyes. *I am so sorry, Mama. So very sorry.* Then she went downstairs to await the arrival of Harry Jacobson.

The doorbell rang at exactly seven o'clock. "Well," said her aunt, confirming the time with a glance at the sleek, round kitchen clock, "I see that Harry is still as punctual as ever. I will put the strudel in the oven now. Would you care to answer the door, Maddy?"

Maddy felt her heart pounding in her ears as she walked to the front foyer. She stopped to collect herself before she opened the door. She'd practiced her greeting in the mirror all afternoon.

"What a pleasure to meet you, I'm Madeleine Hoffman. Please come in," she said, finishing before the door was even fully open.

The man at the door stared at her, saying nothing. Maddy saw his eyes fill with tears. "*Mein Gott,*" he finally stammered. "You're as beautiful as your mother."

Maddy blushed. She didn't know what she'd expected him to say, but that was certainly not it. "Please, come in," she repeated, embarrassed, and backed up enough to allow Harry through the door.

Once inside, he turned to look at her again, then pulled out a handkerchief and wiped his eyes. "I'm so sorry, Madeleine. It was just such a shock, seeing you there, looking so much like your mother, after all these years... oh, no. I've embarrassed you. I'm sorry."

Bernice's arrival immediately changed the course of the conversation. "Harry! Look at you. You are getting fat."

He smiled ruefully. "Yes, Bernice. How very kind of you to notice. And despite your candor, it's a pleasure to see you again. Thank you for the invitation."

"The pleasure is mine. Madeleine was very excited to meet you."

"And I her," Harry replied, not looking in Maddy's direction.

"Well, then. Come in. We have a nice dinner waiting. Was I correct in remembering that you are very fond of apple strudel?"

Harry patted his portly midsection. "Still too fond, I'm afraid,"

The trio moved into the living room. Bernice rang a bell, signaling the housekeeper to bring in the appetizers.

"Would you care for something to drink? As you know I do not drink alcohol, but I am sure Archie—he is in Washington, by the way, working on another contract—that Archie has a bottle or two of something stashed in the cabinet."

"Could you manage a Manhattan?"

"Nothing that complicated, I am afraid. How about a glass of bourbon?"

"That will do nicely, thank you."

"Very good. Eileen? Please get Mr. Jacobson a glass of bourbon. Ice?"

As the housekeeper fixed his drink, Harry found it hard to take his eyes off Madeleine. It was as if Martha had greeted him at the door: the same eyes, the same room-brightening smile. She was even wearing Martha's necklace! He'd not known her when she was Madeleine's age. He'd not met Herr Levy's younger daughter until his first year at the university in Munich.

So many years ago. He'd fallen in love with her before he'd ever even spoken to her. But Martha had never really been his; she'd never said yes, she'd never given him anything but a mercurial glimmer of hope, no sturdier than a dragonfly resting on water. But he'd captured it, and then relied upon that hope as if it had been a promise.

Was it possible to hate a man you'd never met? He hated Hitler. He hated Mussolini. But these were abstract, intellectual animosities. Harry was an engineer. He was devoted to disciplines grounded in physics, dependent upon forces one could measure. He made sense of things. It made sense for him to hate Hitler.

It had never made sense for him to hate Leo Hoffman.

Harry believed what his rabbi taught: hatred stood in the way of healing. Hatred was an acid, corrupting every vessel that tried to contain it. Harry made an effort to turn his back on his hatred, move away from it, set it aside. He'd eventually stopped torturing himself with visions of Martha being intimate with this unknown man, this stranger who must have been better looking, smarter, and a better lover than Harry was or could ever hope to be. He'd finally succeeded in getting to the point where the hatred no longer burned its way through his sleep. But he still thought about her—no, he thought about both of them, for they were inseparable, the yin and the yang of his pain—he thought about both of them nearly every day.

He'd learned that the opposite of love was not hate. The opposite of love was indifference. For the past sixteen years he'd craved it, and for sixteen years, the peace that indifference brings had eluded him.

Bernice was asking him a question. "What project brings you into town, Harry?" He looked at the drink in his hand, trying to pull himself back into the present.

"An office tower. Interesting challenge. It's on an L-shaped lot on Park Avenue. The primary architects want to maximize the amount of square footage for the lot size. We'll be using a thirteen-story base. It took a while to get started because there was such a ruckus about tearing down the old hotel that was there."

"Where?" Maddy asked, trying to sound interested. Harry Jacobson was so very different from her father. His hair was curly but brown, with bits of gray. His eyes were brown, too. Big, brown, and friendly. He was… soft-looking. And so very normal. He was the sort of person, thought Maddy, who would blend in on the subway platform with all the other businessmen going to work, wearing a suit and a hat and carrying a briefcase. Not at all like her father.

"It's on Park Avenue. Madeleine, how would you like to come out to the job site with me? Put on a hard hat? Watch the crews in action?"

Maddy perked up. "Could I, Aunt Bernice? Please?"

"Yes, *bitte* Bernice?"

"I will make no decisions on an empty stomach. Let us go to the table."

"Bernice, Bernice. You live in America now. American is a delightfully informal language. You really must start using more contractions. *Let's* go to the table. Dinner smells wonderful!"

"Contractions, I can probably adapt to. But I won't—you see? I won't use my fork in my right hand. Switching one's fork from one hand to another! What a ridiculous convention."

"Indeed."

All through the soup course, while Harry and Bernice talked about boring subjects like discount rates and labor shortages, Maddy tried to think of a way to bring up the subject of her mother. As difficult as it was for her to picture her mother *in* love with the man across the table, Maddy could not imagine anyone ever falling *out* of love with her mother. Maybe Mr. Jacobson didn't like to talk about her because he was still in love with her. Maybe…

An opening finally presented itself and Maddy dove in. "Tell me, Mr. Jacobson, are you married?"

Harry scraped the last drop of soup from his bowl and set his spoon down before answering. "Yes, I am."

Married? To someone else? This answer did not fit into the romantic drama unfolding in Maddy's imagination. "Oh. Do you have children?"

Harry looked at Bernice. "She converses like an adult, Bernice."

"Yes, and in two languages." For the first time, Maddy had the sense that Bernice was proud of her. She felt a tingle of joy in her stomach, but it was coupled with annoyance; she hated it when adults talked about her like she was not in the room.

"Well, then, don't I deserve an answer to my question?" she asked, sounding a bit more peevish than polite.

Harry wiped his mouth to hide his smile. "Of course. No, I don't have any children."

"Oh. How long have you been married?"

"Three years."

"What's your wife's name?"

"Ruth."

"And Mrs. Jacobson… is she Jewish, too?"

"Madeleine!" Bernice interjected. "This is not an inquisition."

"Bernice, really, I don't mind. I'm sure the child's had to answer many questions herself over the past few weeks. Yes, dear. My wife is Jewish."

"But is she *really* Jewish? Does she go to synagogue and everything?"

"Madeleine!"

Maddy started. That voice! It was the same tone of voice her mother used if she asked a question, but it was the *wrong question.* Her father would scowl, and tension would fill the air like static electricity. *Haven't you learned anything, you idiot? Shut up! Shut up!*

"I'm sorry, Mr. Jacobson. I didn't mean to offend you."

"No offense taken, Madeleine."

"Harry, there is no need—"

"It's really fine, Bernice. I know this is a sensitive topic for you, but she's not being overly personal. Yes, Madeleine. We do go to services. I wasn't raised in a religious household, but my wife was, and she... well, she reintroduced me to my faith. So, what about you, Madeleine?"

"What about me?"

"Tell me a little about yourself."

Maddy felt nervous again. "Um... well, I just found out that I'm Jewish. We always, I mean, I always *thought* we were Catholic. But now... now it's like the more I find out, the more I don't know."

"So you're on a journey of self-discovery. That's—"

"Not a topic designed to aid one's digestion," Bernice declared. "Eileen? We are ready for the next course."

Maddy stayed quiet for the rest of the dinner. She gave brief answers to questions about school, how she liked living in New Jersey, and Bernice's plan to send Katherine and Maddy to camp in Maine during the upcoming summer if Mrs. O'Connor thought she could do without her daughter for a few weeks. It wasn't until they'd made their way through generous portions of Bernice's perfect apple strudel that the conversation again turned to the past.

"Madeleine, you look so much like your mother," Harry began. "Would you happen to have any pictures of her?"

"Yes, yes I do." Maddy jumped up from her chair. "Aunt Bernice, may I be excused for a moment?"

"Yes, of course."

Harry switched to German. "How's she doing? Adjusting, I mean."

"Well, I believe. She seems happy. She doesn't neglect her studies. I try to give her plenty of privacy. I do not want her to feel forced into any uncomfortable intimacy."

"And has she heard from her father?"

Bernice shook her head. "She received one letter, well over a year ago, posted from London not long after he waltzed into New York, announced that he had annulled his marriage to that tramp, approved Madeleine's living arrangements, and disappeared again. The letter was very chatty, but did not contain any real information about what he was doing in London. About four months later, Madeleine received the oddest letter from the U.S. Navy, explaining that Leo was, 'in fine shape,' but that he was being released from the service. Neither Margaret—that's Mrs. O'Connor, the woman I told you about, who has taken care of Maddy for the past three years—neither Margaret nor Madeleine knew that he'd *been in* the Navy. All he'd told them when he left was that he had to do some sort of military service for two years to earn his citizenship. They haven't heard a word since."

"And no ideas?"

"None. It seems as if he has abandoned the poor child. Again."

Maddy burst back in, holding a framed picture in her hand. "Here," she panted, having sprinted back from her room, "My mother. And my father." She put the photograph into Harry's outstretched hand.

Early in his career, while inspecting the construction site of the first skyscraper he'd helped design, Harry had seen a worker fall from the scaffolding. He'd watched as the man lost his balance, watched as another crewman grabbed at him in vain, and then watched as the man plummeted seven hundred feet to the ground. It had taken a million years for him to fall. Time stopped, and Harry felt his heart stop along with it. It wasn't until the man hit the ground, generating a rush of blood, shouts, and sirens, that the world, and Harry's heart, started to move again.

Harry looked at Leo and Martha's wedding picture and felt time stop for a second time. Martha looked radiant. What Harry would have given for her to ever, even once, have looked at him with that light in her eyes! And standing next to her was Leo Hoffman, gazing at his new bride with complete adoration.

"Harry? Are you all right? You look so pale!" Bernice's voice broke through the fog. Harry felt his heart starting to beat again.

"Yes, fine, sorry. I just need a little water, please. I do tend to sleep too little and work too hard on these trips."

CHAPTER 7

THE MESSENGER

ᕉᑎᕊ

NEW YORK, JUNE 1942

Lorraine Callaghan had never been to New York, and she was more than a bit intimidated by the thought of going there on her own, but nothing could keep her away from her sister in her time of need. Not the train fare, or the petrol shortage; not her husband's rheumatism, or her own bad back; not the Nazis, or the bloody Japanese emperor himself. Margaret had lost her youngest son, and although she and her sister didn't keep up with each other day-by-day, Lorraine would see to it that she did not have to mourn her child without a sibling by her side. She was that sort of person, Lorraine was; she took charge of matters. Minutes after she got the phone call, she packed her suitcase and caught the first train south.

She'd lived in a small town in Canada since she came over, married to a young Canadian soldier who'd been lucky enough to finish up the last war all in one piece. Lorraine hadn't worked in the grand houses like Margaret had. She hadn't ever been to a place where they had skyscrapers, subway trains, or hot dog stands. It would have been nice if she could have spent a day or so seeing the sights, but this was not a tourist trip.

A polite, very young police officer picked her up the next morning at the Grand Central, introduced himself, and somberly offered to take her one small suitcase.

"How do you do, Mrs. Callaghan. I'm Ryan Sullivan. I worked on the force with Jamie. He was a good officer. We all feel terribly sorry about your family's loss."

Lorraine felt a bit uncomfortable riding to the house in his blue and white car, even distracted as she was by the size of the buildings and the sheer number of people on the streets. But then Margaret's house looked like a regular police station when she arrived; there were at least a half a dozen police cars parked along the curb, stretching down the full length of the block.

Lorraine let herself in, the nice young man who'd brought her following close behind. It was as if every member of New York's finest was crammed into the place, paying their respects, honoring young Jamie. She knew what they'd be saying. *Terribly sorry for your loss, Mrs. O'Connor. He was a fine man, your son. A brave man. A good man, who could handle his liquor and knew how to fight fair. You should be proud of him. We all are.* In addition to sending a police car to pick up Lorraine, Police Chief Valentine himself sent a telegram, expressing his condolences. The officers were still passing it around, as if it were a picture postcard.

She knew how hollow all the words would sound to her sister, if she could hear them at all. There was nothing in the world worse than outliving your child. Nothing. Lorraine's only daughter died when she was just fifteen, as fair and full of promise as a spring crocus breaking through the snow. Until the polio got her, and there was nothing anyone could do.

She found Margaret just where she thought she'd be: in the kitchen. She was sitting in a chair at the head of the large oak table, her strong features collapsed into a mass of doughy wrinkles. Shoulders bent, she stared with swollen eyes at a plate of eggs and toast that some concerned person had put in front of her, as if she didn't remember what she was supposed to do with it. Four women, dressed in black, fluttered around her like magpies, chirping useless condolences.

"Margaret," said Lorraine. The room fell silent. Her sister looked up. The instant their eyes met, Margaret's filled with tears.

"He volunteered. Ya know that, don't ya Lorraine? He didn't wait to be drafted. He upped and volunteered."

Lorraine walked over and laid a calloused hand on her sister's cheek. "I do know that, Margaret. I know."

Margaret placed her own hand over her sister's. "Thanks fer comin,'" she managed to say, before the fragile threads holding together the pieces of her heart disintegrated completely.

It took a long time to clear out a houseful of Irish in mourning. No one who showed up at the door could be sent away without a bite to eat and a small glass of hospitality, and after the last of the sympathetic visitors had taken their leave, there was the business of putting all the food that had been brought 'round into the icebox, the gathering up of all the empty whiskey glasses, the dumping out of too-full ashtrays, the washing of dishes, and the general sweeping up. By late afternoon Lorraine was the last one standing. Margaret and her girls were off to the church. There was no body to be buried; no part of Jamie would ever make it home. But arrangements had to be made nonetheless.

She answered the knock on the door quickly, expecting to find another friend or relation coming by to express condolences over a glass of whiskey. Instead she was greeted by the postman.

"Good afternoon ma'am. Is Mrs. O'Connor in?" the young man asked, full of shy courtesy.

"No, she's gone off to church. Can I be of help to ya?"

"Well, I heard about her son. I'm new on the route, but I went to grade school with Jamie. I just wanted to tell her how sorry I am." He handed over a small stack of letters.

Lorraine flipped through them. "That's very kind. And who shall I say called?"

"Kevin. Kevin Wilson."

"Well, thank you, Kevin. Hold on—you've got one that's been misdelivered. I met the three boarders today. They've all been here a donkey's age, and there's no one here by this name." She handed him back a fat white envelope.

He glanced at it. "No return address. One more for the dead letter off—oh, I'm so sorry. I didn't mean—"

She smiled to put him at ease. "Can't be helped. I'll tell Margaret you stopped by."

Later that day, she had second thoughts about that letter. Madeleine Hoffman. Wasn't there something familiar about that name? No matter. She could only stay for a few days, and there were more important things to worry about.

CHAPTER 8

THE CASUALTY

⌒⌒⌒

TANGIER, AUGUST 1942

The Medina, the oldest section of Tangier, was an architectural maze of small, square, flat-roofed and white-washed buildings, all piled across, alongside, under, and on top of each other, as if some child of the gods had used gigantic sugar cubes for building blocks. Its passageways were as narrow and crooked as a ferret's tunnel, winding up, down, around (and occasionally under) the congested homes and shops.

Navigating the Medina required a good sense of direction, decent powers of observation, and some physical stamina, for little of the ancient walled city rested on level ground. Good reflexes helped, too. Leo had already dodged one resentful over-laden donkey, two burly Bedouin men who had no intention of moving out of anyone's way, a woman carrying several dozen loaves of bread stacked on a board atop her well-covered head, several stray dogs, their droppings, and the spittle of a beggar whose aim may or may not have been intentional.

Warily making his way up and down stone staircases worn concave by centuries of sandal-clad pedestrian traffic, Leo was once again struck by the similarities between Shanghai, his home for fifteen years, and Tangier, his home for hopefully not much longer. Like the ancient walled heart of Shanghai, the Medina was surrounded by solid ramparts originally designed to keep invaders out, while keeping slaves, concubines, and prisoners in. During the day both places echoed with the raucous noise of merchants hawking their wares, the gossip of matrons, and the grunts of men carrying twice their own weight. Conversations in a dozen different dialects blended into an indecipherable sea of sound.

Like the Chinese residents of Shanghai, the people of the Medina moved quickly, at a pace set by the speed of commerce, or the timing of an opportunity. Both places were saturated with the pungent odors produced by too many people living too close together; although, unlike in Shanghai, the residents of the Medina managed to mask some of the more unpleasant smells with fragrant ones, like orange, jasmine, sage, and clove, their efforts aided by an occasional breeze from the ocean.

But of all the similarities between the two European-controlled seaports, what hit Leo hardest was the look he saw in the eyes of the children, the ones who had not yet learned to keep their eyes lowered, to hide their hatred or feign submission. In Tangier, as in Shanghai, suspicion and desperation haunted the eyes of the very young.

He glanced at his watch. Normally he met Carlton Coon at night, at Colonel Eddy's villa. Coon and Gordon Browne, Coon's longtime friend and fellow spy, stayed at the hillside mansion whenever Eddy was out of town. Leo would meet Coon or Browne in some remote rendezvous location, then climb into the back seat of their consulate car, crawl underneath a blanket or carpet, and wait, cramped and sweaty, until they arrived at the villa and he was given the "all clear."

On one such trip Leo had nearly suffocated from the smell in the trunk. "What the hell have you got in the boot?" he demanded as he crawled out of hiding, gasping for fresh air. Coon and Browne looked at each other and grinned.

"Just what it smells like," explained Browne. "The toymakers at S.O.E. wanted us to send them samples of local rocks, so they can make harmless-looking roadside bombs, disguised as, well, rocks. But we—"

"We discovered there really aren't a lot of rocks on the roads around here," Coon interrupted. "There is, however, a copious supply of mule turds, because there are so many damn donkeys everywhere. But they don't look like good, healthy, British mule turds. They're more sepia-colored, with a bit of green. So today we had to collect samples to ship off to London."

"Mule turds? They're going to make *mule turd bombs?*"

Coon nodded, still grinning. "And the little buggers will blow a jeep's tires to smithereens, or slow down the pace of an entire division while the advance guys flip and poke *thousands* of mule turds, trying to check for explosive ones!"

"Shit, it might just work."

"Exactly!"

It all seemed ridiculously cloak-and-dagger, but so far, their stereotypical espionage tactics seemed to be working.

Today was different. Today's meeting was designed to be overheard. But it could not seem that way. They had to make it seem as if the person listening in had scored a major coup.

Leo saw the key-shaped entryway for which he'd been searching. Verses from the *Koran* decorated the top of the archway. Leo paused. He was prepared. He knew his lines. He could only hope that everything else went according to plan.

The opening led into a tiny courtyard, where four brightly painted doors opened into four different establishments: red, blue, yellow, green. He knocked on the blue one.

A skinny Arab man opened the door seconds after Leo knocked. His sun-ravaged skin made him look at least fifty, but Leo knew that underneath the deep wrinkles and his heavy mustache he could have been twenty years younger. The man grinned at Leo with the insincere manner of a servant willing to pretend that he knows his place, as long as the pretense remained lucrative, or at least entertaining.

"Ah, welcome, welcome good sir!" he proclaimed in French, gesturing for Leo to come inside.

It took a moment for Leo's vision to make the transition from the bright sunlight to the darker interior of the small room. While his eyes adjusted he focused on the smells wafting in from beyond where he stood: the burnt-sugar odor of kif, a tobacco-like, mildly narcotic substance concocted from hemp leaves; cooking oil; and human perspiration.

"Please, come this way," his host gestured toward an open doorway covered by a drape of thin cotton. Leo followed him into the next room.

Behind the curtain, Carlton Coon sat cross-legged on a large cushion, placed on the floor behind a long, low wooden table. A half-finished bottle of wine sat on the table in front of him. He did not stand as Leo approached.

"Mr. Hoffman. We meet at last. Glad you made it."

Leo sat on the cushion on the other side of the table. "Is this really a good place for a meeting?"

Coon glanced around. "Yes. The proprietor is one of our native operatives. It's one of the few places in Tangier where I feel comfortable saying everything I need to say."

How long would it have taken you to discover that he was working both sides, if I had not come across that helpful detail? "Privacy is certainly a rare commodity here. Tell me, are you inclined to share that wine?"

Coon waved at the man who'd answered the door. "Ahmed, my friend, kindly bring us another glass! And some food!"

The moment Ahmed left the room, Coon leaned forward. "I understand that you're in touch with men who have large stores of weapons at their disposal."

Leo almost laughed. "Is that your way of making polite conversation?"

Coon snorted, and lifted his wine glass. "Despite the fact that I trust the owner of this establishment, it's still a good idea to talk about important issues while he remains out of earshot."

Leo knew full well that the absent owner was now listening carefully to everything being said. "Well, I have no reason to trust the owner of this 'establishment,' as you rather generously describe it. So I will be brief. You've heard correctly. There are certain parties with whom I am in touch, who have held on to substantial munitions since Franco put an end to the 'unrest' in Spain. I believe they could be persuaded to part with their inventory for the right price."

"I assure you, we can meet whatever price they ask. The question is, whether the goods can be transported to where they will be needed."

"That depends. What sort of distance are we talking about?"

Carlton lowered his voice, and managed a fair imitation of a stage whisper. "Dakar. We will need whatever armaments you can muster to arrive in Dakar, no later than the middle of November."

Leo pretended to ponder this information. "Well," he said at last, "I think that can be arranged. But of course, such a complicated delivery requirement will require a substantial increase in the price."

"Freedom has no price!" Coon declared melodramatically. "Name yours."

"I will have to consult with the concerned parties first," Leo replied. "But here comes our proprietor. I suggest we change the subject."

☙

Three weeks later, a beaming William Eddy welcomed Coon and Browne into his paneled study, where a black-market bottle of bourbon awaited. "I don't want to celebrate prematurely," he said as he opened the bottle, "But I've received word that the Dakar cover story is taking hold. Our code breakers have intercepted some German ciphers indicating that the Reich is now concerned about an Allied landing in Dakar sometime this fall. Excellent work, gentlemen."

Coon and Browne exchanged worried glances. "We've got some bad news to report on that, sir," Coon said. "It seems Hoffman may have been compromised."

Eddy's grin faded. "Compromised? How do you mean?"

"One of our sources in Algiers, a cleaning woman, overheard Schmidt—the Swiss architect—telling a German member of the Armistice Commission that he thinks Hoffman has been feeding him false information."

"When was this?"

"About a week ago, as far as we can tell. Now Hoffman's after us to give him something significant they can verify. No more license plate numbers. Something serious."

Eddy rubbed his chin, not saying a word. Then he poured three glasses of bourbon. He handed one to Coon, one to Browne, and then picked up his own. "Well, gentlemen, I hate to say this, but I think it might be time for Leo Hoffman to die."

⚭

Leo knew that meeting Schmidt in the middle of the day, in a place as public as the bar across the street from the Continental Hotel, was a risky business. There could, of course, be many reasons for the two men to meet over a sandwich and a glass of beer, but all innocent justifications would be immediately discarded by those who knew that Schmidt was a German agent. And in Leo's view, that group of people was growing distressingly larger by the day. Still, it was not the first time that Leo had gambled with the devil. He woke up each morning hoping that his luck would hold. It had to. Given all that he was involved in, talent not laced with luck would lead straight to an unmarked grave.

As guarded as he intended to be, he was not prepared for the direct manner in which Schmidt brought up the real reason for their meeting. Evidently subtlety was not a Swiss trait.

"I don't believe my associates feel that you have been earning your money," Schmidt said, after washing a large bite of rye bread and cheese down with a swig of warm beer. "There is certain information you agreed to communicate that you have not yet provided."

Leo glanced around before answering. *Who was listening?* "I did not want to convey any information until I could verify it," he answered. "I had to make sure that my facts are correct."

Schmidt snorted impatiently. "Do you think that I'm stupid? Do you think that *we* are stupid? If you stacked up everything you've told me so far, it wouldn't amount to more than a pile of shit. What makes you think that you could deceive us so easily?"

Leo blanched. "Lower your voice, please. I'm sure there are other people here who speak German."

Schmidt seemed to enjoy Leo's nervousness. "Oh, is that so? Well, isn't that the goal, Mr. Hoffman? To create a world where anyone with power over other human beings speaks German? What information have you supplied that would enable that to happen?"

"What is it that you want from me?" Leo looked around again. There, at the next table. A face he recognized. A local who knew Carlton Coon, an Arab who'd worked on one of his archeological digs, long before the war began. A man well-known as a friend of the Americans. Did he overhear what Schmidt had just asked?

"I want what you offered to give me," Schmidt continued, his voice still too loud for Leo's comfort.

"I don't want to tell you anything until I'm sure."

"If you're not sure by now, then you're of no use to us."

"And you? Have you arranged what I asked of you?"

Schmidt looked quizzical. "What are you talking about?"

"Citizenship," Leo hissed, keeping an eye on the man at the table next to them, who was shoveling his lamb stew into his mouth with astounding rapidity. "Swiss citizenship for me and my daughter."

"What have you done to deserve it?"

Leo exhaled. At least Schmidt had lowered his voice "Very well. I had hoped to have more substantiation. But I'm nearly positive it's to be Dakar. Late in the fall."

Schmidt sat back. "And how do you know this?"

"Eddy's been spotted there twice. Coon's negotiated a gun shipment, presumably to arm some anti-Nazi native force. And the woman I have working for me in the consulate says there's been a dramatic increase in the number of transmissions received. Something's up, and everything points to Dakar."

Schmidt considered this as he took another swig of his beer. "Well, that little morsel might save your double-crossing neck. If we can substantiate it."

Leo's eyes turned icy with anger. "I work for no one but myself. I'm not betraying anyone."

"A figure of speech. Nothing more."

Leo pushed back his chair and stood up. "I've now given you what you wanted. See that you do the same for me."

Schmidt grinned up at him. "You've shown your cards too early, Hoffman. We'll see how the hand plays out before you're paid." Leo stared back, trying to control his reaction. Then he left without another word. The man at the adjoining table hastily choked down one last bite of lamb, then walked out right behind him.

Schmidt turned back to his food as Leo stalked out. He didn't even mind being stuck with the measly check, now that he'd gotten what he wanted. And it would be a cold day in hell before Leo Hoffman was welcome in Switzerland. Dakar. That made some sense.

He did not look up from his fried potatoes until he heard the gunshots and the screams.

Murder was common in Tangier. But to see a man shot in the back, in broad daylight, just as he was crossing the street in front of the Continental Hotel, now that was noteworthy. And to see a Ford coupe arrive at just the right moment, and watch as the driver and the front-seat passenger leapt out and flung the blood-stained corpse into the trunk; that was interesting. That was a bit of gossip worth bringing home.

And who would investigate such a murder? The Spanish police, who were allegedly in charge of the city? They had no interest in who'd killed Leo Hoffman. The American consul, because the man who fired the shot and then disappeared into the Medina had once worked as a ditch digger for one of his vice-consuls? Not likely. The dead man was a man without a country and a known racketeer. His luck had run out, that was all. The denizens of Tangier dismissed his fate with a collective shrug.

Rolph Schmidt celebrated that evening. It seemed clear to him that the Americans were behind Hoffman's death. He'd posed a real danger to their operations. And, despite the scarves covering their faces and their Berber clothing, there was something familiar in the movements of the two men who'd grabbed the body. Some of the café gossip even hinted that the two men in the Ford were none other than the American vice-consul, Carlton Coon, and his cohort, Gordon Browne.

Good thing he'd found out what he needed to know before they did the bastard in. He had to admit, he would not have thought that Eddy and his group of amateurs had the skill to uncover someone as clever as Hoffman, or the balls to do what was necessary. Killing Hoffman gangster-style, in broad daylight, sent a clear message to others: do not betray us. He'd make sure to communicate that. One should never underestimate the enemy.

CHAPTER 9

THE HAUNTED

⣿⣿⣿

CHICAGO, AUGUST 1942

Harry and Ruth met at the Art Institute of Chicago, in front of Georges Seurat's, "A Sunday Afternoon on the Island of La Grande Jatte," at two o'clock in the afternoon, on an April day that threatened rain.

Ruth was standing in front of the painting when Harry entered the room, a look of total concentration etched across her face. She stared so intently for such a long time that Harry's attention shifted from the monumental work, one of his current favorites, to the little brunette in front of him, still and quiet as a statue herself.

"Well, do you like it?" he asked, as if he'd been awaiting her judgment.

"That is what I'm trying to decide," she responded, without taking her eyes off the painting.

"Come closer." Harry walked within a foot of the large canvas and gestured for her to follow. "You have to appreciate the technique to appreciate the painting."

She did as he asked. "You see?" he said, pointing to the long skirt of the most dominant figure, a well-to-do matron holding an umbrella, "It's nothing but dots. Tiny, disconnected points of color. Now, close your eyes. Don't worry—just walk backwards—

no, don't open your eyes yet!" He waited as she stepped backwards, one uncertain baby step at a time, until she was in the center of the large room, a good twelve feet from the wall. "Now, open your eyes. You see?"

"That is amazing. All the dots come together to form the figures."

"Yes. Can you imagine the time this took? First, to determine all the colors one must use for everything to blend together in such a way that a real-life scene is created, and then to apply them all, one by one, with just the very tip of the brush."

She studied the painting a moment longer. "Yes, but one can admire the technique without liking the painting. I don't like it."

Harry was not prepared for this response after his clever demonstration. "Why not?"

She turned and looked at him for the first time. "They aren't happy. It's a beautiful day, they're all outside, surrounded by trees and sun and the river, and not one person looks happy. There are brilliant colors there, but no joy."

Harry looked back at the painting. "I suppose I'd never considered that. I guess you're right."

She rewarded his admission with a tentative smile. "There's no right or wrong to liking art."

"What a very sophisticated point of view." He wanted to keep talking to her, but did not know how to continue the conversation without seeming too forward. "Well, enjoy the rest of the museum."

"And you do the same. Thank you."

She looked at the floor as she finished her sentence, as if she'd just realized how inappropriate it was for her to be speaking to a strange man. An older man, too. Harry was in his late thirties, and she looked to be barely past twenty.

"Well then. Good day to you." He couldn't think of anything else to say. As he left the room a group from a girls' school swooped in, a large body of barely contained energy, and it struck him again how—*still*—the young woman was. Not just quiet, but calm. The type of calm that comes from inner confidence; shyness might result in a quiet exterior, but it tended, Harry thought, to mask a sort of nervousness. At least that was the case with himself. And she was pretty, too.

So Harry was delighted to see her in the museum courtyard an hour later, sitting at a table near the center fountain. He started to approach several times, then stopped. What would he say?

Suddenly, to his surprise, she turned, looked over her shoulder, and smiled at him, as if she'd known all along that he was standing there, and needed a bit of encouragement. He smiled back, and walked up to her table. "I think I forgot to introduce myself. Harry Jacobson,"

"Ruth Goldman," she replied, offering him her gloved hand. "Would you care to join me for a cup of coffee?"

They were married seven months later, in the synagogue containing the Torah that Ruth's great-grandfather had brought with him from Russia. Ruth's family welcomed Harry with open arms. He was successful in his own right, so there was little chance he was marrying into the family to take advantage of their wealth. He didn't drink to excess, and he treated Ruth with respect. He even played the violin. He didn't know much about the faith of his own people, but this was a problem that could be corrected, and Harry was perfectly willing to cooperate.

Ruth wanted to have children right away, but Mother Nature did not seem inclined to cooperate with those plans. Harry told her not to worry. She was young, and he was not in a hurry. Being childless did not bother Harry. He loved his work, music, art, and Ruth. He loved her, he suspected, the way Martha had loved him; he felt nurtured and protected by her. Her calmness and her confidence provided a quiet shelter for his soul. And he tried hard in his marriage, as he did in his work, not to make mistakes.

But after two years he made one. And like a crack in the keystone of a bridge, the mistake created a flaw that kept growing, until the integrity of the entire structure was compromised.

A mistake. Honesty should not be considered a mistake, but it could be, when the truth caused so much pain. One answer to one question. One crack in one stone. He should have been able to predict it. He should have lied.

They were having a snowball fight, of all things. Ruth was better at it than he was; he could throw farther, but she could rebuild her arsenal much more quickly, and before he knew it, she'd pelted him three times, leaving him unable to aim for the snow covering his face. Once he surrendered, she'd come up to him and brushed off the snow, laughing and even kissing him on his cold cheeks, right there in public, in the park. But Ruth was like that, Harry knew, after two years of marriage. She liked winning.

And then it came, as she wrapped her arms around his shoulders, and looked up into his face with her golden brown eyes, her little nose pointed up at him like a bunny's. The question he should have answered differently.

"Have you ever been in love with anyone else? Before me, I mean?"

"Only once. A very long time ago. A girl in Germany."

"Oh." She scrutinized his face, as carefully as she had studied Seurat's painting on the day they met. Then she dropped her arms and turned away from him quickly. "Let's go. I'm cold."

How did she know? How could she have known? What was there in his voice, on his face, that had given so much away? Ruth knew. Now she knew. It wasn't that he had once loved Martha. It was that he still loved her. Even now, even though he knew that she was dead. Martha was the crack in the keystone.

❦

"I'll be going to New York again next week."

"Oh? Again?"

They sat at the dinner table, in the formal dining room. Ruth liked to eat there. She liked the fact that the furniture had belonged to her grandmother. She liked the smooth sheen of the linen tablecloth, and the glow of candles reflected against the wood-paneled walls. She liked the elegance of her wedding china. She enjoyed the comfort of her things.

"Has it been so often?"

"Four times since May. That's a lot. Usually, at this stage, you just work from the plans. It's all physics, remember? As long as you have the right information, the actual location doesn't change anything. That's what you've always told me."

"Yes, well, this is more for the clients. It's a novel design. They like having the engineers around."

"But there's nothing for you to inspect yet, Harry. It's still just a hole in the ground. You told me so yourself."

Harry put down his fork. "Why don't you come with me? You love going to New York. You can do some shopping."

"There's nothing to shop for. My cousin told me. You can't even buy a pair of stockings on the East Coast."

"Is it stockings you'll be shopping for?"

"Is it your business you'll be going for?"

There was no point in answering that question. "What is it, Ruth? Why don't you just come out and tell me what's wrong?"

Harry had never seen a dam break, but he knew how to calculate the physics behind such a calamitous event, and could describe all the forces that came to bear. And that's what he thought about, right at that moment, when he saw the tears in Ruth's eyes. *The dam is about to break.*

"I wonder, sometimes, if I would have married you, had I known."

"Known what?" He had to at least pretend not to know what she was talking about.

"That I would share my husband with a ghost."

"Don't be ridiculous."

"At first I thought I could do it. I thought, 'He only thinks that he still loves her because he doesn't know what it's like to be loved.' But I don't know if I was right about that. Not since... not since her daughter came back to haunt us."

"Do you know how foolish you sound?" He wanted to get up and go to her, to comfort her somehow, but he could not. He was pinned to his chair by the force of her emotion, a tree limb pushed up against the rocks by rushing water.

"Do I? I can feel it, Harry. The distance between us, growing like a shadow. It's as if she knows she made a mistake, losing you when she was alive, and now she's sent her daughter here to take you away from me."

"Ruth, this is nonsense. You know I love you. I married you. This is not fair—"

"Oh, I agree with that. It's certainly not fair."

It's not fair, he thought, as he read Bernice's letter, telling him that Martha had eloped with a man they'd never met. *I've loved her for years. I've been good to her. It's just not fair...*

He said nothing.

"So, I've been thinking..." She picked up her fork again, and Harry saw it tremble in her hand. "I'm not going to New York with you. I'm going to Switzerland."

"What? What on earth are you talking about?"

"I'm going to Switzerland, Harry. There are children... Jewish children, who may or may not have parents once this is all over. Children who need a home."

She looked right at him then, piercing the dark place where he hid, where he licked his wounds and tended the flame of his hatred. He came roaring out of the darkness.

"You can't go to Switzerland! It's too dangerous! Bombs... submarines... you'll be killed! Your family will never let you go!" He had never raised his voice to her. But as he grew louder, he felt her defiance grow stronger. So much strength in such a small person. Where did it come from?

"You're wrong about that, Harry. My parents are coming with me."

"Coming with you? What are you saying?"

"We can help, Harry. You know what's happening. People are disappearing. There's no telling how many have died, how many more will be killed. It's not just me. There's a whole group of us going. People with means. We're volunteering with the Red Cross, to help in various ways... and when we come home, we're coming home with the children. As many as we can bring out with us. And then, Harry, you'll have to choose. You will have to choose between loving your family, loving a ghost."

"*If* you come home," Harry whispered, and he felt tears rise in his eyes.

Ruth's calm demeanor had returned. "I suppose that's right," she said, and took another bite of her dinner.

CHAPTER 10

THE DEAD SPY

❧

CAIRO, AUGUST 1942

"Leopold Hoffman... looks like the kind of guy who'd end up shot in the back." Coon took another look at the passport he held in his hands then tossed it onto the ground, laughing. Gordon Browne laughed along with him.

Leo was not amused. His back hurt from where the two rubber bullets bruised his flesh after breaking the bags of stage blood taped to his skin. His knee and shoulder hurt from the way Coon and Browne wrenched them when picking him up, and the back of his head hurt, too, where they'd smacked it against the edge of the trunk as they tossed him into the car.

"Very funny." He stretched forward to retrieve the passport from the sand at his feet, trying to find a way to move that did not cause more pain in his back, shoulder, or knee.

"C'mon now. Zanuck thinks he deserves a medal for teaching us how to kill someone Hollywood-style. I think we deserve an Oscar. We pulled it off beautifully," Coon said, still grinning.

"I will give you this: you died very nicely. Fell the right way and everything," Browne added, taking a swig from a hip flask, then passing it over to Coon.

"Very nicely indeed," agreed Coon, who took a drink, and then handed the flask to Leo.

"What's in it?"

"No idea. Burns, though. Brandy, maybe. Really shitty brandy."

"Thanks." Leo tipped the flask up. He'd trade tomorrow's headache for some pain relief tonight. Given the way he felt, he was not looking forward to sleeping in a tent.

"So, now. What do we do with a dead spy?" asked Coon, aiming the question at Browne.

"Don't know. What do we do with a dead spy?"

"Send him to Cairo, that's what I hear."

"Cairo? Lucky bastard."

"Cairo?" echoed Leo. "What the hell am I supposed to do in Cairo?"

"Wait," answered Coon, suddenly business-like. "Keep your mouth shut, don't tell anyone you're working for us. Just keep your ass out of trouble, and wait."

"And if I run into someone I know who thinks that I died in Tangier?"

"Well then, tell him that the reports of your death have been greatly exaggerated." Coon started laughing again. Browne also found this comment very amusing. He was very good at laughing at Coon's jokes.

"Hoffman," said Coon when he caught his breath, "You know what rumors are like. You're not a big fish. It won't matter, unless you stumble over your old friend Schmidt, who's not likely to go to Cairo now that we've exposed him as a spy. He'll be sent back to Switzerland. So cut your hair short, grow a mustache, and act French, like it says on your passport. And then, just wait."

"Wait for what? For how long?" Leo winced again as a shot of pain reverberated through his shoulder.

"Wait for as long as you're told to wait. Wait until something shakes loose around here."

"Such as?"

"Well, I suppose we'll know it when we see it, won't we?"

❦

The first time Leo saw Christine Granville she was lying on a chaise lounge by the pool at the Gezira Sporting Club, sun bathing. She wore a modern bathing costume, one that exposed the full length of her slim legs, her tanned arms, and an alluring patch of shoulder. Dark brown hair, pulled away from her face by a headband, formed a crown of curls around her wide forehead; her mouth, resting slightly open, would have been too large for her face, had it not been shaped so perfectly. One hand lay upon the ground, two fingers tucked into a book, as though she'd fallen asleep reading yet managed to keep her place just before dozing off.

Leo located an empty lounge chair and pulled it into the small puddle of shade created by a palm tree. He also had a book to read, a well-worn copy of *Gulliver's Travels* left in the hotel's lending library by a previous guest, but his attention kept straying from the page in front of him back to the woman by the pool.

"Aha." A voice behind him made Leo jump. "I see you've discovered our Cleopatra."

Shielding his eyes from the sun with one hand, Leo looked up to see an English officer, Roger Mayes, standing next to his chair.

"What was it that you said?"

Mayes squatted down next to Leo's chair so that he spoke directly into Leo's ear, and gestured toward the sleeping woman. "I said I see you've found our Cleopatra. Christine Granville."

"Cleopatra? That skinny brunette with the long nose?"

"Oh, yes. To quote an ancient Roman who'd fallen under the spell of the legendary Egyptian queen, 'It was not the comeliness of her face or the fineness of her figure that created her allure, but the combination of merely sufficient beauty with extraordinary intelligence, wit, and cunning. Enthralled, men came away from her presence with an impression of great beauty, when in truth, beauty was the least of her attributes.'"

"You sound pretty enthralled yourself."

"Hopelessly. But alas, she has a husband in England and a lover here in Cairo. And, if one listens to the rumors, there are other men as well. I only pass along that last bit of gossip because I'm insanely jealous that I've never been one of them."

"Well, I suppose that's honest," Leo said in French-accented English, punctuating his response with a typical Gallic shrug.

Mayes stood up with a sigh. "Yes, though it's not likely to get me anywhere with the countess."

"Countess?"

"Oh, did I neglect to mention that? Yes. She's the daughter of a Polish count. Have no idea what Polish titles mount up to, but unlike most of the Czarists around here, they're legit. What is it? What's so funny?"

"Oh, I've had a few dealings of my own with a countess. Of course, that was a very long time ago." *Are you a virgin, Leo? Yes, Countess. Leo, you must know how beautiful you are. No, Countess...*

"A very, very long time ago," he added, thinking of how dramatically his life had changed since the day that Countess Julia Podmaniczky seduced him, right on the floor of the library in his foster family's grand home in Budapest. He'd lost his virginity on the same day the last war started. The war that destroyed his life. Funny, he'd never thought about it that way before.

"Already had your own countess, have you? Bloody hell. You Frenchmen. Well, good luck with this one. You don't choose her. She chooses you."

"Thank you for the warning, but I have no intention of getting in line."

Leo watched as Mayes strolled off, stopping to take a long look at the sleeping countess before ducking back into the main clubhouse. Was it true, Leo wondered, that Mayes was with the British spy network in Cairo? He and Peter Wilkinson were often together, and Wilkinson was reputed to be the new S.O.E. head. Whenever Leo saw the lanky Englishman, he was tempted to disobey Coon's orders. Leo wanted to tell Wilkinson exactly why he was in Cairo, and ask the man to verify that he was, in fact, on the British undercover asset list. He wanted to ask Wilkinson if someone was reassuring his daughter that he was safe, that he would come back to her.

He took Eddy up on his offer to send one letter home via the diplomatic pouch, but then the State Department cut him off. Too complicated, the consul said, to use the diplomatic pouch for personal business. *Too much ass-covering involved if something should go wrong, that's what he meant.* No wonder Eddy, Coon and Browne called the State Department the "Snake Pit."

As much as he itched to ask Wilkinson for some enlightenment, he couldn't do anything that might jeopardize his good standing with Eddy. Leo's reward, his U.S. citizenship, would rest on Eddy's evaluation of his performance. As he'd told Eddy, for once in his life, he was going to play by the rules. His two years were up in November. He'd done decent work. The O.N.I and the O.S.S. and the S.O.E. and whatever other alphabet-soup operations he'd been spying for had better let him go. Until then, he obeyed his orders. He waited in Cairo, pretending to be a French businessman, waiting to see which way the winds of war would blow.

The heat sent a drop of sweat trickling into his mustache. It took some getting used to, having facial hair after a lifetime clean-shaven. His new addition was thin and close-trimmed, unlike the huge, curly mustaches worn by the men of Budapest in his youth: mustaches that were groomed, pampered and fussed over like expensive pets. He'd also cut his hair short, as Coon had suggested. Not much of a disguise, but, he hoped, enough of a change to keep him from being immediately recognized while he waited out his time in Cairo.

Upon his arrival Leo learned that Cairo was full of people waiting. The British waited to see whether Rommel and his Panzer Group would get any closer. The Egyptians waited to see whether being overrun by the Germans would be better or worse than living under an English yoke. At the exclusive Gezira Sporting Club, British residents organized polo tournaments, amateur plays, and ladies' teas. At Shepheard's Hotel, British officers drank gin, played cards, and waited for orders from the desert front. Polish military men drank vodka, ran their own spy network, and waited for the chance to fight the Germans again. Everyone waited to see what the Allies would do next. Russia couldn't hold off the Nazis for much longer, and England couldn't defend itself forever without help. America and Britain had to open a second front, to force Hitler to divide his resources. They would have to strike somewhere in Europe, and soon.

Leo looked down at the book in his lap, and then tossed it aside. He'd lost his enthusiasm for plowing through English. It was too hot to just sit outside. He'd go swimming. No, he'd go for a walk in the marketplace. No, he'd go over to the stables and see if anyone's horse needed a bit of exercise.

As he walked by her chaise lounge on his way back into the changing rooms, a cloud passed over the sun, and Cleopatra stirred.

CHAPTER 11

THE ENGINEER

∞⌇∞

NEW YORK, SEPTEMBER 1942

"I can't believe such a thing! Five years you've lived in New York, and no one has taken you up to the top of the Empire State Building?"

Maddy started rolling forward and back on the balls of her feet, an unconscious habit both Mrs. O'Connor and her Aunt Bernice had tried to break. "Yer makin' me dizzy, Maddy. For goodness' sake, keep yer feet still, darlin'," Mrs. O'Connor would say.

"Madeleine, it's very disconcerting to watch you bob around that way. It's quite childish. Please stop," Bernice would admonish.

She stopped herself, not wanting to earn a reprimand from Mr. Jacobson, although he didn't look like he was about to say something critical. She smiled back up at him, ignorant of the effect her smile had on him. It was her mother's smile.

Into the grand lobby, up eighty floors in one elevator, cross over the hallway, up the next elevator bank to the eighty-sixth floor, then on to a third to take them to the observation deck, 1,250 feet high. During their final ascent Maddy's ears popped, and her stomach lurched. As they got off, Harry reached out and took her hand. Maddy felt a tingle of elation having nothing to do with where she was. No man had ever held her hand except for her father. Her uncle, Archie Mason, occasionally administered a clumsy night-time hug topped off by a quick kiss on the top of her head, but that was all the paternal affection she received.

"Don't be scared," Harry said, jiggling her hand slightly. "Just close your eyes if you feel dizzy. The building is very stable."

They stepped out onto the platform. Maddy gasped, then said, "You can see the other end of the world."

"Not quite. Five states I think, and eighty miles out to sea. But it's impressive. Do you know that Henry Ford, the man who makes the cars, was so concerned about this building that he didn't want it built? He said digging a hole that big and filling it with steel and cement would create an imbalance that could knock the world right off its rotational axis."

He looked down at Maddy, whose eyes were glued to the view. "Well, he was wrong, of course. You know what the earth's axis is, don't you, Maddy?"

She nodded, then looked up at Harry, her eyes filled with awe. "How can you do it, Mr. Jacobson? How can you build something that stands up so high in the air like this?"

Harry smiled. "With lots and lots of stable little pieces, Maddy. Everything you see—buildings, boats, bridges—even people—are held together by stable little pieces, all linked together. The important thing is to understand the forces that connect them, in order to guarantee that stability. Now, let's look at some of the other buildings. Okay, that one over there, see? The Chrysler Building. You know it, yes? Well, it was supposed to be the tallest, but held that title for only two years because the owners here got wind of the plan, and added enough height to the Empire State to make *it* the tallest building in the world. Now, you see how that building is cut in right there, and again there? Can you think of why that was done?"

"Because it's pretty?"

"That's a good reason, but there's another one. It cuts down on the size of the shadow the building creates. You see, people figured out right away that the skyscrapers would block out the light, so there's a law requiring them to get skinnier as they get taller."

"Really? And you design them?"

"I don't really come up with the idea for the building, Maddy. Architects come to me with preliminary plans for a building they want to build, and I come up with a way to do it. A way to do it and ways to make sure it's safe. No matter how pretty a design is on paper, it has to be safe when it's finally built."

They walked around the entire platform. New York's capricious September weather had produced a clear, sunny afternoon, yielding a splendid view in all directions. Facing the Hudson, they could see the piers where the big ocean liners came to dock. Four were anchored there now, side-by-side, like neatly lined-up toys. There were no cheerful *bon-voyage* parties at the gangplanks, or pursers sorting trunks full of fancy dresses. All the big liners now served as troop transport ships.

Harry noticed the child turning pale. "What is it? What's wrong, Maddy? Do you feel dizzy?"

"No, I was thinking… about a trip I took once. On a ship."

"Did you get seasick?"

"A little." *I was so frightened. I wanted my mother, but she was dead. I wanted my father, but he didn't want me. He put me on the ship with Amelia, who told me I'd regret it if I didn't stay out of her hair. The waves were so huge. I kept throwing up and throwing up. The steward brought me buckets to throw up into, then he'd rinse them in the sink so it didn't smell so bad.*

When I was feeling better, I went up to the ship's dining room. There was Amelia, laughing and smoking, with her face too close to this other man's face. He saw me, and said something. Amelia turned around and looked at me, and I knew then that she hated me just as much as I hated her. "Well if it isn't the little albatross," she said. "What do you want?"

I didn't want to talk to her. I didn't even want to be there. But my stomach was so empty. I asked her if I could have some dinner. She laughed again. "Do I look like the cook? Go ask the steward for some food. The less I see of you, the better." I stayed in the cabin after that. The steward brought me clear chicken broth and crackers. All I saw was the view from the porthole of our cabin. The ocean was gray and empty. Just like me.

"No, not very much. I didn't really like it very much."

"You poor little thing." Harry wrapped his arms around her, enveloping her little body in a big warm hug, and she buried her face in his shoulder. "You're safe now, Martha. You're with people who love you."

"I know," came the muffled reply, and she snuggled up closer against him, seeking solace.

His body betrayed him. He shoved her away, terrified that she would feel him, through his coat, through her coat, through her dress... it was absurd. This was perverse. She was a child. This was not Martha. *She sent her daughter to haunt us...*

Harry turned red with embarrassment. Maddy stared up at him, startled, then her gaze fell to the floor. Had she felt it? Had she noticed anything?

"You called me Martha," she said, without looking up.

"I did? How foolish of me. I'm sorry. All those M's."

"It doesn't matter."

Maddy said very little as they made their way to the O'Connor home, where she was going to spend the night. She dashed inside the moment the door opened, leaving Harry on the doorstep. Mrs. O'Connor invited him in for a cup of tea, but Harry declined. He could not shake the feeling of shame that overcame him when his body responded so inappropriately to Maddy's embrace. He wanted to walk, and think.

Everything is held together by stable little pieces, all linked together. Even people. The important thing is to understand the forces that connect them, in order to guarantee their stability. Harry Jacobson was not impetuous. He was not an artist; he was an engineer. He never did anything without thinking first and planning ahead.

Until that moment.

He did not need to be in New York to finish this project. It was just a hole in the ground, and would likely remain that way until the war was over. He was an American citizen. He could travel. There were a dozen European consulates in New York. He would start at the Swiss consulate, and if he was unsuccessful there, he would go to each country, one by one, until he got a visa that would allow him to board a boat bound for Europe, and from there get to Switzerland. The Red Cross would know exactly where to find his wife.

CHAPTER 12

THE ROGUE AGENT

᠁

CAIRO, NOVEMBER 1942

By noon the word was all over Cairo. They'd done it. The Brits and the Americans had invaded North Africa. A hundred ships brought thousands of men. They'd landed troops on the beach in Algeria and French Morocco, catching the French completely by surprise.

But the French under Vichy were making good on their promise to Hitler; they were fighting back. For the first time in their long history as allies, American and French soldiers were deliberately killing each other.

Rumors flooded the city. Algiers was taken. Algiers was lost. German planes were slaughtering American soldiers; no German planes had been sighted. No one in Cairo wanted to be more than a few feet from the nearest radio.

Leo spent most of the day at Shepheard's Hotel with a horde of other expatriates from fifteen different countries, analyzing each fresh piece of information, obsessing and reworking all the possibilities. Who was leading the Allied assault? How many troops were there? How long would the French fight? How would Hitler respond? Just four days before the invasion, Montgomery had smashed through Rommel's forces at El Alamein, finally forcing the "Desert Fox" to retreat. Would Rommel now get the reinforcements he needed? Would he turn back to fight against an Allied advance?

It was late in the evening when Leo excused himself from the bar and wandered out to the terrace, to escape the cigarette smoke and nurse his after-dinner drink.

"Would you like to go to a party?"

Christine Granville stood a few feet away. Leo looked behind him, assuming the question had been addressed to someone else. She laughed with a deep, throaty chuckle, as if he'd just performed an engaging little trick for her private amusement.

"Yes, it's you I'm talking to. Would you like to go to a party? Right now? An invasion celebration?"

Her French was near-perfect, betraying hardly a trace of her Polish origins. She could have been French, thought Leo, with those wide brown eyes. What else did he see in them? Warmth, certainly. Laughter. But what else? Frustration? Restlessness?

No, thank you, he was about to say. *I'm not really the sort who likes parties.*

"Why would you invite me to a party?" is what came out.

Everything about her suddenly softened. "Because you're bored, and lonely, and tired of waiting. We're all so tired of waiting…" Before he could respond her gentleness disappeared, replaced by a buoyant frivolity. "So come on. It will be fun."

"That's very kind of you, Miss…"

"Christine."

"Yes, well, Christine, I do appreciate the courtesy, but I'm tired, and I'm sure I'd be boring company at a soirée. I think I've celebrated sufficiently for today."

She responded with a smile that gave him the odd impression she understood the one thing about him that he would never comprehend himself: an elusive piece of self-knowledge, perpetually dangling out of reach. Then her dark eyes flickered with mischief. "It's not because you're pretty, you know, that I invite you. Not that you aren't," she added, with a coy glance that took in his whole body, "but that's not the reason."

Leo was smiling now. He couldn't help it. "What sort of party is it?"

She tossed her head and shrugged, as if the whole subject had just lost all significance. "An American party. And I don't speak very much English. So you can come and interpret for me. And don't go saying that you don't speak English. I've heard you."

"Surely someone else—"

Good Lord, how the expression in those eyes could change! Before she even spoke, they communicated a kaleidoscope of emotion: amusement, anticipation, irritation.

"Yes, yes. Surely someone else. But you see, I have not invited *someone else.*" Her eyes locked onto his.

Cleopatra, he thought, as he flagged down a cab.

⁊

The taxi pulled up in front of the colonial-style villa overlooking the Nile. Dozens of people moved about on the wide terrace, like bees clinging to a swollen hive, buzzing through a fog of river mist and cigarette smoke.

"I can see why you said one more person wouldn't be noticed," Leo remarked as they made their way up the front staircase. They had to walk sideways through the main hallway. Luxuries rapidly growing scarce in other parts of the world were still plentiful in Cairo. Champagne bottles sat in silver ice buckets. Platters of savory pastries filled with lamb and potatoes, beef sausages, fresh cheese, platters of tiny shrimp, deviled eggs topped with caviar, chocolate tarts, figs, and honey-drenched *baklava* covered the linen tablecloths overlaying the English oak tables in the banquet room.

A trio of musicians played lively jazz that was roundly ignored, even by those who could hear it.

Leo looked to his right. The thin brunette wearing the khaki skirt and white sweater still stood there, but Christine's presence and personality were gone. This version of Christine looked shy and ill-at-ease. Lacking any animation, her face was plain. Her nose looked larger, and, now dull, her eyes looked smaller. She fidgeted with a button on her sweater.

Concerned, Leo reached for her hand. "Do you feel all right? Do you want to leave?"

She shook her head as she clutched his hand, and he did not know which question the gesture was meant to answer. "I have to find someone who is supposed to be here."

"Good luck. What does he look like?"

"He's Polish."

"That narrows it down. Could you be more specific?"

"He is pale, shorter than you, with a round face. His hair is light brown, and he does that thing where you part it on one side to cover up the baldness. So silly."

"Okay. Well. Keep your eyes open. Does he have a name?"

"Truszkowski. And he's in the army."

"One balding Polish military man, coming right up, Madame."

A loud cheer from a room off the hall caused a general movement in that direction, pushing people even closer together. Leo put Christine in front of him, clasped her shoulders, and used his outstretched elbows to negotiate their breathing space.

"Whose house did you say this was?"

"He was a movie star in America. Now he likes living here, in Cairo, because he likes men."

"I didn't realize that Cairo was known for that sort of thing."

"It's known as a place where you can buy what you want. Including silence. If you're rich enough."

Leo eyed the marble and silk surrounding them. "I'd say he's rich enough."

"There he is!" With a burst of energy Christine broke away and headed toward the other side of the room. Leo followed her. Being taller, he saw the man Christine was headed for—and the look of dismay on his face when he saw her.

She got right up to him and started speaking in rapid Polish, loudly, to be heard above the din of the crowd. Leo saw the man's expression change from discomfort to annoyance. He gave a long reply. Leo moved closer. He could not hear well over the noise, and he did not speak Polish, although he could make out a few words based on its similarities to Russian and German, both of which he spoke fluently. It sounded as if the man had used an English name: Leo heard what sounded as if it could have been "Wilkinson."

Wilkinson. Could that be Peter Wilkinson? Why would he be a topic of their conversation?

Christine made a dismissive gesture and kept on talking. Leo caught another word, something like "assignments." Whatever the response this time, Christine was not pleased to hear it. She whipped around and shouldered her way back across the room like a slender battering ram. Leo watched her go. She did not seem to notice that he was not behind her.

The man, whom Leo assumed was Truszkowski, looked very agitated. "Is everything all right?" Leo him asked him in French, wondering what he'd do if his simple query provoked a confrontation.

Truszkowski just looked at him. "Have you known Mrs. Granville long?"

He spoke French. Not a surprise. Most Polish noblemen did.

"No. In fact, we just met."

"I would advise you to be careful. A very dangerous woman. She has a lover, you know. Andrew Kennedy. Man with a wooden leg. Also quite charismatic in his own way. They live together openly, although she's still married to someone else. Amazing what we put up with in wartime that we'd never tolerate otherwise."

"My sentiments exactly." He turned his back on the man and went to find Christine.

He found her out on the terrace, arms crossed, staring up at the moonless night sky.

"Do you know how planes fly?" she asked as he approached.

"Vaguely. The engine produces a force that provides lift—"

"No. It's magic. That's all. Just magic."

She sounded so convinced, he almost believed her. "Do you want to stay?" he asked at last, not anxious to disturb her reverie.

She looked away from the sky and up at Leo. "No, and I'm sorry I dragged you here. It's not really my kind of party. Too many loud, stupid people, doing nothing useful. I can't tolerate sitting around doing nothing, when there's so much to be done."

"What assignments were you talking about? Are you a journalist? What is it that you want to be doing?"

She looked at him as if she thought he might be joking, but wasn't quite sure. "I was under the impression, Mr. Hoffman, that we are engaged in the same line of work, and that we are both, at the moment, unemployed."

Then she brushed past him, back into the crowd, a slight figure soon swallowed up by the crush of overheated, inebriated bodies. He heard someone shout her name. *Who is this woman? What does she know about me? And how?*

To hell with all of them. Tomorrow morning he was going to see Wilkinson.

⚬❦⚬

"I'm not sure what it is you want from me, Hoffman." Major Peter Wilkinson had a pinched look on his narrow face. This was not unusual.

"I want to know if I can leave. I want to know if I'm finished. I want to know if you're going to live up to your side of our bargain."

"And the 'you' to whom you're referring would be… ?"

Leo put his head in his hands. "I'm not sure I know anymore."

Wilkinson tapped a pencil on his desk, thinking. "Look," he said finally. "This is a volunteer business. No one can make you do this sort of work. Leave whenever you like."

"And go where?" Leo was on his feet now. He walked around his chair and grabbed the back of it, knuckles white with frustration. "Eddy told you I'd be in Cairo, didn't he?"

"I did receive word that you were a valuable asset, that you'd been operating successfully in Tangier, and that you were being sent to Cairo for an indefinite period, awaiting further orders. That's as much as I know about you."

"Am I on your list of spies? The payroll? Whatever it is I need to get credit for what I've been doing?"

"I'm not sure what you're driving at. You're down as a freelancer, if that's what you mean. You're Eddy's asset. You're not on my payroll."

"Eddy was supposed to work this out for me."

"Colonel Eddy is otherwise occupied at the moment. We've just begun a major offensive. I'm sure you can understand why your personal bureaucratic problems did not rise to the top of his agenda."

"What am I supposed to do? Just sit here and wait? I have to get to New York!"

"Then go see the American ambassador. Try explaining your problem to him. Of course, that may take some time. From what I understand, there's quite a long line outside the embassy."

"You know that would be useless! They're not letting anyone in. I need your help."

"I'm sorry. I don't have any authority to negotiate your passage to the States."

"You mean I'm stranded here?"

"I don't mean to sound insensitive, Hoffman, but the soldiers in Algeria and Morocco are doing a bit more than passing their afternoons drinking lemonade and sunning themselves at the Gezira Club. There are worse things than being 'stranded here,' as you put it."

Leo sat back down in the chair facing Wilkinson's desk, every muscle in his body sagging with disappointment. "So I do nothing."

"Do what you like. You're not under my jurisdiction."

"And what about Christine Granville? Does she work for you?"

Wilkinson's already pale face went a shade whiter. "What are you talking about?"

"She must work for you. How else would she know that I've been doing 'this type of work,' as you so eloquently put it?"

"Christine Granville does not work for me and never has. What is it you've heard?"

Leo told Wilkinson about the comment Christine had made the night before. He could see the man was shaken.

"All I can tell you is this," Wilkinson said after a long silence, "Christine Granville volunteered to do some work for our office at the beginning of the war. She was dropped because certain sources maintained that she was working both sides. I have no idea how she found out about you. Perhaps it would be in your own best interest to discover that for yourself. And I'd appreciate your sharing what you find out."

"I'll think about it."

Leo took his leave and went straight back to Shepheard's. *Do what you like*, Wilkinson had said. *You're not under my jurisdiction.* Before going to his room, Leo stopped by the concierge's desk.

"I'd like to send a telegram to the U.S.," he said. "To an address in New York."

⚭

The next day Leo bribed the day manager at the Gezira Club into telling him where Christine lived. She lived in a boarding house, in another, less fashionable part of the city, the man said. From the look on his face Leo could tell this was not the first time he'd answered the question.

Having no obvious reason to pay her a visit, Leo decided to wait until he could catch Christine at the Gezira Club. He did not have to wait long. She was there the next afternoon, stretched out on a towel on the wide, well-watered lawn, chatting with an English officer Leo saw frequently at Shepheard's. The man looked hypnotized.

Christine saw him watching and waved him over. "Mr. Hoffman, how nice to see you again. Do you know Major Hawthorne?"

"Only by sight. Good afternoon, Major." The man stood up. "Pleasure's mine, Mr... ?"

"Hoffman. Leo Hoffman."

"I find that the Major speaks French very well for an Englishman." Christine delivered this compliment in a manner that made the Major blush. "He's going to help me with my English, which is very poor. Would you like to join us, Mr. Hoffman? The Major is about to find someone to bring us lemonade, aren't you Major?"

The Major hid his surprise with gentlemanly courtesy. "Of course. I'm sure I can arrange that. Won't be a minute."

Leo flopped down next to Christine. She started to pull at a small weed poking up through the blades of grass next to her pretty bare feet. "You do like lemonade, don't you?" she asked, without looking up.

He ignored this. "How is it that you seem to know so much about me, when I know nothing about you?"

"I think we should talk about this later."

"I'm not going anywhere until you answer my question."

"Sit here and rot if you like." She said this without spite, almost without emotion, as she extracted the weed from the manicured lawn and tossed it away.

Leo grabbed her hand. "Why do you think that we are, to use your words, 'in the same line of business'?"

"Only two types of people come back from the dead, Mr. Hoffman. Saints and spies. Are you a saint? Ah, you'll have some time to think about your answer—here comes our lemonade. Now, please, let go of my hand."

꧁꧂

Bernice read the telegram a second time:

Maddy I am okay. I will come home as soon as I can.
I think about you every day and hope you are well.
I love you. Papa

It was a shame, really, that Leo had chosen that form of communication, thought Bernice. Poor Margaret was still white and shaking, three hours later, when Bernice came by to pick up the message. For Margaret, a telegram would always be an omen of evil. Bernice respected Margaret O'Connor, despite their many differences. She was a strong woman, or had been. One could never tell what loss, what hardship, would be the one burden too difficult for a specific individual to bear. There were so many unknown variables when it came to predicting human behavior.

Margaret knew that a telegram had come for Maddy, but that's all she knew. Thank goodness Maddy was not home yet.

Bernice read the message a third time. Sent from Cairo. What on earth would he be doing there?

More importantly, how would Maddy react to this? She seemed to be doing so well. Her marks in school were satisfactory. She was well-behaved. Was it fair to disrupt her life with this message? To raise her hopes, only to have them dashed again? What was that man thinking? No, it was best not to share this with her. The child needed stability. *He's only seen her once in the past five years. It's very unlikely he'll ever come back at all. And if he does, well. I will not let you take her away from us the way you took Martha, Leo Hoffman.*

෴

He'd agreed to meet Christine the next evening, at a small bar close to where she lived, away from the expatriates' center of gravity. The room had a comfortable, neighborhood-pub atmosphere, with dark wood floors and a mirrored bar, behind which a grizzled old Dutchman with little hair and few teeth poured drinks with a heavy hand. He kept a radio going in the corner. Every once in a while he would shuffle over to it, cup a hand to his right ear, and shout, "Pipe down! There's news!" Then he'd shake his head, grumble something unintelligible, and turn his back on the disappointing report. No news worth repeating, it seemed.

Leo sat in a booth in the back of the room, his eye on the door. No one else paid the slightest bit of attention to him, which was a good sign. Christine was already thirty minutes late. Not surprising. *She's the type who'd keep men waiting.*

The door opened, letting in a shaft of evening light and gust of fresh air. A man entered. Large round face, decent height. *He looks Irish*, thought Leo. Maybe Slavic. The man's fine brown hair had receded almost all the way to the top of his head. He wore a thick, broad mustache. And he had a wooden leg.

He headed straight over to Leo's table. "Christine sends her apologies," he said in French as he slid into the booth. "She'll be along in a while. Can I freshen that beer for you? Sorry, I'm Andrew Kennedy. But I presume you already know that."

"I don't know much about anything, at this point. That's why I wanted to speak to Christine."

"Well, there are no secrets between Christine and me, Mr. Hoffman. You can ask me whatever you like."

"I think I'll wait."

"As you wish." The man did not act defensive or jealous. *Perhaps the rumors of Mrs. Granville's infidelity have been greatly exaggerated.* He decided to ask Kennedy a few questions after all.

"I find it very disturbing that you know things about me that only a very short list of people should know."

"We've been at this game for nearly three years, Mr. Hoffman. It's not that complicated. Christine has many contacts within the Red Cross. We recently learned that the main Red Cross representative in Tangier, an architect by the name of Schmidt, was sent packing under allegations that he was spying for the Germans. This was coupled with rumors that the Americans had very boldly assassinated one of the men from whom Schmidt had been getting information. Soon afterwards, Christine learned from another acquaintance that this dead man from Tangier was observed among the living in Cairo."

"Was that acquaintance German? Or Swiss, by any chance?"

Andrew gave him a steely look. "People of many nationalities travel from Tangier to Cairo, if they aren't stuck without a visa in that stinking pit. And most foreigners with financial means end up at Shepheard's. Don't believe everything you hear, Mr. Hoffman."

"I'm having a hard time believing anything."

The door opened again and Christine walked in. Everyone in the bar looked up. A few men looked a good long time before turning back to their drinks and newspapers.

"Sorry I'm late." She slid in beside Andrew. "What have I missed?"

"Mr. Hoffman was just accusing us of working for the Germans."

Christine made a noise communicating irritated contempt. "That again."

"Why would the Brits have cut you off if it wasn't true?"

"Politics," Christine snapped. "The Poles didn't like the fact that we were working for the British instead of their operation. Stupid jealousies."

"That's all? That doesn't sound quite... credible."

"Stick around Cairo for a few weeks more. The politics of the espionage community has the makings of a great comic opera," Andrew countered. "When we arrived in Cairo, I had microfilms showing that the Germans were amassing artillery on the Russian border. Two rolls of solid evidence tucked into my hollow leg. But by that time we were 'under suspicion' and no one took the information seriously. The Germans attacked Russia two weeks later."

Christine jumped in. "Find a Polish aristocrat, here, in Cairo. There are plenty of us here. Ask about my family. Ask about my Jewish mother, who was dragged out of her house screaming. Ask any one of them if they think it's plausible I'd work for the Nazis." Christine spoke with such intensity her dark eyes looked as if they might actually catch fire. It was hard not to believe her.

"So why contact me? What makes me so interesting?"

Andrew answered. "When you surfaced in Cairo we thought it pretty unlikely that you'd been working for the Germans. Neither Germans nor German sympathizers are welcome here at the moment. Wilkinson may be thick, but even he'd connect those dots. Which meant your murder had been *staged* by the Americans. Which meant you'd been working for them. The real work is being done out of Tangier, Algiers, Holland, England, France. Cairo is where spies are sent to cool their heels."

"There are worse places."

"Pipe down!" the Dutchman shouted, once again crouching over the radio.

Andrew lowered his voice. "Worse places, I'm sure. But what's worse than being forced to do nothing while the world is being destroyed? Inactivity is the real torture. That's why we contact people like you. Good operatives, who for whatever reason have been shoved to the side. To see if we can get something accomplished, with your help."

"You'll have to look elsewhere. I'm out of the business. I'm just waiting to get permission to go to New York."

"Why New York?"

"I have family there."

"And you'll be leaving soon?"

"I think so."

The Dutchman let out a roar. "They've surrendered! The French have surrendered! It's ours! North Africa is ours!"

They could hear the noise growing in the street. Cheers broke out everywhere, punctuated by car horns, the banging of pots, and a few gunshots. The door to the bar swung open, and a young boy popped his head in. "The French have surrendered!" he shouted. The patrons raised their glasses and joined in the revelry.

"Great news!" Leo declared, taking a celebratory swig of his beer. *Now maybe I can get Eddy's attention. Now maybe I can get out of here.*

Christine's expressive eyes grew wide with fear. "There's not much more time, then. Oh, my God, Andrew. We have to move quickly. The first thing they'll do is close the borders."

"Quickly? With what?" Leo asked.

Christine leaned forward and squeezed his hand, hard, as if she didn't already have his complete attention. "There are camps, Leo. People are disappearing. The Jews are disappearing. We've got to get to them soon and at least... at least try to save the children."

CHAPTER 13

THE REDEEMER

೭ᔐᔑᕐᕐᕐᕐ

CAIRO, NOVEMBER 1942

"No, I can't help. I can't jeopardize my own chance to get out of here. I'll just have to wait."

He'd believed those words when he'd uttered them. Nothing was more important than getting back to his daughter. And if that meant waiting in Cairo until Eddy or someone else in authority could give him permission to go to New York, then he would just wait.

You'll hide, is what you mean. You've always been very good at hiding.

He was warned not to go home the night his foster mother was murdered. He'd never had a chance to say goodbye, had never even seen her body. She'd disappeared in the raging sea of vengeance that flooded Hungary after the last war. Most of those killed were Jews, slaughtered by their own countrymen for no better reason than the Nazis had now.

But he'd escaped. He'd hidden the truth about his past, his Jewish heritage, and his connection with all the people who had ever loved him. By hiding he'd been able to get away. And he'd been hiding ever since.

The only person to whom he'd revealed himself was Martha, and he'd told her the truth too late to save her. Now he was a spy, still hiding.

He could see Christina's face, hear her voice as she spoke, her words laced with earnestness and horror. "Last July, they had a round-up in Paris. The police—the *French* police, not the Germans—went from house to house, and they collected refugee Jews. Thousands of people. They brought them by bus to a place outside Paris, and piled them onto trains headed east. Sealed box cars. Cattle cars. There are witnesses—we have seen letters—but no one will listen.

"People are trying to pretend that all the Jews are being sent to work in factories, or to do some kind of forced labor. But I know. I've seen it, in Poland, what the Nazis will do. First, they will make them dig their own graves. Then they will line them up, rows and rows of them, and shoot them down with machine guns. I've seen it.

"For the past two years, all the Jews who managed to escape to Vichy France from Germany, Austria, Poland—all the conquered countries—if they couldn't find a place to hide, the French put them in prison camps, where they live like rats. There's not enough food, no decent shelter, no proper hygiene. But at least there they had a *chance* to survive.

"In August, a month after the Paris round-up, Vichy started to empty out the camps. The French sent thousands more Jewish refugees to Germany. Sometimes, they let mothers with young children stay, or they let the children stay behind. Alone. But all this week, since the Allied invasion, the Germans have been moving into southern France. And we've heard things. Terrible things."

"What are you going to try and do?"

"We're going to go to France and help some of them, as many as we can, get out."

"I can't help you."

Why had the condemnation he'd seen in her eyes affected him so? She had no idea who he was, what he'd been through, or why it was so important for him to wait here, in Cairo, and play by the rules. *They live like rats…*

What if it were Maddy there, in one of those camps? Who would save her?

I just have to wait.

He saw Christine a week later, in her favorite spot by the pool at the Gezira Club. She looked like a cat, the Egyptian goddess Bast perhaps, stretched out in the sun, surrounded by her worshippers. He walked over and stood over her until she opened her eyes.

"How long would I be gone?"

Christine gave him a smile that would cause any man to sprint joyfully to his doom. "Three weeks at most," she said. "How soon can you leave?"

☙

They would first fly to Algiers, she said, in the private plane of a friend, then take a boat to Marseille; that port was still open. Andrew would go with them only as far as Algiers. He had other ways of helping, they said, by leaning on Allied ears.

"How long will we be in Algiers?" Leo asked.

"Well, just long enough to get married."

"*What?*"

"Granville is my English name, the one I have on my British passport. With a marriage certificate, I can travel into France with you on my Polish passport, under my maiden name, Skarbek. Nothing Jewish about that. And what nasty bureaucrat would refuse permission for a loyal Frenchman to bring his new bride home to meet his mother? People are desperate to get out of France.

They'll be delighted to let one loyal Frenchman back in with his new wife."

"And how will we get back to Cairo?"

"Once we've accomplished our mission, you'll get papers authorizing you to enter Spain. From there, it will be easy to get to Tangier, and then back to Cairo. If the border guards give you any trouble, bribe them with cigarettes. A pack of Camels works better than gold."

"We won't come back together?"

She shook her head. "I may be gone longer than you need to be."

"How long have you been planning this?"

"We started receiving information about the deportations late in the summer. Then, when the Americans invaded, well, we knew we had to act quickly. Vichy won't do anything to protect Jews now. Not that they've done much as it is."

"Who is this 'we'?"

"Friends from before the war. People with whom we used to going skiing in France. A man who once sold me a beautiful piece of jewelry. A friend whose horse I used to ride when we lived in Kenya."

"And that 'we' would be you and your husband?"

"Do you always ask questions to which you already know the answer?"

This response startled him. What had he been expecting? A denial? An explanation?

She did not wait for him to reply. "There is very little we need to know about each other, Leo. You're doing this because you've found some reason to trust me. Let that be enough."

He felt it again, that sense that she understood something about him that he did not. As if his defenses were pointless. He changed the subject.

"Isn't it possible that someone in Algiers will recognize you?"

"Oh, no," she answered, executing a melodramatic pantomime as she spoke. "I'll wear dark glasses, and a big hat, a scarf, and stay in our hotel room until nightfall. There's just been an invasion. It's a busy place, and we won't be there long."

"Let's hope not."

Leo checked out of Shepheard's and asked the concierge to hold any messages he might receive. "Time to go see the wonders of Luxor," he explained, "before I have to leave this fair land for good. I'll be back in a couple of weeks."

෴

Marseille was a fisherman's town, of no particular refinement. On the night he and Christine arrived, a cold November mist clung with bone-chilling damp to every nook and cranny of the narrow streets. The fog suited the dark mood of the city. Thousands of refugees, who'd fled south when the Germans took Paris, now moved clandestinely through the streets, trying to find ways to escape. German soldiers were already arriving, setting up checkpoints, and the French police stopped people everywhere, demanding identification. Looking, everyone knew, for Jews.

Leo stretched out on one of the two twin beds, listening to the fog horns and the clanging of bells on boats as they moved cautiously through the fog. So far everything had run remarkably smoothly. The only tense moment came when the immigration official at the port in Marseille started asking Leo questions about how long he'd been away from France. But Christine, with her magnetic smile, immediately started asking *him* questions, about his wife, and if she could cook, and if French cooking was hard to learn, because she wanted to cook well for her new husband, she said, squeezing Leo's arm and blushing... the man was under her spell within seconds. He handed Leo's passport back to him, wished them luck, and told Leo that he was a very lucky man, to have a woman like that. A very lucky man.

Christine returned from the communal bathroom down the hallway. She wore a silk housecoat, and she'd wrapped her hair in a towel turban. The sight of her bare neck made Leo's pulse jump. Christine, it seemed, could turn her sexuality on and off like a light switch. Since they arrived in Algiers, she'd not displayed any embarrassment at sharing quarters, or shown any interest in exploring the physical implications of their charade. She was totally professional, and a complete enigma.

"There are more Germans here already than I'd thought there would be," she said, pulling the towel off her head and then using it to dry the ends of her damp hair. "You're sure your German is excellent?"

"*Ja.*"

"Good. One never knows, and I don't speak it at all."

"Hopefully I won't have to talk long."

"Yes." She dropped her towel on the floor and sat down on the opposite bed, chin propped in her hands, elbows on her knees. "Where are you from, really? Not from France. Not from Vienna. Not from Shanghai. Where?"

"Why does it matter?"

"I would like to know."

There it was again… that look. *I know who you are. I know you've suffered. I've suffered, too.*

"Hungary."

"Really?" She sounded genuinely surprised. "When were you there last?"

"A long time ago. I left in 1925."

"I was there two years ago. In Budapest. It's a beautiful place."

Budapest. A wave of homesickness swept over him, with a severity he hadn't felt in years. The Danube. The bridges. The music, the parties, his foster mother's laugh, his sister's smile...

"Leo, what is it?"

"It's nothing. It's just... it's been a long time, that's all."

"Poles and Hungarians have that in common: we never get our country out of our soul."

He did not reply.

"Why did you leave?"

"It's complicated."

"I have time."

"Well, perhaps there are things I don't want to talk about."

She stood up and moved closer to him. She put her hand on his shoulder. Her hand was so warm, her touch so comforting. *Leave it alone, leave her alone, don't do this—*

He looked up at her, his eyes asking just one question, and he saw his answer in hers. Her lips parted slightly. He stood, already breathing heavily, grasped her face with both hands, and plunged his tongue into her mouth. Her body cried out to him. *Lose yourself in me.* There were no boundaries, no uncertainties. He was on top of her; he was inside her. She was so wet, so hungry, yielding and demanding all at once. Too fast, *too fast;* everything was beyond his control. He came with his eyes wide open, groaning aloud as she reached around and pulled him in deeper, and she was watching, watching, connected to him with every breath, a shared existence that left everything else behind.

He could not move. She shifted slightly, and he drifted off to sleep, still inside her. He did not wake up, not even when she moved away to the other bed. Leo slept soundly through the night, undisturbed by his dreams for the first time in years.

Their destination was the Gurs prison camp, located just fifty miles from the Spanish border in the heart of the French *Paye Basque,* the home of a fiercely independent people who traced their mountainous kingdom in the Pyrenees back a thousand years and their unique language back to the beginning of time. The French built Gurs in 1939 to detain refugees fleeing from Franco's wrath at the end of the Spanish Civil War. Later it was used as a prison for Frenchmen who fought or plotted against the Vichy regime. Finally, it had become a dumping ground for thousands of Jewish refugees, rounded up by the French police, obeying Hitler's command that France rid itself of all "stateless" Jews.

They could see the barracks stretched out below them: long, even rows of single story buildings, hundreds of them, on an empty plateau as barren as an abandoned chicken yard. The camp was surrounded by two rows of barbed wire set fifteen feet apart, and pierced by a dozen weather-beaten watchtowers. The guards seldom had to shoot. The real deterrent to escape was the viscous mud that surrounded Gurs like a septic sea.

Leo checked his paperwork. They had precious little to go by, and were relying on the fact that the German invasion of southern France would cause enough confusion to explain any discrepancies.

He checked his hat in the van's rearview mirror. What German soldier had worn this hat, this warm wool coat? Had he been a Nazi, or a reluctant conscript, like Leo himself, back when he was drafted in 1917? Was the man dead now? Or sitting in a prisoner of war camp, wondering how he got there, wanting desperately to go home?

"Are you ready?" the driver asked. Daniel was a short, brave son of a bitch: a German Jew who'd fled first to Belgium, then to Paris, then to Lyon, then said, "Enough," and turned to fight. Now he worked as part of a network that spirited Jewish children out of French internment camps to safe houses in the countryside. Those who had no hope of passing as French Christians were smuggled into Switzerland, where they were put in convents or found homes with families willing to keep them, until their parents—if their parents—could come for them. Daniel had been across the Swiss border half a dozen times himself, and always come back into France, leaving safety behind. "I'll do what I can while I can," he'd told Leo. "But I can't run any more."

"*Ja*," Leo answered, already having made his transition. He was no longer Hungarian, no longer French, no longer a spy. He was a German officer, with orders to pick up as many Jews as they could squeeze into the back of their truck for deportation east.

He banged the back of the cabin. The two men in the back, dressed in Vichy uniforms and carrying machine guns, answered. "Ready."

"Let's go."

Christine was already there, inside the camp, with a group from the Red Cross. He hadn't seen her in three days. They'd spent their last night together in the leaky basement of a farmhouse close to the camp. They made love silently in the darkness, touching and tasting every crevice of each other's body, quiet and frantic, sensing, without confirming, that it would be the last time.

The morning they left Marseille was the only time they'd talked about what was happening between them. They made love as the sun rose, and before leaving her bed, Leo asked, "Why me?"

She put her finger on his lips. "Because we are so much alike, Leo. And you needed me." After that, he'd never asked her about Andrew, or her husband, or what would happen when they both made it back to Cairo, and she never offered any explanation. They'd found each other. It would have to end. That was all.

But he ached for her. Since the day that Martha died, Christine's embrace was the only place he'd found peace.

The truck pulled up in front of the gates. Leo stepped out, followed by the two guards. The driver beeped on the horn, loudly, as if their arrival had gone unnoticed. Of course, it hadn't.

Two guards came up to the gate. "Open up, you idiots, I have orders here," Leo barked at them in German. They stared back insolently. Good. They didn't speak German. That was safer.

Leo gestured to one of his men, who dashed up to the gate. "Tell them to let us in," he told his man, again in German. The fraudulent Vichy soldier thought for a moment, then said in French, "Open up the gates. We're here to collect some Jews."

The two guards looked at each other. "Go get the boss," said one, with a sarcastic smile. A small crowd of women began gathering up against the wall of the building closest to the gates. Leo glanced at them and then spat on the ground, using this gesture of contempt to cover his shock. The women stared at him with hollowed-out eyes, clutched at their mud-stained, ragged skirts with raw hands, or covered their mouths as they whispered to each other. Only a few had coats. He could smell their unwashed bodies, and see the fleshless elbows of their undernourished arms. *Rats live better than this.*

A large man strolled up to the gate. "Here again?" he asked in barely comprehensible German. "We just marched over a thousand of the bastards out of here a few months ago. They had to walk to the train station. What do you have there, a Jewish limousine? Why spoil them? It's only a few miles!" He laughed, and the two guards laughed with him, despite the fact they had no idea what he'd said.

"It'll be your hearse if you keep me here another goddam minute. Open the gate and let's get on with it," Leo growled.

The camp administrator looked at Leo contemplatively. "Let them in," he said finally.

Leo entered on foot. The truck drove in behind him. He shoved his papers at the rotund man, looking around as he did so. "Your name is Gruel, yes?

"That's right."

"So tell me. What did you do to deserve this pleasant duty?"

"Could be worse," was the answer. "These types don't fight back."

Leo snorted. "We'll have German officers in here to replace trash like you soon enough."

The man bristled, but Leo's words hit their mark. Gruel handed the papers back to Leo, eager to have this obnoxious German gone as quickly as possible. Unoccupied France was unoccupied no longer. "Do you have names?"

"Doesn't matter," Leo replied. "As many as we can get into the truck. Including women and children. No more exemptions. I have a quota to fill."

"Come to my office."

Where was Christine?

He followed the man down a muddy path cut between buildings with sealed windows and sagging roofs. From somewhere he heard the sound of children singing, their lilting voices so out of keeping with the vile surroundings that Leo felt a lump rise in his throat. He coughed.

"What kind of diseases are you breeding here?"

Gruel laughed. "Dysentery, mostly."

There she was! She looked so different: homely, even. No sparkle. No warmth. *A complete chameleon.* She walked quickly toward them, bundled into a threadbare woolen coat. She must have given hers to someone at the camp. Her Red Cross armband was already covered in grime.

Christine thrust a paper in front of her. "Monsieur Gruel, I have a list of just a few of the women who are sick. They need medical attention immediately. I'm afraid it might be typhoid."

She spoke in rapid French. Leo looked at her blankly, feigning incomprehension. Gruel looked from Christine, to Leo, and then back to the list she held in her hand.

"Are they all Jewish?" he asked her in French.

"*Juden?*" Leo asked, as if he'd caught just that one word.

Christine looked terrified. "I don't know. I suppose so."

"Give me your list."

She reluctantly handed it to the camp director. "Monsieur, the deportation orders exclude women with young children, and these women need medical attention. Most of them have children they're too sick to care for—"

"Here's your list," the colonel said in German to Leo. Leo grabbed the piece of paper. Fifteen names.

"Round these women up. Children too. I want to leave as quickly as possible. I can't stand the stench."

Gruel executed an exaggerated salute. "At your service. Heil Hitler!"

Christine did not give up. "But sir! These women are not well. They won't survive a journey—

"Just as well. And if the Red Cross doesn't stop meddling in the camp's administrative affairs, you will all be less welcome to accomplish whatever good you think you're doing here. Am I understood?"

Christine did not answer. Head bowed, shoulders sagging, she trudged away, back into the stench of human soil and decay.

Fifteen women and nineteen children piled into the truck, grasping their small dirty bundles, cowering under the rough hands of the Vichy guards herding them in. Many of the children were crying, and several had soiled themselves. There was not enough room for anyone to sit down.

Leo climbed back into the cab and ordered his driver to leave. They needed to make it five miles without running into any patrols. Then he would hand his cargo over to someone else, who would give them food and fresh clothes, and help them find hiding places or escape routes. If Christine had done her job, these women were strong enough to travel. For some, their next home might well be an internment camp in Switzerland—the Swiss would not issue any more entrance visas—but their children would find safety with a willing family, or in a convent. It was a large group, making the exodus a very risky operation, but the people in charge were hoping to take advantage of the chaos of the invasion to get more Jews out before the Germans obtained control of all of France.

The van was only ten minutes away from the camp when Leo felt the truck sag on one side, then come to a stop.

"Shit!" Daniel banged the steering wheel, then leapt out. Leo followed. They walked around to the back of the truck. A length of barbed wire had wrapped around the right rear tire, tearing it in several places. The two other men, Val and Charles, had been riding on the outside of the truck on the rear running board. They were already inspecting the damage and adding their own expletives.

"We'll have to walk. We'll have to split into two groups," Daniel declared.

Leo glanced at the dense growth of trees surrounding them. "I have no idea where the hell we are."

"We do. Stay with me."

"I've got to get out of this uniform."

"Soon. Aren isn't far. We'll find help there. Germany bombed the hell out of a couple of Spanish Basque towns as a favor to Franco during the civil war. The Basque hate the Germans almost as much as they hate the French."

"That's my concern."

Daniel moved to the back of the truck and pulled back the bolt to the lock. He'd opened the door less than six inches when a hand holding one end of a cloth-wrapped bundle swung out of the small opening and smacked him soundly on the head. Daniel's knees buckled, and he fell to the damp ground with a thud.

The doors flew open and women and children poured out. They started to run the instant they emerged, urged on by panicked voices crying out in several languages.

"Stop! We're here to help you!" Leo shouted in German, trying to get to Daniel before he was trampled to death. The other two rescuers screamed in French, and made wild attempts to grab women and children as they raced by.

"We're here to help you escape! Don't run! You'll get lost! Stop!"

The crack of gunfire broke through the chaos. Those closest to the van froze.

"I won't shoot you. You just have to listen," shouted Val, the younger of the two Vichy imposters. "We're here to help you."

"We want to help you," Leo repeated in German as he dragged Daniel's injured body to one side. "Please come back!"

A few of the wary women walked slowly back to the van. Leo shouted again.

"Please come back! We're here to help you. We'll try to get you and your children safely out of the country. But you must trust us! Please come back!"

"We can't wait long," Val responded. "That gunshot will have been heard for miles. But I didn't have much choice, did I?"

By now more than half of the women and their children stood within twenty feet of the van, their eyes wide with a terrible combination of fear and hope. Leo could hear feet thrashing through the underbrush, some coming closer, some getting farther and farther away.

"If you speak French, stand to the right," Val ordered.

One of the women shouted out something in Polish. Two more responded and crept out of the woods, their toddlers in their arms.

"They won't long last out here. Not in this weather. Once the sun goes, they'll freeze," said Charles. "What a mess. How's Daniel?"

"Alive, I think," Leo answered. "At least for now. He's not losing much blood, but he got quite a wallop on the head, and that trampling didn't help."

Hearing this, another woman shouted out a name. A voice answered. Two more women appeared, three children in tow. Most of the women were now conversing between themselves in low voices, or comforting their frightened, cold, and confused children.

"Okay, who has a plan?" Leo asked.

"We'll have to split up or we'll attract too much attention. The ones who speak French can travel with me," Val answered. "Everyone else should go with you and Charles."

"And Daniel?"

"You'll have to take him. You're both sturdy. Take turns carrying him. It's only two miles to Aren. We have a friend there, who can at least get us some food, and may let us stay in his barn. I'll get in touch with another of our members who can contact the leader of the next leg of this operation, explain the situation, and they'll figure out how to get the group out. We have to be careful, though. Not all the Basque are sympathetic."

"Very well," Leo responded. "Charles? Do you know the way?"

"It's like traveling in my own backyard. How many have we lost?"

Leo did a quick count. "Seems all but two of the women are back."

Charles hefted Daniel over his broad shoulders like a sack of grain. "Call 'em. Let's get going."

The women soon sorted themselves out. Leo and Charles led away their group of seven women and ten children, ranging in age from one to thirteen. For as many children as they had with them, it was a fairly quiet procession.

Just when Leo felt his optimism returning, one of the women moaned and fell over. Her daughter, a small child with long curly hair and enormous dark eyes, screamed and pointed.

"Christ, what now?" Charles muttered, setting Daniel down as gently as possible while Leo made his way through the circle of women now surrounding the one who'd collapsed. He knelt down and put a hand to the woman's head. No fever. What then? Exhaustion? Starvation?

Leo took her hand and spoke to her softly. "Madame, what's wrong? Are you ill?"

The woman gasped with pain, and her free hand went to her stomach. "I'm losing... I'm losing my baby."

Leo looked at the ground. A dark stain was spreading beneath her. The little girl plopped down next to her mother's head. Silent tears flowed down her pale chapped skin.

Leo stood up. "Does anyone have anything we can use to... to absorb the blood?"

"*Ja,*" said one woman without hesitation. She unknotted her dirty bundle and pulled out a blue cotton dress. "Take this. Who knows if I'll ever wear it again? Poor girl. No one even knew she was expecting."

Leo took the dress, then looked around, embarrassed. "Could one of you ladies please... tuck this up where it will... soak up the... discharge?"

Another woman nodded and took the dress. Leo politely turned his back. "It's done," he heard, and squatted down again.

"What's your name?" He asked the little girl, who now held her mother's head in her own small lap.

"Gabriella."

"What a beautiful name. How old are you, Gabriella? She held up three grubby little fingers.

"Three already! What a lovely grown-up girl you are! Okay now, I'm going to carry your mommy okay? But we have to walk more before we lose the light. We don't want to get lost in the dark, do we?"

"I'm scared of the dark," Gabriella answered, her chin trembling.

Leo pulled out his handkerchief, wiped Gabriella's face, and helped her blow her nose. "We'll be fine. You'll see. Walk right next to me." He picked up Gabriella's mother and moved over to where

Charles stood. "Charles, can you handle Daniel? I've got to carry this one."

"Leo, we can't take anyone who can't travel. I'm sorry. It's too risky."

"I'm not leaving her."

"As far as Aren, then. We'll have to leave her there. Whether or not we can find someone to take her in, you understand?

"Let's just get there."

After struggling through another mile of dense forest, the group came to the edge of the Basque village of Aren. Only a few hundred feet away stood a small farmhouse, corral, and barn.

Charles laid Daniel down. The unconscious man groaned. "Well, that's a relief," Charles said as he waved Leo over. "He must be coming out of it. I'll go see what the welcome is like. You wait here. Keep everyone quiet and out of sight."

He was back in twenty minutes, a good deal more cheerful than he'd been when he left. "Val's already been there. We're good for tonight, anyway. We'll spit into two smaller groups and move into the barn after dark."

Gabriella lay fast asleep at Leo's feet, wrapped in the German officer's coat that was now heavily stained with her mother's blood. Her mother's lifeless body lay beside her.

"We lost her," Leo said, exhaustion punctuating every syllable.

"Probably for the best, hard as it sounds. She'd only cause a problem in that condition."

Leo looked at him. "Get me a shovel when you come back for the second group. I want to bury her, at least."

"I'll see what I can do."

Charles came back with a shovel and Leo's coat. "Never mind the blood. You'll freeze out here without it," he said. Leo found a place just inside the tree line where the ground was relatively soft, and dug a shallow grave for the woman he knew only as the mother of little Gabriella. Charles would have to tell the girl when she woke up. Leo couldn't, not after he'd had to tell his own daughter that she would never see her mother again.

He shivered as he piled the dirt back in on top of the body. Digging had helped keep him warm, but it was much colder now. He leaned his shovel against a nearby tree and stretched his back.

A noise in the underbrush ignited his senses. He reached for the shovel. *Who was out there?* He waited, motionless, concentrating on every sound. Nothing. Shovel held high, he moved backward toward the field.

Two noises pierced the silence, so close together it was hard to tell them apart: the crack of a shotgun, and the ring of metal ricocheting off metal. Two Basque villagers sprinted out of the woods toward Leo's fallen body.

"Great shot!" said one, setting down his small trace of rabbits as he learned over to get a closer look. "Must've got him right through the heart. Look at all that blood." He gave Leo's chest a quick poke with the barrel of his own rifle and grinned.

"Now that makes for a good day's hunting," said his companion. "Half a dozen rabbits and a fuckin' German!"

"Too bad we can't eat this bastard."

"You could tempt me to cut off a few pieces."

"Enough fun. We better get him out of here. One of his friends finds him in this field, and they'll be shooting everyone in the village."

"Tell you what. Let's go dump him in the middle of the camp road. He can finish bleeding to death there. His friends will know what we think of them around here."

৵৹

"Katherine?"

"Hmm?"

"Are you asleep?"

"Yes."

Maddy sat up in her bed. Katherine lay curled up in the twin bed beside her own, the one Bernice bought especially for her friend to sleep in when she spent the night. But for a swath of curly red hair, she was buried under a down comforter.

"Do you think I would know if my father were dead?"

Katherine rolled over to face Maddy. "What do you mean? Would the War Office send you a telegram, something like that?"

Maddy shook her head. "No, I mean, do you think that I would just... *know.*"

"I don't believe in that stuff, Maddy. If anyone could know that, Ma would have known that Jamie was dead. An angel would have come and told her in a dream, or some crazy Catholic nonsense."

"What do you mean? What's nonsense?"

"I think..." Katherine paused, as if thinking twice before she committed blasphemy. "I think a lot of all the religion stuff is nonsense. Look at your aunt and uncle. They don't go to church, do they?"

"They're Jewish, dumbo."

"Temple, then. They're doing all right without priests and all. Or rabbis. They seem like decent people. I don't think you have to be Catholic to be a good person."

"Yes, but... what about what the nuns told us, about going to hell if you're not baptized?"

"What about it?"

"Do you think that applies to Jews?"

"Geez! How am I supposed to know?"

"But what about me? What if I wasn't baptized?"

"Don't be stupid."

"But what about original sin?" Maddy laid back down, her heart thumping in her chest. "What if I'm going to hell, and there's nothing I can do about it?"

"You're gonna get there quicker if you don't go to sleep, 'cause I'm gonna kill you."

"Please don't joke about this. We're talking about my *immortal soul*."

"Are you really scared?"

"Aren't you? Aren't you afraid of hell?"

Katherine didn't answer this. "C'mon. Look at the facts. You went to Catholic school in Shanghai, right?"

"So?"

"They wouldn't have enrolled you without a baptismal certificate. They wouldn't take a chance on letting any little heathens in by mistake."

"But what if baptism doesn't help… Christ killers?"

Now Katherine sat up. "Maddy, what's gotten into you? All of the original Christians were Jews, right? The Apostles? If you're baptized, then the Pope has your name on a list somewhere, and you're covered."

This made some sense, and Maddy found herself breathing a small sigh of relief.

"I sort of wish I could see that list."

"So write to the Vatican. Now go to sleep. I'm bushed." Katherine laid back down and turned away, curling up into a ball under the covers.

"Okay. G'nite."

The silence lasted only a minute. "Katherine?"

"What is it now?"

"I'm really sorry I wasn't there. When you found out about Jamie."

"You've told me that a million times. It's not like you could've done anything differently."

"But I'm sorry I wasn't there."

"All you missed was a bunch of Irish cops getting drunk. And watching Ma fall to pieces. I don't think it would've hit her so hard if it had been me lost at sea."

"Now *you're* being an idiot!"

"Can we please go to sleep now?"

"Okay. Sorry. Goodnight."

"Goodnight, already."

Maddy pulled her own covers up under her chin. Just as sleep overcame her, Katherine's muffled sobs edged into her consciousness.

"Katherine?"

Her question was met with silence. Maddy knew that any further attempt to comfort her friend would just rouse that Irish temper of hers, so she let herself drift into her dreams.

ᨳ

He put his hand on his sister's stomach, amazed at how taut it felt through the fabric of her dress. "I'll have a nephew for you soon," she said, and then he got into a car to ride away. It was the countess' car, the Rolls Royce, and the chauffeur was driving too fast, way too fast. The car would crash, and he would never get there. He started to sweat. "Slow down," he shouted. The man would not listen. He shouted again, in Russian this time. Then French. Then Chinese. The refugees started crowding around the car. Hands touching him. Hands covered in blood. He saw Martha in the distance, walking into the store. He had to stop her! He struggled to get away, but the hands held him too tightly—

"Quiet, now. Hush."

He saw a woman's face. It wasn't Martha. He lost consciousness again.

He heard the murmur of lowered voices and tried to open his eyes. He had never exerted so much effort to move any part of his body. *If he could just open his eyes.*

The voices drifted away.

She smelled like honey and vanilla. Silk and rippling warmth. Then she was gone and he saw Amelia looking down at him. She was talking to him, saying something to him. In German. He needed to ask her what she'd done with Maddy. Why couldn't he speak? He had to get the words out! Where is my daughter? Where is my daughter?

"Wo ist meine tochter?"

CHAPTER 14

THE PRODIGAL FATHER

∽⌇∾

WASHINGTON, D.C., AUGUST 1945

Lieutenant Colonel Gregory Sharpton and Major Douglas Hagman walked briskly down an empty, windowless corridor, deep in the bowels of the Pentagon. They returned the salute executed by the soldier stationed at the end of the hall, then each displayed a special pass that the young man inspected carefully before stepping aside.

Hagman opened the steel door that led into a small office, furnished with two plain desks and one filing cabinet. The cabinet was bolted to the floor, and sealed with two separate combination locks. Sharpton knew one code, Hagman the other. There was no way one single human being, operating alone, could invade the contents of this particular cabinet.

Each man removed a stack of files from the top drawer and retreated to his respective desk. Sharpton, a career military man in his late fifties, pulled a pair of reading glasses from his pocket. Hagman, younger by almost fifteen years, removed his cap, put his feet up on his desk, and leaned back in his chair as he began to read.

All was quiet for a few moments. Then Hagman broke the silence.

"Greg?"

"Hmm?"

"Do you think ol' Harry really knew what those atom bombs could do?"

"I assume so."

"I saw pictures today. Have you seen pictures yet?"

"Yes, I have. Very effective."

"Effective! Guess that's one way to put it. Who would've thought we could make something that could do all that? The whole place just… disintegrated."

Sharpton put down the file he'd been reading and looked over his bifocals at the younger officer. "Would you rather have been on the beach yourself, attempting to take the Japanese homeland? The war could have dragged on for years. The president did the right thing."

"I suppose so."

"Douglas, Truman is shutting down the Office of Strategic Services in a month. We have less than two weeks before they sweep the place clean. Debate nuclear ethics on your own time. Right now, just read."

There was silence for a few more minutes. Then Hagman emitted a long, low whistle, swung his feet to the ground, and leaned forward in his chair.

"Now this is some hot shot spy. Listen to this. Hungarian national, recruited out of Shanghai in late 1940. Tapped for special duty even before Donovan was named Coordinator of Strategic Information. That's a little strange, but I guess someone knew what they were doing. He was loaned to the Brits and worked in North Africa under Colonel Eddy, where he was instrumental in effectuating the Dakar decoy plan. Then, get this! He's in France, wearing a German uniform—"

"Why?"

"Hmm... doesn't really say. Anyhow, he gets some kind of head wound and is left there to die, when he's discovered by a German patrol. They dump him off at a Vichy hospital, thinking he's German. He manages to get out before they catch on, but then gets captured for real when he's headed for the border. Lucky for him no one connects the dots, so the Nazis send him to Meyreuil, a work camp outside Marseille, where he spent two years digging coal and then escaped again, bringing *fifteen* other prisoners with him by masquerading as a German guard in charge of a work detail. Hooked up with the Penny Farthing network in Avignon in time to assist with Operation Dragoon—geez, the guy is a regular Scarlet Pimpernel."

"A what?"

"You know, "The Scarlet Pimpernel," that movie with Leslie Howard, where he saves all his friends from the guillotine during the French Revolution by adopting different disguises. Don't you ever go to the movies?"

"Not lately."

"This movie is at least ten years old."

Sharpton ignored this. "Where is the man now?"

"Ah, let me see. Released to Naval Intelligence, then given a special assignment in Berlin for post-war debriefings. Handy guy to have around, I guess, since it says here he speaks English, German, French, Russian, Hungarian, Chinese, and decent Arabic. Finally discharged with permission to immigrate, destination New York, about a month ago. I think they made this guy up, Greg."

"It's not our job to decide that. But I'd say his file should make the cut, don't you? We only have a few weeks before they dismantle the whole O.S.S., and if Donavan convinces Truman to go ahead with a peacetime agency—"

"We'll need some good spies. I know." Major Hagman tucked the dossier back into its manila folder and tossed it into a box marked SPECIAL CLEARANCE: DONOVAN that sat on the floor between their two desks. He then leaned back in his chair, put his feet back up on his desk, picked up the next file from his stack, and began, again, to read.

❧

He had to knock twice before someone came to the door: a young woman who looked to be about Maddy's age. Her face was pleasant, but not beautiful, surrounded by a wild mass of curly red hair, most of which was captured in a haphazard ponytail. Her limbs were long and thin, and she moved with determination rather than grace. Leo was pretty sure he knew who she was.

"Hello, Katherine."

She must have recognized him as well, for the expression on her face shifted from anticipation to surprise to contempt in a matter of seconds, before she slammed the door shut.

"Ma! Ma! You won't believe who's here!" he heard her shout. He banged on the door this time, not pleasantly.

Margaret opened the door. She was so thin, so fragile-looking. Not at all the person to whom he'd said farewell when he last left New York.

"Mrs. O'Connor. May I please come in?"

She looked uncertain. Katherine stepped in front of her. "You've got some nerve, showing up here—"

Katherine's outburst brought Margaret to life. "Mary Kate, mind your manners. Haven't I raised ya better than that? Go upstairs. It's me he means to talk to, not your uppity self. Go on now. Come in, Mr. Hoffman."

Katherine didn't move.

"Off you go, Katherine. There's laundry to be folded upstairs."

"Ah, Ma—"

"Am I talkin' to meself, Miss Mary Katherine Anne O'Connor?"

Katherine knew that an order issued using her full Christian name left no room for argument. She turned and clomped up the stairs, each step signaling her protest. Leo waited until he heard a door slam upstairs before talking again.

"Where's Maddy?"

Margaret shook her head. "She's not here. And she hasn't been, hasn't lived here that is, for quite some time."

"She doesn't live here? But why—where—?"

"I think I'll be the one asking questions, if you don't mind."

They faced each other, both sensing that at that moment they would become allies or enemies. Leo blinked first. "I'll answer any questions you have. Just tell me that she's all right."

Margaret continued to give him a speculative look. "Right enough. We'll have some tea, then. This way to the kitchen."

He followed her down the narrow hallway to the room he'd been in only once before, the night he brought Maddy back from Amelia's apartment and decided to let her stay with this family rather than deposit her in a Swiss boarding school. Had that decision been one more of his many mistakes?

Leo took a seat at the table while Margaret put the kettle on. She continued to talk as she lit the stove. "She's living in New Jersey, your daughter is. With her aunt and uncle. Her mother's sister and her husband."

"*What?*"

Margaret took the cups and saucers out of a cupboard and set them down on the table. "Yes, that's right. Bernice Mason. Showed up here three years ago, sayin' how she'd been searchin' for Maddy ever since she heard of her sister's death. She had an old photograph, of a man and two girls, one that was surely herself, the other a spittin' image of Maddy, only with lighter hair, who I figured had to be Maddy's mum. And then, also, she had a letter that yer Martha, pardon me, that *Mrs. Hoffman* had written home to her sister when you were all still livin' down there in Shanghai."

"A letter... a letter from Martha?"

"Yes, sir. I paid an old German lady from the market to read it for me, before I let Maddy out of this house. She was quite willin' to go, ya see. And with your bein' gone all that time, with no sign of comin' back, I couldn't tell her no, not after seein' this letter.

"Mrs. Hoffman wrote that with another war on, Shanghai was quite dangerous, and that you two were tryin' yer best to get out, but that you had visa troubles. She allowed as how things between the two of you weren't quite what they used to be, and she wanted to know how to find Bernice if she got to France before you could get out of Shanghai."

Leo did not respond. His eyes were closed, and he looked as if he was barely breathing. Mrs. O'Connor poured the tea.

"You can't blame her for wantin' to go with her aunt, Mr. Hoffman. She was offerin' Maddy somethin' she'd never had. A piece of herself. And the fact the woman's obviously rich didn't hurt; we've done well by Maddy, thanks to the money you left. But we are who we are. Maddy came from somethin' different, and she had a right to go back to it. Mrs. Mason seems like a decent woman. Not a warm person, but decent, and determined to do the best by Maddy."

Leo finally overcame the lump in his throat. "I understand why you made the decision you did, Mrs. O'Connor. And I appreciate everything you've done for my daughter. More than you will ever know. But I'm still her father."

"No one's arguing that point."

"Have you talked to her? Did you tell her that I was coming?"

Margaret shook her head. "No. I called Mrs. Mason, and she asked me to let her tell Maddy, if you actually showed up. In case you didn't. No reason to disappoint her, you see."

"I understand."

"Do ya now? That's the trouble I'm havin'. I lost two boys in this war, Mr. Hoffman, our youngest and our first born. There's nothin' that prepares ya for losin' a child. It opens a hole in your heart so wide and so deep there's no way to ever fill it back up. The best ya can do is learn to walk around it, for the sake of those left behind. So I can't imagine, havin' yer own child, how ya let her sit here thinkin' you were never comin' back, with no word, no hope…"

"I tried—"

"We never got a word. Not one word, after the letter from the Navy sayin' you'd been discharged. Not until your telegram two weeks ago."

"But I did write! And then I couldn't—" Leo felt the full weight of Margaret's judgment in her stare, and knew there was no point in arguing.

"You're right in everything you say, Mrs. O'Connor." He stared down into his cup. "But maybe there's a reason that I'm still here, and not dead like so many others. Maybe it's so that I could have this chance. To try and convince Maddy that I do love her, and that it wasn't her fault that I left…"

It took a moment for him to reclaim his voice. "I don't know if it's too late for her to believe anything I have to say. But I have to try."

Mrs. O'Connor had tears in her eyes when he finally looked up. She coughed and dried her eyes on her apron. "Mr. Hoffman," she said at last, "You're either a decent man or a damn fine liar. Maybe only the Good Lord himself knows the truth of that. But I'm afraid that for you and your Maddy both, it might just be too late."

❧

"Madeleine, your father is in New York and wants to see you."

Maddy's stomach flipped over, and she thought her egg was going to bounce up and out onto the tablecloth.

My father. She'd wanted to see her father for so long that the desire had gone stale inside her, atrophying into something closer to dread. It hadn't been difficult, explaining her father's absence during the war. So many fathers, brothers, uncles and cousins had been away from home for so long that the details of Maddy's unusual circumstances blended into the background. Depravation was the normal course of things, during the war. But now the war was over.

Katherine had warned her. *Facts facts facts. Don't draw any conclusions until you have the facts.* She kept saying that the government, or the Red Cross, or someone, somewhere, would have found a way to tell Maddy if her father was dead.

"He's in New York, at the O'Connor's. He rang last night. I told him I'd ask you if you wished to see him, and that under no circumstances was he to come here without your express permission."

Maddy sat back in her chair, eyes wide. No one had ever given her a choice about something so vital. She felt the control her aunt was giving her as palpably as if she were holding a weight in her hand, and the responsibility for making the decision terrified her.

"How long... how long will he be here?"

"That's not clear."

"Oh."

"Madeleine, I will follow your wishes in this matter. It's entirely up to you whether you want to see your father. I have no objection, provided he is willing to be reasonable."

Maddy was not entirely sure what Bernice meant by "reasonable," but she didn't have the courage to ask. She tried to decipher what Bernice wanted from her. If she didn't want her father to come, wouldn't she have said so? Didn't that mean it was all right? What was her aunt waiting to hear?

"Of course, I will see him," Maddy finally said, gravely, and then waited for Bernice's reaction.

Her aunt rewarded her with a self-satisfied smile. "That's what I was hoping, my dear. It's better to get this settled once and for all. For that reason, before you talk to him, I think there are some things that you should know."

⚭

At four o'clock a taxi deposited Leo at the Mason's doorstep. He spent a few moments outside the house, taking in the cold, geometrically striking exterior, before ringing the bell.

Bernice came to the door. They looked at each other. Leo tried to discern in that first instant whether there was any room for friendship between them. He was not encouraged.

"Leo Hoffman. We meet at last. I'm Bernice Mason. Come in."

"Thank you," he said, stepping inside. "Is Maddy—"

"Hello, Father. How kind of you to come visit."

She stood in the hallway, her figure framed like a photograph by the entrance to the living room. The dark green suit she wore set off the color of her eyes and made her hair look as shiny as a raven's feather. Leo sucked in his breath when he saw her. She was Martha, except she wasn't.

"Maddy." He wanted to reach for her, but could feel her willing him away. He kept his distance.

"Well," said Bernice crisply, "Shall we sit down?"

She led them into the living room. A low camel-hair couch formed a semicircle around a glass-topped coffee table. On it sat a contemporary silver coffee service, the pot as sleek as a missile.

"Coffee?"

"Please."

Leo looked at Maddy while Bernice poured. She was trying so hard to emulate Bernice. Her rigid posture. The cool reserve. The little girl he'd known should never have turned out like this. She'd been too much like her mother.

But what choice had he given her?

"You look lovely, Maddy. That green is a beautiful color for you."

"Thank you, Papa."

So much silence. So much time lost. So many things to say, with no idea where to start. *Simple. Start with something simple.*

"You sound so very American. Is that all you speak? Have you kept up with your French?"

To his consternation, Maddy looked at Bernice before responding. "Yes. Somewhat. I take classes."

"If you keep up with it in school, it will come back when you need it."

"I can't imagine when I will ever need to speak French again, Father."

He took a sip of his coffee. "Well, one never knows. What a striking home you have, Bernice. Very modern. The landscaping is lovely. I tell you, I'd love to walk outside. Maddy, would you care to show me the garden?"

Again, Maddy looked to Bernice. "It's entirely up to you, Madeleine."

"Very well." Maddy set her coffee cup gently back into its saucer. "Aunt Bernice, would you care to join us?"

For a moment Leo was afraid the woman would say yes. To his relief, she shook her head. "No, it would be fine for your father to have you to himself for a few minutes, if you're comfortable."

"I'll be fine," answered Maddy with a touch of contempt Leo hoped was not aimed at him. But of course, it was. He felt his resentment of Bernice growing by the second.

They did not speak again until they were outside. Leo ran his hand across the top of his head and down the back of his neck. "I don't know where to start," he said, hoping that Maddy would feel comfortable asking him a question that could begin their conversation.

Maddy was not at a loss for words. She'd rehearsed this scene in her head for years. "Well, Father, what *have* you been doing with yourself?"

"I've been in the military."

"That's a lie. You weren't in the military. We got a letter. You left the Navy."

"Not exactly. They transferred me to a different division. I became a spy."

Surprise interrupted her internal script. "A spy*?*"

"Yes. I'm not supposed to tell you that, but I'm not going to let any more secrets get between us. That's why I couldn't write to you, or give you an address to write to. I was supposed to be gone for two years. But then the U.S. entered the war and I was stranded. Then I was captured."

"Captured? By the Germans?"

"Yes."

He could sense her wall of hostility wavering. Then it snapped back into place. "Show me your number."

"My number?"

She pointed at his arm. "On your wrist. Show me the number."

"You mean a tattoo? I don't have one. Not everyone—"

"You're Jewish, aren't you? And you were captured? And put in a camp? Then why don't you have a number? You're lying to me again. You lied about where you were from, about being Jewish, and about Amelia. You stuck me with her because you'd had an affair with her. When you were still married to my mother."

"Maddy, it wasn't like that!"

"Oh, no? My aunt told me the truth about you. *She* doesn't lie to me."

It would have been easy to leave at that moment. Easy to run away from her anger, easy to let Bernice win. But what had he fought for, if not this? If not for her?

"Please. Let's sit and talk." He looked around. "Surely there's somewhere?"

His daughter glared at him, suspicious of even this simple request. "Over there," she said at last, and pointed behind him to a stone bench. He walked over to it and sat down. She perched on the other side, as far away from him as possible. But she was listening.

"I was captured in France, Maddy, when most of the French were still doing whatever they were told to do by the Germans. I was lucky. The Germans needed workers, and I was capable of working. As a prisoner of war, I was not tattooed, or sent east to the death camps. I worked in a coal mine near Marseille."

She said nothing. He kept talking.

"As for the rest, I stopped acknowledging my Jewish background long before I went to Shanghai. After the first war in Europe, people in Hungary were being killed just for being Jewish. My faith meant very little to me. It was more important to stay alive."

Something in his statement served as a tripwire for Maddy's anger. *Aunt Bernice was right. He betrayed my mother, and I'm not the first person he's abandoned. I'm not the only person he's run away from.*

"You were a coward!" she lashed out. "Think of all the people Hitler killed! People who were willing to die rather than disclaim their heritage! You're a liar and a coward!"

"I suppose it's true that I am a liar and a coward, Maddy," he said, still calm in the face of her onslaught. "I could have told the truth and been killed for it. Being labeled Jewish was a dangerous inconvenience. That's all I gave up."

"Just like you gave me up, when I became inconvenient," Maddy spat out, daring him to respond.

He sighed heavily, a long sound, full of patience and regret. "Maddy, I know why you feel that way. All I can say is that I did what I did for your protection, because I love you—"

She stood up before he could finish, rearing away from him like a wild horse. The depth of the hatred in her eyes stunned him.

"To *protect me?* Sending me off with Amelia? Do you have any *idea* what it was like? Living with strangers, knowing that you weren't wanted, hoping and waiting for someone who never comes? And do you know what happens then? *You give up.*

"I thought you were dead. It would've been *easier* if you'd been dead. Then there would've been a reason for you to leave me alone the way you did!"

By now Maddy was shaking with rage. She'd never felt such anger before, had never let it emerge from her soul. She could feel the power of it, power she wanted to use.

"You were a prisoner of war, you said. What kind of prisoner did you make me? *What kind of prisoner was I?*"

"Maddy, please. Listen to me—"

"Listen? *You* listen to *me!* I never want to see you again. Never, do you understand? Go back to your spy job or whatever you do. I do *not* want you back in my life. I found someone who wants me. And she's wanted me all this time, and would have found me, too, if it weren't for your sending me away and hiding me behind all of your lies. You stopped being my father eight years ago. It's too late to start again now."

Without another word, she turned on her heel walked back into the house.

oɕo

Bernice refused to meet with Leo anywhere other than her lawyer's office. *Behind enemy lines,* he thought as walked into the somber suite occupied by the Wall Street firm that Mason Industries kept on a generous retainer. A prim secretary ushered him into a small conference room where Bernice sat, flanked by two of her mercenaries. Only one of them stood to shake his hand when he entered the room.

"It would have been easier to meet me for a cup of coffee somewhere, Bernice. And a lot less expensive, I'll bet," Leo said as he took a seat.

"I think there are some details of the situation that require some technical elaboration," she responded, with a nod at one of her attorneys. "I don't want there to be room for any misunderstanding."

"What is there to understand? I have a right to see my daughter."

"No, you don't, actually," one of the lawyers interjected. "She's fifteen. She can live where she likes, as long as she's in no physical or moral danger."

"But I just want to talk to her."

"She doesn't want to talk to you. I think she's made that abundantly clear." Bernice answered. "And you can add these to your collection," she added, handing him two letters addressed to Maddy, marked with the word REFUSED.

The older of the two lawyers spoke. "Mrs. Mason wishes us to inform you that if you show up at her home again, you will be arrested for trespass."

"I spent two years as a prisoner of war. Do really you think a few days in the county jail will keep me away from my child?"

"Miss Hoffman is no longer a child. She's a responsible young woman, who wants nothing to do with the man who seduced her mother away from her own family, carried on numerous adulterous relationships—"

"What the hell are you talking about?"

"We have an affidavit from your ex-wife, Mr. Hoffman, explaining the... intricacies of your relationship. With her, and with other women. Prior to your first wife's death."

"You mean you talked to Amelia? And believed *anything* she said?"

"She swore out an affidavit under oath. It was enough to convince your daughter." The attorney held a paper out to Leo. He swatted it away, and addressed his words directly to Bernice.

"You mean you showed that spiteful, obscene garbage to Maddy? You don't even know me, Bernice! Why are you doing this? Why won't you give me a chance to try and make amends with my only child?"

"It's not my decision. It's Madeleine's. What chance did you give her? What chance did you give her mother?"

Her words, cold and sharp as a razor, found their target. The blood drained out of his face as Bernice continued her calculated assault. "What right do you have, now, after all this time, to disrupt Madeleine's life? Just how selfish are you?"

He couldn't listen to any more.

He called Bernice's house late in the afternoon the next day. Maddy answered the phone. Even her voice sounded like Martha's.

"Maddy, it's your father."

The next thing he heard was the sound of the dial tone in his ear. He looked at the receiver for several minutes before placing his next call. It took some time before the connection went through.

"Sharpton here."

"This is Leo Hoffman. I would like to reconsider the position we discussed."

CHAPTER 15

THE MUSICIAN

○◦◦◦○

NEW YORK, 1910

Maddy knocked gently on the familiar door.

"Here it is!" squealed Katherine, flinging it open in response to Maddy's knock. She leapt out onto the stoop and waved a single page of paper inches from her friend's nose. "The ticket to my future! My acceptance to Barnard!" Pulling the sacred letter close to her breast with a touch of melodramatic reverence, she added, "And after Barnard, wait and see: the Columbia School of Journalism!"

"Congratulations, Katherine," said Bernice Mason, just behind Maddy. "And as you have lived up to your end of our bargain, I'm prepared to live up to mine. I shall pay your tuition at Barnard, as long as you maintain a B average or better."

"Thank you, Mrs. Mason, but that's really far, far too generous," replied Mrs. O'Connor from the doorway, before Katherine could respond.

"Nonsense, Margaret. As I said when I made the offer last fall, given all that you and your family have done for Madeleine, it's the least I can do. I only hope that Katherine's drive and ambition will inspire her. And today, to celebrate Katherine's achievement, I'll take the girls to lunch at the Waldorf."

"Wow!" Katherine squealed again, nearly jumping into the air before she caught herself. "Ah, thank you, Mrs. Mason. I would go change, except I'm already wearing my best dress."

"You look lovely, dear. Would you care to join us, Margaret?" Bernice inquired, with a touch too much graciousness.

Mrs. O'Connor cast a sympathetic look in Maddy's direction, which Bernice mistook for embarrassment. "Thank you, Bernice, but I have far too much to do today, though I am mighty proud of Katherine. You all go, and have a fine time of it."

Taking their leave, the trio returned to the curb, where the chauffeur was already waiting next to a new Oldsmobile limousine. Maddy's ears were burning with embarrassment. She seldom responded to her aunt's pointed remarks about her own lack of achievement, but they were never lost on her. She wasn't jealous of Katherine's talent, just her ability to win Bernice's approval.

During the six years Maddy had lived with her aunt and uncle, they'd been generous but demanding guardians. She tried to emulate them: to be practical, unemotional, articulate, and intelligent. She was obedient and helpful. They made clear to Maddy that performing well in school was essential, and Maddy, with a significant amount of effort, was able to do decently well in all her subjects, but did not excel in any particular discipline. To her—and her aunt's—disappointment, she had not been accepted at any of the "Seven Sisters," the colleges that offered the equivalent of an Ivy League education for young women. She would go, instead, to a small liberal arts college in Manhattan.

The problem was, Maddy realized, even if Bernice did not, that real achievement required passion. Like Bernice's own passion for science, or Katherine's passion for journalism, or Uncle Archie's passion for making money. Maddy did not feel passionate about anything, except her music.

And that was still her secret.

Her misery increased during lunch, while she played with her shrimp salad and listened to Katherine and Bernice discuss Katherine's plans for the future. Maddy had to admit that her friend held up well under her aunt's interrogation, much better than many adults would have.

"But why psychology?" Bernice was asking now. "I can understand why you would choose to study history, but why a soft discipline like psychology?"

"Because I want to understand why people do what they do, Mrs. Mason. I want them to open up to me. I want to be able to get inside their heads."

"Just prove yourself trustworthy, and show interest."

"I disagree. I think there are all kinds of strange things that go into making people do what they do. The more I understand them, the better I will be at my job. History is essential, too, of course. And I need to improve my Spanish."

"Good heavens! Why Spanish?"

"The war has already rewritten the map of the world, Mrs. Mason. All of the old empires have collapsed. But not in this hemisphere. You watch! Cuba, Argentina, there's where real political change will come, and within the next ten years."

"Why not study Russian? There, at least, you'll be prepared to deal with an *important* country."

"The Soviet Union is a closed society. No free press there. No, this foreign correspondent is going where the action is, and the action will be in South America."

"Katherine, you are truly a remarkable young woman."

Maddy, who had always been proud of her friend's achievements, felt a spark of naked envy. How did she do it? As long as she had known Katherine, her friend had known what her goals were, and had never been afraid to reach for them. Katherine never seemed to feel guilty about what she wanted, or to fret about the price she might have to pay to get it. It wasn't fair.

"Madeleine? Are you listening?"

"Of course. Revolutions in South America."

"No, dear. We've left that behind. I was telling Katherine that I hope you'll discover something that interests you when you go to Hunter. I would love for Madeleine to go into medicine, Katherine. I think it so important that a woman have a profession that she can fall back on, to support herself. And not only for financial security! Women are just as capable of finding professional satisfaction as men are. They're just seldom given the opportunity."

"But I know what I want to study. Music."

Katherine and Bernice both turned and stared at her. Maddy could not believe her own ears. She tried to think of a way to retract what she had just said, but Katherine was already off and running.

"Music? Why not? You know, Maddy used to take piano lessons at the convent. That's how we met…" her voice trailed off.

"Music? My dear, isn't it a little late to take up music? Seriously, I mean? Of course, it's marvelous as a source of amusement, or relaxation. But even as a profession, it is not very practical, is it?"

"Neither is journalism," Katherine interjected, and instantly regretted it.

Bernice turned to her. "Well, my dear, I suppose there is always a way to make ends meet at the top of one's profession; I have no doubt you have the drive and the ability to get to the top of yours. But music! For Madeleine, this is something brand new."

The patronizing tone in her voice rekindled Maddy's resentment. "You said if Katherine got accepted at Barnard, you would pay for her tuition. If I got accepted at music school, would you pay for me to go there instead of Hunter?"

"You're not serious."

"I am serious. I am grateful for all you've done for me—"

"Now Madeleine, please—"

"And I have tried for all these years to please you every way I could. But I want one chance to follow my own dreams. Just the same chance you've given Katherine."

"But Madeleine—"

"If I fail, I fail. Then I'll study whatever you want me to. But I want the chance."

A short, intense period of silence followed. Katherine was afraid to look at either of them, and more than a little concerned that her own scholarship could end up as part of the deal. Under the table, she crossed her fingers.

"Oh, my, of *course* my dear," Bernice finally replied, with an exasperated sigh implying she knew she had nothing to lose, "But we must limit this… experiment… to serious institutions. No fly-by-night nonsense."

Maddy looked at her aunt and smiled. She wanted to say thank you but could not, for she was completely overcome by a strange mixture of emotions: nervousness and elation; pride and shame; excitement and embarrassment.

Across the table, Katherine was grinning from ear to ear. She did not know exactly what Maddy had up her sleeve, but she knew her friend well enough to know she did not take any step lightly, and wondered what Maddy had in store for them.

Saints preserve us, she said to herself, in silent homage to her mother. *Saints preserve us all.*

꧁꧂

Maddy knew enough about music school to know that she had to audition and get references. Bernice did not offer to help; she had no idea what had put such a preposterous idea into Madeleine's head, and chalked it up to some sort of delayed teenage rebelliousness. Madeleine was now almost eighteen, and a senior in high school. She'd never been caught smoking, or kissing a boy, or staying out after curfew, or committing any of the other nuisance infractions that so many other teens foisted upon their parents. She'd not made many friends at LaSalle, the private school where she'd spent the last four years, but the two or three friends who came to visit seemed well-behaved and trustworthy, just like Madeleine, and they came from good families. They giggled and compared crushes on movie stars. For all this, Bernice was relieved and very nearly grateful.

But music? To Bernice's knowledge Madeleine had never done more than sing in the school glee club, hardly a noble start for a musical career. She had no doubt that her niece would be safely at Hunter come September.

With no other guidance, Maddy sought out the music teacher at her high school. Mrs. Thomas proudly displayed her degree from the New England Conservatory on the wall of her small office. She must have graduated twenty years ago, but still, maybe she could help.

Maddy made an appointment to see her after school the next day. "How nice to see you, Maddy dear. What can I do for you?" she asked as Maddy hovered near the door.

"Please, Mrs. Thomas, I would like a letter of reference. For school."

"But I thought you'd already been accepted at Hunter. And really, I've only had you in glee club. I haven't been in a position to evaluate your academic ability."

"No, you see, I want to go to music school."

"Music school?" Mrs. Thomas repeated lamely. "What sort of music school?"

"Well, you know, like Juilliard, or somewhere like that."

"Juilliard?" the astonished woman tried to keep the surprise out of her voice.

Maddy edged closer. Mrs. Thomas could see the plea in her eyes. "I know it sounds crazy, but I think I can play the piano. I know I'm very far behind—I haven't had lessons in years—but if you were to work with me a little, I could audition, and then maybe I could really learn."

Mrs. Thomas sighed. She couldn't refuse the girl a quick listen. They were so sensitive at this age. "Very well, Maddy. I'll pick out a piece for you. Let's go to a practice room."

Maddy practically fell over as she went to sit down on the piano bench. Mrs. Thomas placed the sheet music for Liszt's *Liebestraum No. 3* in front of her. The notes swam like little black fish on the page, and for a moment she couldn't even remember how to read the music. She took a few deep breaths.

"Begin anytime, Madeleine."

Although Maddy did not know the piece, it was not especially difficult, and she played it with no mistakes. When she was finished, she twisted around to look at Mrs. Thomas.

"Why, that's not bad at all," the woman said, in a supportive tone. Maddy could tell she was not really impressed.

"Mrs. Thomas, would you please play something?"

"Maddy, I really don't see—"

"Please? Just play something for me. Anything. It will help me relax."

Another sigh. Mrs. Thomas silently resolved that she would not let this little interlude eat up her entire afternoon.

"Very well." The two traded places. Mrs. Thomas thought for a moment. Her instrument was the violin, but she was quite competent on the piano. She played Beethoven's *Für Elise,* a piece she knew by heart.

She played it from start to finish, adroitly. Maddy was nodding enthusiastically as Mrs. Thomas stood up. "Okay. Thank you. Now I'll play it."

And she did.

"There," Maddy said, half to herself. "That was better." She turned to face the startled teacher. "Can you play another one?"

"Maddy, tell me you knew that piece when you came in here."

"No, ma'am. I mean, I've heard it before, but I've never played it. It's easier for me to play if I'm not reading. The sheet music kind of gets in the way, I guess."

"Gets in the way?" Mrs. Thomas plopped down on the bench next to Maddy. "Are you pulling some kind of trick on me? Is this the senior class prank or something?"

Maddy looked horrified. "Oh, no! Nothing like that. I've never, I mean, I've never really shared my music with anyone. I guess it must seem a little strange. Anyway, thank you. I can see I made a mistake—"

"No! Sit down, Maddy. I'm just trying to get a clear picture of all this. How long have you been taking lessons?"

"I took lessons for almost three years. From when I was seven until I was ten, I guess. But I've been playing myself for a few years now. It's, my hobby, I guess you could say."

Mrs. Thomas blew out a gust of air. "Play this." Still sitting next to Maddy, she played a short Viennese waltz.

"Okay." Maddy's fingers danced along the keys, and Mrs. Thomas felt that she could have been listening to a recording of herself, except Maddy's rendition was slightly livelier: a shade more like what a waltz should be.

"This is unbelievable," she whispered aloud.

"Does that mean you will help me?" Maddy asked hopefully.

Mrs. Thomas patted her on the back. "Most definitely, Maddy. I will. It would be my great pleasure to help you."

But there was not much time. Mrs. Thomas had the schedules for all of the major music schools' auditions. It was already mid-April; many deadlines had already passed. Ultimately, they found three schools where Mrs. Thomas thought Maddy might stand a chance: the Northeastern Academy of Music, in Stanford, Connecticut; Oberlin College, in Ohio; and the New Music School, in Cambridge, just outside of Boston. All were auditioning before the end of May. Mrs. Thomas pulled a calendar out of her drawer and circled the three important dates.

"We don't have much time, Maddy. So you know what we must do until then."

"Practice, practice, practice," cried Maddy joyfully. "And then, some more practice!"

Ten days later, Mrs. Thomas received a telephone call at her home from a perturbed Bernice Mason.

"Mrs. Thomas, I'm sorry to disturb you at home, but I need to discuss something."

"Of course, Mrs. Mason. I'm delighted to hear from you. I think it's important for us to discuss Maddy's progress."

"That's exactly why I am calling. Madeleine tells me that you plan to take her to an audition in Connecticut this weekend."

"Yes, that's right, at the Northeastern Academy of Music. We would have liked to try for Juilliard, of course, but I'm afraid the deadline has passed."

"You must be joking."

"I beg your pardon?"

"My dear Mrs. Thomas, you're a professional, are you not? What on earth gives you the idea that Madeleine should be embarrassing herself, and you, and me, by showing up to audition for music school, when she has no musical training whatsoever?"

Startled, Mrs. Thomas momentarily took the receiver away from her ear and looked at it, as if that would help her make sense out of what she'd heard. Shaking her head, she brought it back to her mouth. "Mrs. Mason, I know that Madeleine is a *raw* talent, but she is marvelously gifted, and has made amazing progress given the self-taught nature of her studies."

"Self-taught? Mrs. Thomas, are we speaking about the same girl?"

"I certainly hope so."

"Have you actually heard her play the piano?"

"Why, of course. In fact, we've worked for hours every day, for almost two weeks. I waived my usual fee, of course. Not that I meant to insult you, but it is really such a thrill to be, well, as immodest as it may sound, the discoverer of such a talented prodigy. I only wish she had come to me years ago! She seems unusually shy about her music."

"Shy? I should say so! She's lived with us for five years and I've never heard her play a single note on the piano that we have in the library."

"Really? My goodness. You mean, she's kept her ability a secret from everyone? Even you?"

"Me, her uncle, her best friend... I daresay no one has known, until now. Which is why I have such a difficult time taking this whole thing seriously. You don't truly think she has some sort of musical talent, do you?"

"I know she does. She has an emotional feel for music that is truly extraordinary, and the way she can play by ear! Why, it's phe-nomenal. She will be a marvel one day, I assure you."

"I find this quite hard to believe."

"Well, I suppose I would too, in your position. But I think you're to be commended for giving your niece this opportunity. I'm sure that she will not disappoint you."

"Well, thank you. Do you suppose I ought to come with you to the audition?"

There was a pause on the other end of the line. "Please, don't be offended, but I don't think that would be a very good idea. Maddy is already so nervous. I'm sure you understand."

"Yes, yes, of course. Well. You shall keep me informed of her progress, yes?"

"Certainly."

Bernice's next phone call was to her husband. "Archie?"

"*Ja?*"

"Archie, something has developed with Madeleine..." In rapid German she poured out everything that Mrs. Thomas had communicated to her.

Archibald Mason was a stout, serious, and clever man, to whom sex meant little, good food meant a lot, and money meant just about everything. His main talent was the ability to spot talent in other people and persuade them to work for him. He'd never shown much interest in Maddy, but had never been unkind to her either; she was simply one more variable in his wife's well-organized life.

Now he listened to Bernice's story about the girl's alleged talent without comment. By the time she finished, the wheels in his financially fixated mind were spinning.

"Well," he said thoughtfully, "If it's true, and she is some sort of prodigy, she could well make a fortune!"

"I suppose so," answered Bernice, still skeptical that Maddy's music might turn into a serious endeavor.

She hung up the phone and called Harry in Chicago. "Ruth? Hello? This is Bernice Mason. Yes, it's good to talk to you, too. No, nothing's wrong. I just wondered if I might talk to Harry for a moment. Is he in?"

While Ruth went to get her husband, Bernice flipped through the mental filing cabinet in her brain. Their child, the little girl they'd adopted in Switzerland during the war. What was her name? Gertrude? No, no. Gurs was the camp she'd escaped from. Gladys? Greer? Gabby? That was it! Gabriella.

"Bernice?"

"Harry! It's been so long. How are you? And how is little Gabriella?"

"Not so little! She's nearly ten now. Such a beauty! You should see her. How are you? And Archie? And Maddy?"

"We're all fine. But it's Maddy I wanted to talk to you about… "

Harry listened to Bernice's entire story, glad the grin on his face was a thousand miles away. Bernice sounded… flummoxed, that was the word. He didn't think he'd ever heard his old friend so completely confused.

"You're the only person I know, personally, who's gifted musically, Harry. I remember how you used to talk about playing the violin instead of going into engineering—"

"A totally impractical choice, of course."

"Yes, but, is it possible? Can one just be born with this *gift?*"

"Mozart was. There have been others. You remember Martha was very musical." He caught sight of Ruth and Gabriella, heads close together as they giggled about something, and his voice caught in his throat. "There is no explaining the gifts that God brings to us, Bernice. Ruth and me, for example. We're… Ruth is going to have a baby."

"A baby! Now? Are you sure you want another child, at your age?"

Harry laughed. "Well, luckily for me, Ruth is a good deal younger. But yes, Bernice. We do want this child. This baby is a gift."

Bernice said all the polite things required, but shook her head as she hung up the phone. Harry was almost fifty. A baby! She would just never understand some people.

Maddy was not accepted at the Northeastern Academy. Mrs. Thomas assured her that she had done quite well, it was just that each school had its own idea of what one's musical development should be when one arrived, and a specific idea of what type of talent the school wished to foster.

"You'll find your place, Madeleine," she said reassuringly as the train rumbled its way back into Grand Central Station.

But I never have. Mrs. Thomas. I never have.

The following week they were on their way to Boston for her next audition, at the New Music School, in Cambridge, Massachusetts.

The New Music School was not really new anymore; its founders gave it this name to distinguish it from the staid New England Conservatory, started a quarter-century earlier. The New Music School had made its reputation encouraging virtuosity and experimentation. Even the fact that it held its auditions late, nearly a month after the other prestigious music schools, was done intentionally by the administrators as a way of setting it apart. Year after year a few talented students reneged on their acceptances at the Conservatory and Juilliard in order to attend the small, elitist institution nestled on the banks of the Charles River.

Maddy gazed out of the cab window as they made their trip into Cambridge from the train station. By now it was early May, the one time of the year when flowers actually flourished in the cold New England climate. Lilacs, bent over with the weight of their blossoms, filled small gardens with varied color and sweet fragrance. Window boxes bulging with petunias added small accents of joy to the serious facades of the Boston brownstones. The air was still crisp, but the sun was out, and so were most of the residents of Boston, enjoying a few weeks of decent weather before the muggy heat of summer drove them indoors or out of town.

Her audition was scheduled for the late afternoon. She had a chance to freshen up, to listen to the last minute advice of Mrs. Thomas, and warm up on a beautiful Steinway in the practice room next to the auditorium that was already crowded with applicants.

Student after student was called to the stage. Finally it was Maddy's turn. "Madeleine Hoffman, from LaSalle. Very good. Take your place, please, Miss Hoffman. You may warm up for five minutes."

As Maddy made her way to the piano, three of the judges whispered to each other.

"This is Thomas' pupil, is it not? Janet Thomas at LaSalle? She hasn't sent us anyone good in years," commented the first in a disappointed tone.

"Oh, Ernest, don't be such a snob," responded the man to his right. "Just because you haven't had a piano whiz from LaSalle doesn't mean Janet would waste our time. This is the little prodigy she's so excited about. It's worth a listen."

"We're looking for musicians, not circus monkeys," sniffed the third, an older woman whose wide round glasses gave her the look of an owl.

"Are you ready?" asked the man in charge. Then, without waiting for a response, he continued. "Please begin. We have a list of your selections."

Maddy took a deep breath and closed her eyes. She could not bear failure again.

A few seconds ticked by. She opened her eyes and took a single quick glance at the sheet of music in front of her as she exhaled. Then she closed her eyes again, and reached with her mind for the place inside herself where she kept her music, the place where she could feel it. Her fingers started to move.

There was silence when she finished. She looked beyond the piano and saw Mrs. Thomas, who stood with her hands clasped, a smile on her face and tears in her eyes.

A man was coming towards her. His hair was gray and slightly too long on the sides.

"Miss Hoffman, do you know Mozart's *Piano Concerto No. 12, in A*? The finale?"

"No, sir."

"If I play it for you, would you try to play it by ear?"

"I could try."

"Here—no, don't get up, just scoot over a bit—that will do." Maddy was completely unaware of the many eyes glued on them. As the man next to her played, she watched his fingers. Then she closed her eyes. She could see the keyboard in her mind, and see where his fingers were landing. She could see them stretch and curl; feel the downward pressure of his foot as he reached for the pedals. The music wrote itself into her brain.

There was polite applause as he finished.

He turned to Maddy. "Please. Just try it."

Maddy positioned her fingers, then readjusted them. She felt completely confident. When she'd finished, the grin on the man's face told her all she needed to know.

"Welcome to the New School," he said. "I'm Ernest Auerbach, and I will be your piano instructor."

"It's a pleasure to meet you," she replied, and gave him one of her mother's radiant smiles.

CHAPTER 16

THE SHADOW

LONDON, 1949

He never thought he would see her again, and in the deepest depths of his imagination, he never dreamed it would be so easy. All he had to do was ask.

Word got around that there was a pub in London, not far from Westminster Abbey, that had become a haven for the veterans of the army of shadows. It was the place where an undercover operative who'd won the Victoria Cross could leave behind his job as a file clerk in the office where no one remembered his name, and chat for a while with the men who shared his memories; where the man who now sold cars for a living could down a pint with someone he'd lived with in a cave for three days, not to talk, just to sit, because the sound of the other man's breathing had been all he'd heard for those three days, all he'd had to let him know that he was still alive. There were those who told the same stories, over and over, and those who never spoke. They'd fought the war using assumed identities, risking their lives to make one radio broadcast or deliver one case of dynamite to blow up a train. And they'd survived, only to drown in the boredom of post-war life in London.

Leo sat at the bar, nursing a beer. Someone in this group would know what happened to Christine. He started with the bartender.

"Christine Granville? Lord yes, she survived the war, with enough medals to anchor a bloody battleship. Do you know her?"

"We met briefly in Cairo. She seemed very competent."

"That's one word for it. Think they'd have kept her on, don't you? One like her? Saved the head of the whole operation in France, just before the end. But no. Dumped her off with the same month's pay they handed the lot of us. As if there's no more work to do, with Stalin eyeing every choice piece of real estate we won back from the Krauts with our own blood and guts."

"Do you ever see her around here?"

"Not her. Runs with a fancier crowd, she does. She's in and out of London all the time, though. Just got back from Nairobi, last I heard. Been living with some rich duffer who's starting up a tourist business there. That'd be the life, eh? Hunting lions, coming back to camp to find a hot meal and a cool glass of whiskey ready in your tent?"

Leo imagined Christine stretched out on a thick rug on the floor of a safari tent, skin warm from the sun, her bright brown eyes alight with desire. *Enough of that.*

The bartender leaned forward. "You're not the first one to ask about her. She made her mark, didn't she?"

"I guess she did." He paid for his beer and left.

She was alive. Did she know he'd survived? Probably not. He lived a life so fine-tuned by fabrications he didn't think his own supervisor knew his real name or where he was from. Leo Hoffman was probably already dead on paper somewhere, if there was even a piece of paper still around with his name on it, and surely nothing would be left from his time as a British asset. The Brits started shredding their files right after the war, and an "accidental" office fire at S.O.E. headquarters had expedited the process of reinventing the past. The army of shadows had evaporated in a cloud of smoke.

He had a week in London before he went back to Berlin. After that he'd start working his way east, digging farther and deeper until he could attach himself to some vital organ of this new enemy and suck information out like a tick.

He had seven days. How hard could it be to find her? He was a spy, after all.

๑๖๑

He watched her as she left the apartment. The turn of her wrist as she locked the door, the way she looked at the sky before putting on her sunglasses, the half-knot she tied into the belt of her jacket, the shape of her slightly too-thin calves, all registered in his brain like individual notes in a piece of music he'd memorized long ago. He half-expected her to turn around and wave to him, for it did not seem possible that he could be so acutely aware of her without her knowing that he stood just a few feet away.

He spoke as she was about to get on a bus, patiently allowing a bent old woman to make her exit before boarding herself.

"Christine, wait."

She turned at the sound of his voice. He could not see her eyes behind her dark glasses, but every inch of her body suddenly grew still. Then she took a step back and waved the bus driver on.

"Is that really you?"

She asked the question in French, which surprised him somehow. He smiled at her and took a step closer.

"It's me."

She flew at him, throwing her arms around his neck with such force it put him off balance, and for a second he thought they were going to end up in a pile on the pavement. He steadied himself and held on to her, saying nothing, resting his face against her soft brown hair.

"You made it," she whispered into his ear.

"I did. As did you."

She slid out of his embrace, but did not let go of his hands. "And now?"

"Can we… can we go somewhere and talk?"

She dropped his hands and lifted her glasses, revealing the familiar sparkle in her eyes; one of the lights he'd used to help him stay alive during two years of darkness.

"We can go to my apartment. I live close by."

"I know," Leo answered. Christine rolled her eyes, he laughed, and she punched his shoulder.

"Enough spying. Come, have a drink with me."

But the apartment wasn't hers, of course. It was Andrew's. He saw a picture on the mantle of the two of them, taken together somewhere in the Middle East, both looking into the camera with vibrant joy. It hit him then. His fantasy that somehow he and Christine could be together was no more than a delusion. It would, of course, always be Andrew, thought Leo, just as for him it would always be Martha. The difference between them was that Martha was dead.

"Where's Andrew?"

She looked surprised that he had to ask. "In the hospital. You didn't know? He was in a terrible car accident. Unconscious for days. I was in Nairobi at the time."

"Nairobi?"

She nodded. "Sherry all right with you? So British, but I'm used to it by now."

"That's fine."

"Have a seat, it's all right here."

He sat on the couch in front of the fireplace, took off his hat, and put it down next to him. She went to a cabinet and pulled out two glasses and a crystal decanter, chatting as she did so.

"Have you ever been to West Africa? You know I was there with my husband, in Kenya, when the war broke out. I enjoyed being back. So warm, so beautiful. I've always loved the sun."

"But you weren't with your husband this time, were you?"

This seem to catch her off guard. Leo had the feeling she'd read some unintended criticism into his question. He tried again.

"I mean, you're divorced now, aren't you?"

She handed him his drink. "I was there with a friend. He invited me to help him organize a tourist business. But I suppose you know that already, too, don't you?"

A friend. The chill in her voice informed Leo that he'd stepped out of bounds. He took the sherry she offered him, trying to figure out how to start the conversation over.

"I hope Andrew is recovering well. I didn't know that he was—"

"He's doing quite well. He'll be home in a few days, the doctors say."

"Well, here's to Andrew's health." He took a sip of his drink. She did the same, then sat down across from him, without taking her eyes off him. They were dark now.

"Tell me what happened, Leo. After you left the camp. I heard that Val and Charles made it across the border with most of the women and children. Daniel was hurt. And you—you disappeared."

"I was shot and captured. Not shot, really. I think I was hit in the head by a shovel I was carrying when a bullet ricocheted off of it. At any rate I woke up in a Vichy hospital, where the nurses, at least, thought I was German. I was able to get out of there before they could discover differently. Then I was captured again. Then I escaped again. Then I went to America. Then I came back to Europe."

"And your daughter? Did you find her?"

"Yes I did." That was all he was going to say about that.

She didn't push. "I never got to thank you, Leo. For agreeing to help us."

"We didn't, any of us, really do it to be thanked, did we?"

Something about this comment enraged her, but as her words exploded in the small room, it became obvious that her rancor was not aimed at him.

"No, we didn't fight in the war to be thanked. But a *little* more gratitude would have been helpful. At first they didn't trust me, then after I managed to accomplish something they said I was 'too hard to handle.' They cut me out the minute the war was over."

She stood up and began to pace back and forth in the small room, arms crossed, not bothering to temper her bitterness.

"It took me three years to get a proper British passport, did you know that? I couldn't get any sort of decent job without credentials. I worked as a telephone operator, I sold clothes at Harrod's, I worked in the linen room at a hotel. I'm not afraid of hard work, you know that. But to be so useless…"

Her anger left her as suddenly as it had arrived. She sank back into her chair with a loud sigh.

"I can't imagine that you'd ever be useless, Christine."

This made her smile. She picked up her drink but did not taste it. "I suppose some of us are just not suited to the rhythm of ordinary life. What about you? Your life has never been ordinary, either. Have you found a place for yourself?"

"I think so."

She did not ask him to elaborate. "Good. I'm happy for you."

I'm not so sure I'm all that happy for me. When was the last time he'd felt real happiness? Had in it been in this woman's arms?

"So, do you plan on going back to Africa?"

"No. Andrew needs me. He needs me here. We're going to have to find some way to make a living."

What if I needed you, Christine? Would that matter to you? Would it make difference? Would it change both of our lives, right now, at this moment?

If the Russians could read him as easily as she could, he'd soon be a dead man. He saw the sympathy in her eyes and it made him stare down into his drink, just to have somewhere else to look, other than into those eyes.

"Leo," she said softly, "I'm sorry."

There were suddenly no more words. He could speak seven languages, and there wasn't a single word in his head. He drained his glass, put it down, picked up his hat, and stood up.

"Thanks for the drink."

She looked away from him, not moving, then closed her eyes and grimaced, as if she'd felt a sharp pain run through her chest. Leo headed toward the hallway. He stopped when he got to the door, waiting, hoping, hearing nothing. Just as he reached for the handle he heard her speak.

"Good luck, my dear friend."

He turned and looked at her: so small, so fragile. Stronger than anyone he'd ever known.

"Thank you," he said, and left.

Three years later Leo learned that Christine Granville had been murdered, stabbed to death in the hallway of her apartment building by a man who had briefly been her lover, then decided that he'd rather hang than to lose her to another man.

CHAPTER 17

THE BOYFRIEND

e⌒⌂⌒ɘ

NEW YORK, 1950

"Oh, c'mon, Maddy. It's New Year's Eve, for cryin' out loud. The beginning of a new decade! You can't just sit in the dorm and listen to the radio. Anna says these guys from the med school are really nice. She's been dating Theo for six months. What's the matter with a blind date? Just for once?"

Maddy smiled at her friend and shook her head. "No thanks, Vick. I'm just not the New Year's Eve kind. I would have gone home, except Bernice and Archie are in California, so there's no one to go home to. But Katherine will call me, and, well, I like listening to the radio."

Vicki rolled her eyes. "You can't hide your light under a bushel forever, you know. You'd really be helping me out. I've been dying to see this guy again, you know, Allen? But we need three girls, on account of this other guy, Brad, just got stood up, and Allen and Theo don't want to go out without him, to leave him alone crying into his petri dish in the lab. Honest, a New Year's date with Allen! The med school guys don't have a lot of time to socialize, you know. It's not like dating some jock from BU."

"You should know," said Maddy with a smile that took the sting out of her words.

"Geez, Maddy. Just because you are little miss stuck-in-the-dorm. The only guy you ever went out with was that guy from MIT, and he didn't last long."

"I didn't know you kept such close tabs on my social life," responded Maddy, only half amused.

"It's not difficult. Look, please, for me, one night out. Otherwise, the next time you need help in Composition 110, I'll tell you to blow it out your tuba."

Maddy could not help but laugh. "Okay, okay, Miss Vicki Violin. What's the dress code?"

"Great! Okay, we'll be going to a private club for sure. These guys are loaded. Try to, uh, not dress quite as conservatively as you usually do. You want to borrow something? What am I saying? Anything I own would fall right off you. Think festive, okay?"

"Sure." She didn't really care what some medical students from Harvard thought of her.

"Great! You're a gem. I'll call Anna. You've really saved us, Maddy."

"Don't mention it."

She started to regret her decision less than an hour later, after she'd strewn every outfit she owned across the length and width of her small dorm room. What Vicki said was true. She dressed like an old woman. She bought her clothes on shopping junkets when she went home on vacation or when Bernice came to visit, and her choices were heavily influenced by her aunt's conservative taste. She had dresses that were simple and suitable for day or evening wear. She had suits that looked suitable for lunch or an evening at the theater. But festive?

She looked again into her small closet. Underneath a sheath of paper was her recital dress from last year. It was a somber black silk, but fashionably cut, with a pinched-in waist and a full skirt that fell in supple pleats to mid-calf. The dress was cut loosely through the shoulders, to allow for maximum arm movement, and three little pearl buttons led the way to a demure, narrow collar of white satin.

Maddy tried on the dress. She unbuttoned the collar, exposing a small "V" of flesh, and put on the triple-strand pearl choker Bernice and Archie had given her for her eighteenth birthday. There. It was still conservative, but not, she hoped, too stuffy. She wanted to look sophisticated. Confident. Everything she felt sitting at a piano, and nowhere else.

As she turned in front of the mirror for a final inspection she noticed, not for the first time, how much she now resembled her mother. But no amount of affirmation from the mirror could make her feel beautiful. The beauty belonged to her mother. Maddy could not claim it.

She applied her lipstick and thought about the long-ago days when she would help her mother get dressed for a party. Bernice did not go to parties, other than those she had to attend for business purposes, and had never once solicited Maddy's advice about what to wear. Thirteen years. Her mother had died more than thirteen years ago.

The boys picked their dates up at eight-fifteen. Theo, Anna's date, was driving. Anna joined him in front, leaving Vicki, her date, Maddy, and the third young man to crowd into the back of the big golden Cadillac.

"So where are we off to first?" asked Vicki cheerfully, after introductions all around. "I don't want to walk much. Not in this weather."

"Don't worry little lady, I won't let cha get cold," chided Allen suggestively. The rest of the group laughed.

"To the Pier for dinner, then the Back Bay Club for dancing until the sun comes up," announced Theo.

"Oh, swell," exclaimed Anna appreciatively, snuggling up against her date.

"Don't thank Theo the Third, thank Grandpa Theo," laughed Brad, Maddy's escort. "He's treating tonight."

"Oh, and thank *you* for the financial report," answered Theo sarcastically. "Allow me to do you the same favor someday."

Bradley Harrington Gordon IV smiled back at his friend. "Yes, doctor."

The two men then debated the best way to make it to the bay front from Cambridge, given the traffic and the icy weather. Maddy took advantage of the moment to study her date. He looked nice enough. He had a square face, with a long, masculine nose. His eyes were dark brown, fringed by dark lashes. His hair was thick, wavy, and brushed straight back from his forehead.

Suddenly he caught her looking at him and smiled back at her with a teasing look in his eyes. She blushed, and looked down at her gloved hands, folded in her lap. He followed her gaze.

"Nice hands," he said lightly, tapping one of her knuckles with his forefinger.

"They're too small," she said automatically, then wished she hadn't.

"Why?"

"Too small to reach a tenth on the piano."

"A tenth?"

"Ten keys. Two keys, ten keys apart. I mean, any key, and the tenth one away from it. When I started I could only reach one octave, an eighth. Now I play a ninth, but I'll never make a tenth."

"So are you doomed? No Brahms or something like that?"

"No. Well, some pieces I'll never be able to play, but most of the time, I can cheat. I alter the fingering."

"Aha! I've discovered your secret. And when you play in Carnegie Hall, I will jump up and shout, 'Cheater! Cheater!' in the middle of your performance, and let the music-going public know about your foul schemes."

Maddy had to laugh, and he laughed with her. Then he held his own right hand out in front of him. His fingers were long and smooth, each topped by a square fingernail. A few golden hairs protruded from underneath the cuff of his shirt.

"A surgeon's hands don't have to be large. Just steady," he commented.

Maddy smiled up at him. She was beginning to be very glad that she had come along.

They had cocktails and dinner in a restaurant that overlooked Boston Harbor. The men amused their dates with entertaining, sometimes gory stories about what could go wrong when trying to remove internal organs, and macabre stories about stupid things people had done to themselves to land in the emergency room. Theo had just finished telling them about the time their landlady had gone onto his back porch and fainted when she found a brain he had been keeping in a bucket for his biology lab, when Anna pleaded enough.

"Oh, please. I've never seen a dead person, and I hope I never do."

"Oh, you sheltered little musicians. Have any of you ever seen a corpse?" whispered Allen, doing a decent impression of Bela Lugosi.

"I have," Maddy whispered back, soberly.

"You're kidding."

"Oh, God, Maddy. Yuck."

"In a funeral parlor, right?"

"In Shanghai," she responded, silencing the general clamor.

"That's my friend," quipped Anna, trying to inject levity back into the evening. "Madeleine, the Mysterious Lady from Shanghai."

Brad was looking at Maddy, his eyes full of curiosity. She met his gaze and was struck by the sympathy she saw there.

"Okay," he announced. "Enough of the gory stuff. Let's finish dinner and go dance."

The rest of the evening went well. The conversation stayed light. The Back Bay Club, on other nights a stodgy meeting place for Boston's older elite, had been handed over to the next generation for a one-night New Year's celebration. The dance floor was so crowded one could barely do more than sway to the music. Several times, Maddy caught Brad staring at her. He never looked away or got embarrassed.

The girls had received permission to stay out until one-thirty. When they pulled up to the dorm, Brad jumped out and helped Maddy out of the car. It was obvious that the other two couples had some special Happy New Year kissing to do, and Maddy was grateful that Brad did not seem to expect her to participate.

He walked her to the door. They moved quickly as an icy blast of air swept in from the river.

"I've really enjoyed the evening, Maddy," Brad said warmly. "I hope I can see you again."

Maddy nodded. "I'd like that."

"I'll call you."

"Okay."

"Happy New Year." Tucking his hand under her chin, he lifted her face and kissed her quickly on the lips. Before she could object he was on his way back to the car.

"Hands in the air gentlemen! I'm comin' in!"

❧

"So, are you telling me you like him?"

"Yes, Katherine. I think I do. I don't know. He seems nice."

"Maddy, give me the scoop. Where's he from? What does his family do? What kind of medicine does he want to practice?"

"Whoa, slow down. It was a date, not an interview. He's from Marblehead, just north of Boston. His family is in the banking business. He's the fifth generation to go to Harvard College, but the first to go to medical school. He's an only child, like me. And he has a good sense of humor. He made me laugh."

"Is he going to call you?"

"I think so."

"Keep me posted!"

"Oh, yes. No secrets from you, Queen Snoop"

"You mean Queen of the *Scoop,* don't you?"

Over the next few months Maddy had several dates with Brad to report. He took her to a Harvard hockey game. He took her to the movies. He took her out for dinner. Then, in May, he took her to the symphony.

As they entered the music hall, he looked around, a sheepish look on his face. "We may run into my parents at intermission," he said apologetically. "We're sitting in the orchestra. They have a box. They'll only stay to hear the guest soloist, but they might come looking for us in the lobby."

"I'd love to meet them," Maddy responded sincerely. Brad grimaced, leaving her to wonder why.

They did see his mother and father, in the lobby, at intermission. Mrs. Gordon was tall, and had Brad's warm brown coloring. Her hair was twisted into a severe French knot. Mr. Gordon was big, and his once-blond hair was now silver. He had a deep, mellifluous voice, but moved awkwardly, as if he had never adjusted to his size. They were cordial, but not friendly. Mr. Gordon asked Maddy a great many pointed questions about her family. She told him that her father had disappeared during the war and that her mother was dead. He did seem impressed when she told him that her guardian was her uncle, Archibald Mason, of Mason Industries. Brad's mother said little, but studied her carefully. They made no plans to meet after the concert.

"Well, not exactly cozy, are they?" muttered Brad after his parents had departed, and they were returning to their seats.

"Why do you say that? They were very civil."

"What a diplomat. Yes, they were civil. But they won't be, once they smell the threat."

Maddy was astonished. "What threat?"

He looked at her intently and squeezed her hand, as the orchestra started to play. "That you might take me away from them," he said lightly.

She dared not ask him to explain what he meant. Not that she really needed to ask. She knew that she felt fondly toward him. But she had not thought about marriage.

Maybe she should. She was nearly twenty-one. Many girls her age were already married. But her aunt had married late, and Katherine did not plan to get married at all. Maddy remembered their conversation the previous summer, when Katherine had astounded her with her unorthodox views on the subject of wedded bliss.

"Why get married if you don't want to have kids? I have enough nieces and nephews to keep me happy when I want to hug a baby or change a diaper. I don't want to live at anyone else's beck and call, trapped in the house by a bunch of screaming brats. I think I'll skip that particular adventure."

"But, don't you want to fall in love?" Maddy had asked her, thinking of love as a sort of magic spell that happened to you all at once, like in the movies.

"Oh, Maddy. Of course, I'll fall in love. And I'll have lovers, and they'll leave me, and I'll leave them, and one day my love letters will be found in an attic somewhere and be worth a fortune. But marriage? I don't think so."

Maddy wondered how Katherine, with her good Catholic upbringing, could comfortably plan her life in a way that would assure a direct descent straight to hell. During her years of Catholic school Maddy had absorbed the message preached by the nuns. Nice girls keep their legs crossed. Sex meant children, and children were reserved for marriage. Fornication was a sin. Even when she discovered that she was from a Jewish family, and gradually abandoned her Catholicism, many of the messages planted by the good sisters stayed in her psyche; this one, more than any other.

Not that any of the sisters actually discussed the sexual act: that was the subject of intense speculation and whispered gossip. At least, it had been that way until, much to Maddy's chagrin, her aunt had taken her to lunch before she left for Cambridge and bluntly explained to her "the facts of life."

"Ignorance is dangerous, Madeleine. I trust you to be sensible. But you must know enough to protect yourself."

Then, fully armed with what Bernice considered to be appropriate knowledge, Maddy never had anything to protect herself from. She did not know that her shyness was often mistaken for snobbery, that her beauty was as intimidating as it was attractive. But she saw what other girls went through while chasing boys, and she didn't think she was missing much. Her passion was her music.

The morning after the symphony she called her aunt. Sunday morning was one of the few days she could generally count on finding her home.

"Hello?"

"Hello, Aunt Bernice? It's Maddy. How are you?"

"Fine dear. Are you just calling to say hello, or do you have something on your mind?"

Maddy smiled. Trust her aunt to cut right to the chase.

"Well, I was wondering. This boy I've been dating, Brad, well, I think he's starting to get serious."

"My goodness. Well, how do you feel about that?"

"I'm not sure."

Bernice cleared her throat. "Maddy dear. I know you're old enough to know your own mind. But you must decide what is truly important: your music, or being someone's wife. Be careful. He may accept your talent now, as a student, but who knows? Once he's a doctor, he may change. And…"

Another pause.

"And what?"

"There's the religion issue to consider."

"Religion? What does that have to do with anything?"

"Madeleine, don't be so naïve."

Maddy tried to temper her indignation. "The world is not the same place it was before the war, you know. I don't think that I have to worry about… the same things you and my father worried about."

"The world never changes, Madeleine. When circumstances become difficult, people become irrational. I just want you to be careful. Don't rush into marriage. Finish school first. If you two are truly in love, you can wait."

Maddy did not respond. Bernice, as usual, read her silence as assent, and changed the subject. "So. Are you doing well in school?"

"Well enough."

"We'll be there for your recital, and meet this young man then, yes?"

"I hope so. He has exams, but he's going to try to make it."

"Very well. Get plenty of rest."

"Yes, thank you. Goodbye, Aunt Bernice."

On an impulse Maddy dug into the bottom of her tiny closet, where she kept a box of mementos: the program from her first recital; her letters from Katherine; autographs of some of the famous musicians who had made an appearance at the school. At the bottom was her parents' wedding picture.

She had not looked at in a long time. Now she studied it carefully, trying to distill from the expressions on their faces how they'd felt about each other. For Maddy knew that when she was young, there had been love in her house.

After a few moments she put the picture away. Even after all these years, she couldn't look at it for too long without feeling an uncomfortable fullness in her chest.

Her aunt was right. Brad still had another year of medical school, then his residency. She wanted to graduate and go on to some sort of career in music. They were both too busy to think about marriage yet. Soon it would be summer. She was going to spend it in Manhattan, rooming with Katherine, in a sublet apartment in midtown. Katherine had landed a summer job with the *New York Daily News*, and Maddy would spend the summer studying with a new teacher who, Mr. Auerbach swore, would do marvelous things for her technique.

"He's a dragon. A dragon's dragon! But a gifted one. If he doesn't scare you to death, you will blossom under his instruction," Mr. Auerbach had advised. Maddy did not intend to be intimidated.

⚜

Six weeks later she and Katherine were set up in their apartment. Bernice had paid their rent for the summer, and put a tidy sum in a checking account for their "reasonable" expenses. She and Archie would be in and out of New York all summer; they were doing more and more traveling for their business. Bernice had discovered a new way of using ceramic material as an electrical conductor. The post-war consumption boom kept them very, very busy.

Katherine and Maddy were delighted to be living together again. Around Katherine, Maddy felt the weight of living up to her own expectations fall away from her. She laughed more easily. She took time off to go see silly movies. And she took over the cooking, for Katherine's idea of dinner involved opening a can of tuna or ordering take-out Chinese. Brad was spending the first part of the summer in Europe with his parents. He hoped to visit Maddy in New York when he returned, sometime at the end of July. In the meantime he sent her postcards, full of affectionate little jokes, and Maddy felt her tenderness for him growing.

On a Saturday afternoon in mid-June, Maddy was at the corner grocery market, picking up the staples she and Katherine needed to get them through the week. She reached up for a jar of olive oil on the top shelf but couldn't quite get it. Slipping off her shoes, she stepped up on the ledge of the bottom shelf, stretching her arm up as high as it would go.

"Can I help you with that?"

Maddy jumped down, olive oil in hand, embarrassed that she'd been caught climbing.

"Oh, no. Thank you. I got it, after all."

"You live in the Bordeaux Apartments, don't you?"

"Yes," answered Maddy, warily, slipping her feet back into her shoes.

"I do, too. I thought I recognized you. You're the piano player. Or, should I say, the *pianist*."

Maddy was now eager to retreat. "I'm sorry if my playing disturbs you."

"No, no, not at all. Quite the contrary. I try to listen. It's beautiful. Like you."

The young man paid her this compliment as if he were talking about the weather. Maddy did not know how to react. He didn't look at all familiar. Did he really live in her apartment building? If so, how could she—or Katherine—have missed him? He was gorgeous: tall, broad-shouldered, with rough-textured curly black hair, and large, gray, not-quite-blue eyes. His face was full and rounded, but all the features in it were firmly-cut and masculine. Maddy found herself gawking, and went a shade pinker.

"I… well…"

"Gosh, I'm sorry if I embarrassed you," he said gently. Maddy could feel the blood throbbing in her ears.

"Uhm, well. Thank you—"

"Gene. Gene Mandretti. I live in the penthouse. But from my balcony, I can see you when you and the red-haired girl are on your balcony, and when you play with the window open, I can hear you play the piano. It floats up to me. Like an angel playing. But I don't want you to think I spy on you, or anything like that. I just… love your music." He finished his speech in a rush, as if he sensed he'd said the wrong thing.

Maddy did not know what to say. He was a complete stranger, yet there was something familiar about him: the comfortable grace of his stance, and the careless charm with which he spoke. "Well," she said, completely at a loss, "You should come by sometime. We always have people dropping in for dinner. If you like spaghetti."

"I love spaghetti. I'm Italian." He smiled. Maddy had to smile in return.

"Okay, then."

"You haven't told me your name."

"Oh, I'm sorry. It's Madeleine. Madeleine Hoffman. Most people call me Maddy."

"Hello, Maddy. Nice to meet you, finally." He put his hand forward, as did she, then they both laughed as she realized she was still holding on to the bottle of olive oil.

"Can I give you a hand home with your groceries?"

"No, thanks, really."

"It's no trouble. I'm going that way, after all."

"Well, if you're sure you don't mind."

"No, it would be my pleasure," he said, as if he really meant it.

It only took a few minutes for them to get through the checkout counter. He carried his one bag in the crook of his left arm and balanced hers against it, carting the two of them easily.

Maddy walked next to him, suddenly acutely aware of her own small stature. Everything about Gene was so… big. His eyes. His hands. The way he moved through space.

"So, you're just in New York for the summer?" he asked.

"Yes. But how did you know that?"

"I know the Jasons, the couple you're renting from. They went to Greece for the whole summer. He's a professor at Columbia. He's the one who plays the piano. But not like you."

"And are you here for the summer?"

"No, I live here. I'm finishing up my degree at NYU. Then I'll go to work."

"What are you studying?"

"Business. Marketing. Finance. The boring stuff."

"Are you really bored?"

"Not today." He smiled at her again over the bags of groceries. Maddy felt a peculiar tingle at the base of her neck.

"So, where did you come from?" he asked her, injecting a dozen meanings into the question.

She blushed. "Boston."

"You don't sound like you're from Boston."

"I'm not. You don't sound like you're from New York. Not much, anyway."

"Thank you." She was rewarded with another smile. His teeth were white and even.

"So what do you do in Boston, Maddy?"

"I study music."

"Of course. Stupid question. Well, here we are."

They made their way into the building. Maddy opened the door to her apartment, and he carried the bags into the kitchen.

"Thanks again."

"Don't mention it. All it will take to pay me back is one spaghetti dinner."

"How about next week?"

"Great. Can I call you?"

"Sure."

"So, can I have your number?"

"Ah, that would help, wouldn't it?" She grabbed a pencil from the counter then, after fishing in her bag of groceries, pulled out the receipt and scribbled her number on the back.

"Until Saturday," he said, as he took it.

"Yes. Great."

"*Ciao*." He left.

Buzzing with excitement, Maddy dashed to the telephone to call Katherine. Then something made her put the receiver down. She wanted to keep this to herself. This feeling.

She ran to the piano and grabbed a pile of sheet music. It slipped through her fingers and fell to the floor. She sat down. She closed her eyes. Beethoven. It had to be Beethoven. A sonata. A sonata that would sweep her up and carry her away. Music that would sound the way she felt. Music written to make everyone who heard it feel this way.

CHAPTER 18

THE NEIGHBOR

❧

"Oh, Katherine," wailed Maddy in despair, "You can't do this
to me. I told Gene there would be a bunch of us here! Vicki and
Allen have already canceled. He wants to meet you. I can't have a
man over alone, even if he is just a friend. What will he think?"

"Oh, Maddy. Don't be such a baby. He can come over any
night, can't he? He lives right upstairs! This is the first time I have
been invited to cover the police beat and I can't miss it. The editor
is doing me a big favor. Just call this guy up and tell him you're sick
or something."

Maddy glared at her friend. Maddy knew Katherine was totally
driven when it came to her work. She knew the police beat was an
opportunity Katherine had been lobbying for all summer and that
it was, truly, a great opportunity. *But what about my plans?* Why did
she always come in last?

Katherine began to feel guilty underneath the weight of Maddy's silent anger. "Look, Maddy. I'll make it up to you. And I'll call
him if you want, to explain."

"No, thank you," said Maddy curtly. "Just go and report
on some hideous crime of some kind or another. I'll make the
excuses."

Katherine paused at the door, hoping to leave on a less angry note, but not willing to alter her position. When it became clear that Maddy was ignoring her, she stomped out.

Maddy waited a moment, trying to compose herself before she called Gene. She picked up the phone. She already knew his number by heart. The bottom dropped out of her stomach when she heard his voice.

"Hello?"

"Hi, Gene, it's Maddy."

"Is something wrong?"

"How did you know?"

"I can tell by the tone of your voice. What's happened? Are you okay?"

"Oh, yes, thanks. I'm sorry, it seems that everyone has canceled out on our dinner party tonight. Katherine has to work, and my other friends were invited to Long Island for the weekend."

"Oh. And feeding me all alone wouldn't be a good idea, I guess."

"Oh, Gene," faltered Maddy. "It's just—"

"No problem. I understand. But is there anything that says I can't invite you out for dinner?"

Maddy glanced over at the kitchen counter, where a Caesar salad awaited its dressing, garlic bread sat buttered, ready to be heated, and her homemade spaghetti sauce simmered on the stove.

"But Gene, I asked you—"

"I know, but things happen. Put the spaghetti in the 'fridge. Can you be ready in an hour?"

"Yes, but—"

"No buts. I've been looking forward to this evening all week. See you at seven."

He knocked promptly at seven. Maddy opened the door. She'd thought about nothing but his smile for seven days, yet the sight of it made her feel as if she had never seen anyone smile before.

"Hi, Angel," he said warmly, holding out his hand to take hers. The warmth of his grip sent an electric shock through her. She took a deep breath, trying to slow her heartbeat.

"Well," he said lightly, his blue-gray eyes shimmering with amusement, "I sure am sorry to miss that spaghetti but I can't say that I'm sorry to have you all to myself. Not too disappointed, I hope?"

"No, in fact, I think I'm glad it worked out this way. Where shall we go?"

"Wherever your heart desires. Atlantis? Mount Olympus? My chariot awaits your command," he said breezily, as they started toward the elevator.

She laughed, and he smiled again, happy to have pleased her.

"Well," she answered, as he pushed the call button, "My plan fell through, so now you're in charge."

Without a word he reached for her hand and brought it to his lips. He did not kiss her hand, so much as merely connect his mouth to it, right behind her knuckles. His eyes never left hers. Just when she thought she must snatch her hand away or faint, he released her.

He did not touch her again the entire evening.

They walked to the park and ate dinner in a small French café across the street from the zoo. He asked her many questions about her life and she found herself answering freely, without her normal self-consciousness. It had taken Brad weeks to pry the same information out of her. Yet here she was, telling Gene all about her childhood in Shanghai, her mother's death, how she came to live with the O'Connor's, her decision to live with her aunt rather than return to her father, and her desire to go to music school. He asked enough questions to keep her talking, but seldom commented, except for an occasional expression of sympathy. Gene listened intently, as if he were determined to remember every word; not only what she said but how she said it: every nuance of her voice, every gesture.

"And you never heard from your father again?"

"No. My aunt actually checked out some of what he told me that day. She was able to get the information from her contacts in the Defense Department. More lies. He never worked for the O.S.S."

"What a bastard, if you'll pardon my saying so."

"Pardon given. What about you?"

"What would you like to know?"

"Did you fight in the war?"

"Nope. I was lucky. I wasn't drafted until '45, and hadn't even finished up at Fort Benning before Hitler caved."

"That was lucky. Well, let's see. Were you born in New York?"

"No. New Jersey."

"Brothers and sisters?"

"Two sisters."

"Do they have names?"

"Doreen and Lucia."

"Younger or older?"

"Both younger."

"You're not making this easy, you know."

"It's not important. It's not where you came from that's important. It's what you make of yourself."

He said this in a tone not really in keeping with the conversation. Maddy was silent for a moment.

"I'm sorry if I was being too inquisitive."

"No, don't be. I'm sorry. I'll tell you anything about me that you want to know. I'm the one who should be apologizing."

"Let's call it even, okay?"

"Okay. So shoot. Next question."

"You said you were Italian. Are your parents Italian? Born-in-Italy Italian?"

"Yes, they were. They're both dead now. My Dad died a few years ago. Mom died just last year."

"I'm sorry."

"Don't be. She never got over my Dad's death. She wasn't a happy person."

"Oh." Maddy again tried to shift the conversation to something a little less somber.

"Have you ever been to Italy?"

"Yes. When I was a boy."

"Did you like it?"

He told her stories about his summer in Italy. He described the wind in the cliffs on the seashore; the sight of old women, wrapped in black, coming out of church on Sunday; the houses put together from pieces of ancient Roman ruins. He made her laugh with a tale about trying to get a moody donkey to do what it was told, and described in detail the process of harvesting and pressing the olives that were the source of sustenance for so many.

"I was lucky to get there, before the war. I hear it's ruined now."

"Do you want to go back?"

"No. I'm an American. My life is here." He signaled for the waiter to bring them a check.

"What will you do when you graduate?"

"Well, that's an easy decision. I'm going to join my uncle in the family business."

"What's that?"

"He owns some restaurants down in Jersey, and does some import business. He's hoping my education will help me come up with some brilliant plan for diversifying his resources."

"And will it?"

"Maybe. I have some ideas. We'll see. Shall we go somewhere else for dessert?"

"I don't think I could eat another thing."

"A drink?"

"No, thanks. I mean, I don't drink, really. Maybe some coffee?"

"As you wish. We can wander back toward the apartment. I know a little café."

"DeMarco's?"

"Yes. Do you like it?"

"I love it."

"Let's go."

He got up, walked around to her side of the table and pulled out her chair for her. She thought, I can't believe how badly I want him to touch me. When dating Brad and the few other boys she'd been out with, she looked forward to a goodnight kiss with a little tingle of anticipation, but nothing like this. She felt as if her skin were on fire, and only his touch would soothe her; soothe her, or cause her to explode.

As they walked, she tried to detect some sign that he felt it, too: this longing, this tantalizing tension. But he gave her no clues. After they had their coffee, he escorted her back to her apartment. Her heart was pounding when they reached her door. She started to unlock it, but his voice stopped her.

"Madeleine."

She turned to face him, leaning against her unopened door for support. Her mouth was so dry. He towered above her. Slowly he came closer. He propped one arm up against the door, somewhere above her shoulder, and leaned close to her face.

Maddy willed him to kiss her.

But he didn't. He looked at her, his face inches away from hers. She wanted to reach out and touch him, but her hands were riveted to her sides.

Then he backed away.

"Thank you for a wonderful evening," he said calmly.

She nodded, too shaken to speak.

"May I call you again?"

"Yes, of course," she stammered, recovering her voice.

"Goodnight." Still, he did not move.

He stood there, looking at her. She did not know what to do. Finally she turned and found her key dangling from the keyhole. She unlocked the door and stepped inside her apartment. Then she turned again to face him. He was still standing there. Looking at her. Looking at her with those eyes.

Suddenly she was afraid. She bit her bottom lip. She reached for the open door.

"Goodnight," she said, and closed it.

She stood without moving, listening. The sound of his footsteps told her that he was gone.

"God, how crazy," she said, aloud, to no one. "He was a perfect gentleman. What on earth were you afraid of?"

She ran one hand over the top of her head and down her neck, unconsciously imitating a gesture of her father's. She wandered aimlessly toward the kitchen, put her purse down on the counter, then walked toward the piano.

She played until the sweat poured from her skin and her fingers shook with exertion. Then she realized. She was not afraid of Gene. She was not afraid of what he might do to her.

She was afraid of how she had felt when she was with him.

Don't see him again, Maddy. You can't. You're only here for the summer, anyway. Brad is your boyfriend. Just leave Gene alone, she lectured herself as she stepped into the shower. She turned the water on, cold, full blast, and stifled a yelp.

Katherine arrived home the next morning at dawn. She bounded into the room, long legs full of energy, looking as if she were ready to lead the charge of the Light Brigade. Maddy was sitting on the couch, book in hand.

"Oh, Maddy, I can't thank you enough. It was fantastic. You wouldn't believe what goes on in Times Square at night. Why, there is a whole diff—what's wrong?"

"What do you mean, what's wrong? Nothing's wrong."

Katherine sat next to her on the couch. "I don't know. You look a little... intense. Are you still pissed off?"

"Katherine!"

"Sorry. Ya hang out with the boys, you start to talk like 'em. Did you have to cancel?"

"No. No. Gene took me out to dinner, instead."

"Great! Did you have fun?"

"Yes."

"Is he going to call you?"

"Yes."

"Do you like him better than old Brad the Fourth?"

"What a question! No. I don't know. I've only seen him once. I mean, he's just a friend."

"Did your first date with Bradley keep you up all night?"

"Oh, you idiot. I was waiting up for you. I was worried. Don't be a creep."

"Okay, okay. I withdraw the question. Well, kiddo, give him until Wednesday. Tuesday is too early to call. Wednesday says, 'I like you, but I'm cool.'"

"Now you sound like a beatnik."

"Harlem, baby. Harlem has the beat. Dave's gonna take me to a club."

"Oh, go to sleep," said Maddy, now genuinely annoyed. Annoyed with Katherine, and herself.

Gene did not call the next day. He did not call on Monday. He did not call on Tuesday, or Wednesday, or Thursday. Maddy's piano teacher lambasted her for her poor performance during the week. By Friday she was morose and difficult to live with. By Saturday she'd convinced herself that she did not care. He was just a friend, after all. A new acquaintance. Just a boy.

On Sunday morning, Katherine and Maddy were stretched out on the living room floor in their bathrobes, reading the *New*

York Times and the *Daily News*. The remains of a bagel-and-cream-cheese breakfast lay strewn about the floor.

There was a knock at the door.

"You get it," both girls said simultaneously.

Katherine sighed. "Who the hell could get in without being announced, anyway? Isn't there a doorman on Sunday?"

Maddy's head jerked up with a start.

"Oh, my God. Katherine. You get it. Please. Please. I've got to change." She raced into the bedroom.

"Hey, what's your problem?" barked Katherine, immobile. The visitor knocked again. She unfolded her legs and kicked through the papers on the floor.

"Coming. Hold your horses. Commm-ing," she sang out, resigned to her fate.

She yanked the door open, and her jaw dropped.

"Whoops. We weren't really expecting company."

"You must be Katherine," said Gene warmly. "I'm sorry we missed each other last Saturday."

"Yeah, me too. Well. That means you're Gene, right? Nice to meet you. Please excuse the glamorous look. My tuxedo is being cleaned." Katherine gestured to her bathrobe, then walked back into the living room.

"Oh, Maddy! It's a friend of yours," she tooted in a high-pitched voice. Over her shoulder she asked Gene, "Would you like some coffee? There may be a cup left."

"No, thank you. I've had mine."

"Maddy is indisposed. She shall emerge momentarily. Sports section?"

"Sure. Thanks."

Katherine tried not to stare as Gene settled down on the couch and sifted through the sports pages. She tried to remember if she had ever seen such a good looking man in her life. At least, in civilian clothes. All guys looked good in a uniform.

"So do you think the Yankees stand a chance this year?" she ad-libbed, trying to make conversation.

"Do you care?"

"Of course I care. I'm a fan from way back."

They discussed baseball for a good five minutes before Maddy returned, metamorphosis complete. She was dressed in a striped, two-piece pants suit. The cropped top revealed a hint of her midriff. Her hair was still pulled back, but the ponytail had been replaced by two white barrettes. She wore red lipstick.

Katherine raised her eyebrows. "Well, it's about time. 'Scuse me, Gene, but I believe it's my turn in the shower. Come by again sometime when I have clothes on." She walked into the bedroom, shutting the door firmly behind her.

"She's just like you described her."

Maddy glanced at the closed bedroom door. "Yes, she's an original. My best friend since I was nine."

"I'm sorry if I came by at an inconvenient time. I was wondering—hoping—it's so beautiful out today. Would you like to go sailing?"

"Sailing?"

"Yes. My uncle has a boat on Long Island. He's out of town, so he won't be using it. Would you like to come?"

The coy, calm conversations she'd been rehearsing all week fled her brain. "I would love to."

"Let's go."

"Do I—"

"You won't need a thing. Well, a bathing suit, maybe."

"I'll be right back."

She stepped quickly into the bedroom. Katherine was sitting on the bed, still in her robe, a slightly amused, slightly envious look on her face.

"No wonder you were pissed off," she said.

"Hush! We're going sailing."

"La-Dee-Da. Have a great time. Nice new outfit, by the way."

"Katherine—"

"Hmm?"

"I may be late getting home."

"I should hope so."

Maddy made a face. She grabbed her swimsuit from her chest of drawers and stuffed it in her handbag. Then she went to the closet and pulled out a straw hat. She checked her image in the mirror and dashed back to Gene.

It took just over an hour for them to reach the boat dock where Gene's uncle's sailboat was moored in Long Island Sound. He'd obviously called ahead. There was a picnic lunch already on board and the boat—more like a yacht, a forty-foot, twin-masted schooner—was ready to sail.

"Have you ever been sailing before?" asked Gene, as they got underway.

"Not since I was a little girl. And then... this will sound funny, but I sailed on junks."

"What?" He laughed.

"It's a kind of a Chinese boat, with a sail that looks like a bat's wing. Very fast, and capable of sailing in shallow or deep water. But the water was never like this in Shanghai."

"What was it like?"

"Dirty. Not pleasant."

"Well, we'll see if we can't find a pleasant place for swimming today."

Maddy had forgotten what it was like to move on the water in a small craft, in rhythm with the waves. She felt a heightened sensual awareness: the sun on her skin, the wind in her hair, the cry of the gulls, the taste of the bread in her sandwich, the chilling briskness of the water as she dove in for a quick, cool dip. She studied

Gene as he worked the lines, watching the fibers of his muscles ripple across his back. She imagined laying her cheek against those muscles, and tried to push the image from her mind.

They turned back at four o'clock, and made it back to Manhattan by nightfall. He parked his car, a red convertible, underneath the building. When they got to her door she thought, *This is it. Now he has to kiss me.*

But he didn't.

He invited her to dinner on Wednesday. On Friday, after her lesson, they went to a showing of Impressionist paintings at the Metropolitan. He told her in advance that he could not see her over the weekend, because he had to study for an exam. On Tuesday, he asked her to go roller skating in the park.

Maddy awoke every morning with a feeling of boundless expectation. She played the piano like a fiend, accomplishing everything her tutor set out for her, and more. Her mind was filled with her music. With music, and thoughts of Gene. There was no room for anything else.

Late in the afternoon on the Fourth of July, Katherine and Maddy were getting ready to go to a dinner picnic with the O'Connor clan. The whole group was going out to Coney Island for an evening of fun and fireworks. Just as Maddy was putting on her shoes, the doorman buzzed the intercom.

"Yes," answered Katherine, expecting her brother, who was to pick them up shortly.

"It's a Mista Brad Gordon, Miss O'Connor," announced the doorman. "Do ya want him sent up?"

"Brad? Here? Now?" Maddy blurted, buckling the straps on her sling backs with lightning speed.

"Sure, Marty. Send him up," responded Katherine.

"But Brad's supposed to be in Europe," stammered Maddy. "Until the end of the month."

"Surprise! Guess your plans have changed. Don't worry, I'll make your excuses to Ma."

"No! I mean—oh, gosh, Katherine. What does Brad want?"

"To see you, I assume. Shall I tell him you are indisposed?"

"But why he isn't in London?"

"Guess you'll have to ask him that yourself."

In a moment Brad burst in and made straight for Maddy. "There's my girl!" he cried out happily as he lifted her into the air. Katherine hooted. Brad put Maddy down and scowled at her.

"Who's this?" he asked abruptly.

"Never mind me. I'm the roommate and I'm leaving. Nice to meet you, Brad."

He looked sheepish. "I apologize. I just didn't realize that we weren't alone. You must be Katherine."

"Where have I heard that before?" said Katherine, rolling her eyes and then giving Maddy a wink. Maddy gave her a startled look, followed by one that could only mean, "Shut up."

"Happy Fourth of July!" Brad burst out, turning again to Maddy, and giving her a big hug. "Are you surprised?"

"Yes, yes I am. What happened to your trip?"

"Well, I decided Europe wasn't big enough for me and my parents to be there at the same time. So I caught a flight back."

"Oh, Brad, don't tell me you're on the outs with your parents," sighed Maddy, truly distressed.

"What of it? Serves them right. Stuffy old windbags. Never been so fed up in my life."

"Brad! They're your parents."

"So what?" he chided defensively. "I don't see your old man anywhere around."

"That's not fair. That's completely different."

"I don't think so. Some parents outlive their usefulness. So what's on the program for the evening? Picnic? Fireworks? Boat races?"

"Well, I'm gone. See you later," interrupted Katherine, ducking out the door. Dismayed, Maddy watched her leave.

"Boy, am I glad she's gone," Brad whispered. "God, Maddy, I missed you." He pulled her to him and pressed his lips against hers. She kept her mouth clamped tightly shut and wriggled free.

"Wait! Hold on!" she cried out, trying to sound cheerfully unoffended. "You sure know how to bowl a girl over."

"Maddy, I should have kissed you like this months ago. I'm so glad to see you. How have you been? How are your lessons going? Have you enjoyed your summer in New York?"

"Fine, yes. Ah, would you like something to drink?" She needed a moment to collect her thoughts. Here was Brad. Her boyfriend. She should be happy to see him. And she was. Wasn't she?

Brad nodded. "Thanks. Water will do." He seemed oblivious to her discomfort, chatting behind her as she walked into the kitchen.

"Europe is so depressing. Place is still a bunch of bombed-out ruins. People running around in rags. Think they could've done more by now! The war's been over for five years. But how are you? Did you miss me?"

"Of course I missed you," said Maddy, handing him a glass of water, then swallowing hard herself. She *had* missed him. Until lately.

He took a sip, then set the glass down, and stared at her.

"Oh, Maddy." He was at her again, kissing her cheeks with clumsy passion. "Maddy, let's get married. Let's get married right now, this week, before my parents come home. Let's drive to Maryland and elope. Then they can't object, not if you're already my wife."

"What?" Maddy pushed herself away. "Brad? Are you proposing?"

"Yes! Oh, I guess I should have bought a ring and all that, but we can do that on the way to Maryland—please say you'll have me, Maddy. I love you so."

Maddy put her hands over her ears. "Brad! I can't just run off! And what do you mean, your parents object to me?"

Brad was startled out of his euphoria. "Maddy, I thought you knew... I assumed... you know, they have... misgivings. Because you're Jewish."

"What?"

"But darling, it's never mattered to me!"

"Wait, wait just a minute, Bradley," she said, now holding out her hands as if to ward him off. "You mean, the reason I've never met your parents, other than at the symphony that one night, is because I'm Jewish?"

"Oh, Maddy. I don't give a damn what they think. I want you. I love you. I couldn't stand being away from you. Please say you'll marry me."

"No."

Now it was his turn to look jolted. "You don't mean that."

"Yes I do. I don't want to live that kind of life! I don't want to be an outcast in my own family. And I don't want to get married now. I want to finish school."

"But you can finish. Lots of guys in med school are married."

"Not to musicians. No, Brad. I'm sorry to be so abrupt, but you really put me on the spot. Thank you, but no."

He looked crestfallen. "You'll change your mind, Maddy. I just went about this the wrong way. Please say you'll think about it."

She shook her head.

"Well." They looked at each other in silence.

"I'm sorry," she whispered.

"Don't be," he said, trying to adopt a jaunty air, "I don't give up that easily. Well, I'm going to stay with Theo for a few weeks, at his place in Newport. Vicki can get the number from Anna, if you think... well, I'll be in touch, anyway. Goodbye for now, Maddy."

"Goodbye." She walked him to the door. He kissed her on the forehead, and left.

Maddy slammed her hands down on the dining room table. What was happening? Marriage? Now? Impossible. And that business about his parents! How could she have been so blind? So naive? Why this, why now, when everything was going so smoothly?

Or was it?

She thought about trying to catch up with Katherine and her family, but felt in no mood for holiday festivities. Flopping down on the couch in exasperation, she put her feet up on the edge of the sofa, and stared at the ceiling.

"Damn," she said, "Damn, damn damn."

Another knock. She jumped up. Could Brad be back so soon?

But it wasn't Brad. It was Gene.

"Hello, Angel," he said as she opened the door. From behind his back he produced a dozen yellow roses.

"Gene! Oh, thank you! They're beautiful! But… wait. How did you know I was here? We were supposed to go to Coney Island. And I thought you were going to spend the day on the boat with your uncle."

"Well, I pay Marty to keep tabs on you. For a few bucks a week he lets me know about all the comings and goings in this apartment. He just called to tell me that Katherine took off without you."

Maddy's eyes nearly popped out of her head. Then she laughed. It was a joke. It had to be. "Creep. You had me going there."

Gene laughed, too. "You should have seen the look on your face! Okay, the real story is, I was going to drop these at the door. See? They have the little water thingies on them, so they'd last until you got home tonight. But, having come this far, I just took a chance and knocked."

They stood looking at each other.

"Are you—"

"Where is—"

"You first," said Maddy with a smile.

"Where's Katherine? Have you changed your plans?"

"Yes. Well, she just left. I should try to hook up with them, I guess. How about you? What happened to your day of sailing?"

"Uncle Sal's arthritis kicked up. That's what he tells us when he's too hung over to go sailing. The rest of the family decided to skip sailing and go upstate. I wasn't in the mood for a big family day, so I passed. I was going to hang around and study. Unless you have a better idea."

Maddy's heart skipped a beat. How could she think that what she felt for Brad was love, compared to how she felt around Gene? What else could this be?

"I can pack a picnic. We can go to the park."

"Or... just come up to my apartment in ten minutes. We'll have a cocktail, then go for a special celebration."

Maddy knew better than to say yes, but she did not want to say no. "Ten minutes?"

"Ten minutes."

"And thank you again for the flowers."

"My pleasure."

Maddy did not allow herself to think about what might happen that evening. She went into her room and put on a strapless white cotton sundress with a matching bolero jacket. She brushed her hair and put it up into a twist, to show off her neck. She refreshed her lipstick. And she went upstairs.

Gene opened the door as soon as she knocked, and looked her over from head to toe. "You are so beautiful."

Maddy could not answer. Her desire for him was so intense she thought he must be able to smell it, emanating from her body like a wicked perfume. But she could not act upon it. She was incapable of taking that step.

"Welcome to life on top of the world," he said as he ushered her in and took her hand. "I have a surprise for you."

He led her into the living room. A wall of windows spread Central Park and midtown Manhattan before them. There, in the center of the room, stood a glistening white grand piano. On top of the piano was a silver wine cooler containing a bottle of champagne, and two crystal glasses.

Maddy released his hand and walked over to the magnificent instrument. "I didn't know you had a piano, Gene." Her voice trembled.

"It's a very recent addition. Just got it last weekend. They had to practically take the whole thing apart and put it back together again to get it in here."

Maddy sat down on the white leather bench. Outside the sun was beginning to set. A rosy hue spread across the horizon. Long shafts of golden sunlight reached out to christen the skyscrapers of Manhattan.

"It's too perfect," she said softly.

"No," he said. "You—only you—are perfection." He handed her a glass of champagne.

Maddy seldom drank, but now she took a long sip of the effervescent wine. Within a few seconds she felt lighter, almost giddy. She took another sip, and looked up at Gene, trying to tell him everything without having to say anything. *Surely now he will kiss me.*

"Play for me," he said. Then, with a soft, "Shhh," he gently removed her jacket, and tossed it on the couch behind them. She shivered.

"What should I play?"

"Whatever you like."

Out of her heart came the sensuous strains of Debussy's *Reverie.* Her fingers moved along the keyboard, enchanted. He stood behind her, listening. Then he touched the base of her neck with just the index finger of his right hand. It scorched her skin like a torch, but she did not stop playing as he continued to trace his finger slowly down her spine. Her lips parted slightly, as softly as a blossoming orchid. She poured her passion into her music, wanting so much more, afraid to ask for anything.

His finger reached the bodice of her dress. Then she felt his whole hand, fingers and palm, slide underneath the fabric, pressing against the skin between her shoulder blades. She arched her back.

He was on his knees, behind her. He unzipped her dress, slipped his hands along the sides of her chest, and cupped her breasts. Her eyes closed as her fingers fell away from the keys.

"Angel," he whispered in her ear. She felt his tongue on her neck, moving in tiny increments. Small whimpers escaped her: sounds of helplessness, surrender, and delight.

Now he was next to her, straddling the piano bench. He cupped her delicate face in his large hands. "Do you want me, Maddy?"

She opened her eyes. "Yes," she whispered, her face burning with shame and desire.

"Tell me," he demanded, drawing his face closer to hers. "Tell me that you want me."

"I want you," she breathed, and closed her eyes again. His hands still touching her face, he traced the outline of her mouth with his thumbs. She was beyond thinking. She could experience only his touch, his scent.

"Tell me you want me to make love to you," he whispered.

"I want you to make love to me." Her voice floated out from some murky, unfamiliar part of her. Her heart beat even faster. She could not open her eyes.

His hands slid from her face. He peeled down the top of her dress, then caressed every inch of her naked torso, as if he were sculpting her body from clay. His hands came to rest below her waist. Then he leaned forward and, for the first time, kissed her mouth.

By now her desire had become an unbearable torment. She writhed on the bench, only dimly aware of the release her body craved. She shifted her weight and flung her leg over the bench so that she too, now straddled it, and pushed herself up against him.

She pressed her bare breasts against his chest, reached her fingers up into his hair, and kissed him, and kissed him again, each kiss both a plea and a promise.

And then she was moving: moving through the air. She felt softness beneath her and a rush of fear and pleasure as he slipped off her underpants. She heard the sounds of clothes being removed. Only then did she open her eyes. He was on the bed, on his hands and knees, just above her. She could see the movement of his chest as he inhaled and exhaled, and the small beads of sweat clinging to his shoulders. She saw all of him, ready and strong and full of desire.

"Is this what you want?" he asked again.

She had no voice. She nodded.

"Say it," he commanded.

"Yes," she said, and closed her eyes as he slipped into her. *Yes Yes Yes.*

She wrapped her legs around his back and clung to him, and then heard herself cry out in a voice that was not hers as he ground her into the bed. She was no longer Maddy. Maddy had disappeared, overwhelmed by his power and the depth of her surrender. Her punishment. The sweet agony of her punishment.

She had journeyed to a dark place, a private place, a place of terror and truth. She knew, finally, where she belonged. And she knew that only Gene could take her there.

CHAPTER 19

THE DEMON

ⓔↄ◇◇ↄⓔ

"I said call her, and tell her that you aren't coming home."

Maddy lay naked on Gene's bed, with the sheets pulled up to her chin, trying to hide from the daylight and whatever reality had in store for her. Gene sat next to her, holding the phone by its cord, dangling the receiver a few inches from her face.

"Tell her your aunt came back into town and invited you to New Jersey for the weekend. Tell her to call your piano teacher and tell him you're going to miss a few lessons."

"I can't do that!" She sat up now, ducking out of the way of the dangling receiver, clutching the bedclothes tightly up against her naked breasts. "If I miss a lesson, Aunt Bernice will have to pay for it anyway, and she—"

"Do you want me to call him?"

Maddy stared up into Gene's face. She could read no threat there but she knew, without a doubt that he would call her teacher if she did not do as he asked.

She took the phone. He dialed for her.

"Hello, Katherine?"

"Maddy! Where the hell are you?"

"Katherine, look, I'm sorry I didn't leave a note. I decided to go to Jersey for the weekend. Just for some time alone. To think."

"Geez, kid. I was about to call the police. Did you and Brad have a fight last night? What's going on?"

"Oh, something like that. It's so stupid. I'll talk to you about it when I get back. I really don't want to go into it now. But, well, would you call Mr. Laboucherd and tell him that I am not going to make my lessons today, or tomorrow?"

"What? You're kidding, right?"

"No, I need some time to... think."

"Okay, I'll do it for you, this one time, but you'll have some world class explaining to do when you get back here, you know."

"Oh, Katherine, okay..." Gene had started biting her shoulder.

"I'll see you tomorrow. No, I mean, Saturday."

"Monday," he whispered in her ear.

"That is, I'll probably stay until Monday."

"Maddy, do you want me to come out this weekend? Are you going to be okay?"

"NO! No, I mean, I'll be fine. I just want some peace and quiet. I'll explain everything... when... I... see... you."

Gene snatched the phone out of her hand.

Later that day, when Maddy was sure Katherine would be at work, she snuck down to her apartment and picked up some clothes. She tried not to disturb anything as she stuffed a few items into a canvas bag, hoping that Katherine-the-Reporter would not notice the bag was missing. "I've fallen off the world, and I'll have to climb back on. Soon. Somehow," she said out loud to herself as she left.

On Monday Maddy made it to her lesson with Mr. Laboucherd. She sat down at the piano in his stuffy studio on Madison Avenue and felt a yawning emptiness inside. Her fingers were stiff as she started her first piece. In a moment, to her embarrassment, the Maestro stopped her.

"Madeleine, you are a disappointingly inconsistent student."
She flushed crimson.

"This is why I seldom take women students, Madeleine. They
are slaves to their emotions. But you showed such promise...."
Lines of discouragement appeared on his aging brow.

"Anyone can play the piano, Madeleine. It is a machine. You
bang on the keys and the noise comes out."

He paused, as if waiting for the profound implications of his
observation to sink in. "Anyone can play the piano, Madeleine,
but only an artist can make music. Artists are different. We have a
different soul, a different spirit. And in that spirit there is—there
must be—passion. Passion that is impossible for a normal person
to comprehend. But it is a passion that must be mastered, for the
music to be mastered. Your passion can be the source of a divine
elevation, or it can sew the seeds of your own destruction. If it
cannot be tapped, you may as well be sitting at a player piano, with
a strip of moving paper cranking out the music in front of you. But
if you let your passion overcome you, if you do not master it, then
you will never be a great artist."

He turned to look at her. Her face burned with shame, and hot,
silent tears slid down her cheeks. "You have a gift, Madeleine," said
Mr. Laboucherd, ignoring her tears. "But you must prove yourself
worthy of that gift." He walked toward the door. A few feet from
it, he paused.

"I do not know if you are in love, Madeleine. I do not care. I
will give you one week. One week. If you are ready to become a
musician, be here a week from today. If not, then go make some
pretty babies." He left the room.

Maddy put her head down on the keys and sobbed.

She was supposed to meet Gene after her lesson, but after Mr.
Laboucherd's lecture, she could not bring herself to go back to his
room. She went, instead, to her own apartment, looking for solace
in the quiet privacy of her own unrumpled bed.

At three o'clock, she heard a knock on the door. She knew it must be Gene. Because he lived in the building, he was the only one who could make it to the door unannounced. She froze, as still as a mouse, afraid that the wild beating of her heart would give her away. After a moment, she heard him knock again. Then, footsteps, and silence.

Her thoughts were an addled mass of confusion. When she went to his apartment… was it only four days ago? She'd been convinced she was a woman in love. But the four days she had spent with him weren't romantic. There had been only hunger. A greedy, insatiable hunger.

Maddy brought her hands to her temples and squeezed, trying to press the pictures out of her brain. The ways Gene had taken her… the things that she'd done! And she'd wanted all of it, every thrusting, melting moment. And she wanted him still.

Maddy groaned aloud. *Passion.* Her music could not come from the same place inside her as this… insanity.

She dragged herself out of bed and into the living room. She felt claustrophobic. She realized that she had not been out of the apartment building, except to attend her lesson that morning, in nearly a week. She would go to the park. She would buy a pretzel from a street vendor. She would soak in the sunshine. She would escape from herself.

Maddy scampered back into her room and put on a long cotton skirt. She slipped her feet into a pair of flat sandals, whipped a brush through her hair, grabbed her purse, checked for her keys and lipstick case, and left the apartment.

She waited impatiently for the elevator. When it arrived she stepped in and pressed the button for the lobby. The door closed. It stopped on the next level down.

The door opened. There stood Gene.

Maddy stared at him.

"Hello, Angel," he said, as he stepped inside with her. The elevator started to move.

"Gene—what are you—"

She did not finish the sentence. He held his finger to her lips. Then he pulled the emergency stop button on the control panel. An ear-splitting bell filled the small room.

"What are you doing?" Maddy shrieked, trying to make herself heard above the siren.

Gene did not answer. He moved closer to her. Instinctively Maddy retreated, her hands covering her ears, trying to shut out the noise. She stepped back until she hit the balance rail that traveled the circumference of the elevator. He was so close to her. Too close to her.

He lifted her up by the hips and planted her body up against the wall, precariously propped up by the small railing.

"No!" Her hands came away from her ears. She dropped her small purse and pushed with the full strength of both arms against his shoulders, trying to force him away.

His eyes, absurdly calm up to now, darkened with anger. "Don't fight me, Angel," he responded, in a voice all the more threatening because of its lack of emotion.

And she knew she would not fight him. Her body was already beginning to betray her. The more he wanted her, the more overpowering her own desire became.

He pinned her against the wall with his chest as he dug under her skirt, grabbed her panties, and ripped them off as if they were made of tissue paper. Then he backed away a few inches, and placed one hand firmly up against Maddy's breastbone to keep her balanced on the railing. With the other he quickly unfastened his belt and trousers. His pants fell to his ankles.

He thrust up and into her. Maddy screamed, not knowing herself whether it was a cry of protest or passion, the sound of her voice buried in the protective camouflage of the elevator's emergency bell.

Then she closed her eyes, wrapped her legs around him, and dove again into their obscene madness.

When her spasms subsided Maddy was gasping shamelessly. The emergency siren continued to ring mercilessly. Maddy could still feel Gene inside her, firm and demanding.

He lifted her up and off him, and set her down, gently. She grasped for the railing behind her, trying to steady herself. She did not know what to think of him, of herself, of what was happening. She did not dare think at all.

Gene pulled up his trousers and pushed the emergency button back in, disconnecting the alarm. They rode the elevator in silence to the ground floor. When they reached the bottom, Marty, the ever-reliable doorman, was waiting.

"Get stuck?" he asked, sounding worried.

"No, no," Gene replied suavely. "I just banged the emergency knob by accident. We were actually going up, weren't we, Maddy?"

Maddy nodded, too ashamed to speak. She tried not to look at her panties, still sitting in the corner where Gene had tossed them. She prayed that Marty wouldn't notice.

"You sure you're okay?" asked Marty again, with sincerity.

"Top notch," Gene replied. "But thanks for looking after us."

"No sweat," said Marty, as the elevator door closed.

When they reached Maddy's floor, she picked up her panties and tucked them into her purse, trying to appear nonchalant, knowing it was a ridiculous effort. The doors opened, and she stepped out of the elevator as if she did not expect Gene to follow her. He did. He stood, motionless and silent behind her, as she turned the key to her apartment.

He followed her inside, slammed the door shut, grabbed her by the shoulders, and spun her around to face him.

"You never, never say no to me, Maddy. You are mine, Angel. All mine."

She stared at him, trying to reconcile the fear and exhilaration his words evoked in her. She thought he was going to kiss her, but instead he twisted her around, roughly, and brought her down onto the hardwood floor. She was on her hands and knees. He was behind her. He pushed her skirt up around her waist, revealing her wanton nakedness.

His tongue was inside her. She moaned, then gasped, as he suddenly pulled away and pushed her flat onto the floor.

"Don't you ever say no to me again." He spread her legs apart and lowered himself onto her body, covering hers completely. She wanted to shout, no, *not like this*, but that part of her evaporated beneath the heat of his desire. *Yes. Take me. I am yours.*

At last Gene moved off of her. Maddy hid her face in her arms and stayed where she was, wishing she were invisible. He did not speak. She heard him pulling up his pants, heard him walking to the bathroom, heard the sound of water running. She heard more footsteps, and then his voice coming from the direction of the door.

"Come to my apartment for dinner tomorrow. Be there at six o'clock."

Maddy stayed on the floor, and curled herself up into a tight, tiny ball. Her whole body trembled with humiliation. She hated Gene at that moment. And she hated herself even more, for she knew that she would do whatever he demanded.

CHAPTER 20

THE BRIDE

Maddy stood, listening at the door, trying to make sure that Katherine had already gone to work. She heard nothing. Breathing a sigh of relief, she unlocked the door and went into the apartment.

Katherine was sitting on the couch. She looked up from the book she was reading as Maddy entered the room.

"Okay, kid," she said brusquely, slapping the thin volume shut and setting it to the side. "Start talking. Where the hell have you been all night?"

"Aren't you late for work?" Maddy responded, lacing her fingers together behind her back.

Katherine rolled her eyes. "Yes, idiot. I am late for work. And I was getting ready to call in sick. I've been worried, Maddy. So spill the beans. Is it the pretty Italian playboy from the penthouse?"

Tears filled Maddy's eyes. She shook her head.

"Maddy, talk to me. We've never had any secrets—well, except about the fact that you're a piano genius. So, are you developing another secret life? Is it that? First you're gone for four days, then you come back spouting, 'guess what, Brad asked me to marry him, the nerve of that man,' then you're gone again. I haven't seen you since yesterday morning. What gives?"

"No," Maddy whispered, fighting back tears.

"Maddy, I can't stand this. You're gone all night, and you come back all weepy, and you won't even tell me what's going on! I'm your best friend, Maddy. There's nothing you can't share with me. I don't care who you've got the hots for—unless, maybe, you've fallen for Marty the doorman, which would be pretty unforgivable. Don't tell me Brad came to town for a visit. Did he come to kiss and make up? Did he? Did he come to ask you to reconsider, using a new set of persuasive skills?"

Maddy did not answer. She did not move.

Katherine stood up. "Fine. Don't talk. I can see I wasted my time. Do what you want. God, Maddy. I thought I was the crazy one."

Maddy wanted to tell her, to tell her everything, but she did not dare. It would make it all too real, and it was too shameful to be real.

Still Katherine waited, giving her friend a chance to explain. Maddy looked down at the floor.

"Great," snapped Katherine. "Have it your way. I'm going to work. But if you're leaving again, leave me a note, okay? I can't afford to lose any more sleep." Brushing her way angrily past Maddy, she marched out the door. Maddy winced as she slammed it shut behind her.

Maddy walked into the bathroom and filled up the tub. She stripped and stepped into the scalding bath, winced, then held her breath and sank low in the water.

Gene's mocking voice rang in her ears.

"Married? Angel, married is for diapers and cutting the grass and roast beef on Sunday. Do you think married people live like this? You think if I see you doing the dishes and sewing clothes and wiping up after the dog I'm gonna want to tie you to my bed? You're fantastic, Maddy. Outside you are beautiful and delicate, but inside, you are a wild thing. I knew it when I heard you playing that piano. I wanted to set free all that yearning, all that fire inside you. And I'm not gonna screw up what we've got by getting married."

"But what if I get pregnant?"

"There are ways to handle that which don't involve marriage."

Maddy shuddered, despite the heat of the water, just as she had shuddered when the words came out of his mouth. She did not ask him to elaborate. His suggestion was too horrible to consider.

She thought about what Katherine had said before she stormed out. Brad wanted to marry her. Brad loved her.

Next she heard Mr. Laboucherd's words echoing in her brain: "Master your passion… or go make pretty babies."

It did not take her long to find Theo's number. Long distance information, in Newport. Newport. America's Cup. Sailing. Sailing with Gene. Don't stop to think. If you stop to think you will be lost.

"Hello, this is Madeleine Hoffman. May I speak to Bradley please?"

The butler's grave voice answered. "One moment, ma'am. I believe the gentlemen are having coffee on the terrace. Please hold on."

It was an eternity. Twice she almost hung up the phone. But she couldn't. She had to escape. She had to turn her back on the ugliness that Gene had summoned from within her. She had to put the genie back in the bottle.

"Hello, Maddy?"

She had forgotten how soft and deep his voice was.

"Brad?"

"Darling! How lovely to hear from you! I was… well, never mind. I'm so glad you called."

"Brad. I thought about it. You know, what you said. What you asked me. And I do want to marry you. Right now. Today. I want to be your wife. I will make your parents love me, you'll see. I'm not afraid. I won't be afraid of anything."

Her words came out in a torrent. When she stopped there was silence on the line.

"Brad?"

"Oh, God, Maddy. Do you mean it?"

She closed her eyes. "Yes," she whispered.

"You won't change your mind?"

"No."

"Okay, okay. Let me think. Three hours to New York, if I make the ten o'clock train… meet me at Grand Central at one o'clock. We can take the afternoon train to Baltimore, and get married tonight. I'll go buy a ring on my way to the station, if there's any place open. What am I saying? I'm thinking out loud. Do you want Katherine to come, or anything? Should I bring Theo?"

"No. No. Just you. Just you and me."

"What about your aunt and uncle?"

"They're in California. They won't object. They'll be happy if I'm happy."

"Oh, my darling, you will be happy. I promise you. I will do everything in my power to make you happy. Maddy?"

"Hmm?"

"I love you."

"I love you too, Bradley."

"Until one?"

"Until one."

"Under the clock, okay?"

"Okay."

"I love you."

"I know," she whispered softly. "I know."

She put the receiver back on the phone. Now she would pack. She would pack, and spend the day at the public library. She would not take a chance that Gene might find her. For the first time in weeks, she felt calm.

Katherine came home at six. She called out Maddy's name. Silence.

"Figures," she muttered to herself.

She threw her purse on the couch, kicked off her shoes, and ambled into the kitchen to see if there was anything still edible in the refrigerator.

She saw a note on the counter and picked it up.

Dear Katherine,

> *I've eloped with Brad. We're getting married in Baltimore. I'll be in touch. Please tell Aunt Bernice, if she calls.*

Love Always,
Maddy

P.S. You told me to leave you a note.

Katherine plopped down on the floor. The piece of paper fell from her fingers. "Holy shit. Holy shit, Maddy. I hope you know what you're doing."

Later that night, at a small roadside hotel just outside Baltimore, Bradley Harrington Gordon IV carried Madeleine Hoffman Gordon, his new bride, across the threshold of their hotel room.

"I promise, Maddy, within a few days we'll go on a real honeymoon. We can go to Paris, Vienna—anywhere you want. I just couldn't get enough cash in one day, without... it's in a trust, you see... well, you don't need to worry about that."

"I don't care, Brad," she said, smiling up at him warmly and putting her arms around him. "I don't care where we are. I just want to be with you."

They kissed. Gradually, hesitantly, his tongue crept out of his mouth and touched her lips. When she did not pull away, he pushed the tip of his tongue gently into her mouth. She sighed.

He pulled away from her face and brought her head to his chest, holding her tightly against him. The top of her head reached up to his Adam's apple.

"I can't believe you're mine, Maddy. Mine forever."

She shuddered.

"Are you cold?" Brad asked, pulling back so he could see her face.

"No, silly. It's hot as blazes in here. I'm just a little nervous, I guess."

He blushed. "Well," he stammered. "Do you want to go and freshen up?"

Maddy nodded and slid from his embrace. "My suitcase?" she asked, sweetly.

"Oh, right." He dashed out the door and was back in an instant.

"Looks like it might rain tonight," he said awkwardly, handing Maddy her small bag.

Maddy flashed him a quick thank-you smile, and went into the bathroom. She caught herself reaching down to lock the door, and stopped herself. There was no need for privacy now, she thought. We're married.

She looked at herself in the mirror. She could not believe that she looked exactly the same as she did five days ago. Five days. Before her life exploded. Her life had exploded on the Fourth of July. What a joke! Funny. Her parents were married in July.

She picked up a wash towel and rinsed her face with cool water. She *was* nervous. Unlike Gene's voracious demands, Brad's embarrassment made her self-conscious. She knew that her wedding night would not be anything like the frenzied experience she'd had with Gene. And she wanted it to be different. Completely, totally different. Maybe it was good that she was nervous.

She quickly removed her simple gray suit and folded it neatly in a small pile, along with her hose and her undergarments. She'd borrowed a long, kimono-style robe from Katherine's closet to wear on her wedding night. It had been a gift from one of Katherine's brothers, her oldest brother, who'd died in the war. The two girls normally raided each other's closets without permission. Maddy knew that Katherine would understand, given the importance of the occasion.

She reached into her bag and pulled out the exotic garment. The green silk rippled out of the suitcase like a waterfall. She wrapped the robe around her naked body, tied the sash around her waist, splashed on some perfume, and opened the door.

Brad was sitting up in bed. He was wearing a full set of short-sleeved pajamas.

"You are so beautiful," he said simply as she emerged, his eyes filled with tenderness.

Maddy came to him shyly, wanting to please him, but afraid of letting him know that she was not an innocent bride. She crawled on to the bed and lay down next to him, sending a silent invitation.

He rolled over on top of her and kissed her forehead. Then he kissed her nose, then her mouth, then her neck. He kept on kissing her until he reached the belt of her kimono with his lips. With trembling fingers he undid the loosely tied knot, and the silk fabric slipped to her sides. He rolled on top of her again, and this time she could feel his erection, rubbing insistently up against her thigh. She kissed him, holding her hands gently on his shoulders, then reached behind him to stroke her fingers along his back.

When finally he pushed his way up into her, she started to cry. Hot, silent tears spilled from her eyes down the sides of her cheeks. Brad felt wetness on the side of his chin, and stopped moving.

When he saw she was crying, he pulled himself out, and begged her forgiveness.

"Oh, Maddy, I'm so sorry! I didn't know I was hurting you. Of course it hurt. Oh my darling, it will get better, I promise. Please, please, don't cry, my love. Don't cry."

She shook her head, trying to make him understand, knowing that she could not explain anything. So she reached for him and tried to stop her tears.

"Please. I want to. Please."

Brad looked doubtful, but he was still aroused. He entered her again and she arched her back to meet him. He came immediately, thrusting with sharp, sudden movements, emitting small groans of pleasure.

"Are you okay?" he asked softly when he'd finished, his voice coming from somewhere above her head.

Maddy sniffed. Her eyes were closed. "Yes. I'm fine now. Just, hold me. Please hold me."

He stretched along beside her and put one arm underneath her. With the other hand he caressed her tear-stained face. She turned to him, pressing against him, until every inch of their bodies were touching. Then they were silent, for a long, long time, comforted by one another's presence, resting in the quiet cradle of the night.

CHAPTER 21

THE WIFE

"I don't believe it!" Bernice cried out, exhibiting an uncharacter-istic loss of control. Archibald Mason glanced up from the financial pages as his distraught wife entered the parlor of their suite at the posh and modern Los Angeles Hilton.

"What's bothering you?" he asked calmly, without actually set-ting the paper down.

"That was Katherine O'Connor on the phone. She called to tell us that Madeleine has gotten married. *She eloped.* Yesterday, with Brad what's-his-name, the boy from Harvard Medical School. It's impossible."

Now Archie put the paper aside. He cast about his brain for an appropriate response.

"Well, I'm sure he'll be a good provider. And didn't you tell me he comes from money?"

"Money! Archie, of course he'll be a good provider. Madeleine doesn't need a good provider. She has us. What she needs is inde-pendence. And what she does not need is to be treated like a pariah by some blue-blooded Boston anti-Semites."

"Now, Bernice. It may not be as bad as all that. Don't let your own bigotry get the best of you."

She gave him a look of total dismay, and sank into a chair.

"Oh, my word. She's just like her mother, after all. There must be a genetic explanation for this. And after I warned her! Let's just hope she intends to keep going with her musical career. Perhaps we can salvage something from this."

Archie looked fondly at his wife. "Messed up your plans, did she, dear? Children will do that."

She glared at him. "Oh, Archie Mason, go jump in a lake."

"Yes dear," he answered, and returned to his financial pages. "Oh, look. GM's up two points. I love America."

Across the world, another, entirely different kind of couple, in a completely different kind of hotel, was having a similar conversation. Mr. and Mrs. Bradley Harrington Gordon III had just finished visiting old friends in Piccadilly Circus, and were now having afternoon tea in their suite at Claridge's. The tuxedo-clad butler served the tea then bowed, presenting Mr. Gordon with a telegram.

"Why, it's from Brad," he said, tearing open the message.

"An apology, I hope," sniffed Mrs. Gordon.

"DAMN!"

"Bradley! Your language!"

"Carolyn, the boy has gone mad. He's eloped! Eloped! Married the little Jewish girl. This is outrageous."

"Oh, dear God, no," whispered his wife, her face pale as the lilies on the table in front of her.

"Oh, yes. And there's more! He wants $5,000 for his honeymoon! Over my dead body! First he snubs us, then he disobeys us, now this. He's gone too far. If he wants to live his own life, then let him! Let him! Let him see how easy it is!" Bradley III was up now, roaring and stalking around the room like a wounded bear.

"Oh, dear," whimpered Carolyn. "And I always wanted Brad to have such a beautiful wedding. Oh why, why would he do this to us, Bradley? Why would he want to hurt us this way?"

Her husband looked at her, his sympathy for her momentarily taking precedence over his anger.

"There, there now, dear. Perhaps they won't stay married long."

She began to wail in earnest.

A week later an outraged Bradley Harrington Gordon IV sat in a distinguished office in an historic brownstone in downtown Boston, facing the dour face of Henry Walthen Waters, Jr. He'd been the attorney for the Gordon family since the day his own father, Henry Walthen Waters, Sr., had passed away, nearly twenty years ago, long before Bradley IV was old enough to cause trouble.

Waters disliked this young man. He had disliked him ever since Bradley IV had enlisted in the Navy in 1945, on the very day *after* the draft board had issued his carefully engineered exemption from military service. Luckily for the insubordinate runt, one of his law partners in Waters, Winthrop & Simmons was able to pull some strings and get him assigned to a supply depot in San Francisco. The war was over soon after he joined up, anyway. But Henry Walthen Waters, Jr., never forgave the boy. He abhorred disobedience, especially among the children of his wealthier clients. It made for such messiness. Like the business he was dealing with now.

"But he can't cut off my trust money. It's mine. Grandfather left it to me."

"You are the beneficiary of the income accumulated by the trust, yes, but you have no authority to spend it. Under the terms of the trust established by your grandfather, the principal will be distributed to your children, the children who survive you, of course—and if you have no surviving heirs, then to—ah—the children of your father's first cousin, I believe—I could check that—but it's really of no relevance at the moment. The interest income is yours to spend as you see fit, but not until you reach the age of thirty, or when you finish your education, whichever comes first. I believe the exact words are, 'obtains a degree or license to practice in whatever career upon which said child embarks.' So you see, your grandfather did not wish to reward his grandchildren for *quitting,* but for *succeeding.* No dilettantes in the Gordon family. You chose to go to medical school despite your father's objection. He relented, as you know, once you were accepted at Harvard, and has paid for your education out of his own pocket, although he could have, as trustee, authorized payment out of the trust for such a purpose. However, until you finish medical school—and your residency—at which point, you will be twenty-eight—until that time, your father, as trustee, is within his authority to deprive you of all access to the accrued interest in your trust fund."

"Well, thank you, Grandpa," muttered Bradley.

"I have instructions to tell you that this means all access, Brad. Including your tuition for medical school."

"Wait just a damn minute! You mean, he won't pay for me to finish school?"

"Not unless you are… willing to…" He cleared his throat. Oh, what was the world coming to? "Not unless you are willing to divorce your wife."

"The bastard." Bradley punched one fist into the palm of his other hand.

"Please, Bradley. You are speaking about your father. He just doesn't want you to throw your life away following the whimsy of youth. You have an important career ahead of you. An important place in society. The right sort of wife—"

"I have the right sort of wife, thank you," Bradley interrupted, eyes blazing. "My parents are absurd. They've never even really met Maddy. They wouldn't even invite her to their home for dinner, because they said they didn't want to 'encourage' me. They have no idea what kind of person my wife is. I don't give a damn if she's not from the right sort of family, or if her father was a pickle salesman from Hong Kong, and her mother was… never mind. Just tell my dear old dad I'll finish school without his help. And that I won't be naming my son Bradley V." He stalked out.

That evening, he explained the situation to Maddy. She listened quietly. She did not seem upset.

"Don't worry," she said, placing a hand on his knee. "I can ask Aunt Bernice for the money. She'll pay for your medical school."

"No!" he snapped, pushing her hand away. "I won't take her money. I don't want her help, thank you."

"But Brad, she's paying for Katherine's school, and mine."

"No. Don't you see? You let people do something for you, and then they own you. Pushing and prodding, telling you what to do, then bemoaning your ingratitude. My parents have done this to me all my life. And when I got into trouble, they were always there, with their apologies, and their bribes, and their excuses. If I can't finish by myself, then I'm finished, anyway. I don't need your aunt and uncle to step into my parent's shoes."

"Then will you let me help you?"

"How?"

"I can get a job."

"No. Impossible."

"But Brad, how else?"

"I'll take a year off and do lab work. I'll borrow money. I can do it."

"But that will delay your graduation, and your freedom. If it weren't for me, they never would have disowned you. Please let me help. I'm your wife, Brad. If you can't take my help, then what kind of marriage do we have?" *And then I can quit school. The decision would be made for me. I wouldn't need to explain anything.*

As if reading her thoughts, he said, "But I don't want you to give up your dreams,"

"I don't have any dreams, Brad. I never did. Oh, I wanted to play the piano but I don't have what it takes to be a real musician. I was a talented prodigy. I can't… I don't want a musical career."

She looked at him, and tried to make him believe what she was saying, just as she tried to make herself believe it. "I just want to be your wife." *I just want to be safe.*

Brad was weakening, she could tell. After all, her offer would give him no more than a bunch of the other fellows at the med school had: a supportive wife, helping to make ends meet until medical school was over, the residency finished, the bills paid.

In the end, he agreed. They moved into a small apartment, near the medical school, in downtown Boston. Maddy got a job at Filene's Department Store selling ladies' sportswear. She was pleasant, and helpful, and her customers and coworkers liked her. Every day she got up early and rode the subway to work, enjoying a sense of productive usefulness that she'd not experienced since her childhood days of living in the busy O'Connor household.

At first she saw some of her friends from the New Music School, but the life of a student was at odds with the hours and responsibilities of a working wife, and she soon lost contact with them. She received one letter from her teacher, Mr. Auerbach, in which he expressed his disappointment about her decision to withdraw, and said he felt he was to blame, that perhaps a summer with Mr. Laboucherd had shaken her confidence. Maddy threw the letter away, and never wrote back.

Aunt Bernice did not offer them any significant financial assistance. She was extremely displeased with Maddy for ignoring her advice about Brad, and doubly so when she quit music school. Given her displeasure, she did not feel obligated to soften the harsher edges of the new life her niece had created for herself. Unlike Brad's parents, who until he was twenty-five had always tried to protect him from the adverse consequences that his rebellious nature brought his way, Bernice believed that consequences built character. She wished the newlyweds well, and gave them one nice check as a wedding present, but other than that, she left them to their own devices.

Besides, she and Archie were busy themselves. Mason Industries was at the forefront of the electrical engineering industry. There were contracts with the defense industry, contracts with the budding airline industry, and contracts with General Electric. There were even plans on the table to take the company public. Bernice was busier, and she and Archie were richer, than ever before. She missed Maddy. She was disappointed in her. But, as usual, her work came before everything else.

Katherine came to visit at Christmas. She took in the tiny, shabby apartment, the skinny, half-decorated Christmas tree, the medical books piled up everywhere.

"Well. Cute place. Is Brad joining us for dinner?"

"No, he's doing an obstetrics rotation, and won't be home until sometime tomorrow, having delivered a few babies of various colors, shapes, and sizes, all in time for Christmas."

"Good. So we can talk."

"Would you mind if we finished decorating the tree while we chat? I wanted to finish it last night, but Brad was so tired."

"Sure, if you tell me where you want things to go. I have no eye, as you remember, for this sort of thing. I can plant punctuation marks in a paragraph much more easily than I can discern discordant decorations awkwardly placed on a Christmas tree."

"Okay, okay, Miss Pulitzer. You just sit there, unwrap and hand me things. I'll decorate the tree."

"Good." They worked quietly for a while. Maddy started to hum.

That was all the room Katherine needed.

"Maddy, I don't get it. I've known you since we were kids, and I've always felt that I was one step away from knowing who you really are. Like some part of you was all locked up. I just figured it was on account of your parents. That would've been tough on anybody. But when I heard you at your first recital, two years ago,

I knew what I'd missed. Behind all that sweetness—which believe me, I envied—there was this explosive power. When you finally let it out you were happier than I'd ever seen you before. And then, it seemed like, just when you were on the path to getting what you wanted, you got spooked, and settled instead for what you thought you *should* want."

"That's not fair," Maddy interrupted hotly. "Don't criticize something just because you don't understand it. We can't all be globe-trotting career girls, you know. I love Brad and I'm proud to be his wife. He's kind, and handsome, and intelligent—"

"And arrogant."

"Katherine!"

"Come on, Maddy. Don't ask me to pretend otherwise. Anyone who's been telling his parents where to get off as long as he has suffers from a big, fat arrogant streak. Now he's married you, just to piss them off some more. Didn't you ever worry that his wanting to marry you had as much to do with how he felt about *them* as how he felt about *you?*"

"How *dare* you suggest that Brad doesn't really love me!" Maddy was furious at Katherine for conjuring up the ugly question that sometimes slithered like a poisonous snake out of the darkest corner of Maddy's own mind. Why did Brad marry her? Why had she married him? Go away, questions. Go away, snakes. Go away Katherine, if necessary.

Maddy turned to the tree, climbed up on a step ladder, and busied herself with the ornaments, trying to control her rage. She'd felt this kind of anger only once before, on the day she'd last seen her father. She was afraid that if she didn't calm down, she could, and would, throw Katherine out of the house.

"You're just jealous, Katherine," Maddy finally blurted out, on the verge of angry tears. "You're just jealous because you're afraid you won't ever have what Brad and I share."

"Think that if you want to, Maddy. But since I don't understand it, I'm not sure how I'm supposed to be jealous of it. I'd just like to see you save a part of your life for yourself. Maybe you don't want to do the famous concert pianist routine. But why do you have to give up your music altogether?"

"Oh, now you sound just like my aunt! I can't have that and this too, Katherine, for reasons... reasons that I can't explain."

"Can't or won't."

"As you like."

"Look, Maddy, I didn't come up here to make you mad or ruin your Christmas. I just... I don't know..."

"You just wanted to try out a little of your psychology training on an interesting subject. Well, don't bother, Katherine. I'm fine. I'm happy, and I'm not crazy. Believe me or don't."

"Okay, okay, I'm sorry. I won't bring it up again." The two worked in silence for a while, both uncomfortable with the tension their discussion had created. Just when Maddy thought the argument had blown over, Katherine asked a question that almost made her fall off the ladder.

"Listen, you haven't, by any chance, heard anything from our old neighbor, Gene Mandretti, have you?"

Maddy felt her cheeks flush. She kept her back turned as she replied. "No, no, I haven't. Why?"

"Because he came to find you, you know, the night you eloped. I showed him your note. It was kind of frightening, Maddy. He struck me as, well, dangerous."

"Don't be ridiculous. If he did have some feelings for me, he kept them to himself. And he hasn't contacted me at all." Her anger evaporated. She stepped back down to the floor. She felt sick. But it was true. Gene had not contacted her at all. She had walked out of his life and he had let her leave, without a protest. Good. Good. That's what she'd wanted. This is what she wanted. Brad and a calm, well-ordered life. Happiness.

"Okay, okay. Good. Good," Katherine was saying, obviously relieved by Maddy's confirmation. She stepped closer to her friend.

"Well. I've spoken my piece. No more bad behavior. I promise. Need some help with those lights?"

Katherine's smile helped clear the air. It always had.

In the spring, Maddy and Brad got the news they had been waiting for. Brad had been accepted at Stanford for his residency. He was on his way to becoming a surgeon.

"Wait until you see it, Maddy. Palo Alto is okay but you'll love San Francisco. It's a lot like Boston, only prettier."

"Prettier than Boston?" laughed Maddy, taking a sip of some rather inexpensive champagne.

"Oh, it's a wonderful place. You really will love it. We'll have dinner on the water."

"On a resident's salary?"

"Well, I won't be a resident forever."

"Thank goodness."

That night in bed he nuzzled her neck. She responded as well as she could. He never seemed to expect much from her.

When he reached for a condom from the top drawer of the nightstand, Maddy reached over and put her hand on his wrist, to stop him. She did not have to explain.

"We have to think responsibly," he said quietly.

"But, we're secure now. You'll be finished, and we can go to California, and—"

"It won't be so easy, Maddy. I won't get my trust money until I finish my residency, and then I'll want to make sure I'm settled in my practice. We have time. We're young. We can, and should, wait."

Maddy stifled her disappointment, but her thoughts drifted as he made love to her. She felt as if her body and mind had separated and she was hovering above the bed, watching two people from whom she was totally disconnected. She thought about her job, and what she'd sold that day, and about the clearance sale inventory, and what she could possibly get Brad for his birthday. She kept her mind full, until finally she felt safe. Safe from thoughts of Gene.

⊙╬⊚

Brad was right. Maddy liked Palo Alto, and she loved San Francisco. She made friends with the wives of some of the other residents, and hid the pangs of envy that struck her when, one by one, they each got pregnant. Aunt Bernice even came out to visit once and tried to seem positive, although not much good could be said about their tiny apartment.

When the ordeal of his residency was over, Brad was offered a position at the hospital in San Francisco. He wired to Boston for his long-awaited trust payments, and bought a beautiful house overlooking the bay. And on the day he passed his medical boards, Brad kept the condom in the drawer.

But no babies came. And so Maddy waited.

Gradually Maddy began to fill the emptiness of her life with small rituals. It began in simple ways; she always put the coffee on before heading down the driveway to pick up the newspaper. She always brushed her teeth before brushing her hair. She always went to the grocery store on the same day every week, and went down each aisle, from right to left, pausing to make sure she did not need anything else before moving on to the next one. She had the car washed on Thursday afternoon, and had her hair done on Friday morning. The strictness with which she adhered to her small routines helped numb her mind and constrict her emotions. It made the wait for a baby bearable.

For her twenty-fifth birthday, Bradley surprised Maddy with a piano. It was a small, Baldwin baby grand. Maddy found she could play, when requested, without any serious emotional turmoil. She limited herself to cheerful contemporary songs, and always played using sheet music. Her strategy had worked. She'd put the genie back into the bottle.

And still, no babies came. The lack of children began as a small absence, like the missing piece of a jigsaw puzzle. But over the years it grew, until it was a great, unmentionable gulf that lay between them. And they each wondered, at times, if they recognized the person across the abyss.

CHAPTER 22

THE SNAKE

୧᠊ᢩᢣᢣᢩᠣ

SAN FRANCISCO, 1960

Maddy walked through the tall, colorful archway marking
the official entrance of Chinatown and was instantly transported
from the lofty ambiance of San Francisco to the frenzied, crowded
streets of her childhood. Men stood in doorways or squatted in
corners, swapping stories, spitting, smoking, playing cards. She
smelled fish and ginger, garlic and incense, admired the trium-
phant colors of ravishing silks, and heard the incomprehensible but
familiar sounds of Chinese voices scolding, laughing, and cajoling.
This chaotic, noisy place was her refuge. She could step through
the archway and relive the few pleasant childhood memories she
had, brought back by the sights and sounds and smells of Chinatown.

   She headed toward an alchemist's shop. Hundreds of drawers,
each marked with unintelligible Chinese characters, were filled
with unimaginably exotic ingredients, each used by the oriental
pharmacist to ward off evils ranging from warts to lung disease.
They contained powders that fought impotence, snake blood that
cured cancer, pollens to help with liver ailments, and the roots of
plants that produced a tea guaranteed to bring forth healthy sons
from a barren womb.

On more than one occasion Maddy had succumbed to temptation and brought home an ancient cure purported to enhance fertility, knowing her determination would turn into a source of ridicule if Brad discovered that she gave a second's thought to such nonsense. But the unfailing faith of the Chinese was sometimes persuasive where Western science had not yielded a solution, and she found herself drawn back to the mystical ways of the Orient.

"The two of you together just present an awkward combination. Irregular ovulation and a slightly low sperm count which, when combined, makes things a little more difficult but not impossible. Just keep trying," was the verdict of the fertility specialist she'd finally persuaded Brad to consult. After that, their lovemaking, which had never been inspired, turned into an agonizing chore.

Then Maddy turned thirty and, frightened by the possibility of a childless future, she raised the possibility of adoption. He hadn't just refused; he'd acted as if she'd accused him of committing a crime, and barely spoke to her for two weeks.

She did not bring it up again.

Maddy walked inside the small shop and was surprised to find another non-oriental customer inside. The few white people she saw wandering around Chinatown were generally tourists. They gazed around with a combination of curiosity and badly concealed disgust, taking pictures of the strange vulgarities like whole-roasted ducks hanging in the store windows, and curbside cooks serving boiled dumplings to men who squatted in place and gobbled them down using chopsticks. Tourists were careful not to touch anything that might be home to a wayward microbe.

This woman was in the shop to do business, and she wasn't being pleasant about it. She was yelling at the proprietor, who withstood the woman's verbal onslaught with indissoluble dignity.

But that voice. Although deepened with age and dried out by cigarettes, Maddy still recognized that voice.

"Amelia?" The question escaped like an involuntary reflex. The woman turned.

Her hair was too blond, and her makeup too loud. Her narrow face was lined, her once-luminous skin now sallow, but her eyes still held the sarcastic, calculating expression that had tormented Maddy as a child.

Amelia's penciled-on eyebrows drew closer together. "Martha? Jesus Bloody Christ. You're supposed to be dead!"

Walk out now, you idiot. You have nothing to say her. Let her think that you're your mother's ghost.

Maddy didn't move. Amelia took a step closer. "Well I'll be damned. It's you." She looked Maddy over from head to toe. "Of course. Martha would be shriveled up like me by now. Quite the resemblance, though. Imagine two old friends like us running into each other in a place like this. How's your darling father?"

"He's… dead."

"Is that so? Well, we'll all be dead soon enough." She turned back to the alchemist, who was measuring a beige powder into a small box. "You telephone me when you get more, you understand? I'll pay double." She brushed past Maddy and left.

Maddy did not move. *Why did you lie to her? You don't know that he's dead.* The proprietor hurried over to her.

"You okay, Miss?"

She nodded her head. "Just surprised. She was someone I knew… a long time ago."

"You very much younger. You daughter-in-law, maybe? Maybe her son die in war, make you widow? Very sad."

"No. Nothing like that." *She's the wicked stepmother. From a land far, far away.*

To her consternation he reached for her wrist and felt her pulse. "You sit down. Drink water. Rest a moment. Big shock."

He pulled her over to a narrow wooden chair. Maddy sat down. It was then she realized that her limbs were trembling. She took the water offered her and drank it quickly.

"There, better now, Miss?"

"Yes, thank you. I'll go now."

"You not come in to buy something? Again something to help babies grow? It not work last time?"

Maddy's stomach lurched. "No, it didn't work. I have to leave now. I have to get home."

"Wait a moment more. Have some tea."

"No, thank you." *Amelia. How long had she been in San Francisco? What was she doing in this place?*

"Why was that woman so angry? What did she want?"

The man shrugged. "She is very bad sick. Want special Chinese medicine, very expensive, very hard to get. But no medicine can help. She rotting from inside."

"She's dying?"

He nodded. "Soon."

Amelia, dead. What secrets would she take with her? There was so much that Maddy didn't know, so many pieces missing. Would knowing make any difference? Would it help her hide from the noise of the echoes that the emptiness inside her created?

Maddy stood up. "Thank you. I feel much better now. Do you think… could you please give me that woman's phone number? She's… well… we're sort of distantly related."

Mr. Tang looked skeptical. "Mrs. Langtry? She relative of yours?"

"In a way, yes. I should have asked for her number before she left. I was just so surprised to see her."

The Chinese gentleman made his way slowly over to the counter and copied a number on a piece of paper. "Be careful," he warned as he handed it to Maddy. "Fang of dying snake still carry poison."

❦

Amelia glanced down at the diamond ring on her left hand. Poor Richard had been so generous. So shy. So trusting. So homely. And so pathetically unlucky.

Amelia Langtry, widow of Reggie Simmons and ex-wife of Leo Hoffman, married her third and final husband, Richard Langtry, in December of 1943. Richard met Amelia while he was waiting to be shipped out. Social barriers that might have otherwise deterred their courtship were eradicated by the war. They were married within two weeks.

Then Richard died, and she was once again a widow. Amelia found it laughingly ironic that she had a kamikaze pilot to thank for her freedom, although it was an observation she kept to herself. Luckily for Amelia, her aged in-laws liked her. They liked her very much. She lived with them on their estate in Connecticut while Richard was away at war, then stayed on after they received the news of his death, consoling them over the loss of their only son. The elderly Langtrys were at the age in life when they believed what they wanted to believe.

Within five years of their son's death they both passed away. The bulk of the estate went to nieces and nephews. But Amelia was, as the Langtry family lawyer had explained, "quite well taken care of."

She traveled. She went to Europe and viewed with disappointment the remains of a war-ravaged continent. She went to Mexico, Brazil, Vancouver, Saratoga, and Hawaii. She lived well, and took a lover only when she wanted one. She was not a dance-hall girl now. She could look back on the flophouses, the unsatisfying sex, the abortion, and the Pacific dance tour that ended in Shanghai as if she were watching a movie starring someone else.

When the doctors in New York told her how really ill she was, she came back to San Francisco, where she'd twice managed to turn her luck around. She didn't believe what the doctors told her. No one could tell *her* anything about her chances of survival. She'd beaten those odds long ago.

Amelia looked down at her lap. She'd bunched up her napkin into a tight little wad. Why had she agreed to see Madeleine, for Chrissake? What could she have to say that Amelia could possibly want to hear? She wasn't going to sit still for any goddamn tongue-lashing, that was certain. And she hadn't waited for the little snit to ambush her, either. She'd gathered all the ammunition she might need before agreeing to meet her former step-daughter. *Just tell me what happened to him.* Amelia drained her martini and waved the waiter over to order a second.

Maddy walked into the restaurant and saw Amelia talking to the waiter. The determination she'd felt just seconds before dissipated with every step she took toward the table. *What were you thinking, you idiot? What makes you think she would ever tell you the truth about anything? Leave before she sees you—*

Too late. Madeleine started to raise her hand in greeting, felt foolish, and touched it to her small hat instead, needlessly checking the security of its position. *Go on. This was your idea.* She moved to the table and slid in across from Amelia.

"Thank you for coming."

Amelia ignored this. "I can't imagine we'll be sharing a meal, so you may as well have a drink. I can recommend the martinis."

"I don't really drink very much."

"Suit yourself." The waiter brought Amelia's drink. Maddy ordered a soft drink. Amelia raised her glass. Her hand was shaking slightly. "You said all you wanted was to ask me a couple of questions. I'll answer yours if you answer mine. First. Respect for your elders and all that crap."

She's nervous? Maddy had not expected that. Not from Amelia.

"What do you want to know?"

"What happened to him?"

Him. Her father. Of course. "I don't know. I wasn't completely truthful when I saw you in that shop. He might be dead. But maybe not. I haven't seen him in fifteen years."

"Oh. And here I thought you were going to tell me some gruesome story about how heroically your father died in the war."

What was behind that sarcasm? Curiosity? Relief? "No, he didn't die in the war. I saw him once, briefly, when he got back from Europe. But that was all."

"Don't tell me he left you all alone? Didn't stick around to play with his grandchildren, any of that?"

"Does that surprise you?"

"No." She reached into her purse for a cigarette, and lit it before she spoke again.

"Your turn, my dear. But don't make things difficult for me, or for yourself."

"I just want to know why things happened the way they did. When you took me with you to New York."

"Christ, as if I knew the answer to all that. Look, your father didn't treat me any better than he did you. I tried to do him a favor. Get him out of Shanghai before the whole place blew up and the Japanese shot whoever was left moving just for the hell of it. Then he dumps you on me and stays put. I never knew why, either."

"What do you mean, do him a favor? I thought you—I thought you and my father were—"

Amelia blew out a cloud of smoke with a derisive snort. "Were what? Madly in love? Planning to run away together the moment your mother died? No. He slept with me to get some information he needed about my husband's business, then politely excused himself from my bed. Which in those days was not the usual treatment I received."

"Then why did you take me with you?"

Something approaching regret deepened the wrinkles on Amelia's face, and doused the bitterness in her eyes, giving Maddy a glimpse of the worn-out, dying woman she was. The Amelia she knew flashed back before Maddy could feel any sympathy.

"You should just be glad that I did. I did you a favor, too. You could've been dead before you were ten."

I was. I am. Maddy stood up to leave. "Amelia, you never did me any favors."

"Well, I'm about to do one for you now. Your husband is cheating on you."

CHAPTER 23

THE ACCUSED

"A few years ago someone hired a private detective to find out what you were up to. The guy was very good at his job. He found me while I was still in New York. He wouldn't tell me who was paying him, and I didn't tell him much, but he left me his card. I called him right after you called me. For the right price he was willing to come out to San Francisco and prepare a quick update for me on the life of Madeleine Hoffman Gordon. Everyone's secrets are for sale, Maddy. You're in a dead marriage, living with your husband in an empty space. A wasteland. Now you have a reason to get out. Start over."

"You're lying. I'm leaving."

"Ask him yourself. Here's his card. I told him to talk to you."

She took it.

Maddy walked out of the restaurant, barely conscious of what she was doing or where she was going. She was four blocks away before she remembered that she'd parked her car with the restaurant valet. She walked back and looked in her purse for her ticket. It was in her wallet next to the card Amelia had given her. She threw the card in a wastebasket on the corner and went to retrieve her car.

Lies. She's never told you anything but lies. Maddy drove back to the intersection where she'd thrown the card away and with a wild squeal of her brakes stopped her car at the curb, jumped out with the engine running and, watched by a group of startled pedestrians waiting to cross the street, dug the card out again. Back in the car she tossed the card on the seat next to her and peeled off her gloves, now soiled, before roaring off again.

All surgeons had odd hours when they were on call. Maddy had never challenged him about who was on the phone, where he was going, or who he was with.

Living side by side in an empty space. What would Amelia know about marriage? About making a life with someone? *No one hired an investigator.* Dying snakes still have fangs, all right. She never should have met with that woman. *I hope you die soon, Amelia, and very, very painfully.*

She found herself driving outside the city, on a road that ran along the cliffs of San Francisco Bay. She pulled into an area carved out for motorists to stop and enjoy the view, cut the engine, and picked up the card again. Richard Bates. He would just tell her whatever Amelia had paid him to say. There was no point in calling him.

Maddy got out of the car with the card in her hand. A stiff breeze threatened to blow her hat away, so she removed it. She walked to the railing at the edge of the cliff, hat in one hand, the business card and a few hair pins in the other. The ocean was gray. Gray and empty.

She opened her hand. The hairpins fell to the ground. The wind caught the card. She watched as it moved, flipping and twisting, taunting her with its macabre dance before it finally reached the water, looking like nothing more than a flicker of foam by the time it vanished into the white-tipped waves.

❦

Please be there, Brad. Please be there.

"I'm sorry, Dr. Gordon is not on call tonight. Would you like me to leave a message? He'll be back in for his rounds in the morning."

"No, I'm sorry… I must have misunderstood. Never mind."

❧

She waited, awake and alone in the darkness of their bedroom, for him to come home. When she heard him come in the front door she almost went downstairs to confront him, but her limbs were locked in place. *You could just ignore this. Women do. Lots of women do.* She could just wait. It didn't mean that he would leave. Whatever was going on could blow over, if she just waited and said nothing.

He entered the room and headed over to the sitting area where Maddy had, as usual, laid out his pajamas and left a small light on for him so he could throw his clothes over a chair, dress, and then find his way to bed. She watched as he took off his jacket, then his tie. *Had he undressed just like that earlier tonight?*

She sat up and flipped on the overhead light.

"Who is she, Brad?"

He blinked at her, surprised. "Are you still awake?"

"Who is she?"

She could tell by the look on his face that he'd heard her the second time. "What are you talking about?"

"The woman you're sleeping with."

"What the *hell* are you talking about?"

What had she expected? An admission? An apology? Not this. Not anger. Self-doubt flooded Maddy's mind. Was she wrong? Had she fallen into some trap Amelia laid for her?

No. She knew. She'd seen the truth in his eyes before he'd hidden it behind his indignation. She *knew.*

"You weren't on call tonight. I called the hospital."

"For God's sake, Maddy! I took Bill's shift. He probably just forgot to change the damn list. What's gotten into you?" He stalked into the bathroom. Maddy got up and followed him.

"Who is she, Brad?"

He ignored her and went to the sink, splashed water on his face, grabbed a towel, rubbed his face for longer than it took to dry it, then flung the towel into the sink before turning to her.

"Do you have any idea what it's like for a man to feel competent everywhere but in his own bed?"

Maddy bit back the words that sprang into her mind. *Do you have any idea what it feels like to never feel competent at anything?* She knew that tears were pouring down her face but could not feel them. Her vision blurred and she reached for the doorjamb to steady herself. The world had split open again, leaving her no safe place to stand.

"It doesn't matter," she whispered, more to herself than to her husband. Nothing mattered. Nothing at all.

"Doesn't matter? What wonderful words of wisdom. Let me ask you this, Maddy. Were you a virgin when you married me?"

The question caught her completely off guard. A hot blush of shame flooded both cheeks. She stumbled out of the room as Brad's vindictive words sliced through her.

"I suppose you are going to tell me it doesn't matter. Now, after nearly ten years of wedded bliss, when you've been such a good little wife. Did you think I wouldn't *notice* that you didn't bleed, Maddy? Of course I noticed. But I loved you. God, how I loved you. Why did *you* marry *me,* Maddy? What were you running away from?"

He was shouting now. Maddy reached blindly for her chest of drawers and started throwing clothes on the bed. He followed behind her. "You know the worst of it? My parents were right. 'Marrying a woman who does not come from a good family is like taking a time bomb to your bed, son!'" Brad continued, mocking the stern, pompous tone of his father's voice, "'Sooner or later, that lack of a pedigree will explode and you'll be hoisted on your own petard.'"

Maddy collapsed onto the floor and put her hands over her ears. Brad stood over her, breathing hard. "Her name is Caroline," he finally said, and then left.

By the next morning Maddy was on a Pan Am flight bound for New York.

CHAPTER 24

THE SENTRY

Bernice met Maddy at the gate. It had been nearly a year since they'd seen each other. Bernice looked stern. Unchanged. Just what Maddy needed to see.

"Aunt Bernice, thank you so much for coming to meet me."

"Well, this is a bit unusual, Madeleine. Can you give me more details about your sudden decision to come to New York?"

"Of course. Once we're in the car, if you don't mind."

It did not take more than a few moments to collect Maddy's bags. There was no driver to assist them. She made no comment. She had never quite figured out the pattern behind her aunt's small economies, although she was sure there was one.

"Ready for dinner?" Bernice asked as she started the car.

"No, thank you. I'm really not very hungry."

"Well, I've taken a room for you at the Plaza. I assumed you'd have people to see, and I'm sure you don't want to be stuck all the way out in New Jersey. Traffic in and out of the city is getting worse and worse. Thank goodness I seldom need to go in. Archie doesn't mind all the socializing. I abhor it."

Despite her weariness, Maddy had to smile. She could imagine her uncle happily wining and dining his biggest clients, unencumbered by the restraining effect of Bernice's disapproval of his expanding expense account, and the expanding waistline that went with it. What a funny pair they were. Archie, having lived to make a fortune, now relished spending it. Bernice often behaved as if the money didn't exist.

Maddy pulled herself back to the conversation. "Katherine is in London. I suppose I should drop in on Mrs. O'Connor."

"I'm sure she would love to see you. Now, what's this all about?"

Maddy looked over at her aunt, and had the sense that the car had stretched, that her aunt was not next to her but hundreds of feet away, her face small and her voice faint. What could she say to her? "I'm afraid that Brad has found me something of an inconvenience as of late."

"What? How ludicrous. You are a terribly supportive wife. Ridiculously so."

"I'm not sure he feels that way. I'm not sure I… we needed a break from each other."

"I see," Bernice responded, giving Maddy no more clues about what she really thought. For once Maddy was grateful that intimacy did not come naturally to her aunt. She didn't really want to discuss what had happened. Not yet.

"Well then, why don't you go see Katherine? Take the *Queen Elizabeth*. She's in port, leaving day after tomorrow. I'll be no comfort. I'm up to my eyelids in conductivity formulas. Don't worry about the ticket. I think I owe you a birthday present, anyway."

"I'm not sure I'm in the mood for a trip right now."

"Think about it. Where shall we stop for dinner?"

When Bernice had what she thought was a good idea, she seldom let go of it. Dinner became an hour-long opportunity for her to persuade Maddy to visit Katherine. The trip would give Madeleine a chance to sort herself out, she said. A change of scenery would be good for her. "Just call me tomorrow, after you've slept on the idea. I'll make all the arrangements."

The next morning Maddy woke with the odd sensation that she was back in her old home, in Shanghai. As she pushed away the bedclothes the weight of her pain hit her. She was not home: not in Shanghai, not at her aunt's in New Jersey, not in her house in San Francisco. She was alone. Once again no one wanted her.

She snatched the phone off the nightstand and asked to be connected to London. Katherine was not in her room. Maddy left a message with the desk clerk. "Coming on the *QE*. See you in five days." She didn't care if it was a good time for Katherine to have a visitor.

By the end of the day Maddy had seen the inside of virtually every exclusive shop within a six-block radius of the Plaza. She'd bought everything she needed for an ocean voyage and sent all her packages straight to her suite. Bernice and Archie were to meet her for lunch, the next day, before she sailed, but she was on her own tonight. She should go get some rest. Or pop in and see Mrs. O'Connor.

But there was something she needed to do before she left Manhattan.

She flagged down a cab driver and gave him the address, then sat in silence as they made the trip uptown, fighting the remains of rush hour traffic.

There it was. The apartment building where she and Katherine had lived together a lifetime ago. It looked just the same.

The double glass door to the lobby was propped open, undoubtedly so the doorman could enjoy some of the cool evening air. She crossed the street and peeked in.

Marty looked up.

"Well, if it ain't Miss Maddy Hoffman. What are ya doin' back in da ol' neighbahood?" he grinned.

She jumped back, startled. "Marty! I can't believe that you're still here. Or that you remember me."

"Oh, I don't forget the pretty ones! You and dat liddle Irish lady—da redhead."

"Katherine. Katherine O'Connor."

"Yeah! You was friends wit da boss, too, which neva hoits."

Maddy's heart hurtled into her stomach. Her mouth went dry. "The boss?"

"Yeah! Gene Mandretti. He owns da place, now. 'Dis buildin' and who knows what else. So, what brings ya back? If ya lookin' t'catch da boss, he lives out on Long Island now, but he still comes in occasionally. I could give him a message."

"No, thank you. I'm sure he wouldn't remember me. And besides, I'm not going to be in town long. I'm leaving for London on the Queen Elizabeth tomorrow."

"No kiddin'? Life's been treatin' you okay, huh?"

Maddy nodded, anxious to retreat. Why had she come here? What was she thinking?

"So, goodbye. Good seeing you, Marty."

"Right. You still see da redhead?"

"Yes."

"Tell her hi from me. Marty da doorman. She may rememba me."

"I'm sure she will. Goodnight." She escaped.

That night, Maddy did something she had never done before, ever in her life. She bought a bottle of gin at a package store. Once in her room she ordered a pitcher of lemonade from room service. And she proceeded to sit alone in her room, and get very, very drunk.

Around midnight Gene Mandretti walked into the lobby of the apartment building where Marty stood guard.

"Evenin' Mr. Mandretti, sir," said Marty, with his usual chatty chipperness. "Saw an' old friend a' yours around da place today."

"Oh yeah? Who's that?" answered Gene, not really interested, but always careful.

"That cute little brunette what usta live here one summer, with her Irish friend. Maddy Hoffman. You rememba her?"

The elevator bell rang. The door opened. Gene did not move. The door closed. The elevator disappeared back upstairs.

Gene turned to Marty. "No kidding. You sure about this?"

"How could I not be sure? She's the only lady you ever paid me to keep tabs on. She just comes walkin' right in, pretty as you please. Prettier, even. She's got more a' da good stuff now, if you'll pardon my makin' such an' observation."

"Where is she?"

"Funny you should ask me dat, Mr. Mandretti. I just happened t' get her t'tell me dat she's goin' t' London, tomorra, on da big *QE*. Funny, ain't it? Almost ten years ago, exact, since she lived here."

"Yeah. Did she mention me?"

"Oh, yessir. Well, I did. She allowed as how you probably wouldn't rememba her. No message or nothin.'"

"Yeah. Well. Thanks, Marty. It's always nice to see an old friend. Too bad I missed her." He returned to the elevator.

"Yeah. Too bad. Well. G'night."

"Goodnight."

Gene Mandretti rode the elevator up to the penthouse. He unlocked the door, tossed his jacket over a chair, and picked up the phone.

"Hi, Tina. Yeah, I know it's late. I'm sorry. Listen. We've had an interesting opportunity develop… I know you hate it when I say that… I'm afraid it may mean travel. London. No, no, I'm sorry. This time you can't come. It's all business, not like the trip to Vegas. I'm leaving tomorrow. Yes, tomorrow. I'm not sure how long I'll be gone… no more than a couple of weeks. I'll come in tomorrow morning for breakfast. Have Max get a suitcase ready—tell him some black tie and business—he'll know what to pack. I'm sorry, sweetheart. Yeah. I love you too. Kiss the kids for me. I'll see you in the morning."

He dropped the phone back on the hook. He had some business in London to take care of, all right. Some unfinished business.

CHAPTER 25

THE PASSENGER

৹ᴖᴧᴖ৹

Maddy took a long, slow sip of her ginger ale, relieved that her stomach had finally stopped fighting back. Her headache was gone. The wobbly feeling in her legs had disappeared. She would live after all.

"Never, never again," she said out loud to herself, her voice lost in the strong breeze that blew along the deck as the mighty ocean liner churned through the Atlantic. Lunch with her aunt and uncle had been one of the worst ordeals of her life. Not having any experience with hangovers, she made a terrible choice of what to eat. Her eggs Benedict stayed put for barely ten minutes before her gin-ravaged tummy revolted, and Maddy subsequently spent a good part of the meal in the ladies room.

She hid in her cabin during the bon voyage festivities, trying to avoid the noise and commotion that only made her head pound more. It was well past seven o'clock when she finally emerged, thankful for the calm seas, and the polite, experienced valet who was ready with advice for what he assumed was seasickness. "Please, step out and allow me to unpack your things. You should go get a little fresh air. Keep your eyes on the horizon. That will help," he had suggested, and the therapy seemed to work.

"I never want to taste gin again. Or lemonade. Uggh. Pity. I like lemonade," Maddy told the stars. Perhaps by the time the late supper was served she would feel like eating something. Some bread, maybe. A little soup. Not a true challenge for the Queen's chef who, it was said, could produce virtually any dish requested by a passenger within twenty-four hours.

Feeling decent for the first time since she had come aboard, Maddy went for an exploratory tour of the ship. The *Queen Elizabeth* was the biggest cruise ship in the world, proclaimed the brochure Maddy picked up in the lobby. Not a penny had been spared in refurbishing her majesty once her days as a troop transport ship came to an end. The maple wood paneling in the lounge was restored, and all of the ship's brass fittings replaced, and her original art deco murals repainted. There were 2,000 new carpets, 1,200 plants, 700 clocks, and 30,000 lamps. She was truly a floating palace.

Maddy spent well over an hour roaming, then decided she was hungry enough to find some food, and sufficiently recovered to bear the company of her fellow travelers. She made her way back to her stateroom, and was amazed to see a large vase of yellow roses glorifying the vanity.

"How thoughtful," she said to herself, assuming the bouquet came from her aunt and uncle. But it was so unlike Bernice to send roses. Roses didn't last more than a few days. For that reason Bernice, who rarely sent anyone flowers, preferred, when she did, to send lilies: sturdy flowers that "enabled one to get one's money's worth."

Maddy gently dug around in the bouquet, careful not to prick herself, looking for a card. Nothing. She picked up the phone and dialed the ship's florist.

"Hello, this is Mrs. Gordon in suite twelve. I have some beautiful flowers here, with no card. Could you please tell me who sent them?"

"Just a moment, Madame." He was back in a flash.

"Yes, Madame. Here it is. Ah, I'm so sorry. A fellow passenger sent you the roses, and the sender asked to remain anonymous."

"A passenger? Now? On the ship? There must be a mistake. I don't know anyone on board… I don't think."

"Well, it is a large ship. Would you like the flowers removed?"

"No. No, thank you. They are lovely. Thank you for your help."

"My pleasure. At your service. Goodnight."

Maddy stared at the flowers as if her careful scrutiny would force them to disclose the identity of the sender. Did she really know someone on board?

She peeled off her suit and donned a simple black evening gown, for dinner on the Queen was strictly black tie. On an impulse she gathered her hair up into a twist. The style exposed the smooth, white skin of her neck, making her feel elegant and feminine. Her mirror image registered her approval, and she went in search of supper.

The *maitre d'hotel* greeted her with cordial civility at the door to the dining room.

"Ah, yes. Mrs. Gordon," he repeated after she gave him her name, "Your table is ready. Please, this way, Madame."

Politely obedient, Maddy followed the tuxedo-clad host to a small table for two, set for an elaborate supper. A bottle of champagne sat chilling in a stand beside the table, and two crystal flutes waited to be filled.

"No, excuse me, there's been a mistake."

"Oh? I beg your pardon. This table does not suit you?"

"No, it's lovely. It's just that, I'm sure that I'm at a group table, and I didn't order any champagne."

"That is not a problem. May I?" He pulled out a chair. Hesitant, she sat down.

"Your companion will join you momentarily, Mrs. Gordon. I need only notify him that you are here."

"But I'm not expecting—" Could it be that Brad had found out that she was traveling on the Queen? Could he have followed her? Did he think their quarrel would end so easily?

"Thank you," she said, switching thoughts in mid-sentence. Maddy was surprised at her own mixed emotions. Did she even want to see her husband? Could she forgive him? What could she tell him about her past? And why did he bring it up now, after all this time? If he would only agree to adopt a child…

She was rehearsing their conversation in her head when she heard a voice behind her.

"Hello, Angel."

Maddy took in two huge gulps of air. She could not turn around.

Yellow roses. Yellow roses. Only one man in her life had ever given her yellow roses.

She felt his lips touch her neck, briefly. A shiver ran through the length of her body.

He sat down across the table from her. Ten years had added a touch of fullness to his face, and a few small lines had appeared around the corners of his eyes, but the rest remained unchanged.

Maddy put her hand to the bodice of her dress to reassure herself that she was not as naked as she felt. "Oh, my God. Gene, what are you doing here?"

"Don't you think that's a rather silly question?" He gave her a smile that was not a smile at all.

"But how—why—"

"You were kind enough to tell Marty how to find you. Ten years is a long time to wait, Maddy. But I can see you were worth waiting for. You're even more beautiful than you were the last time I saw you."

Maddy's senses stumbled through the flustered maze of her brain. She tried to say something. She tried to move back from the table. She tried to pull her eyes away from his gaze. She could do nothing.

"You can't do this," she finally whispered.

"Can't do what?" countered Gene amiably. "Can't meet an old friend for dinner? Can't offer a beautiful woman a glass of champagne?" He signaled to the waiter, who hurried over.

Maddy stayed silent while the waiter served their wine. Once their glasses were full, Gene lifted his.

"To you, Madeleine Hoffman, the most fantastic creature God ever placed on this earth." He took a sip. Maddy did not touch her glass.

"My name isn't Hoffman. It's Gordon. I'm married. You know that."

"Married?" Gene looked around, pretending to be shocked. "Where's your husband?"

"He's in—he's in London. He's waiting for me there. I'm going to meet him."

"You're lying, Maddy," Gene said, as if he were comforting a child. "He's in San Francisco."

"How did you—what makes you say that?!"

"Oh, Maddy. You didn't think I would let you just walk out of my life and disappear, did you? I've kept track of you over the years. And it's a simple call to the hospital to see if Dr. Gordon's on duty. Which he is. Unless he's cozying up to some nurse there."

"You're a bastard," Maddy hissed, and found the willpower to rise. He stood as well.

"Where are you going, Maddy? We're in the middle of the Atlantic Ocean."

"I'm going to whatever part of the ship you're not on. To my room."

She turned to flee. In two strides he was next to her. "I'm sorry if I upset you, Maddy," he said gently, holding on to her arm. "All I want is dinner and an explanation. Our last parting was rather sudden, don't you agree? I will make a scene, if that's what you want. But it would be easier if you would just, please, sit down and join me for dinner."

She shook her head adamantly.

He did not let go. Instead, he pulled her around to face him. He leaned down until his mouth was only inches from hers. "I love you, Maddy. I've loved you for ten years. I never thought I'd have this chance. There's no one in the world who wants you more than I do. No one." He released her.

She stood, mute, frozen. Fear, pain, and confusion danced across her face. Then she turned and walked away.

The knock came sometime after one o'clock. She had been telling herself for hours not to move, not to make a sound when it came. She closed her eyes and tried to will him away. After a moment, he knocked again.

"I'll just tell him to leave," she lied to herself, pulling on her long satin robe.

She opened the door and saw him, standing there, his pale blue eyes smoldering. He moved into the room.

"Gene, you can't—I just wanted—no, please—"

He held her face in his hands and kissed her under her eyes, next to her mouth, on her chin. His right hand went to her hair, and he tangled his fingers through the loose tresses.

"Tell me that you don't love me. Tell me that you never loved me," he whispered in her ear.

"I don't love you. I've never loved you," she pleaded, closing her eyes.

"You're lying, Maddy," he whispered again.

And then it was gone, everything was gone; the ocean and the ship and the stars were gone; Brad and Bernice and Katherine were gone. All of the pain was gone. There was no one, and nothing, anywhere, except Maddy and Gene.

CHAPTER 26

THE ADULTERESS

"Water, water everywhere," Maddy murmured as she stood on the deck and looked out over the endless acres of water. "It's like being in a different world. A water world."

Gene came up and stood close behind her.

"I don't want to talk," she said.

"I didn't ask you anything."

"I know. But you were thinking about it."

"About what?"

"About whether you could ask me now why I ran away, why I married Brad Gordon."

"That's right."

The morning sun had just crept over the horizon, painting the sea a pale blue-gray. The color of Gene's eyes. She turned and looked up into them.

"Are you hungry?" she asked.

"Not yet."

"Would you like some coffee?"

"You'll do anything to change the subject, won't you?"

She turned again to face the ocean. "Yes."

He wrapped his arms around her and let his chin rest on her shoulder. Maddy could not believe how comfortable she felt in his embrace.

"Angel, we don't have to talk at all. We can spend the next three days just the same way we spent last night."

"I'm not sure I could take three days like last night."

"Well, we could take little breaks for dining and dancing. Maybe even sleep a little."

The mention of the word set Maddy to yawning. "Sleep would be nice," she said. "Now that I've seen the sunrise."

"Your place or mine?"

"Mine. But alone. I won't get any sleep if you're there, too."

Leaning against him, she could feel his body tense, but he kept his tone light when he answered. "Very well, sleeping beauty. Since I know that you can't jump ship until we reach England, I'll risk letting you out of my sight, but only if you promise to meet me for lunch. You skipped out on me at dinner, remember."

She laughed, genuinely this time, and reached up behind her head to pat his cheek.

"Oh, I promise. I'll be famished by noon."

"Okay. I'll walk you back."

He kissed her at the door to her cabin, a long, deep kiss that was both possessive and reassuring. Once she was alone in her room, she touched her lips with her fingers, marveling at how long the sensation stayed with her. How could she feel so completely connected to someone she'd known for such a brief period of time, so long ago? Someone she really knew very little about. Someone she'd been sure was so absolutely wrong for her. And probably still was.

She knew that he'd reentered her life at the worst possible moment; she'd never felt more vulnerable. Lost, in the middle of the ocean, betrayed by the one man in her life she'd relied upon to take care of her—

Just as she'd been when she was seven years old.

"God, don't be so neurotic," she muttered, annoyed with herself for drawing the parallel. She needed some sleep.

Sleep came quickly, heavy and dreamless. When she woke up it was nearly noon. She took her time getting bathed and dressed, then rang for Gene.

"Ready for lunch?" she asked brightly.

"I'll meet you there," he answered.

During the meal they found an amazing number of amusing, meaningless things to talk about. Finally, once their solicitous waiter had brought them their coffee, Gene attempted to bring up the topic that Maddy had ducked earlier that morning.

"Are you ready to talk now?" he said quietly.

"Not really," she replied. "I don't know what explanation I can give you that would make any sense. At times the answer was so clear to me, and times, well, times when married to Brad it seemed as if I were living someone else's life, as if I had woken up in the wrong bed, in the wrong house, at the wrong time, in the wrong place. I don't know, Gene. I was scared, I guess. That's all I can say."

"I can understand that, Maddy. I've grown up a lot over the past ten years. It takes a while to realize how selfish you are when you're young. But I understand now, how you could have been… overwhelmed by what we'd experienced together, and how I must have scared you. I was pretty overwhelmed myself by the passion between us. I just handled it differently."

She looked down at her own cup, touched by his humility. *Passion*. That didn't begin to describe what it had been like. But last night had been… different. As if there might actually be something left of the two of them once the flame burned itself out. Maybe.

"So, what now?" she asked, looking down at her cup.

"Now, we spend three days making up for lost time. The rest can wait."

"Okay." She reached across the table for his hand. "The rest can wait."

They discovered that there was no better way to drop off the face of the planet, to live a separate life, to become a different person, in a different place, than on board an ocean-going cruise ship. Completely removed from the rest of the world, each day became a creature of their own invention: a fresh palette for the imagination. They spend many hours in bed. They ate many meals on the private balcony in Gene's stateroom. But they also tried badminton, bingo, and shuffleboard. Once Gene tried to show Maddy how to use a rifle to shoot the clay pigeons sent soaring off the rear deck by a uniformed steward, and to her astonishment she knocked two of the twenty she shot at out of the sky. They went to the ballroom to dance, holding each other close, swaying to the gentle rocking of the sea, or twirling to the pulsating sounds of the Cuban jazz quartet that cranked up in the cocktail lounge after eleven.

The weather held, and so did their good mood, until the morning they were due to arrive in Southampton. Then the clouds covered up the sun. The sea turned a brownish green. They went up on deck after breakfast, trying to find a place to themselves, away from all the other passengers vying with each other to be the first to spot the coast of England.

"So where do we start?" she asked finally, her tone of voice matching the downcast color of the day.

"Well, first, why don't you tell me why you're here without your husband."

"We had a fight."

"Okay."

"He wasn't getting what he wanted from our marriage. Perhaps we both went into it for the wrong reasons."

"And what would those have been?"

Maddy shrugged, without taking her eyes off the sea. "Why didn't you ever try to get in touch with me?" she asked at last.

He smiled ironically. "You mean, to try and persuade you to leave the man you married and come back to me? It was pride, at first. I guess you could say I wanted you on my own terms. I was young. I was selfish. So I sulked. Then, I eventually went on with my life."

"And I went on with mine. And now this happens." She turned and looked up at him. "So what now?"

He grasped her shoulders so she couldn't turn away from him again. "I know what I want. I want you back in my life. I don't ever want there to be a moment when I can't reach for you. But I'm married, Maddy. I'm married, I married into the family business, and I have two children."

Of course, of course he's married. You're married. Neither of us should be here. We never should have done this. Her stomach lurched in a way that had nothing to do with the movement of the ship.

"Gene, don't think you could have mentioned that three days ago?"

"Would it have mattered?"

Yes. No. I don't know. She couldn't answer. He released her, but his eyes stayed locked onto hers.

"You left me once. You can leave again. But I can't get a divorce."

Maddy felt piece by piece of her self shutting down in response to the pain shooting through her. She wobbled. Gene put his arms around her and held her close.

"Will you go back to him?" he whispered into her ear.

"I don't know."

"What if you couldn't? What if you couldn't go back?"

"I don't know. I don't know anything. I can't make sense of any of this."

"Can I see you in London?"

"No. No. This isn't... it isn't right, Gene."

He pulled away from her slightly and lifted her chin with his hand. "Please come back to me, Angel. I know you must think that refusing to get a divorce means that I don't love you enough, but maybe, if you give me a chance, you'll understand. Don't judge me by rules created for other people. Just believe that I love you."

Don't judge me. Her old piano teacher's scolding reverberated in her mind. *Artists are different. We have a different soul, a different spirit.* She shook her head, unable to do or say anything else. *No. It's a lie. Lies built on lies built on lies.*

Gene took out a handkerchief and tried to dry her eyes. She pushed his hand away.

He put his handkerchief back in his pocket and withdrew a slim velvet box. She did not make a move to accept it, so he opened it for her.

It was a choker, made of diamonds and emeralds, set to form a garland of roses. Even in the overcast light that surrounded them, the jewels in the necklace sparkled with their own brilliant fire.

"Take it, please. I want something of mine to be near you when you're away from me. Please."

"No."

He didn't argue any further, but he reached for her again. She rested her head on his chest, listening to the sound of his heart-beat, looking out over the water. They stood together for a long time, in just that position, and then, when the rest of the ship had begun the hurried drill that meant an imminent approach to shore, he released her. He handed her a slip of paper, on which he had written a telephone number.

"Call me when you get back to New York," he said simply. And he walked away.

Maddy was one of the last people off the ship, for she spent a good long time in her suite, sobbing, childishly wishing the voyage had never come to an end. At last, summoned by a fourth and rather forceful knock from the deck steward, she washed her face, put on some makeup and her sunglasses, and headed to where she hoped Katherine was waiting for her.

The sight of her old friend standing on the other side of the customs gate, waving and smiling like a cheerleader, set Maddy off again. Katherine left instructions for the luggage to be delivered and bundled Maddy off to the car. She chatted on as if Maddy were not crying her eyes out on the seat beside her; talking about London, about the historic sites they were passing, about the people with whom she worked at Reuters. By the time they reached the hotel, the elite Grosvenor House, Maddy had calmed down.

Katherine bustled her into the room, tipped the doorman, and then sat down in the overstuffed chair that filled one corner of the suite's small sitting room. She kicked off her shoes, and lit a cigarette.

"Do you smoke?" she asked, offering Maddy one of hers.

"No, thanks," replied Maddy, subdued.

"Neither did I, until recently. It's just difficult to be taken seriously if you don't in this game. It's part of the window dressing. I can drink like Hemingway now, too. Irish genes are good for something, I guess. Okay. Your turn. What's going on?"

Maddy told her. She started at the beginning, ten years ago, during the carefree summer she and Katherine had shared in New York. Katherine asked her questions now and then, but mostly just let her talk, as she related every detail of her story. When Maddy finally finished, Katherine was lighting her fifth cigarette. She got up to open a window, for the room was, by now, quite smoky.

"Holy shit," she said, turning back to face her friend. "I always knew that truth was stranger than fiction, but this takes the cake."

"Thanks," said Maddy, smarting at her friend's apparent lack of sympathy.

"Well, I don't know what you expect me to say. I'd ditch the both of them, if I were you. Stay here with me for a while. Sounds like you could use a fresh start, Maddy."

Maddy had to laugh at her candor. "Is life always so simple for you, Katherine?"

"Life is simple, Maddy. Human beings are the only things that complicate it."

"How profound."

"Laugh if you want," responded Katherine, reclaiming her seat. "Look, I feel for you. I really do. I feel badly that you put up with Bradley the Fourth for ten years, and I feel even worse that you've fallen for a world-class bastard, although the latter is a bit more understandable. You want my advice, you got it. Ditch 'em both. You want my sympathy? You got that, too. You want a place to run away to? Stay here as long as you want, then stay with me in my cute little flat. I love you Maddy. You're my oldest friend in the world. I'm here to help."

With this, she put out her cigarette and stood up. "You want dinner tonight? Dinner and a show? A little London theater?"

"Yes. Thanks. That would be nice."

"Okay. Great. I'll call you."

While unpacking her hand luggage, Maddy heard something fall on the floor. She looked down. It was Gene's necklace. *How did he do that?* She started to cry again.

That evening, dinner and a show was followed by drinks and music. The next day Katherine took off from work and they did the requisite sightseeing: the Tower of London, Westminster Abbey, and Buckingham Palace. The next morning Maddy wandered about on her own, shopping and seeing the city. In the evening she met up with Katherine. They ate and drank and laughed at a small pub in the West End. Finally, by her third day in London, Maddy was beginning to feel as if she would survive.

And then came Bernice's telegram.

Maddy,
Please come home immediately. There has
been an accident. Bradley is dead.
B.

CHAPTER 27

THE WIDOW

❧

Katherine accompanied Maddy on the plane trip home, insisting that she was due a vacation anyway, and that her mother would kill her if she ever found out that Katherine had let Maddy make the trip alone.

Bernice picked them up at the airport and it was from her that Maddy learned the details of how her husband had died. He had driven their car off a cliff, at night, while on the Pacific Coast Highway. There was alcohol in his bloodstream at the time of death, and the weather had been, as was usual for that time of year, damp and foggy. There was not enough left of the vehicle to establish whether some mechanical failure was to blame. Suicide had been ruled out, not only because he had not left a note, but because he had, despite the critical nature of his injuries, tried to crawl away from the car before it exploded. He escaped the inferno, but did not live long. He was dead before the rescue crew could reach him.

"A horrendous accident," Bernice concluded, communicating the story as if she were reporting it to a medical conference rather than the widow of the man who'd died. "Especially at a time like this—not that I expected you two to reconcile, but still—this was no way for things to end."

Maddy was nearly catatonic. Everyone treated her carefully. They had no way of knowing that guilt, as much as grief, was the emotion eating away at her. Down in the untouchable part of her mind where a frightened seven year old girl still lived, Maddy knew that she had killed Brad by reaching for Gene, by taking what she wanted, just as surely as she had killed her own mother.

By the time she and Katherine reached New Jersey, Brad's parents had already had his body transported, in Maddy's absence, to the funeral home in Boston used by the Gordons for generations. She did not complain. She knew she had to face them, and did not care whether the confrontation occurred at their home or across the country.

The one thing she could not bring herself to do was to call Gene. It was as if, if she did not talk to him, if she didn't involve him in this, that somehow she could keep the memory of their voyage intact, let it exist alone is a separate space, unaffected by everything that came before and after, an oasis in her imagination.

To Maddy's relief, Bernice stepped in and made all of the necessary arrangements, including handling several conversations with Brad's parents regarding both the funeral and Maddy's financial interest in Brad's estate.

"You don't have to do a thing," Bernice told Maddy firmly. "Funerals are a ridiculous business anyway. Burials are arcane. A waste of perfectly good real estate. Still, if you want to go, I will go with you, and Katherine will come, as well. But I won't have those people putting you through any more nonsense. You've suffered enough at their hands."

Maddy went to the funeral. She sat in the front of the crowded church, flanked by Bernice and Katherine, her guardians against the Boston establishment. Only once did she glance at Brad's parents, seated across the aisle. Bradley Harrington Gordon III kept his eyes straight ahead, his complexion the color of ancient granite. Bradley's mother wore a black veil, which covered her face. Maddy did not look at them again.

The service continued at the gravesite without incident. Once Bradley's coffin had been laid in the ground and the final benediction made, Maddy followed Bernice's lead and headed straight to the car. Before they had taken more than a dozen steps, she heard Katherine's voice behind her.

"Wait, Maddy. Here she comes."

Maddy turned to see Mrs. Gordon approaching. The older woman walked slowly, uncertainty plaguing her every step. Maddy stopped.

"Do you want me to stay?" Bernice asked quietly.

"No, thank you, just please, wait in the car. You too, Katherine. This is something I have to do myself."

Her two companions obeyed.

Once they had gone, Mrs. Gordon moved more quickly, obviously relieved to have Maddy to herself. Behind her Maddy could see Mr. Gordon walking toward the family limousine, accompanied by a woman who may have been his sister, and two young men who were probably his nephews.

It was impossible to believe that she was at her husband's funeral. It was impossible to believe that she had been a member of this family for ten years, and never been a part of it at all. It was impossible to believe that Brad was dead.

"Thank you for coming, Madeleine," Mrs. Gordon said, raising her veil when she was close enough to speak quietly. Her eyes were puffy, her skin blotched beneath her makeup. She had probably been crying for days.

Maddy merely nodded.

"I know you probably would have preferred for this to happen in San Francisco. That's where your life is. My husband... he takes charge of these things. Rather like your aunt. They've had some interesting conversations over the past few days, as you might imagine."

Maddy found herself smiling at Mrs. Gordon's attempt to lighten the air between them. Neither of their smiles lasted very long.

"Madeleine, Bradley called me the day before he died. I was so surprised, and so pleased. Ten years ago I had to choose between my husband and my son. You know the decision I made. I abided by it—though at times I've hated him—my Bradley—for it, and myself for giving in to him so easily."

Maddy wanted to speak but she could tell the woman was not finished, so she stood quiet.

"Bradley told me that you had quarreled. He said you left him because he'd just … because he refused to try and adopt a child."

"That's not true," Maddy cried out.

Mrs. Gordon put her gloved hands to her ears, unable to bear hearing her dead son contradicted.

"It doesn't matter, Maddy. I'm not here to blame you. I'm here to apologize. I always thought that Bradley married you because he hated us. Now I know that he married you because he loved you. I'm sorry… as was he… that he could not give you what you wanted."

"But, you can't… it wasn't that way…" Maddy tried to explain, the lump in her throat rendering speech even more difficult.

"It doesn't matter, Madeleine. At times like this, one sees clearly what matters and what doesn't. At least, I think, women do. We can't just write off the people in our lives the way men can. The way my husband can. We suffer for it. I just don't want you to suffer any more than you have to."

By now Maddy was crying again. She did not have the strength for another denial.

Mrs. Gordon leaned over and kissed her on the cheek. "There," she said, on the verge of breaking down herself. "I should have done that ten years ago. If I had, maybe we wouldn't be here now." Her composure gone, she too began to sob, and turned to stumble back across the lawn in the direction of the long black limousine that waited to carry her home.

"What did she say?" asked Katherine as Maddy joined them in the car. Bernice listened in stern silence.

"She wanted to say she was sorry that she had let Brad's father cut us off from the family. That she wished things could have been different. And she said... she said that Brad had called her, before he died, and told her that I left him because he wouldn't let us adopt." Maddy answered between sobs.

"Is that true?" Bernice asked.

"No, no of course it's not true. Why would he say that?" Maddy moaned.

"I guess to make you look like the bad guy," Katherine answered gently. "So his parents wouldn't blame the failure of the marriage on him."

"Oh, God," Maddy wailed, resting her head against the window. "When will I ever stop crying? Why am I always, always crying?"

But Maddy did stop crying, eventually. She stayed for several days at her aunt's house, with Katherine and the television for company. The two girls spent one afternoon at Mrs. O'Connor's, surrounded by Katherine's nieces and nephews, whom she laughingly referred to as, "the Wonder Kids, because they make you wonder why you'd ever want to have kids." But even after a far-from-peaceful dinner at the child-infested house, Maddy could not agree.

Once they were back at Bernice's home, Katherine followed Maddy into her bedroom. "Ma sent something with me, to give to you. You know Ma. She has her own way of doing things. Well, she's had all these letters from your father, letters he sent years ago, back when you'd just started living here with your aunt. Seems you didn't want them at the time, so he sent them all to Ma, and told her to give them to you, if she ever felt like you'd want to see them. I never even knew she had them.

"Ma thought that everything was hunky-dory between you and Brad in California, and she never wanted to upset the apple cart by sending you these. But today, she dragged me off and gave them to me, and told me to give them to you, because it might be a good time for you to hear what your father had to say."

She cleared her throat. "Ma says he loved you Maddy, and at a time like this, it might make you feel better. So here they are."

She handed Maddy a manila envelope.

"I can't believe this," she said, looking at it as if it might explode in her hands.

"Yeah, well, me neither, but that's Ma for you. And she might be right, you know. I hate to admit it, but she usually is."

"Thank you, Katherine."

She shrugged. "Don't thank me yet. You haven't read 'em yet."

Maddy brought the envelope to her room and dumped its contents out on the bed. Inside were letters she'd seen before, fifteen years ago. Scrawled across each was the word REFUSED, written by her own hand. All except one.

She picked up the fat envelope. The postmark indicated it had been sent in 1948, well after the others, from Washington, D.C. She ripped it open. Page after page spilled out. Maddy picked up the first one, and began to read.

Dear Maddy,

    I won't ask your forgiveness, for I don't deserve it. I'm hoping it might help you to understand why I've done what I've done—not to forgive me for it, but to understand it—if you hear my whole story.

    Only two people in the world have known everything there is to know about me. One was a man in Shanghai, a Chinese by the name of Liu Tue-Sheng. The other person who knew me best was your mother. If I had told her everything sooner, perhaps our lives would have turned out differently.

I came from a peasant family in a small village in Hungary. My father was a blacksmith, but when I was ten a teacher came to our village, and discovered that I have a gift for learning languages...

Maddy read and read and read. She read about how her father was taken in by a foster family in Budapest, and how the first Great War ruined their country and their lives. She read about how her parents met in Paris when he was there on business, about how he was blamed for a counterfeiting scandal, and why he had killed a man. She read about his decision to flee to Shanghai. She read about why her father became involved with the gangster, Liu Tue-Sheng, and what that mistake eventually cost him. He told her how he'd been recruited to work as a spy, and how that decision made it impossible to return to her until after the war was over.

Near the end of the letter, he wrote:

At first I told myself that I was protecting you by sending you away. The truth was that I was afraid of failing you, as I had failed your mother. You were right, Maddy. I am a liar and coward. But you must understand that I do love you.

For a long time she could read no more. Then, finally, she picked up the last page.

I think, if I did give you anything at all, it was your musical gift. Your mother and I together gave it to you. She was the musical one. And you do have a gift, Maddy. You owe it to yourself to use it. It would have made your mother so happy. She was so proud of you. As am I.

You will not be able to contact me after you receive this

letter. I will spend the rest of my life, however long that may be, trying to do something worthwhile for what is left of the human race. I suppose in some ways it's easy for me to take this step because I'm going back to the only arena in my life where I've been successful. But I do love you, my little princess, for what it is worth. I do love you.

When Katherine knocked gently on her door the next morning, she found Maddy sitting on the floor, her father's letters spread around her, still dressed in the clothes she had worn the previous day.

"Hi," she said uncertainly, not sure whether she should be interrupting, "Do you want to have some breakfast?"

"I've got to get cleaned up first. Get out of these clothes."

"Did you sleep at all?"

"No, no, not really. I guess I dozed off a little. I feel okay, though. Better than I have in a long time."

"That's terrific! So. What's in all those letters?"

Maddy stood up. "I think he did love me, Katherine."

"Glad to hear it. Had a strange way of showing it."

"Yes, I know. But he didn't leave me because he didn't care, Katherine. He left because he was lost. And I... I know what that feels like."

"I know you do, Maddy," she answered, and did the only thing she could think of; she gave her old friend a big hug.

CHAPTER 28

THE JAZZ PLAYER

∽⌇∾

Maddy didn't tell Bernice about the letters from her father until after Katherine left for London. Sitting at the breakfast table, Bernice listened patiently.

"I would take everything he said with a grain of salt, Madeleine." Bernice said when Maddy was finished. "He was nothing if not a very capable liar."

"But there's more. In San Francisco, before I left. I saw Amelia."

"Who?"

"Amelia. She lives there. We ran into each other. She told me some things about what happened between her and my father. And it's the same story he told me in his letter."

"What does that matter now?"

"It means she lied to you, Aunt Bernice. She lied to us, to keep me from forgiving my father. To keep me away from him."

"Which was not a bad outcome, Maddy."

"How can you be so sure?"

"Maddy, when you're trying to purify a formula, you have to isolate and exclude the impure ingredients to protect the final product. It's no different with human beings. So many unanticipated events can adversely affect the outcome. One controls what one can."

Something in her tone of voice planted a long-overdue realization in Maddy's head. "You knew, didn't you? You knew that she was lying about her affair, about my father's affairs."

"No, I did not know that."

"But you wanted to believe her, didn't you? You didn't want me having anything to do with my father. You wanted to control my life. To keep me away from him."

"And was that so wrong? Was I to stand by and watch him destroy your life as he had destroyed your mother's? Was I not entitled, no, *required* to protect you from that man?"

"Did he really destroy my mother's life, Aunt Bernice? I don't remember her being so unhappy. What if she loved him? What if, up until the end, he did make her happy?"

"Madeleine, he abandoned you. And what forced him to disappear off the face of the earth, might I ask, if he was so determined to reconnect with you? Where is he now?"

"I don't know, Aunt Bernice. But if you helped to keep him away from me, then I expect you to help me find him. Or find out what happened to him."

"Madeleine, what would be the point? Haven't you been through enough?"

"That *is* the point. I've been through enough not to be afraid of what I could find out."

"I can't imagine how you'd go about looking for him."

"Surely your contacts at the Defense Department could come up with something."

Bernice looked surprised. "It's not that easy. I tried once and came up with nothing. One doesn't just go peeking through the Pentagon's personnel files."

"But you must know someone who can. Please. I want to find out what happened to my father."

Bernice gave her an exasperated look, but Maddy knew that she'd won. "I'll try," her aunt finally said. "I can't promise anything, but I will try." Then, as if proceeding to the next agenda item at a business meeting, she changed the subject.

"Will you be going back to live in San Francisco?"

"No."

"That sounds very final."

"It is. There's nothing left for me there."

"You're welcome to stay with us, of course. Until you get your bearings."

"Thank you. I will. Until I get a job, at least."

"A job? What sort of job do you have in mind?"

"I'm going to play the piano. In public. At a jazz club."

"Now, Madeleine. I'm sure that Brad left you financially secure. You don't need to do something just to earn money. Do something that will give you a sense of accomplishment. Focus your efforts on something a bit more practical."

"I know it's not practical. But it's my passion, Aunt Bernice."

Maddy would not be dissuaded. She wasn't even sure how to go about looking for a job. But before she could take any steps in that direction, she had to sell her house in San Francisco, pack up her things there, and say her goodbyes. And she had to make a decision about Gene.

She did not call him until nearly two months after Brad's death, and it took several tries before she found him at the number he had given her.

"Hello?"

The sound of his voice sent a shock wave through her body. *I can't see him. I'll never be able to say this if he's looking at me.*

"Hi, Gene. It's me. Maddy."

"Maddy, God, I've been worried! What took you so long to call? Have you been in London all this time?"

"Actually I've been home for a while. I had to come home. Brad was killed. In a car accident."

"Oh, my God. I'm so sorry, Maddy. Why didn't you call me right away?"

"I didn't want you to get involved. Things were difficult enough."

"I want to help, Maddy. When can I see you?"

She paused. "Now!" screamed her body. "Right now!" screamed her broken heart.

"Gene, I can't. It's just not right. And I would always want more of you than I could have."

"You don't know until you try," he said, sounding like a disappointed little boy.

"I don't want to try, Gene. I don't want to be your mistress, or whatever it is I'd be. I have to make a new life for myself."

"Maddy, can I at least see you, so we can talk this over?"

"No. If I saw you I'd feel the same way I always feel when I see you."

"Doesn't that tell you something?"

"Please don't, Gene. This is hard enough as it is."

"Will you call me?"

"I don't think so."

"Can I call you?"

"No. Please don't."

"I can't lose you again."

"That's the stupid part, Gene. You never have. I just can't live by your rules."

"You'll change your mind."

"I don't think so... Gene?"

"Yes?"

"I need to know... on the ship you said that you'd 'kept tabs' on me. Does that mean... did you ever hire a private detective?"

Silence.

"Richard Bates?"

"I'm sorry, Maddy. That was years ago. I just didn't want—"

"Don't ever spy on me again."

"I promise. Maddy, please—"

"Goodbye, Gene." She hung up the phone. She felt a dead weight descend upon her chest. She did not know how she would ever feel happy again.

"Work. Work. Work will take your mind off your other problems," was Bernice's advice. Maddy was prepared to listen.

She knew that she could never make up for the ten years of lost time. But the music was still there, if she could find a way to let it out. She wanted to find a place for herself, and she knew her music was the key.

By 1960 the night club, which had for twenty years been the definitive entertainment venue for the most sophisticated, most glamorous, most urbane segment of New York society, was enjoying a quiet old age. That odd invention of the previous decade—the television—enabled musicians to wander into people's homes with the push of a button. Great quantities of people had migrated to the latest human habitat, suburbia, where Technicolor screens brought marvelous musicals to life in the darkness of the local cinema, obviating the need for an evening in the city. But in the heart of Manhattan, from 50th to 59th Street, from Seventh to Third Avenue, there remained a small nest of the smoothest, purest musical environments ever invented: the jazz club. Teens had flocked to rock 'n' roll, and the older crowd still craved the sweet sound of the swing kings, but to those who felt and understood the heart, the very soul of music, nothing had ever replaced the electrifying, sense-surrounding strains of jazz.

When Maddy returned from San Francisco she started to make the rounds, asking if anyone needed to hire a house pianist; someone who was versatile enough to accompany the guest artists who wanted a piano in the background, and good enough solo to entertain the clientele between sets.

A discouraging round of "no openings, no thank you, let-me-take-your-name" was all she received, as she trudged from club to club for two solid weeks. Then, one Friday night, a call came.

When the phone rang it was nearly nine o'clock. Maddy did not make a move to answer it; any call received at that hour was normally from one of Archie's contractors in California. She responded quickly to Bernice's rather peevish summons.

"Madeleine, there is a telephone call for you. A Mr. Silvers. He says it's urgent."

Curious, Maddy set aside the book she had been browsing through and went to the phone.

"Hello?"

"Yeah, hello. Is this Maddy Gordon?"

"Yes, it is."

"Okay, here's the story. This is Matt Silvers, at the Blue Door. I've got a gig for you."

"A what? Oh, of course. Wow! That's great. When?"

"Tonight, sugar. As soon as you can get here."

"Tonight?"

"Look, honey, I can go to the next person on my list if you can't do it, but you sounded good when you came in last week, and it's an all-male trio you need to back up. A classy kid like yourself would be a nice touch. My house man is, ah, sick. His backup already has another gig. Interested?"

"I'm sorry. Which club is it?"

"The Blue Door. On 52nd."

Maddy remembered it. It wasn't the nicest, but it was far from the seediest. The club was located in the basement of a large brownstone building. One walked from the street down a small flight of stairs to the Blue Door which gave the place its name.

"When do I have to be there?"

"An hour ago. When can you get here?"

"In an hour?"

"Make it less." He hung up.

Maddy leapt into her closet. She pulled out a simple black sheath. There was nothing much she could do with her hair. She used two fake pearl clasps to push it back, away from her face. Black hose. Flat pumps. Powder. Lipstick. No time for eye shadow. No time to do a purse transplant. No one would see her bag, anyway. She ran out of the room, and then raced back. With trembling hands she dug around in her top drawer and found the box that contained her mother's gold medallion. She slipped it around her neck, and bolted.

In two seconds she was banging on Bernice's and Archie's door.

"Aunt Bernice? Listen, I've got a gig—"

"A what?" her aunt replied, opening the door. Behind her, Maddy could see Archie, lying on the bed, a bowl of popcorn propped up on his stomach, the glow of the television lighting his face.

"A gig. A job. I've been hired. Can I use the car? The Buick? I have to go into the city."

"Maddy, I told you. It's yours. Take it when you need it. Are you sure this is safe?"

"Of course! Oh, thanks!" She planted a kiss on Bernice's cheek and was gone.

Maddy made it to the club in the somewhat miraculous time of forty-five minutes. The crowd was still light. The headliners didn't start until ten.

She recognized the man standing at the hostess station as the man for whom she had auditioned, and assumed he must be the owner.

She dashed over and handed him her car keys.

"I'm Maddy. Didn't have time to park the car. It's sitting out front. Where do I go?"

"Hey! Great! Glad you could make it, sweetheart. Let me take you back to meet the group. You'll have to play it by ear tonight, sister. Just do what Casper tells you to. He's the lead, on sax. You got a good sound; you'll do okay. And thanks."

The next five hours went by in a whirlwind of music. With no time to prepare, all Casper wanted her to do was listen and improvise: play in the background, jump in when the groove got slow. Even playing on the club's shabby upright piano, Maddy was in heaven. She could feel the emotion of the crowd, feel the music pulsing inside her. It was like great sex, like sharing great sex with a roomful of playfully lusty people.

"Terrific," said Casper, at the end of the evening. "Man, Maddy, we were lucky to get you on such short notice. Where do you play?"

"At home," she laughed, wiping the sweat off her face with a napkin.

"No kidding? Aw, sister, c'mon. Did you take this gig behind your agent's back, or what? Got somebody who'll want a piece if he finds out?"

"An agent?" Maddy asked blankly. She had never even thought about getting an agent. Of course. What a dimwit she was.

"This lady doesn't need an agent," interjected Matt, stepping on to the small platform that constituted a stage. "She's got a job. Here. She's the house pianist."

Maddy gave him a dazzling smile. "What's my salary?" she asked sweetly, as Matt grimaced and the band members broke into guffaws.

"Don't let him tell you we play for love," laughed Casper, as he put his horn away.

But Maddy would have, if they asked her to. She would have played for free. She'd found where she needed to be.

The next day she found an apartment in the city, not far from the club. It was more like an overgrown studio than an actual apartment, but it was the first place she had ever lived in that was all hers: not paid for by her aunt, or her husband. It was hers alone.

Bernice kept her word about starting an investigation concerning Leo Hoffman, but the short paper trail she'd uncovered led to a dead end. He'd worked in intelligence during the war, was all the Navy would confirm. For Maddy, though, it was a comfort. She'd found one twig of truth in the nest of deception in which she'd grown up. It helped.

Bernice was not pleased with Maddy's success. She thought that the whole plan was some sort of disturbing psychological response to Brad's death, and said so. Maddy tried to explain to her that the marriage to Brad had been the mistake; this was what she should have done years ago. This was who she was. She was sure.

She was accepted into the midnight world of the jazz musician as if she had been a part of it all of her life. Each new artist with whom she played helped her reach further; the responses to her solo gigs during the week were fantastic. Matt Silvers knew he had a find on his hands, but he kept that fact to himself. He asked Maddy to sign a contract, to work for him for two years. She did so gladly, grateful for the opportunity.

There was no doubt, however, that her new lifestyle was taking a bit of a toll on her. She slept until late in the afternoon, but still woke up feeling exhausted and nauseous from the long nights spent nibbling on pretzels and inhaling other people's cigarette smoke. But the exhilaration she felt by the time she was on stage filled every tired cell of her body with adrenalin, and all discomfort was forgotten.

One evening, when she had been at the Blue Door just over a month, Maddy started up a conversation with one of the waitresses, a pretty young blond named Charlene. She wanted to be an actress. Charlene knew every story about every Broadway and Hollywood starlet who had allegedly been discovered in a sandwich shop, a country club, in a department store, or on the beach.

"I check out the customers really well. I know the look. If there's someone here, I'll sniff him out," she said confidently, as Maddy once again smiled her encouragement and helped herself to a handful of olives from behind the bar.

Charlene made a face. "Maddy, I ain't never seen nobody eat olives by the handful that way. Except my cousin Josephine, when she was pregnant. It was hilarious. No martini was safe for miles."

"Well, I'm not pregnant," laughed Maddy, as she helped herself to another handful.

Still, the idea stayed with her, as she drove home that morning. She thought about her nausea in the mornings, or rather, in the afternoons, when she woke up. Her periods had always been irregular, and since she and Brad had not needed birth control… it was silly. It was impossible.

Before going to work the next day she slipped into a nearby clinic and asked for a test. Two days later, a nurse called her.

"Congratulations, Mrs. Gordon. You're going to have a baby."

CHAPTER 29

THE BUSINESSMAN

⌐∿⌐

Gene Mandretti lived in a roomy house on the north shore of Long Island. He was married to the former Tina Rose Marro. Gene's uncle, Salvatore Mandretti, worked with Tina's uncle, Frank "Papa" Carbolo. By the fall of 1960 Gene and Tina had been married for four years. They had two children: Sal, who was nearly three, and Angela Maria, who'd just celebrated her first birthday.

The two uncles, Sal and Frank, had grown up as friends in the same neighborhood. Through hard work, perseverance, and a little old-fashioned luck, they had both risen to positions of achievement within their shared profession. Frank was the head of the Carbolo crime syndicate, one of the most powerful of the Five Families of the New York Italian Mafia. Salvatore was his chief lieutenant.

The Carbolo Family, like many of the other organized crime gangs, had been operating in New York's Little Italy since the turn of the century, but had profited tremendously from Prohibition. When drinking became legal again, the Family expanded into other areas: gambling, prostitution, loan sharking, and narcotics. By 1950, the money was rolling in.

Salvatore was not well-educated. He had street smarts, he was observant, and he was practical. He knew it was no joke that Al

Capone, Waxey Gordon, and a handful of other smaller figures had gone to jail, not for murder, or extortion, but for tax evasion. Salvatore knew that neither he, nor his lifelong friend, Frank Carbolo, knew enough to keep the Internal Revenue Service accountants off their asses.

Sal was no rocket scientist, but he could tell that his nephew, Geno, was a very smart boy. Geno's father, Sal's little brother, Tony Mandretti, had been one of Papa Carbolo's bodyguards. He'd died during an attempt on the Don's life by a rival gang. Sal took Tony's widow, the boy, and his two sisters into his own home. He got the boy a good education, at a fancy prep school, then sent him to an even fancier college. He made Gene keep out of trouble. Sal figured that the Family didn't need another hit man or another bill collector. What the Family really needed was a businessman to run the finances and keep them all out of jail.

As Gene grew up, it became obvious that Sal had made a good decision. Gene had real *Mafioso*: that idealized Sicilian blend of boldness, bravery, and physical beauty. Gene was not a man to be taken lightly; he was a man willing to be a law unto himself if necessary, a man who takes care of his own.

The timing was perfect. Gene graduated from business school in 1951, the same year that Senator Estes Kefauver's well-publicized hearings on the operations of the "New York Underworld," triggered an unprecedented effort by the Internal Revenue Service to convict hundreds of suspected Mafia members for tax fraud.

"We have to do two things," Gene said, the first time he was asked to meet with Papa Carbolo. "First, we have to hide the money coming in. Just shipping it to offshore banks isn't good enough. It makes it hard to spend. You buy a yacht, the IRS wants to know where you got the money. We have to make it look like the money was earned legally. Then, we have to diversify into legitimate businesses. Illegal money can generate legal money. Lots of it. Then the origins of the initial capital are easier to disguise."

"But, won't that mean we gotta pay taxes?" Papa Carbolo spoke like a boxer, for his nose had been broken several times, before he became a man no one would dare assault unless he wanted to die.

"Some. Yes. But that's better than going to jail. And paying a few taxes lays the groundwork for the rest of our enterprise which, on the outside, looks legitimate. Remember, they only use the tax code as a weapon because they can't get us any other way. If you can make the money look clean, you've disarmed them."

"Yeah, yeah, Geno. But that ain't new. You got a restaurant with no business, you tell the Feds it's full. There's only so much 'a that you can do. We can only run so many empty restaurants, and I ain't givin' all the Family's proceeds to the Feds."

"The key is diversity. You get money from the gambling operations, you say you earned it in rents from an apartment complex. You make money on the apartments, you invest in a chain of dry cleaning stores, which, oops, on paper loses a little. Some still goes to Switzerland, some to the Bahamas. Make the paper trail so difficult to follow, they'll give up, and go pick on someone else."

Papa Carbolo was silent for a while.

"You think you can do all this?"

"I know I can."

The Don glanced over at Sal, who'd been listening politely the whole time.

"You were right, Salvatore. He's a smart boy. You done good to bring him to me."

Salvatore beamed.

Gene was as good as his word. Within four years, three Family-owned corporations held investments in, among other things, commercial and residential real estate, a cigarette vending business, a chain of restaurants, a jewelry store, two Las Vegas casinos, and a waste-removal service. Through these various ventures they were able to launder the vast sums earned through their more nefarious enterprises.

Papa Carbolo was pleased. So pleased, in fact, that when his niece, Tina, came home from college for Christmas in 1956, took one look at Gene Mandretti, and fell in love, Papa suggested to Sal that such a union had all the earmarks of a match made in heaven. The old friends were delighted when Gene and Tina responded positively to their rather obvious matchmaking plans.

"A dynasty is born," said Uncle Sal with delight, when he welcomed his namesake into the world in 1957. Life was good. Very, very good.

Gene had fulfilled everyone's expectations, and did so in a way that managed to keep his name from being associated with the lords of the Mafia. He was a businessman. A very successful businessman. He had everything he wanted.

Almost.

In the fall of 1960, Gene decided it was time to go into the entertainment business. Not the brothels and casino shows that had been the Family's bread-and-butter for years, but legitimate entertainment. Who could predict how much performers were paid? Who knew how many martinis were consumed in one night? Who knew what the bills would be for dry-cleaning tablecloths, for tuning a piano, for publicity? How could the IRS argue with well-kept receipts?

He had a specific place in mind. There was a little jazz club, on 52nd Street, between Fifth and Madison. It had a good reputation; had been around for years, and the owner, a man by the name of Matt Silvers, liked to gamble. In fact, he owed a little money to one of the bookies in the area. Not a Carbolo operation but there were, Gene explained at the Family's quarterly board meeting, times when it made good sense to pay off someone else's debt. They could acquire the Blue Door, indeed, the whole building it was in, for a song by bailing Silvers out, and giving him enough to start a new place. Somewhere else.

"But jazz? Jazz is history," said Papa Carbolo quizzically. "A buncha coloreds moanin.' It ain't music, even."

"I believe you're thinking more of the blues, Papa, but you have a point. That's the beauty of it. Jazz isn't dead, it's just on its way out. Whether we have a hundred people a night or twenty, it won't matter. We either make money, or we wash it. Either way, we win."

"Okay, Gene. You ain't taken a wrong step yet. We'll go with it."

According to the corporate bylaws, a vote on a new investment required approval by a majority. In reality, Papa's was the only vote needed; it was the only one that counted.

Two weeks later a rather agitated Matt Silvers asked everyone on the Blue Door staff to stay after closing. All the regulars assembled: Charlene and Theresa, the waitresses; Jimmy, the doorman; Tex, the bartender who wasn't from Texas; Al, the cook; Luis, the Cuban busboy; and Maddy, the house pianist. They all sat and listened as Matt explained that the Blue Door had been sold to a corporation.

"But this is a family operation, not some big company, like GM. And the new owners, they say they won't be makin' any changes, at least not right away. I'm ready to move on, guys. I've got a sister in Florida who wants me to help her open a place down there. You know how it is."

"So, who's gonna run the place?" asked Al.

"Well, the guy from the company will be here tomorrow, at five o'clock, to introduce himself. They're gonna bring in a manager. It won't be the same kind of hands-on arrangement, but you'll all be able to keep your jobs for six months. That's part of the deal. I didn't want to leave you guys high and dry."

"Thanks, Matt," said Maddy gratefully. She did not think she wanted to look for another job, not at the moment. In six months the baby would be here. She could play until it just became ridiculous, she thought. Until the sight of an obviously pregnant woman playing the piano at a jazz club went beyond good taste. She thought she could keep it a secret for a few more weeks. Luckily the fashions of the moment helped hide her expanding waistline. Nothing was more forgiving than a trapeze dress.

As the group broke up, Matt approached Maddy.

"Listen, the new owner, or the company's representative, I guess, he wants to meet you. They know you're my ace in the hole. I think this guy wants to make sure you'll stay."

"Okay. Have him call me."

"Well, he's here, now, actually. Upstairs, in my apartment."

"Now? Oh, Matt, I'm bushed."

"Yeah, well, as a favor to me, could ya just go up and say hello? He came in and heard ya play tonight. He said you were fantastic."

"Okay, okay," Maddy replied, flattered out of her exhaustion. "I'll go. What's the guy's name?"

"Ah… darn… I don't remember," said Matt, with a strange look on his face. "But he's good looking. A real charmer. You'll like him."

The small brownstone had been divided into four apartments. Matt lived in the largest, the one to the right on the first floor, so that his bed was directly above the Blue Door's stage. "No tenant would stand for it," he explained, "And I'm never home when the music is playing."

The door was not locked. Maddy went in without knocking.

"Hello?" she called out. No one answered.

"Hello? Is anyone here?" she asked, stepping further into the room.

The door closed behind her.

"Hello, Angel," said Gene.

Maddy jumped. "This can't be happening. I'm leaving. Please move."

"Wait, Maddy. Just hear me out."

"No! Damn you, I thought you would at least respect my—oh, my God. You mean, you bought the club? You bought the club from Matt?"

"I bought the whole building," said Gene, proud of himself. "Got a good deal, too."

"Oh, you… you son of a bitch," Maddy cried out, using one of the colorful phrases she'd picked up from her new circle of friends. "I thought you said—how could you—"

"I just called your aunt's secretary and asked about you. She was only too happy to tell me that you were becoming a jazz sensation, and where you worked. And Mason Industries isn't exactly an unlisted number."

"But you said—"

"You told me not to call you. I didn't. I'm not trying to be funny, Maddy. I'm just trying to be able to see you, on your terms."

"My terms? *My terms?* I can't see you at all, Gene. I can't. I have to leave. I quit."

"You have a contract to play for two years."

"So sue me. Anyway, I won't be able to play for more than a few…" she stopped, horrified at what had almost come out of her mouth. She had promised herself that the last person in the world to find out about her baby would be Gene Mandretti.

"Why, Maddy? Why won't you be able to play?" he said, stepping toward her.

"Because… because… I'm going on a trip."

"Where?"

"To Brazil. To study Samba. Oh, God, Gene. It's no good, it's no good. This isn't what I want, this isn't what I want—"

"Yes it is, Maddy," he said gently, coming closer. "Yes, it is."

He walked to her and wrapped his arms around her. "I have a present for you," he whispered in her ear.

"I don't want it."

"Wait until you see what it is, before you say no," he responded. He dropped his arms.

"Go look on the table."

"No."

"Maddy, I'm not going to let you out of here until you go look on the table."

She sighed heavily, not sure how much more she could stand.

"Okay, okay. But I'm not keeping it."

She turned around and saw a large, flat manila envelope lying on the coffee table in the living room. She walked over and picked it up. Inside was a document. She pulled it out and began to read.

"But, Gene! You can't do this," she said within seconds.

"Yes, I can. I own the place."

"But I don't want it!"

"Why not? A lot of the big jazz artists have—or had—their own clubs: Goldie Hawkins, Eddie Condon, Jimmy Daniels. You hold in your hands a lease to the Blue Door, for ten years, at what I would call an outstanding rate. Plus, the new landlord will pay to refurbish it. The landlord will also pay the salary of the manager of your choice, within the stated limit. But I do get to say who keeps the books. You artistic types are notoriously bad in that department, and part of the rent comes from your profits."

"But Gene, I don't know anything about running a club!"

"You won't have to. You handle the music. The manager will handle the business. I'll handle the finances. The important thing is, it will be yours, Maddy."

"No, it won't be. It will be yours," she said stubbornly.

"Ours, then. But it will be your music, Maddy. Music you can share, music no one can take away from you."

"Gene, I—"

"Just sign it."

"I have to think."

"No, Angel, no. You don't have to think. That is the last thing you need to do." He moved closer. She turned away from him. He put his arms around her anyway, and his hands came to rest on the firm, round, mound of her stomach.

Gene was already a father. His fingers knew the truth. She pulled away.

"Maddy, how could you not tell me—"

"Gene, this is not your baby. This is *my* baby."

"Maddy, I can't believe—"

"This has nothing to do with you."

"Nothing to do with me? Maddy, you don't think—"

"It's Brad's."

He stepped back, shocked into silence.

"Are you sure?" he asked, finally.

"Yes," she lied, holding her chin up defiantly. "I've counted the days. There is no way this baby could be yours."

"I see." He looked at her. Maddy could not tell what he was thinking.

"So," she said crisply, determined to leave before she started to cry. "I guess we can just tear this up—"

"No," Gene said sharply, grabbing her wrist. "No. This doesn't change anything. Maddy, I will take whatever part of you I can have. If I can't share you, at least I can share your music. I promise you, I will never ask anything of you that you are unprepared to give. I mean that. Just sign it."

Maddy stared at the pen he had placed in her hand. Could she do it? Could she somehow keep the Blue Door, and her baby, and have Gene for a business partner? Maddy put her hand on her stomach protectively. She was so alone. The alternative was to go back to Aunt Bernice. The alternative was to give up.

She signed.

Five months later, in February of 1961, Maddy's baby was born; a beautiful baby girl with black hair and blue eyes. "Just like her grandfather," remarked Bernice coldly, not at all happy about the apparent resemblance to Leo.

Maddy named her daughter Martha Nichole Gordon, and called her Nikki. She did not get in touch with Brad's parents. She did not want to open that Pandora's Box again.

When Nikki was a month old, Maddy moved into Matt's old apartment over the Blue Door. She hired a nanny, an old Polish woman named Tia, who came with a list of references as long as her arm. Business at the Blue Door was good. Maddy was able to book many well-known musicians into the club, and even pop down and play herself when she felt like it.

Bernice was horrified at her lifestyle. Maddy did not care. She was happy. She loved her work, and had most of the day to spend with Nikki. Maddy was overwhelmed with love for her child, and she wallowed in the unconditional adoration that Nikki gave her in return. Maddy found that being a mother awakened a whole new range of emotions in her. She felt stronger, braver, more capable; and at the same time, more vulnerable than she had ever felt before.

Gene tried not to complicate matters. He never pressured Maddy, never forced himself on her. Their conversations were infrequent, and strictly business. When Maddy came back full time to play, he sometimes dropped in to listen. He never stayed long.

On the afternoon of Nikki's first birthday, Gene showed up unannounced, his arms full of presents. After Gene and Maddy watched the baby smear herself with cake and plow through her presents, Maddy put Nikki down for her nap, and Gene took Maddy in his arms. It was the moment Gene had been waiting for, for nearly twelve years.

Maddy had the Blue Door, and her music, and her baby. She also had a piece of Gene. She decided that was enough.

CHAPTER 30

THE RENEGADE

∽⟨⟩∼

BERLIN, 1963

On a street corner in West Berlin, an old man waited for a bus. He was sitting on a wrought iron bench, reading a newspaper. A German newspaper. It was dated February 3, 1963.

It was six o'clock, and already quite dark. There was little traffic at that hour; most Berliners were home for dinner by six. The air was frigid. The man wore a worn, gray leather coat, and his head was wrapped in a hat lined with sheepskin. Cracked leather gloves barely covered his hands.

A few feet behind the old man, attached to the outside wall of a small tobacco shop that had been closed for at least an hour, was a public telephone. At a few minutes after six, the phone rang.

The old man ignored the phone, at first. After a dozen rings it went quiet.

Within a few seconds it began to ring again. He looked back at the phone this time, obviously annoyed. A gust of air formed a cloud of condensation in front of his face as he sighed. He stood up and looked down the street, to see whether his bus was coming. It was not. The phone kept ringing.

With a cantankerous grunt the man folded his paper, set it on the bench, and shuffled over to the phone. He picked up the receiver.

"*Ja?*"

"Is that you, Walter?" asked a man's voice, in German.

"Nein, nein, this is not your friend Walter. This is a public phone, for God's sake. At a bus stop. You must have the wrong number."

"I know this is a public phone. My friend was supposed to be there, waiting for my call. Is there anyone else there? A tubby man in his fifties? Brown hair, glasses?"

"No. There is just me, an old man waiting for the bus which, now I see, is coming."

"Well, I guess he got tired of waiting. I don't blame him. I can't wait any longer, myself. I'll have to get going. Goodbye."

The old man heard a dial tone, and hung the receiver carefully back on the hook.

In a few moments, his bus arrived. He rode it for ten blocks, then alighted near a small coffee shop. He went in and ordered a cup of coffee. As he waited, he pulled out a pen, and doodled on his paper napkin.

The coffee arrived, and he drank it, slowly, taking his time, reading the newspaper he still carried with him. When he had finished he wiped his mouth on the napkin, crumpled it up, and stuffed it inside the now empty cup. He fumbled through his pocket for an appropriate amount of change, left it on the table, and with a quiet *"Danke,"* gave his thanks to no one in particular, and hobbled out the door.

After he had gone the waiter came over to clear his place. He saw the napkin in the cup, and made a face.

When he got off work that night, the waiter walked home, as usual. As usual, he walked by a small office building, the front of which was guarded by two American military police. They were dressed warmly against the cold, and stayed well within the frame of the door, to try and stay out of the wind.

As he crossed in front of the doorway, the waiter reached in his coat pocket and pulled out a pack of cigarettes. The old man's napkin fell out of his pocket, onto the sidewalk.

"Hey, you, pick that up," muttered one of the soldiers, in very bad German.

"Pick it up yourself, asshole," the man answered, not breaking his stride.

The marine rolled his eyes, stepped forward, and with a couple of muttered curses, stooped down to scoop up the paper. He shoved it in his own pocket.

The napkin changed hands again, twice, before making it out of Germany. The message it carried was decoded at a military base in England. The message was then re-encrypted and transmitted by wire to the Central Intelligence Agency in Washington, D.C.

This wire was personally decoded by the Deputy Director for Eastern European covert operations. "Shit!" the man shouted, as the translation became clear. "SHIT SHIT SHIT!"

He then called his own boss, the Assistant Director, who then called the head of the CIA and asked to see him in his office, immediately.

There was no easy way to deliver the message. "We've had an emergency communication from Chameleon. His cover is blown. He's trying to get out."

"Oh, Jesus H. Christ." The director put his head in his hands. "Well, there goes the most successful mole operation in American history. Fifteen years. Damn it to hell! Any details?"

"Not yet, sir."

"Anything we can do to help him?"

"We don't even know where he is, sir."

"Has he been caught?"

"Not as of yesterday. Not according to anything we've been able to pick up. Even if his cover was badly blown, I doubt they'd advertise. Too damn embarrassing."

"And if he's caught?"

"He knows what to do. And he will. I know this man. He'll take the pill."

"Oh, Christ, I hope so." He stared with mournful resignation at the phone on his desk. "Well, I guess I better call the president and ask for an appointment. If Khrushchev calls him up all pissed off, Jack will have my ass in a sling if he doesn't know what it's all about."

"Yes, sir. Sorry, sir."

"Keep me posted. God help the sonofabitch. He's done one helluva job."

"Yes, sir. Thank you sir." He hurried out.

The director shook his head. "Shit," he muttered to himself, and picked up the phone.

"Peggy? Get me the White House."

CHAPTER 31

THE PROSECUTOR

❧

NEW YORK, 1963

Assistant United States Attorney Ryan Matthew Sullivan leaned forward on his desk and looked impatiently at his watch. He was excruciatingly punctual, and therefore completely intolerant of tardiness in others. The two FBI agents he was supposed to meet with, Kevin Royster and John "Jimmy" Jamison, were already ten minutes late.

Well, he thought. *They will learn.*

Ryan's physical appearance was somewhat at odds with his stern professional reputation. He had a sweet, boyish face, accented by big hazel eyes and an embarrassing splash of freckles across the bridge of his nose. His ginger-colored hair would have been curly, had he not worn it cropped so close to his head. He was tall and lithe, and could easily be mistaken for an athlete, or a poet. More than anything else, he was unmistakably Irish, and he owed his looks and his career choice to the law-and-order Irish family into which he had been born.

Ryan Sullivan's great-grandfather had been a magistrate in the old country. His grandfather had been a policeman in Boston. His father had been a special agent for the Bureau of Alcohol, Tobacco and Firearms, and had waged war against the bootlegging gangs of New York City and Chicago during Prohibition.

Ryan Sullivan knew from an early age that his mission in life was to do what his father, and his father's father, had both done before him. He was going to get the bad guys. And he knew, because of the tales that his grandfather and his father told him, that the worst of all the bad guys belonged to a shady organization known as the Italian Mafia. Some people said that the Mafia didn't exist, that there was no such thing as organized crime. But Ryan Sullivan had been raised to believe in the existence of the Mafia the way some children were raised to believe in Santa Claus.

He'd joined the police force in New York when he was seventeen. After his stint in the Pacific he went back to the force, using his G.I. benefits to pay for night school. With a college degree he landed a job at the Federal Bureau of Investigation, where to his disappointment he spent five years investigating alleged Communists, not gangsters, because J. Edgar Hoover, long-time Director of the FBI, confidently pooh-poohed the whole concept of organized crime. So Ryan Sullivan decided to quit the Bureau and become a prosecutor.

When in November of 1957 the New York State Police stumbled into a meeting of the heads of all the major crime families in America, Ryan Sullivan was in his third year at New York University Law School. He gloated over the press coverage, relishing every detail of what was soon to be known by nearly everyone in America as "the Apalachin Raid." Over fifty known gangsters had gathered at a private estate in Apalachin, New York, and they started to flee when the police showed up.

Ultimately, each one of the men arrested that day had to be released; for by getting together for a barbecue at the home of Joseph "Joe the Barber" Barbara, they were not committing any crime. But among the "guests" apprehended in the raid, fifty had police records; all were Italian or of Italian descent, and nearly half were related by blood or marriage. It had obviously been a meeting of the Mafia bosses.

In the face of this public relations disaster, Sullivan thought, Hoover would have to do something. He fervently hoped that the hounds of vengeance would finally be released, and intended to be at the front of the pack.

But still, Director Hoover stalled.

Upon his graduation from law school, Sullivan was hired as an assistant prosecutor by the Manhattan District Attorney's office. The pay was lousy, and the work seldom glamorous. He worked more on assault, battery, and theft cases than anything that smacked of organized crime. Sullivan didn't care. He got to know the cops: who could be trusted; who couldn't. He got to know the politicians: who was honest; who had a reputation for being on the mob's payroll. He saw how the Mafia bosses let underlings take the hit for petty offenses to keep themselves out of jail. And he observed that the Mafia soldiers did so, willingly. By dealing with the crooks in the trenches, Ryan began to get a handle on how the mob made its money. He began to know his enemy.

Ryan Sullivan worked hard. He believed in what he was doing. He had a deep, abiding respect for the majesty of the law. He believed in personal responsibility. He believed in justice. He believed in playing by the rules.

In 1961, when John Fitzgerald Kennedy was sworn in as president, Sullivan applied for a job as a federal prosecutor with the Department of Justice, in Attorney General Robert Kennedy's "Organized Crime" division. He knew that the Attorney General, like himself, was serious about taking on the Mafia. Robert Kennedy had been chief counsel to Senator John McClellan when the senator spearheaded an investigation of the Mafia's alleged infiltration of the country's biggest labor unions. During that time, the younger Kennedy had not hidden his belief in, or his fiery contempt for, the Mafia. Ryan Sullivan knew that he and Robert Kennedy had a common enemy. He knew that he had finally found a hero.

He got the job as an Assistant United States Attorney. After two years in Washington, D.C., Sullivan was assigned to the Organized Crime Section's brand new New York field office. His mission, like that of his peers, was to crack the mob. It was late February of 1963. He was finally where he had always wanted to be.

It was slow going. By and large, the Mafia chieftains learned from their mistakes. The code of silence remained unbroken. It was virtually impossible to get information. The bosses were much more likely to get killed by each other than to land in jail for any serious offense.

But Ryan Sullivan had a plan.

He looked up. Two men were standing just outside the open door of his small, spartan office. One was fair-haired and slim; the other had a Mediterranean complexion, dark hair, and the stocky physique of a wrestler. Both wore the FBI "uniform," dark blazer, straight black tie, white shirt, topped off by a bristly military-style haircut. Whatever the individual personality of Hoover's men, the impression they created for the outside world was homogeneous: clean cut, straight-laced, and professional.

"Come in, gentlemen," said Ryan, before either man had a chance to say hello. "I've been waiting for you."

The man Ryan knew to be Jamison, the slimmer one, glanced at his watch. "Gee, Mr. Sullivan. Sorry about the time. Traffic is hell at this hour."

"New to New York?" Ryan inquired pleasantly.

"No, sir," responded Jamison. "Lived here all my life."

"Then you should be prepared for the traffic. Next time get an earlier start."

Jamison and Royster exchanged glances. It seemed as if the new prosecutor was an even bigger hardass than they'd anticipated. They silently took their seats across from Ryan.

"We're going after the Carbolo family," Ryan said, the moment they were in their chairs. "I want to fill you in on the target of this particular investigation."

He handed each of the men a folder. "This is a background report on Gene Mandretti. I think he is the key to the Carbolo's money-laundering operation. I want him followed for the next three weeks. I want to know where he eats, sleeps, pisses, drinks coffee, and buys cigarettes. What he eats for breakfast and how often he does it with his wife. Round-the-clock surveillance. You can choose two agents from the pool to help you. But this has to be tip-top. This is no typical gangster we're dealing with."

"Who is this guy, Gene Mandretti, exactly?" interrupted Royster, giving Ryan a skeptical look.

"He's the nephew of Frank "Papa" Carbolo's right hand man, Salvatore Mandretti. He's married to Papa Carbolo's niece. Went to Williams College and then to NYU Business School. Serves on the board of several of the Family's privately-held corporations."

"How do you know he's on the team? They're always using blind family to hide assets," asked Jamison.

"I don't. Call it an educated guess. The first Carbolo-held company wasn't incorporated until a year and a half after little Geno here graduated from business school. He's the best-educated of the bunch. Over the past eight years, the IRS boys have been able to tag nearly a hundred of the under bosses from the other four Mafia families for various forms of tax fraud and evasion. They haven't touched the Carbolos. Why? Financial sophistication. That sure isn't Papa's strong suit. I think Geno is the brains behind the cleanliness of their operation. Here are photos and start-up information, home address, and other details. Let's see if there is any pattern we can tag on to. Come back in three weeks. Call me with any questions. I want a daily log."

"Okay," said Royster with a sigh of resignation.

Ryan stared at him. "I don't require enthusiasm Mr. Royster, just competence. I've been told you are an excellent agent, despite your... eccentricities. I don't expect to be disappointed."

Royster stared back, not sure whether he should feel insulted or flattered.

"Three weeks," he said, standing up. "We'll be here."

The next time they came to Ryan's office, three weeks later, Royster and Jamison carried with them a stack of journals; several files of documents; and a book of photographs. They showed up on time.

"Well, what do you have for me?" Ryan asked as they sat down, skipping all small talk.

"Well, it wasn't easy, I'll say that much," replied Royster. Jamison stayed silent. They had obviously agreed that Royster would do the talking.

"Looks like the man expects to be followed. He lost us on numerous occasions. I think he routinely takes counter-surveillance measures, which I guess is actually an encouraging sign. Goes home to the little wife and two cute kids on Long Island most nights, but sometimes stays in the city during the week. Real snappy dresser. Has a driver, definitely a bodyguard type. Carries lead. The driver, that is.

"Any unusual patterns of behavior? Anything we can use?"

"I'm getting to that. The one place, other than home, he went to once a week was this nightclub, in a building owned by the Family, on 52nd Street. We managed to follow him there one night, so we posted a lookout for the whole three weeks. Mandretti showed up three times. Went in early, between seven and eight. Came out late, around eleven."

"Any chance there's a meeting going on?"

"Could be. It's a small place, and the one time I sent Al Peyton in after him for a peek—he's the other agent helping us on this— Al didn't see Geno boy anywhere, so there's got to be a back room of some kind, although we couldn't find any sign of a back entrance."

"Who else was there?"

"That's the odd part. No one. No one we could identify, anyway. But boy, is the piano player one helluva looker. Want to see her?"

He began flipping through the notebook of photographs. "We caught a picture of her coming out of the place with her kid one morning. At least, I assume it's her kid. We got a shot of everybody who works there: bartender, bus boy, doorman, manager, two waitresses, and all the musicians. Everybody else went home. She seems to live in the building. No sign of a husband. Here she is." He handed the open book of photographs across the desk to Ryan.

Ryan looked at the picture. He saw a beautiful woman: slender, with black hair, ivory skin, and a heart-shaped face that looked like a china doll's. She was holding on to the hand of a little girl, who looked to be about two years old. The girl, who also had dark hair, was concentrating on her feet, trying to navigate the steps that led from the door to the sidewalk. The woman was smiling down at her, and pushing her own hair out of her face with her free hand. Both she and the girl were dressed in navy wool coats, for it was the middle of March, and spring had not yet arrived.

Ryan's brain was processing everything Royster had told him. He kept staring at the picture of Maddy. Hadn't he seen her somewhere before?

"Check her out," he said at last.

"Who, the dame?" asked Royster, surprised.

"Yes. What's her name?"

"Madeleine. Madeleine Gordon."

"Get me everything you can on Madeleine Gordon. By the end of the week I want to know her better than her own mother does."

"Can I ask why?" interjected Jamison with curiosity.

"Isn't it obvious? Gene goes to this place once a week. No one else we know shows up to see him. She lives in the building, which is owned by the Family. My money says she's Geno's 'special friend.' Let's see where this leads." He handed the notebook back.

"Good start. I'm encouraged."

"We aim to please," responded Royster, not bothering to disguise his sarcasm as he gathered up their files.

Jamison finally spoke up.

"Mr. Sullivan, didn't you tell us that this guy is married to Papa Carbolo's niece?"

"That's right."

"Brave sonofabitch then, ain't he?" opined Royster. "One portrait of a suspected Mafia mistress, coming up."

❦

Three men met again in Sullivan's office. This time Royster could not hide his excitement.

"Here's the report," he said, tossing his treasure casually on Ryan's desk. Jamison walked in behind him.

"What does it say?" Ryan asked, without picking it up. He would read it later, cover to cover, underlining items, taking notes, and preparing a list of follow-up questions. Now he wanted the investigators' informal impressions.

"Well, it was pretty easy, really. Had Jamison call her up, usin' his best 'been to Princeton' accent, and he told her that he was a freelance journalist doing a piece for the *New Yorker* on 'Jazz in the City,' and wanted to interview her. You give him the scoop, Jimmy." He gestured to Jamison.

"Well, we met at a little coffee shop down the street from her club. She was pleasant, and cooperative. She's not at all what I expected. I mean, she's... classy. Anyway, I tried not to ask her anything that might arouse her suspicions. Her maiden name is Hoffman. She had two years of classical musical training at the New Music School in Cambridge, Mass. She quit school to marry Bradley Gordon, a doctor, whom she met while he was at Harvard Med, and she was in music school. They moved out west and lived in San Francisco, where she got her first real exposure to jazz. She moved to New York and went back to a music career when her husband died three years ago. He died in a car accident.

"I asked her about her family, and she got a little evasive. Said her parents died in the war, and left it at that. So I looked sympathetic, and asked, 'So you're all alone in the world?' you know, that kind of thing, and she told me she had a daughter, which we'd already guessed, as well as an aunt living in New Jersey. Then we talked about jazz. She's had an impressive list of musicians in her place—"

Royster jumped in. "We followed that up by talking to a few people at the New Music School, including an old guy named Auerbach, who was apparently very sorry to see her quit. Said she was an amazing talent, blah blah. Also told us that her husband's family is loaded, and that her aunt in Jersey is none other than Bernice Mason of Mason Industries."

"What?" Ryan interrupted. "Didn't Archibald Mason... wasn't he the one who dropped dead of a heart attack on the floor of the New York Stock Exchange the day his company went public last year?"

"That's the one. Stock hit the market, quadrupled in an hour, and the poor ol' guy's ticker just popped when he realized how much money he was makin', leavin' his wife a very wealthy widow. Which means Mrs. Gordon doesn't *have* to work, unless she's on the outs with her aunt."

Ryan paused. "Interesting. What else?"

"We tracked down her late husband's family. Gordons of Boston. Old banking family. Real blue-bloods. Father wouldn't talk to us. The mother-in-law turned pretty hostile when I mentioned a granddaughter. She said, 'My son died without children, and he was not able to have children when he was alive.'"

"Hmm..."

Jamison and Royster exchanged looks.

"Here's the kicker. Check out Mrs. Gordon's 1961 tax return." He picked up the report, and flipped to one of the last pages.

"Here it is," he said, pointing and talking, "Declared income of over $100,000, based on salary and the club's net."

"That's a pretty big number."

"Yeah, especially since it's a pretty small place. Nice, but no Copacabana. Becomes even more suspicious when you look at her bank account. Either she keeps cash under her bed or the money goes elsewhere." He sat back, a smug look on his face. "Or, it doesn't exist."

"I think we have what we need, gentlemen," Ryan said thoughtfully. "Let's see if we can arrange to meet Mrs. Madeleine Gordon and ask her a few pertinent questions. Every man has a weakness."

He picked up another picture of Maddy and stared at her. "Every man has a weakness," he repeated. "Maybe this woman is Gene Mandretti's."

CHAPTER 32

THE INFORMANT

e⌇⌇⌇e

On a clear and breezy Thursday afternoon Maddy left her favorite hair salon and walked toward Fifth Avenue, in the direction of Central Park. She was going to go shopping for some new clothes for spring.

Maddy was half a block away from the shop when she saw a man she recognized. It was Bob Carlson, the journalist who had interviewed her a few weeks earlier for a piece in the *New Yorker*. He was standing still, holding a briefcase, looking in her direction. Maddy waved cheerfully as she approached him.

"Well, hello again!" she said brightly.

"Hello," he responded. "Gosh, was this lucky running into you like this. Mrs. Gordon, do you think you could talk to me for a few minutes? I have some follow-up questions for you."

Maddy glanced at her watch, but there was really no hurry. "Okay, if you like."

"Great."

Another man came over and joined them. He was tall and slim, with reddish hair and a sweet, friendly face. Maddy smiled at him.

"Is this a friend of yours?" she asked Bob Carlson.

Bob now had a funny look on his face, like a small boy who has just gotten away with a practical joke. He did not reply.

The other man spoke.

"Mrs. Gordon, I'm Ryan Sullivan, with the United States Attorney's office. Mr. Carlson works for the FBI. We need to ask you some questions."

"What?" *This must have something to do with my father,* she thought, for no clear reason. *My father the spy.*

"Will you come this way please?"

He took her gently by the elbow. "We'll walk over to the park, if that's all right, Mrs. Gordon. Find a comfortable bench to chat."

Maddy looked up at him. His expression was friendly but serious. She allowed herself to be led across the street.

She did not speak until they had entered the park. He headed immediately for a bench, where another man sat: a stocky Mediterranean type. He grinned up at her as they approached. The look in his eyes put Maddy on the defensive.

"Royster, keep your eyes open," ordered the redhead firmly. "Jamison, stand next to us. Run the tape."

"Aye, aye, cap'n," the man called Royster said, as he heaved himself up off the bench. "Nice day for a walk, isn't it?" He sauntered away.

"What's this about?" demanded Maddy, anger creeping into her voice.

"We'll get to that, Mrs. Gordon," replied the tall redhead mildly. He took the seat vacated by Royster.

"Please sit down."

Maddy did as she was asked, growing more alarmed by the minute.

"Tape running?" Ryan asked the man Maddy knew as Bob Carlson.

"Yessir."

"Okay. April 17, 1963. First contact with racketeering suspect Madeleine Gordon—"

"What?"

"Let me explain. As I said, I'm with the United States Attorney's Office. My name, in case you missed it the first time, is Ryan Sullivan. I work for the Attorney General's Organized Crime Division. Mr. Jamison, whom you met as Bob Carlson, is an agent with the Federal Bureau of Investigation. You are currently under investigation, because evidence has come to light suggesting that you are involved with an organized crime syndicate."

"This is ridiculous. There must be some mistake."

"I don't think so. Do you know a gentleman by the name of Gene Mandretti?"

Maddy turned pale.

Her reaction was not lost on Sullivan. "Speak up, please. We'll need your answer to register on the tape. Do you know Gene Mandretti?"

"Yes. Of course I do. He's my landlord," Maddy stated firmly, trying to regain her composure.

"Is that the full extent of your relationship?"

"Yes. Well, we're friends, but it's essentially a business relationship."

"I see. Mrs. Gordon, I think I should explain to you what is involved here. Jamison, let's have the tax return."

Jamison knelt down, opened his briefcase, pulled out a document, and handed it over.

"Mrs. Gordon, do you recognize this as your tax return for 1961?"

She glanced at it. "I wouldn't know."

"What do you mean by that?"

"I don't do my own taxes. I have an accountant do all that."

"Is that your signature?"

She glanced again to where he was pointing.

"It looks that way. I sign the papers but I don't really check them over. I have no idea how to read one of those things. Gene—Mr. Mandretti—has always had his accountant handle the club's finances."

"How much money did you make that year, Mrs. Gordon?"

"I paid myself a salary of twenty thousand dollars. Mr. Mandretti tells me the club is profitable, but not remarkably so. It's a small place. I don't really play for the money, Mr. Sullivan. Maybe that's hard for you to understand—"

"Do you have any idea what the club cleared, over and above your salary?"

"Thirty thousand, something in that range. I think that's what the accountant told me."

"Not a hundred?"

"Heavens, no."

"Then why does it say one hundred thousand on this tax return?"

"I—let me see that—how do I know this is mine?"

"Mrs. Gordon, you are the taxpayer responsible for this return. The club is leased, isn't it? From a corporation that Mr. Mandretti helps run?"

"Yes."

"He's using your club to wash funds."

"What is that supposed to mean?"

"It means you are helping make money from gambling rackets, prostitution, drug sales, and extortion, look like it was earned legally. It's called money laundering. And that tax return makes you an accomplice. The one you filed two days ago is even worse. You claim nearly one hundred and ten thousand dollars of income from the club's operations."

"I don't believe you."

"You'll believe me when I have you arrested."

"What?" Maddy jumped up. "You can't do that! I don't know anything about this—"

"That's not what this document indicates, Mrs. Gordon. Please sit back down."

"I'm leaving."

"Mrs. Gordon," said Ryan patiently, "If you leave now, the next time we see each other will be at your arraignment. There will be someone waiting for you at your apartment with a warrant for your arrest."

"No," whispered Maddy.

"I'm afraid so. And I know that would prove upsetting to your little girl."

The mention of Nichole made Maddy's knees grow weak. She sat back down.

"Now," Ryan Sullivan said calmly, his voice supportive and sympathetic. "How well do you know Gene Mandretti?"

"Not very. I mean, I've known him for… about three years. Since he bought the building from Matt Silvers, the man who hired me."

"How often do you see each other?"

"Not often. Once a week at the most. Sometimes not even that. He comes by the club."

"Do you meet in your apartment?"

Maddy looked at him, trying to decide if he meant what she thought he meant. "No, we do not."

"Mrs. Gordon, Gene Mandretti is married."

"I know that."

"He is married to the niece of Frank Carbolo, who is head of one of the five Mafia families operating in the New York area."

"What are you saying?"

"The Mafia, Mrs. Gordon. The mob. The Mafia is Gene Mandretti's family business. His uncle, Salvatore Mandretti, is Frank
'Papa' Carbolo's under boss, the number two man in the Carbolo
Crime Family. We think Gene is instrumental in helping to hide
the Family's illegally obtained assets. We know he's been using your
club for that purpose, based on this tax return. We need more
information. We need your help."

"And if I don't want to help you?"

"Then you will go to jail."

Maddy felt as if she had been punched in the stomach. She
wanted to deny everything this man was telling her, but the facts
he'd hit her with explained so many things that she'd been willing
to ignore: the driver who seemed to double as a bodyguard;
Gene's reluctance to talk about his family; the large quantities of
cash he carried with him. He sometimes carried a gun, hidden in
a holster that he wore under his jacket. The first time she'd seen it
and balked, he calmly explained that he needed protection when
he went into certain "ugly" parts of town where he owned investment property. The next time he came to see her he brought a
gun for Maddy to keep in her apartment. After all, he said, she
was an attractive woman, living alone in the nightclub district.
For her own protection she should have a gun, and know how
to use it.

Sullivan's revelation even made sense of the elaborate secret
entrance that Gene had installed: a hidden staircase that led from
her office in the club, through her apartment, to the apartment
upstairs. Privacy, he'd said.

Gene was involved with the Mafia. That's the reason he teasingly
kept her from "bothering herself" about the Blue Door's finances.
She'd been blind. Willfully, deliberately, stupidly blind.

Sullivan was talking again.

"We need your cooperation, Mrs. Gordon. We need the truth. We need you to tell us everything you know about Mandretti. If you cooperate fully, I will keep you from being charged. If you don't come across the bridge, then you will go to jail."

"But I haven't done anything!"

"That's not what this document suggests. And it will strike some people as odd that you do not keep track of what your club is earning. A trial is a very public forum, Mrs. Gordon. I'm offering you a chance to avoid that type of notoriety."

For a while no one spoke. "What do I need to do?" Maddy asked at last, sounding weak.

"Excellent. Okay. Now, we are going to start with some questions. If I find out that you're not being truthful, then you will go to jail, directly to jail, you will not pass Go, and will not collect $200. Is that clear?"

She nodded.

"Now, let me ask you again. What is the nature of your relationship with Gene Mandretti?"

She looked at him, understanding that he already knew the answer. That made it easier, somehow.

"He's my… my boyfriend."

"That's a start. How often do you see each other?"

"As I said, about once a week. Sometimes less."

"And you meet in your apartment over the club?"

"No. Well, yes and no. Gene had a sort of a secret staircase built, from my office in the club, up through my apartment, to the apartment upstairs. He comes into the club; I meet him upstairs. His driver stays outside, usually. Sometimes the driver goes into my apartment and watches T.V."

"And I'm assuming you can see the front entrance from the room where you have your T.V.?"

"Yes. I guess that's right."

"Does Mandretti ever go into your apartment?"

She shook her head. "No. Not anymore. He's… very careful."

"If I were cheating on Papa Frank's niece, I'd be careful, too. Has he ever discussed any aspect of the Blue Door's finances with you?"

"No. Just, as I said, that we're in the black."

"I need for you to copy documents for me. Anything you can find: receipts, payroll records, names of suppliers. Anything relating to anything bought by or sold at the club. And another thing: we'll be planting some microphones."

"Microphones? Where?"

"In your little rendezvous chamber."

"What?"

"Not the bedroom, unless you two talk a lot in the bedroom. Is there a phone in the upstairs apartment?"

She nodded. "An extension of my number."

"Does he use it?"

"Sometimes."

"Okay. So, we'll bug the phones, too."

"When is all this going to happen?"

"Soon. Real soon. Gene is smart. Among the smartest operating. If he gets a whiff of trouble, he'll cover his tracks, but quick. Within a week or so, we'll have everything in place. Some plumbers will come in to fix something in your apartment. You'll show them how to get upstairs without being noticed."

"Where will you be listening?"

"Never mind that. We won't be far."

"What should I do?"

"Absolutely nothing. If he gets an inkling that we're setting him up, this will blow up in our face. It may take a while. But if he has no idea that we can hear him, if he trusts his environment, he's likely to say something, sooner or later, that we can use. So do nothing different, is that clear?"

"Yes. Yes, I think so."

"Fine. And if all this works out, maybe we can keep you out of jail."

He stood up. "Mr. Jamison will walk you home. We'll be keeping an eye on you. Don't try to flee. Remember, if Papa Carbolo finds out about you, chances are both you and Gene will pay dearly for your indiscretion. Papa Carbolo is not an understanding man. If Gene finds out you're helping us, you'll wish you were in jail. Your only choice is to cooperate, and be careful. You can contact one of the agents, or me, if you feel you are in danger."

"Thanks," said Maddy bitterly.

"I'll be in touch." He walked away.

Maddy stood up and turned to Jamison.

"So it's not Bob then?"

"No."

"Is that damn thing off?" she said, pointing to the briefcase she assumed contained the tape recorder.

"Yes."

"So what *is* your name?"

"John. Everyone calls me Jimmy, though."

"Okay, Jimmy. I'm Maddy. You know the way home."

They walked, and for a long while neither spoke. When they were about a block from the Blue Door, Maddy halted.

"Do you think he believes me, believes that I knew nothing about all this?"

"If he believed that, you wouldn't be here."

"Do you believe me?"

He stood looking at her, pondering her question. "What I believe doesn't matter," he said finally, unable to look at her as he said it.

She sighed. "Well, that's honest, I guess."

Maddy went home. Nikki had just woken up from her nap, and was playing in the kitchen, where Tia was fixing dinner for the three of them. It was five o'clock. She would have dinner, play with Nikki, bathe her, put her to bed, and then go to the club. She must go on as if nothing had happened. As if nothing had changed.

But it was all different. Everything was all ruined. All she could do now was try and save herself, and her daughter.

CHAPTER 33

THE AVENGER

൜

Maddy went to a pay phone in Grand Central Station to make the call. She carefully dialed the number Ryan Sullivan had given her, and looked around fitfully as the phone rang. She was sure, or at least, hoped she was sure, that no one had followed her. Still, the thought that Gene—or anyone—might discover that she was helping the FBI tied her stomach into agitated knots.

"Sullivan here."

Maddy took a deep breath.

"Mr. Sullivan? This is Madeleine Gordon."

"Mrs. Gordon! What's wrong? Has Mandretti—"

"No, no. Nothing like that. It's just… I need to talk to you about all this. I'm a wreck. I don't know how long I can go on this way."

"Okay, okay. Can you get free this afternoon?"

"Yes Anytime."

"Okay. Are you familiar with Chinatown at all?"

"Yes."

"Good. My office is near there. There's a restaurant on Mott Street, the Dumpling House. Do you think you could get there within an hour?"

"I think so."

"Great. Okay. I'll see you there."

He was already there when she arrived, sitting in a booth in the corner. He waved her over as she came in.

"Thanks for coming," she said stiffly. He smiled. It was such a warm smile. It didn't fit him, somehow. It was someone else's smile, briefly displayed on Sullivan's face and then gone again.

"No problem," he replied. "I know how difficult this must be for you."

"Fat chance."

"Okay, I had that coming. Look, I was an agent before I was a lawyer. I'm not just some guy in a suit pushing papers. I've been in the trenches. I've done surveillance. I know what it's like to sweat it out—"

"Do you have children?"

"No. I'm not married."

"Then pardon me for saying so, but you don't know a damn thing."

He could see the exhaustion in her eyes. He did not argue.

"Are you hungry?" he asked, artfully changing the subject. "Do you like Chinese food?"

Maddy laughed. It seemed like such an irrelevant question. "To be honest, I haven't been hungry in weeks. But I do, or at least, I did, like Chinese food. I was born in China. But you probably know that already."

"No, I didn't know that. What were you doing there?"

"Being born."

"Okay, I mean, what were your parents doing there?"

Maddy paused. She was going to give a pat answer: my father's business brought the family to Shanghai, etc., etc. But she found herself telling this man, her accuser, the truth. He sat quietly as she related the story of her family: her father's flight to Shanghai;

how her mother joined him there after Leo made his fortune; about her mother's death; and her own journey to America with Amelia.

"Did your father ever come for you?" he asked, reflecting a measure of genuine concern.

"Not until it was too late. Too late for us to… accept each other, I guess. I stayed for a while with a foster family, and then my aunt found me. You know the rest. I told Bob, I mean, Jimmy, everything else."

An impatient waiter hovered nearby. "You wanna orda?" he asked.

Maddy did so and Ryan followed suit. When the waiter left, they sat in silence. Maddy began to play with her chopsticks.

"I guess you could say an attraction for gangsters runs in the family," she said mirthlessly. Ryan smiled again. She looked up at him and he was alarmed to see tears in her eyes.

"I don't know if I can keep this up," she said, her voice cracking.

He handed her his napkin. "Why? Because you're in love with him?" The question escaped before he had a chance to analyze it. He knew the answer. Of course she was in love with him.

Maddy wiped her eyes, and took a moment to reply. "No," she said at last, tasting the truth of her words as she spoke. "I suppose I was at first, at least, I thought I was. Gene is very charismatic, and I was not, shall we say, immune to his charms. But our romance, if you can call it that, it's always been like living out some kind of fantasy. It was something I… needed. And when you told me the truth about him, well, it made too much sense. That's all it took to shatter the illusion. I'm not sorry for him. Or for myself. I'm just angry at myself for being so stupid."

She dipped her chopsticks aimlessly in her water glass and stirred, concentrating on the movement of the water.

An intense feeling of awareness radiated through Ryan's nerves as he watched her. *What if she's telling the truth? What if she's been telling the truth all along? What if she's innocent?*

But he said nothing. This case was too important, and she was too vital a link. She was the mistress of a Mafia kingpin, he reminded himself. She was the enemy.

"Why did you want to see me?" he asked, trying to pull himself back to business. She looked up, tearing herself away from the distant plain of her own thoughts.

"I want to speed things up. I'm going to go crazy. I can't put up with this tension. This worry that something will happen. That something will happen to Nikki."

"Can you send her away? To your aunt's?"

Maddy smiled ironically. "For a few days, I suppose that would work. My aunt is not a very maternal person. And she'd wonder why. No, I want this all to end. There must be something I can do."

"Not really. You've done a great job, so far. These past three weeks have been really productive. We've copied all the documents that you've secured for us, and we've got a good tap on the phone. He's called out several times to some key people. Nothing too important, but with time, something will give. All this takes is patience."

"And where did you, Ryan Sullivan, learn all this patience?"

She was getting under his skin. This was dangerous. "The hard way," he answered brusquely.

"I see." Their food arrived. She looked down at her plate as if she did not know where it had come from, then stood up.

"Where are you going?" he asked, startled.

"I'm not hungry. Thanks. Don't worry. I'll carry on."

"Maddy, wait!" neither of them noticed that he'd used her first name. He followed her out of the restaurant. Just as she turned to walk up the street, he caught her arm, then dropped it.

"Maddy, I—"

She was waiting, waiting for something. Waiting for something he could not give her.

"I'm sorry," he said at last, as if that would help.

"Don't be. I got myself into this. I'll stick with it. You're just doing your job."

"Call me if you need another pep talk," he murmured, feeling foolish.

"I'll be okay."

He wanted to believe her.

Ryan Sullivan found himself walking by the Blue Door that night. He knew it was a ridiculous thing to do. He told himself he was there to check up on the surveillance team. He could see Al Peyton's undercover car, parked across the street. He would be around the place, somewhere. Let the boys think he came by to keep them on their toes.

He could hear the piano playing before he entered the room. A saxophone mingled its own melancholy sound with the music of Maddy's fingers. The blend was hypnotically beautiful.

The music stayed with him for hours, haunting him as he tried to sleep. He thought about her expressive eyes. The sound of her voice. The shape of her shoulders. The sweet sadness that came gliding out through her music.

It was nearly morning before he fell asleep. And she was there in his dreams.

❦

Maddy never bothered to ask herself what she would do when it was all over; what she would do when the Blue Door and Gene and Ryan Sullivan were out of her life. She tried to take one day at a time.

An early afternoon in mid-May found Nikki and Maddy at the zoo in Central Park. Nikki's favorite animals were the pigeons, and her favorite game was chasing them. Maddy sat on a bench and watched as her daughter's chubby little legs trotted with lurching speed in the direction of a clump of the dirty gray birds. Nikki never caught one, but she never gave up.

A tall, older man, wearing a lightweight raincoat, sunglasses, and a felt fedora approached Nikki. He held a bag of popcorn in his hands. Watching him, Maddy felt her maternal radar go up. She was ready to spring from the bench, should the man come too close to her daughter.

He didn't. He stood several feet away, and started tossing popcorn to the pigeons. They gathered around him quickly, torn between their fear of Nikki's thundering toddler feet and their desire for a free meal. Nikki stood still, fascinated, watching his success.

"My turn! My turn!" she burbled.

The man smiled and handed her the bag. Nikki immediately spilled a quarter of it, and the pigeons gathered around her greedily, happy to let bygones be bygones if she were willing to offer such a generous peace prize.

Now the man was walking toward the bench. When he was only three feet away he stopped, looked at Maddy, and took off his sunglasses.

Maddy nearly fainted.

"It's you," she whispered.

"Hello, Maddy," said Leo Hoffman. "May I join you?"

Moving as if in a trance, Maddy scooted over to make enough room for her father to sit down. "What are you doing here?" she got out at last. "Where did you come from? I thought you were dead! I mean, I assumed you were. We tried to find out, but there weren't any records—"

Leo smiled, that half-amused smile that Maddy still saw occasionally in her dreams.

"Not dead. Just somewhere else. Living someone else's life, behind the Iron Curtain."

"Still a spy?"

"Until quite recently. Looks like I'm going to retire."

"Good God," muttered Maddy, sinking back into the bench. "My father is James Bond."

Leo laughed. Nikki looked up from her pigeons when she heard him then, satisfied that she was missing nothing, went back to the business of feeding the birds.

"I haven't seen the movie," he said. "But I have read a couple of the books. My work was nothing nearly so glamorous, I'm afraid. No, the spy business isn't exactly what Mr. Fleming describes."

Maddy was quiet, completely at a loss for what else to say. Leo gave her a moment to collect herself, then he began to talk.

"I've been back in the country for a few weeks, Maddy. I had some business to do in Washington. Then I thought I would come and see you."

"You could have called."

"Well, I wasn't too successful with that strategy last time. So I thought I would try a personal reintroduction. The fact that you haven't yet seized your child and fled is, I admit, somewhat encouraging."

"No, Papa. It's a shock, seeing you like this, but I won't run away this time."

Leo looked at her with grateful relief. "Thank you, Maddy."

They watched Nikki for a moment, who'd by now strewn popcorn all over the pavement, and was using stealth to try and pet one of the gluttonous pigeons. Each one managed to shimmy away from her just in time to avoid being touched.

"She's beautiful. What's her name?"

"Nikki. Her name is Nikki. Aunt Bernice thinks she looks like you."

"No, she looks like you. And your mother."

"But she has your eyes. Blue eyes."

Even this mild intimacy made Maddy feel dangerously exposed. "What do you want?" she asked, the tenderness gone from her voice.

Leo removed his hat. His hair was now streaked with gray. Lines around his eyes testified to his age and the significant stress of his chosen profession. Still, he looked like the man Maddy remembered.

"I just wanted to see you, Maddy. I don't want to make you uncomfortable. I'll leave if you want me to."

Maddy paused. The sight of her father aroused so many conflicting emotions. There was so much pain there, and the scars ran so deep. She wasn't sure how she could cope with Leo's sudden reappearance, especially given everything else that was going on in her life.

"I finally did read your letters, Papa. I'm sorry that it took so long. Mrs. O'Connor gave them to me when my husband died."

"I am very sorry that you lost your husband," Leo said gravely.

"Well, I suppose it's just one of the many things you don't know about me. I mean, we haven't exactly kept in touch, you know."

"That is the greatest regret of my life." He said this without any melodrama, merely stating a simple truth.

She sighed. "It's not as if it was all your fault. I told you to go away."

"I shouldn't have listened, Maddy. You were only fifteen. But there was so much pain there, for both of us, and my other path seemed so... clear."

"Oh, Papa. That's just how life works, I guess. One day a decision seems so straightforward, and the next day, nothing is clear at all." *Nikki's life is all about pigeons and popcorn right now. I wish it would stay that way for her. Simple.*

"Maddy, this is probably asking too much, but I'd like you to consider, that is… to ask you, if you might be willing to make room for me in your life now, on whatever terms you suggest. I would just like to be a… presence."

Maddy winced, wishing he'd been there to ask her that question three months ago, before she had learned the truth about her life. About her lover. About herself. But she had to say something. "Well, I have this little place, the Blue Door, down on 52nd Street. It's a little jazz club. Nothing too commercial. It's a real musician's haunt, you know, for real jazz lovers. I waited too long to make a go of a career in classical music but somehow jazz was the right choice for me. Or, at least, I thought so."

"But now something has changed?"

"Well, there's Nikki, you know. It's not really the life a mother should lead. She'll get older, and I'll have to do something else."

Leo could tell she was lying. He decided not to push.

"And what about you?" Maddy asked. "What's next?"

"I don't know. In part that depends on you."

Maddy had no time to respond, for Nikki had decided she had enough of the pigeons.

"Oh, dear—there she goes—come on!" She flew after Nikki, who had started to run down the sidewalk, in the general direction of the bear cage.

Nikki kept them going for over an hour before slowing down, a signal to Maddy that she was ready for her nap. Leo walked home with them, carrying the tired girl in his arms for the last few blocks. *This, just this one moment, is more than I deserve,"* he thought, looking down at his granddaughter's sweet, sleepy face. *So much more than I deserve.*

"I'm staying at the Pierre, if you want to reach me," he whispered, after he had placed Nikki in her crib. "I'd love to come and hear you play. I can just sit in the back. I don't want to make you feel uncomfortable."

"Oh, Papa, I would like that, I think. Not tonight, though. Tomorrow. I'm doing a solo gig, I mean, a solo performance, tomorrow. If you think you could make it."

"Nothing will keep me away, Maddy. I promise. I'll be there."

Leo showed himself out. He saw a brown, two-door Chevrolet that was parked across the street. Leo had been keeping tabs on Maddy for several days in order to find a convenient way to approach her. The brown car had been there the whole time; not always in the same place, but always nearby. And there was always someone in it.

Leo had spent years training himself to observe such things. His professional instincts made him wary. Then he chided himself. This was New York, not Eastern Europe. The Russians were unlikely to snatch him off the street, even if they eventually found out his real identity. That part of his life was over. He deliberately turned his back on the car, and walked away.

After Leo left, Maddy sat in her room, staring at the walls, for well over an hour. Her father. Her father. After almost eighteen years. To think of all the times she'd thought she'd seen his face in a crowd. The times she awoke to the sound of his voice, a voice that was never really there. If he was willing to try, then so was she. She was stronger, now. She could take a chance.

But she needed to straighten her life out, first. There had to be a way out. No matter what Ryan Sullivan said. There had to be a way out of the mess she'd created. She had to have a new start. For herself, and for Nikki. And, for her father.

Gene was planning to come over tonight. Tonight she would end this charade, one way or another. She would prove her innocence to Mr. Ryan Sullivan. She would rid herself of Gene Mandretti. And she would go on with her life.

She picked up the phone and dialed Bernice's number.

Later that evening, the phone rang in Leo Hoffman's suite at the Hotel Pierre. He let it ring several times before picking it up.

"Hello?"

"Leo, this is Bernice Mason. I would like to say welcome back, where have you been and all the usual rubbish, but I think I will skip the formalities. Madeleine called me a few moments ago, and explained that she has talked to you. Could you please tell me what you did to her?"

"Do? Nothing. I met her in the park. At the zoo. With little Nikki. It was very pleasant, or at least I thought so."

"Then would you please explain to me why she asked me to take Nikki for a few days? The child is on her way over now, with that Polish nanny of hers. Madeleine said she needed some peace and quiet. She sounded extremely distraught. I think your sudden reappearance has disturbed her very deeply. I am disgusted that you would consider it appropriate to leap back into her life like a jack-in-the-box. I must ask you not to see her again."

"Bernice, when I left them, Maddy was just fine. She asked me to come by the club tomorrow. I don't know what happened. I'll go and see her—"

"No! For God's sake, don't upset her anymore than she is already. I've never heard her so distraught. Asking me to take care of Nichole as if she never expected to see her own child again. You must have given her a dreadful shock."

"I'm sorry, Bernice. I don't know what to say."

"Just stay away from her. Stay away from my family."

"She's my daughter, Bernice."

"As if that has ever mattered to you." She hung up.

Leo put the phone back on the hook. Something was not right. The Madeleine that Bernice had described had nothing to do with the poised young woman he'd seen this afternoon. Maybe Bernice was lying, trying to make him leave. Trying to make him leave Maddy and Nikki alone.

Or maybe there was something going on in Maddy's life he needed to find out more about.

❦

Maddy took special care dressing that evening. She spent a long time brushing her hair, and put on the emerald-and-diamond necklace that Gene had given her on the *Queen Elizabeth*. That was one piece of information she did not share with the FBI: that her affair with Gene had begun in June of 1960, not the following year. There was no way she was going to let anyone know that Nikki was his daughter.

Especially not Gene himself.

She was not performing that night; Gene would come early, and expect to stay for hours. She had dinner delivered from Chez Paulette, a bistro down the street. She put a bottle of champagne on ice. She put on her makeup. And she waited.

He arrived at eight and greeted her with the same sensuous embrace he always did. They had dinner and talked about what they usually talked about: the club, Nikki's latest accomplishments, what news she'd had from Katherine. Maddy did not mention her father. She floated through the evening like an actress in a play; not missing a cue, laughing at the right times, as charming as she could be.

After nibbling at dessert she mixed a pitcher of martinis and poured one for each of them. Gene liked his liquor.

She watched him as he took his first sip, nodding his approval. Now, she thought. Now, before he starts… before he gets what he came here for.

"Gene, tell me, is the Blue Door making money?"

He looked at her, surprised. "Of course it is, Angel. You're terrific. You pull 'em in like bees to honey."

"Well, how much of it do we get to keep?"

"What do you mean?"

"You know, taxes. Income taxes. I may not be a financial genius, but I know there are ways around paying your taxes. Doctors love to get paid in cash, so they don't have to report every dime. It helps make up for all the times they don't get paid at all."

"What the hell is she tryin' to do?" barked Royster, listening from the FBI surveillance post set up in a building on the next block. "Didn't Sullivan tell her not to try and make him talk? This is gonna backfire. Shit. Stupid bitch. Call Sullivan. Tell him this whole operation may blow any minute. Tell him to get his butt over here."

"Maddy, Maddy, the doctor's wife," Gene responded, with a touch of sarcasm in his voice. "What other bad habits did ol' Doctor Brad teach you? Good thing his brakes failed when they did, or by now you'd be in jail with him for income tax evasion, instead of here in my arms, where you belong."

Maddy did not respond for an instant. Gene's statement had triggered a terrifying train of thought. "How did you know his brakes failed? The car exploded."

Gene looked at her with a mixture of irritation and defensiveness. "Well, Maddy, his car went over a cliff. Something must have been wrong with the Cadillac."

"How did you know he was driving a Cadillac?"

"Maddy, what is this, the third degree?"

Maddy's heart raced. She'd not connected what Sullivan had told her about Gene with the circumstances surrounding Brad's death. But it made too much sense not to be true. "What if you can't go back to him?" Gene had asked that last morning on the *Queen Elizabeth*. She'd taken his question to mean, "What if he doesn't want you back?" But that wasn't what he meant at all. He meant that he could have Brad taken out of the equation. Gene had made sure that she had no husband to go back to.

At last she found her voice.

"You killed him. You know it's true. You killed Brad, so you could have me."

Gene grinned at her. "Look, I may have wanted the man dead. There was a time I wanted to see both of you dead. But don't you think it's a little far-fetched to go accusing me of murdering your husband? Not to mention unkind."

"You didn't murder him yourself. You had your fairy god-father do it for you. Your Uncle Sal."

Gene's expression turned deadly serious. He put his drink down on the coffee table. "Who have you been talking to, Maddy?"

"No one," she said, looking away. "I'm just not as dumb as you think I am. Your uncle is Salvatore Mandretti. Everyone knows he's connected to the Mafia."

"The *what*? Maddy, who's been talking to you about the Mafia?"

"No one, Gene. I just put two and two together, that's all."

"Maddy, is there something you need to tell me? Has someone been asking you questions about me? About my uncle? About my family's business?"

"No," she whispered, forcing herself not to look away from him.

"Good. Good. And if anyone does, you'll tell me about it, won't you, Maddy?" He reached out and grasped her jaw tightly, too tightly.

"Stop. You're hurting me." She said, her voice comically muffled by his grip on her chin.

"You'll tell me, won't you Maddy?" he repeated, not releasing his grip. "Because I would never, never want anything to happen to you, or our daughter."

Her eyes grew wide. With a surge of strength, she tore his hand away from her face.

"She is *not* your daughter. Don't bring Nikki into this."

"That's bullshit, Maddy. That's bullshit, and you know it. She's my kid. She's got Mandretti written all over her. And if you and Brad didn't have a kid for ten years, I'm not going to believe he planted one right before he died."

Maddy's eyes filled with tears of fury. "You're a bastard."

"I know I am, Maddy. The last time you told me that was the night I finally got you back into my bed. And that's what you've always loved about me. Don't kid yourself, Angel. This ain't no sweet romance. You give me what I want, and I give you what you want. What you've always wanted. It's what you want right now."

"NO! Don't you touch me."

Gene grabbed her wrists.

"I told you once before, Maddy. Never say no to me."

"*Looks like we're in for a show,*" *Royster hollered to Jamison. You reach Sullivan yet?*"

"*Yeah! Got him now, on his car radio. Ryan? This is Jamison. You read me?*"

"*Loud and clear.*"

"*Listen, Ryan. You better get over here. Looks like something may blow.*"

"*What's going on?*"

"*She's going off-script, trying to get him to spill something, and he's getting mighty damn suspicious. It may have worked, though. Looks like we could maybe link one of Sal's boys to her husband's death. And Geno's made some pretty good threats against her. But things are breakin' fast. You better zip on over.*"

"*Uh, oh,*" *interrupted Royster. "Sounds like we got a little nonconsensual sex going on.*"

"*What's that?*" *said Sullivan, unable to catch what Royster was saying in the background.*

"*Well,*" *stammered Jamison, "Seems Mr. Mandretti wants some... uh—you know—and Maddy—Mrs. Gordon—isn't cooperating.*"

"*Shit,*" *said Royster, still listening. "She's really gonna fuck this up if she starts playin' hard to get now.*"

"*I'm on my way,*" *Ryan snapped. A wave of anger and remorse engulfed him. He never should have gotten her involved. He should have believed her when she said she didn't know anything. He had to get her out of there.*

Ryan drove his car like a rocket in the direction of 52nd Street.

Maddy fought Gene with all her strength. She finally escaped him and ran toward the door. He tackled her before she reached it.

Maddy stopped struggling. She lay beneath him, silent, passive, not moving as Gene entered her. When he came she looked at his contorting face with detachment.

Gene moved off of her. He zipped up his pants and walked over to the coffee table to reclaim his drink. Maddy sat up on the floor. She felt uncannily calm and clear-headed. She watched Gene as he picked up his martini, drained it, and put down the empty glass. He kept his back to her.

She would not let him threaten Nikki. If there was one thing she would do with the rest of her screwed up life, she would protect her daughter from the monster who'd fathered her.

Maddy stood up, tried to straighten her skirt, pushed back her hair, and walked over to the small foyer table next to the door. She kept Gene's spare cigarettes in the drawer. And her gun.

"Cigarette?" she asked sweetly, as if she had just made love to the man she adored, rather than been raped by a man she now hated.

"Why certainly, my love," Gene answered, in a fair imitation of Cary Grant. He turned around. She lifted the gun from the drawer as Ryan Sullivan burst in.

Sullivan looked over at the gun in her hand. "Christ! Don't shoot!"

"*What the fuck!?*" yelled Royster. "*Jimmy! Sully's in the apartment!*"

"*What?*" echoed Jamison, leaping to his feet. "*What's he doing there?*"

Maddy looked at Ryan. She saw the plea in his eyes. But she thought only of her daughter.

Gene took a step forward. "Who the hell are you? Fuckin' shit—I don't care who the hell you are! You're a dead man."

Maddy held her gun straight out in front of her, and shot him.

The bullet opened a small, red wound in the side of Gene's chest. It turned red. He looked down at the hole in his body, then up at Maddy.

"Angel," he said, and fell forward, dead.

Ryan Sullivan snatched the gun from Maddy's hand and shot another round into the wall. His eyes raked the room. He saw Mandretti's coat jacket hanging over a chair and raced over to it, searching for the gun he desperately hoped was there. It was. Using his handkerchief, he placed it carefully in Gene's right hand, shouting as he did so.

"Royster! Jamison! I had to shoot the bastard! I think he's dead!"

"*Oh, Jesus Christ. What next?*" cried Royster. "*Sully went and blew the asshole away!*"

"*What?*" screamed Jamison. "*What the hell is he thinking?*"

"We're gettin' out of here!" Ryan shouted to the invisible ears. He turned to Maddy, who stood transfixed, staring at Gene's corpse and the red stain rapidly spreading on the carpet beneath it.

He took her hand. "Come on, Maddy. We have to go." Half dragging her behind him, he headed down the stairs.

Gene's bodyguard was at the bottom of the staircase, his gun pointed up at them.

"Would you mind telling me where Mr. Mandretti is?" he asked, his voice as menacing as his gun. "I heard some gunshots."

"He's dead," said Maddy, pushing her way past Ryan, "He raped me, and I killed him."

"Don't!" Ryan shouted, trying wildly to reach for her and aim his gun at the same time.

"You fuckin' bitch," the bodyguard said, and fired. The bullet caught Maddy in mid-step. She tumbled down the stairs.

"Maddy!" Ryan fired, but his shot went wild. He plunged down the stairs as he heard another shot and flinched, expecting to feel pain, for he knew the bullet was aimed at him. But he felt nothing.

In front of him the bodyguard's knees buckled, and the big man fell over. Another man stood in the doorway. An older man, someone Ryan had never seen before.

"I'm Leo Hoffman. Maddy's father. My car's across the street. Let's get her out of here. And then you can tell me what the hell is going on."

CHAPTER 34

THE HERO

Leo sat in the waiting room of Manhattan's St. Joseph's Hospital and waited for the surgeon to bring him news of his daughter.

He heard footsteps, and half-expected to see Bernice with Nikki in tow. Instead, he saw the haggard face of Ryan Sullivan.

"How did it go?" he asked, as soon as Ryan had collapsed into a chair across from him. His own interview with the city police had taken place hours before, and was mercifully brief. His CIA credentials had thrown them for a loop. They happily turned him over to the FBI, whose agents were both irked and confused by the sudden appearance of a CIA man in the middle of their failed sting operation. The FBI and CIA higher-ups were having joint conniptions in Washington, trying to figure out what Leo could say to whom, and about what. Eventually, he would have a lot of explaining to do. But he wasn't worried. Not for himself.

"Better than I expected, actually," Ryan answered, heaving a sigh. "No one challenged my story. The police were happy to turn the whole thing over to the Bureau. They found a gun in his hand; ballistics test proved I'd fired one. The tape backed up my story. I said, 'don't shoot' to Mandretti, then he told me I was a dead man, and then I got two shots off before he fired. I said my first one hit him in the chest, and the second one went wild. So the self-defense story stands up reasonably well. Now we just have to make sure she doesn't contradict me. I'll catch hell—more than likely I'll get bounced—for botching the whole investigation. But I don't care." He paused. "It was worth it."

Leo studied him; this man who had first jeopardized his daughter's life, then tried so hard to save it. Ryan told him the whole story as they sped to the emergency room. Leo had seen the remorse and panic in the younger man's eyes then. Now he was trying to keep Maddy from being charged with murder. Ryan Sullivan was in love with her, though he doubted the young man yet realized it himself. He was desperately in love with her.

Leo still remembered how that felt.

"I have some friends in D.C. who owe me a favor," Leo said. "I may be able to help you. About the job, I mean."

Ryan nodded, then shrugged. "Thanks," he said. "But it won't mean anything… if she… you know." He could not finish.

At that moment Bernice entered the waiting room.

"Who are you?" she demanded of Ryan.

He dug in his breast pocket and flipped open his credentials. "Assistant United States Attorney Ryan Sullivan, Organized Crime Task Force. You're Bernice Mason, Mrs. Gordon's aunt, aren't you?"

She ignored him and turned to Leo. "Will you please tell me what is going on? How did Madeleine get hurt? And *shot* of all things? Was it some thug from that nightclub?"

"Not exactly, Mrs. Mason," replied Ryan, regaining some of his professional demeanor. "Your niece has been assisting us in an investigation involving organized crime activities in the New York entertainment industry. A target of the investigation caught wind of the fact that she was cooperating with federal authorities, and threatened to kill her. She was shot by his bodyguard while trying to escape him."

Bernice sank into a chair. "I don't believe it."

"I'm sorry... sorrier than I can tell you. That's the truth, Mrs. Mason."

"Why would she get involved in something like that?" asked Bernice, hurt and bewildered.

Ryan did his best to keep the guilt out of his voice as he tried to answer her question. "She's a brave woman, Mrs. Mason. She had access to important information, and she wanted to see justice done. She's a hero."

The surgeon entered the room, leaving Bernice no time for more questions. He looked around at the small gathering, removing his surgical mask as he did so.

"I know Mr. Hoffman," he said, glancing at Leo. "I don't think I've met either of you. I'm Dr. Henderson. We just finished removing the bullet."

"How is she?" asked Ryan, speaking for all of them.

"We won't know for sure for several hours, but it looks like she'll make it. The bullet missed her lung by a fraction. Splintered some ribs, but no spinal trauma. She should be okay."

"When can I see her?"

"I have to talk to her."

"I want to see her."

Dr. Henderson held up his hand. "We can't overwhelm the poor woman. Once she has regained consciousness, I will let Mr. Hoffman, her father, in to speak with her. You two will have to wait."

"But I insist—" Bernice persisted.

"Ma'am," he said politely, "I have just told representatives of the Federal Bureau of Investigation the same thing I am about to tell you. Mrs. Gordon's medical chart lists her father as her next of kin. I have no idea who you are but here, in this hospital, we play by my rules. Mr. Hoffman may see Mrs. Gordon, for five minutes, once I give him the green light. Everyone else, and I mean *everyone,* will wait until I decide her condition has stabilized."

"But—"

"Ma'am, I suggest you go home and get some sleep. I will have a nurse contact you when Mrs. Gordon is ready to receive visitors."

Bernice bristled. She was not used to getting no for an answer. "Very well," she said, barely civil. "I expect to be contacted *immediately* once she has stabilized."

"You have my word," responded Dr. Henderson, at once patient and firm.

"And you!" Bernice now focused on Ryan. "I want you to tell me exactly how this happened. Why was Madeleine involved? How did this mobster find out? This is an outrage, subjecting a law-abiding citizen to this type of danger. What do you think she is, some kind of *spy?*"

"No, ma'am," said Ryan, trying to follow Dr. Henderson's lead. "And I'm afraid I can't give you any more information until I get permission from the FBI to do so. This is highly sensitive information. If it gets out, then Maddy's life may well still be in danger. Right now we hope no one but the two dead members of the Mafia knew that Maddy was involved. You can see how important it is to maintain complete secrecy."

Bernice's mouth dropped open. She put a hand to her head.

"I've had as much as I can take for one evening. But don't think for a minute you've heard the last of me." With this comment, she left.

Dr. Henderson waited until she was gone before he spoke again.

"Mother-in-law?" he asked.

Leo snorted. "My sister-in-law."

"Impressive lady. You may wait if you wish, Mr. Hoffman. It will be two more hours before the anesthesia wears off enough for her to be coherent."

"I'll wait."

"Very well then. I'm going home. She's being monitored. And guarded, I have to say, very closely. These agents are a nuisance."

It wasn't until the doctor left the room that relief began to release the tension in Leo's body. He was too exhausted to feel joy. Joy would come later.

Ryan turned to him, pleading. "You have to tell her for me."

"What? Tell her what?"

"You have to tell her that I shot Gene Mandretti. It's the only way the story fits together. Otherwise, she'll be charged with murder. You have to help me save her."

"Of course I will. Now, go get some rest."

"I'd rather wait."

"As you wish."

The next hour and a half dripped by. By one o'clock in the morning the two men had fallen asleep, dozing off in their chairs. Leo snapped to attention when he heard a voice.

"Mr. Hoffman?" asked a nurse gently. "You may see your daughter now. Five minutes. No longer."

He leapt up.

Maddy looked so small and helpless. Machines ticked and whirred around her. A tube in her wrist slowly replaced some of the blood she had lost. To Leo's relief, the two guards posted outside her room stayed outside.

He sat down next to his daughter and stroked her hand.

"Maddy?" he whispered. "Princess?" Her eyes opened slowly, and she looked at him without turning her head.

"Papa. Papa." She took a breath, and tried to speak.

"Is Ryan... do you know... is Mr. Sullivan—"

"Mr. Sullivan is fine, Maddy. He was not hurt."

"But the driver..."

"I killed him."

"You?" She moved, as if trying to sit up. He gently restrained her.

"Maddy, I'm fine. Everything's fine. Listen to me carefully. Ryan killed Mandretti. Do you understand that?"

Maddy looked puzzled. She shook her head.

"Trust me Maddy. Ryan Sullivan killed Gene Mandretti in self-defense. You were with him, and when you both tried to escape, you were shot by Gene's bodyguard. It's vital that you remember this, because people will ask you questions, and you must be able to answer."

"But Ryan—"

"Ryan's not in any trouble, Maddy. He'll be all right." He paused.

"You have to do this, Maddy. For Nikki, and for me."

A glimmer of comprehension crossed her face.

"Promise, me, Princess," he said.

"I promise."

"Good. Now go to sleep."

He stayed with her until her even breathing convinced him that she had in fact gone back to sleep. Then he watched her for a long time, studying her face, every cell of his body reverberating with the force of his memories. He had never been there for her. He had never given her what she needed. But for once, at last, perhaps... perhaps he'd been there when she needed him most.

The New York police, following instructions from the FBI, reported to the local press that Gene Mandretti, wealthy Manhattan businessman and landlord of the Blue Door nightclub, had been killed, along with his chauffeur, during a robbery attempt. The press also learned that Madeleine Hoffman, the club's owner, had been injured in the holdup, and the thieves had gotten away with a diamond necklace, given to Maddy by her father, a well-to-do gentleman who'd made his fortune in the rubber business prior to World War II.

Papa Carbolo was suspicious of the story, and suspected that Gene had been grazing in a forbidden pasture, but there did not seem to be any direct fallout from the boy's death other than some temporary financial confusion. Then, in June, a mob triggerman by the name of Joe Valachi started singing from his penitentiary cell in Atlanta. He began telling tales and naming names. The code of silence had been broken. The Five Families had more pressing problems to worry about.

It was a week before Maddy was released from the hospital. During that time her father Leo, her aunt Bernice, and her friend Ryan Sullivan, came to see her every day. Her fans from the Blue Door filled her room with flowers. When the tubes were withdrawn and the machines rolled away, Bernice brought little Nikki to visit. Maddy hugged her tightly, trying to reassure the frightened little girl that her mother would soon be home.

On the day that Maddy was discharged, Leo and Nikki were there to escort her. She walked slowly through the glass double doors toward the car where Bernice and her driver waited to take her home.

"You're walking so slow, Mommy! It's like you just learned how!" Nikki sang out, mimicking her mother's measured pace.

"I guess I'll have to learn how to do it all over again," Maddy replied. Then she looked at her father. "There are a lot of things I have to learn how to do all over again."

"Me, too." He answered back.

She squeezed his hand. "I won't let go if you won't."

"Never again, Maddy. I'll never let go again."

And for the first time in a very, very long time, she believed him.

HISTORICAL CHARACTERS

~

One of the joys of writing historical fiction is the opportunity to blend real characters and historical events with their fictional counterparts. Below are some of the real people with whom Leo Hoffman interacts in *Deceptive Intentions.*

Colonel William Eddy, who had an outstanding service record in WWI in military intelligence, was personally tapped by William "Wild Bill" Donovan, founder of the American Office of Strategic Services, to head up the spy network in North Africa. In 1944 he went on to become Minister Plenipotentiary to Saudi Arabia, where he continued to serve as an important source for the Central Intelligence Agency.

Carlton Coon was a professor of Anthropology at Harvard, who, along with his professional colleague Gordon Browne, worked closely with William Eddy in North Africa. They did in fact develop "mule-turd bombs" which were used effectively during the Allied campaign in Tunisia. There is still speculation about the level of Coon's involvement in the assassination of Admiral Darlan, the controversial officer who was to lead French military operations after the Allies won North Africa.

Christine Granville was one of the most glamorous and successful undercover agents to work for the Special Operations Executive, the war-time British spy organization. Born Krystyna Skarbek, the daughter of a Polish count, she began her career as a spy by skiing from Hungary across the Tatra Mountains back into Poland to do reconnaissance. She evaded capture by the Germans multiple times (once by pretending to have tuberculosis by biting her tongue so hard that she 'coughed up' blood). Among other accomplishments, she saved the life of Francis Cammaerts, who headed up the behind-the-lines S.O.E operations in Southern France. Fellow Polish expatriate Andrew Kennedy was her long-time friend and lover, although by all accounts fidelity was never her strong suit. After the war she had an affair with Ian Fleming, and he used her as the inspiration for "Vesper Lynd," the double agent in his first James Bond novel, *Casino Royale.* In 1952 she was stabbed to death outside her apartment by a man she met while working as a cabin stewardess on a cruise ship.

Ahmed Balafrej was one of the leaders of the movement to obtain Morocco's independence. He was arrested by the French in 1944, but then served as one of the country's first prime ministers when Morocco achieved independence in 1956.

Major Peter Wilkinson was for a time head of the British Special Operations Executive in Cairo. His completely unjustified belief that Christine Granville was a double agent caused her and her longtime paramour, Andrew Kennedy, to be sidelined in Cairo for nearly two years.

Darryl Zanuck, the famous filmmaker, did in fact show up in North Africa to make a documentary film about the invasion, much to General Eisenhower's consternation. The only conscious liberty I have taken with the facts regarding the events described in this book is the date of his arrival in Morocco, which I pushed up by a few weeks.

—MLM

READER'S GUIDE
&
CONVERSATION WITH THE AUTHOR

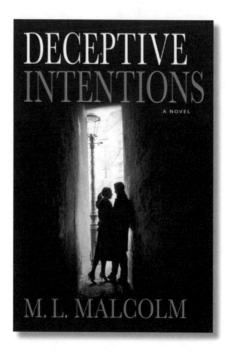

www.MLMalcolm.com

M.L. MALCOLM

—— ～ ——

Silent Lies, the prequel to *Deceptive Intentions*, ends with the phrase, "to be continued." Did you have this sequel completely planned out when Silent Lies was released?

Planned, yes. Completely written, no. I first wrote *Silent Lies* as a huge, multi-generational saga. When the original publisher decided to split the book into two parts, I had to make sure that the second half—the part that would become *Deceptive Intentions*—could stand on its own, so I had to expand it. Luckily for me this involved doing more research into the early days of espionage during World War II, because Leo was about to begin his career as a spy.

☙❧

Why did you pick North Africa as the setting for Leo's espionage work? Why not France or Germany, if he spoke both languages fluently?

For the same reason that I wrote about Budapest and Shanghai in *Silent Lies:* I enjoy learning about and then sharing fascinating corners of history that are a little less-well explored. For example, but for WWII buffs, few people realize that the first American casualties in Europe were not inflicted by the Germans; they came at the hands of the French, when the Vichy government elected to honor their agreement with Hitler and defend North Africa.

The other reason I picked North Africa is because that's where the real action began. The American O.S.S. wasn't operating in Europe until 1942, but President Roosevelt personally sent Robert Murphy to North Africa in 1940 to keep tabs on what was happening there.

❦

Is that also why you decided to write about the Gurs concentration camp? Because it's not as well known?

Yes, and because it was geographically feasible for Leo and Christine to get there from Morocco. Also, while *Deceptive Intentions* does not focus too much on the Holocaust, I thought it would leave too big a hole in the story to ignore it altogether. And it's a fact—once again, a lesser-known fact—that the Vichy French were *horrible* to their refugee Jews. After a war, the winner gets to write the history, and in World War II France was on the winning side. I wanted to shine a little light on what really happened there.

❦

Tangier sounds an awful lot like the city described in the classic movie, "Casablanca." Why didn't you put Leo there?

Because Tangier was really the city described in the movie. In the play upon which the movie was based, "Everybody Goes to Rick's," Rick's Café was modeled on the bar at the Hotel El Minzah, where Leo is having coffee in the first scene of *Deceptive Intentions*. Tangier, like Shanghai, was run by an international council, so it was also an "anything goes" sort of place. But, there was not an official Nazi presence in Tangier. Moving the action to Casablanca gave them the bad guys they needed for the movie because that city was under Vichy control.

৽

How realistic would it have been for Leo to disappear behind the Iron Curtain for so many years?

Very. In the early days of the CIA, the agency recruited foreign nationals to go back to their country of origin and become spies. The activities of the agency were so unsupervised and uncontrolled back then, the leadership didn't have to account for much of anything.

৽

You seem to have a real fascination with exotic places. Have you been to all the places you write about in your books?

I have not made it to North Africa yet, other than to Egypt. Now that I know so much about it, Morocco is top on my list of places I would love to go. But I have been to Shanghai, Budapest, Paris, and about thirty different countries. I love to travel, and I'm lucky in that my husband and children love to travel as well.

৽

You have a degree from Harvard Law School. Is that why you were interested in writing about the Mafia? Because of your law background?

Not really. I sort of caught that fever from my husband, who was a federal prosecutor for ten years. Crime and corruption are standard topics of dinner table conversation at the Malcolm house.

But I also imagined Maddy as unknowingly living a life that parallels her father's. Leo got involved with a Chinese gangster, Maddy with a Mafia prince. Their flaws and insecurities cause them to compromise themselves, and the consequences of their decisions play out along similar lines.

Maddy had already been through so much—why would she get involved with someone like Gene Mandretti?

At the risk of seeming way too psychoanalytical, Maddy feels a lot of guilt over the death of her mother. She is a very passionate person who is emotionally repressed because of that guilt, and Gene, this very confident, attractive man, sees what she's hiding and *wants* her. I'll admit that there is a self-destructive element to Maddy's relationship with Gene, but I also think it realistically reflects what many women with self-esteem issues go through.

☙❧

So is that aspect of the book autobiographical?

No one who has ever met me would say that I am emotionally repressed! And I never dated a Mafia guy. Not to my knowledge.

☙❧

Would you call Deceptive Intentions a spy novel?

Not really. You know, I also had trouble characterizing *Silent Lies.* Some readers called it a historical thriller, others a family saga, others a rags-to-riches tale. I didn't intend to put it any particular slot. I just wanted to tell a good story. While there is a strong espionage element to *Deceptive Intentions*, it's also a story about family, the power of denial, and redemption.

෴

You've worked as an attorney, a journalist, and a fiction writer. Does one type of writing help or hinder the others?

Well, it's hard to say because I've done all three for so long. I wrote my first short story when I was six. Long before I became a professional journalist I worked on the school newspaper, and I was on the debate team in high school and in college. As a lawyer, I was a litigator, or trial attorney. In some ways that is similar to being a journalist, because you have to be able to marshal facts quickly, verify information, and accept criticism of your writing. Both those career moves also taught me how to write succinctly, and how to work on a tight deadline. On the other hand I was pretty left-brained after practicing law, so I think my prose was a bit florid when I first went back to writing fiction, sort of the pendulum swinging the other way. Hopefully now I'm getting the hang of it.

෴

So what are you working on now?

A ghost story that's split between the 1920s and the present-day set in Atlanta. Also a true-crime freelance piece about a serial murderer, and a book of short stories.

෴

Which will come out first?

Whichever gets sold first!

❦

You're not writing a third book in this series?

Not yet, although I do have one planned. This time it will be Katherine's O'Connor's turn to take center stage. It's the story of how she's betrayed by someone she loves when she's working as a foreign correspondent in South America during the early 1970s, and how she has to reexamine her own view of what honor and integrity mean.

❦

And by then Leo is back into spy mode?

Nope. He's a happy grandpa! Don't you think he's earned that by now?

READER'S GUIDE

❦

BOOK GROUP DISCUSSION QUESTIONS

⁓ Maddy's piano teacher tells her, "Artists are different." Christine Granville tells Leo, "Some of us are just not suited to the rhythm of ordinary life." Do you agree that people with special talents ought not to be judged by what Gene refers to as, "rules created for other people?" Under what circumstances?

⁓ What is your opinion of Bernice Mason, Leo's sister-in-law? Were her motives in separating Leo from his daughter altruistic, or deceptive? Similarly, when Amelia informs Maddy about her husband's infidelity, was she being helpful or vindictive?

⁓ What do you think of Leo's decision to go to France when his actions jeopardize his ability to reunite with his own child? Why do you think he decided to fight in the cold war rather than fight to win back his daughter?

⁓ At Katherine's graduation celebration, Maddy is envious of her friend's ability to "never feel guilty about what she wanted, or to fret about the price she might have to pay to get it." What do you suppose makes her feel this way? As the novel progresses, does Maddy change in this regard, or does she just exchange fear for self-denial?

∾ Why was it so imperative that Maddy break off her relationship with Gene? Was it credible that she would rethink this decision later in life?

∾ What explains Leo's attraction to Christine, given that he knows that she's not likely to be faithful? Is there anything about their respective characters that make them better spies?

∾ Harry tells Maddy that everything, "even people" is held together by "stable little pieces" and that "one must understand the forces that connect them, in order to guarantee that stability." What do you think of that statement? Does it apply only to physical "pieces" or metaphysical forces as well?

∾ The author makes substantial use of real historical figures. Do you think she did so effectively? Which was your favorite character (real or fictional) and why?

∾ There's an old piece of advice for writers: "If your plot requires more than two coincidences to keep moving, start rewriting." Were there any such coincidences in *Deceptive Intentions?* Did they seem credible to you, or contrived? Has your own life or the life of someone you've known ever been dramatically affected by coincidence?

∾ For those who have read the prequel, *Silent Lies,* how do they compare in mood, plot development, and characterization? Are there a lot of parallels in the lives of the characters of the two books? Do you prefer one over the other? If so, why?